"GET DOWN!"

Crane had already moved down to the ground. Mike slid down beside him. He felt a pain slash at his left arm just above the wrist. The sound of rifle fire was deafening. Telling himself not to think, just to react, Mike raised his rifle and fired a round on semiautomatic toward where the others were firing, across the rice paddy at a clump of trees. Questions crowded into his mind: What were they firing at? And where? What was that pain in his arm? Then he remembered something: dirt kicking up on either side of him. So, he thought, this was what it was like to be wounded. Was he bleeding? Badly? Was he going to make it...?

Other Avon Books by
Robert A. Anderson

COOKS & BAKERS

SERVICE FOR THE DEAD

ROBERT A. ANDERSON

AVON
PUBLISHERS OF BARD, CAMELOT, DISCUS AND FLARE BOOKS

AVON BOOKS
A division of
The Hearst Corporation
105 Madison Avenue
New York, New York 10016

The Arbor House edition contains the following Library of Congress Cataloging
in Publication Data:

Anderson, Robert A., 1944–
  Service for the dead.

  1. Vietnamese Conflict, 1961–1975—Fiction. I. Title.
PS3551.N3797S4   1986   813'.54   86-10856

First Avon Printing: October 1987

For Rose

SERVICE FOR THE DEAD

"From each one of us there emanate two spirals: one going down and one going up. The first one is reality; the second, illusion. So—which do you choose?"

—JOSEPH RAEL (BEAUTIFUL PAINTED ARROW), from a talk

"As we see whenever a war breaks out, the fear of war is overcome the moment one is really in it. If war were really as terrible as people imagine it to be it would have been wiped out long ago."

—HENRY MILLER, *The Wisdom of the Heart*

"The small survivor has a difficult task
Answering the questions great historians ask."

—EDWIN DENBY, *Collected Poems*

PART
ONE

1

OUT OF IT

Mike could hear mortar rounds explode just outside the hospital. Or were they artillery? He tried to distinguish the sounds, but couldn't; he was too weak. Why were the VC attacking the hospital? What were they doing in Da Nang? It seemed not fair to Mike finally to be out of the fighting only to be back in it. What if the hospital got hit? The hospital! It was only a Quonset hut; it wouldn't stand a chance against a direct hit. Mike imagined what it would be like: blood and confusion, screaming; everyone now the same—doctors, nurses, patients—all trying to save only themselves. And he, Mike, would be left lying helpless in the rubble, his tubes ripped out, slowly dying.

Then he would fall asleep. . . . Lieutenant Farmer was there. Mike was badly wounded and his face was covered with blood, but the lieutenant seemed not to notice. You've got to move out, he said. But how could Mike? Couldn't the lieutenant see—or did he think Mike's wounds weren't serious, that Mike was just trying to get out of the fighting? Mortar and artillery rounds were coming in all around them; machine-gun bullets streamed over their heads; someone was screaming up front. Where was Longo? You

have to move out, the lieutenant said. Yes, sir, Mike said, I'll go.
I'll go.

Then he'd wake and his heart would be pounding. *It's all right,*
he'd tell himself, *it's all right. I'm here, in the hospital. I'm out of
the fighting.* But what about Longo—was he all right? Outside
the hospital Mike could hear mortar rounds crashing. What were
the VC doing here? . . . The screaming from in front became
louder: *I'm dying! Help! Please! Help!* It was Longo, Mike realized: of course, Longo was up there, wounded. Mike knew that:
that was why he had to move out—to save Longo. *Help! Help!*
The lieutenant studied his wristwatch. It was huge, black; it covered his whole arm. It's time, he said, you have to move out. Yes,
sir, Mike said, I'll go. I'll fight. But how could he? The lieutenant
was staring at him. Couldn't he see the blood? Mike held his
breath and got ready to move. . . .

Someone was sitting by the head of his bed.

"How're you doing, Allison?" Who was it? A corpsman? He
was from the South, Mike could tell.

"All right. . . . What's going on—out there?"

"Say again?"

"The VC—the mortars. How close are they?"

"Oh, yeah, those mortars again. I believe you asked me about
them before. Don't worry, I went out and wiped out the whole lot
of 'em, single-handed."

"But . . . I heard them."

"Sure, so did I—kept me up all night."

Mike tried to think. It hurt him to talk. His jaw was very sore.
He was weak. His back ached. He said, "What time is it?"

The corpsman looked at his watch. "Ten-thirty."

"At night?"

"Negative. In the morning."

"Oh. . . . How long have I been here?"

"You came in two nights ago. Boy, were you a mess." The
corpsman laughed. "Doctor worked on you all night, just about."

"Oh?"

"But you're going to be okay."

"Really?"

"Uh-huh. They've got to cut you up again, put a metal plate in your head. But that'll happen later."

"But . . ." The corpsman began to get up. "Wait," Mike said, "I've got to find out . . . Is there anyone here—? My buddy, he was with me, my platoon—his name's Longo . . . whether he's all right."

"Hey, I'm sorry—I told you before—no way I can help. I'm sorry."

"But . . ." But the corpsman had left.

Mike went back to sleep. This time the Professor was there too, sitting cross-legged, reading a book. Why didn't the Professor have to fight? Because he had dysentery, Mike remembered. But was dysentery worse than getting hit? The lieutenant looked down at his watch again; it was time for Mike to move out. You want to be the best, don't you? the lieutenant said. Yes, sir, Mike said, yes, sir. I'll go—I'll fight. But why couldn't he move?

Mike woke and heard swearing. It was a nurse, standing by the bed across from him.

"What is it?" Mike spoke as loud as he could.

The nurse moved closer to Mike. "It's that damn VC or NVA or whatever he is," she said. "He just doesn't quit." Her tone was scolding. "NVA, actually, I think they told me."

"What? What do you mean? Where is he?"

"Right here—across from you." The nurse gestured. "He's a patient. POW. Don't worry, he's not going to hurt anybody. Except himself—that's the problem."

"What do you mean?"

"Keeps trying to kill himself—you know—commit suicide. Rips out his IV tubes and then we have to put them back in, over and over." She sounded bored.

"Really?"

"It's crazy."

"Look, uh, Miss—could you help me? My back hurts. Bad. I want to turn on my side, but I don't know if I can. If it's all right."

"Sure, it's all right." She bent down and helped him turn.

"Thank you."

The nurse went on her way. Mike lay still, thinking about the NVA in the bed across from him, three or four feet away. In his mind he pictured his face: deeply tanned and wrinkled, with black and yellow, rotting teeth. A fanatical look, born of years and years of fighting. Why wouldn't he lie still like all the other patients? Didn't he realize that everyone here—doctors, nurses, corpsmen—wanted to take care of him? He didn't have to fight anymore; he was going to be all right. He was out of it.

Mike slept again. He had the same dream: the lieutenant told him he had to fight. When he woke he was sure it was night. He listened for sounds of incoming.

A woman sat down by the head of his bed.

"Hello, marine." Mike stared at her. She was wearing a blue dress, a red-white-and-blue armband on her left arm that bore the letters *USO*. "My name is Mrs. Chandler," she said, "Lucy Chandler." Her voice sounded familiar.

Mike said, "I'm Mike. Mike Allison. Lance corporal."

"Nice to meet you, Mike." She smiled. She was handsome, Mike thought—not pretty, but handsome; with graying hair. Where had he seen her before? She looked like someone from the movies. "I'd like to know if I could be of assistance."

"What?"

"If I could help."

"Yes . . ."

"Would you like to send a message home?"

"Oh . . . I guess so."

"Are you married?"

"What? Oh—no."

"Parents?"

"Yes."

She held up a clipboard and ballpoint pen. "Wouldn't you like to let them know that you're all right?"

Mike thought for a second. "Yes . . . I guess I would."

She smiled. "Would you like me to write it for you? I'd be glad to. Just tell me what you want to say."

"No. I mean—I can do it. Thank you."

"Then, I'll put this here. There, like that."

Mike felt the clipboard on his stomach, the pen in his hand. He put it to the board and tried to move it. He should be able to do this—what did it matter that he couldn't see what he was writing? Exhaustion filled him; the pen dropped from his fingers.

She spoke again, softer. "Would you like me to write it for you?"

"I . . . All right. Thank you."

She took the clipboard and pen. "To whom will it go?"

"Mr. and Mrs. Ernest Allison, 402 Meadowbrook Lane, Kingston, Virginia. Dear Mom and Dad. I got wounded. I'm in the hospital, in Da Nang. I'm all right. Love, Michael."

She stared at him a moment, then said, "Is that all?" Mike was silent. She said, "Would you have any objection to my adding that you're about to leave for Clark Air Force Base in the Philippines? I think that will make them feel much, much better."

"I am? I mean—are you sure?"

She nodded, smiling. "Yes, Mike, I'm quite sure. You're getting out of here. You're going to be all right." She began to write.

"But . . ."

She finished writing and put the clipboard back on his stomach. "Here, Mike, would you like to try and sign?" He felt the pen in his hand. "Right . . . there." Mike wrote. She took the pen and clipboard back again.

"Wait," Mike said. Lifting his head with his right hand, he turned onto his side. "I need to find out . . . Maybe you can help . . . My unit—what happened—when I got hit. The others . . . It was bad—pinned down—my buddy . . . Maybe I shouldn't leave yet—I don't know if I'm strong enough."

Mrs. Chandler put a hand on Mike's arm. "I understand, Mike," she said. "I understand." Her hand felt warm and dry. "What was your unit?" Mike told her. "Why, that's a fine battalion," she said. "I know your colonel—John Rodman. His family are old friends of my family. I've known John Rodman since he was a boy."

"Really? . . . Then—can you find out? My buddy—his name is Longo. Corporal."

Concern showed on her face. "I don't know what I can do, Mike." She smiled resolutely. "I'm sure your battalion is doing all right." She paused, then said in a softer voice. "Would you like to tell me what happened, when you were wounded?"

Mike stared at her knees. They were like girl's knees: the taut white skin. What could he tell her? About the blood, the cries, the confusion? What did it matter, what happened to him? What had happened to Longo? Should Mike have gone out there? But he was going to, he—

"It's all right," she said, gripping his hand. "I understand. You must be very tired."

"Yes." Mike hissed it.

She removed her hand and straightened in her chair. When she spoke her voice was very serious. "I just want to tell you," she said, "how I feel about you, about *all* of you. I am so proud, so very, *very* proud of what you're doing, the way you're helping these poor people fight for their freedom." She paused and leaned closer to Mike. "I know a lot of people in the media back home and I think it's shameful the way they're handling this, what they're doing to public opinion. When I go back I'm going to do everything I can to see that you men get the support you deserve. Everything I *possibly* can." She leaned closer. "God bless you," she said. "You've done a wonderful thing over here, truly wonderful."

Mike closed his eyes and soon he was asleep.

Arms lifted him from his bed along with his tubes, bottles, and pouch, and put him on a litter. *Be careful, be careful,* he wanted to say. What if something happened? He felt his life as a fragile thing, like a thin glass tube, being handled by rough, insensitive hands. He didn't want to die like that—because of someone's carelessness; not after getting this far.

Then he was on a plane. How had he got there? He didn't know; he must have fallen asleep. Or was this a dream? No, definitely not; he could tell the difference between waking and sleeping: this cold air he felt, this fear—they were real. He slept again. When he woke he imagined he was having trouble breathing, that his life was slipping out of him, silently, secretly: among all the patients on the plane he had been chosen to die. Maybe there wasn't enough oxygen. Or did he need more blood? Then he fell asleep.

It was hot, very hot. The sun was out. There were palm trees. Too bright, Mike thought; he found himself wishing for darkness. He was carried into a large, new, air-conditioned building and put into a room with eight beds, four on each side. It was a spacious, uncrowded room; at the end of it were several windows. No one talked. How different this was from the crowded Quonset hut in Da Nang, the mortars and artillery exploding outside, the fanatical NVA ripping out his tubes; now all that seemed a dream. He gazed at the hot, still afternoon outside his windows and thought of late-summer days from his boyhood when he'd have nothing to do; perhaps he'd watch television, throw a football around.

A nurse came by and pulled down his pajama bottoms. She held his penis. "This may hurt," she said.

"*Ouch!*"

She showed him the glass tube she had just pulled out. "Now you can go to the john when you need to," she said.

"But . . . I can't walk. I mean, I haven't, yet."

"You should be able to. Just take it slow." She left.

In a little while a doctor came by. "How are you doing, Mike?" He was young and seemed friendly.

"All right. . . . What's going to happen, sir? When are you going to operate?"

The doctor shook his head. "We're not going to do a thing to you, Mike. All you've got to do is rest up and get a little stronger for the flight out. Tomorrow."

"Really? But . . . where?"

The doctor smiled. "You're going home, Mike. The war's over for you."

"Really?" Mike repeated. "But . . ." He tried to think. Home already? "But . . . am I ready?"

"Sure, you are," the doctor said, then moved on to the next bed.

In the evening Mike got up for the first time. Very slowly he walked down the hall outside his room. His head felt as though it might fall off. He went into the bathroom and looked in the mirror. He was frowning. The bandage around his head was dirty and stained with blood. He turned away. At first he couldn't piss, and when he finally did it stung. What was wrong? Had the nurse broken the tube when she pulled it out? He thought of telling the doctor—but then they'd have to operate. He didn't know what to do. He walked slowly back to his bed.

That night he woke with a fever; he was shivering all over. It occurred to him that he might die. He had heard of it: people coming down with pneumonia after an operation, then dying from it. He pushed a button and when the nurse came told her he needed blankets. All he had was a sheet.

"Sorry," she said, "but there's a new theory now: patients with fever should be made colder, not warmer."

Mike wondered whether he was dreaming. "But I'm *freezing*," he said. "I can't stop shivering. Please. *Please*."

"Sorry. It's hospital policy. There's nothing I can do."

She left and after a few minutes Mike got up, walked to the only empty bed, took the blanket off of it, and carried it back to his own. A voice from the bed next to him said, "Way to go, man." Mike fell asleep.

In the morning his fever was down. An orderly cranked up the head of his bed and put a tray in front of him. Toast, coffee, orange juice, an egg.

"I don't want anything," Mike said.

"You should try to eat," the orderly said.

Mike stared at the plate. He had a memory of wanting very much to eat food like this. It seemed a long time ago. He sipped a little juice.

Another orderly, this one with a medical kit, came into the

room and sat down at the bed across from Mike's. He told the patient that it was time to clean his wounds and change his dressings. The orderly began to work and in a few moments the patient began to scream.

Mike lay very still. The screaming became louder and more frequent. He closed his eyes, then opened them again. He stared, as though transfixed by the orderly's calm, blank face. A sickening feeling began to take hold of Mike: that this orderly was not who he seemed, someone just doing his job, but rather was inflicting this pain on purpose. Mike's heart beat fast. Whom was the orderly going to torture next?

Finally he left the room. It was as though a spell had been lifted. Mike closed his eyes and slept.

At lunch he ate nothing but drank some soup. A nurse told him again to try and eat. When he went to the bathroom his penis still stung, but less.

In the afternoon he slept again. When he woke someone was standing over him, looking down. A civilian. With short red hair, a freckled red face, wearing a short-sleeved blue nylon shirt.

"I know you," Mike said. "You're Red Parsons."

The civilian smiled. "That's right," he said, hesitating an instant, then offering his hand. His forearm was thick and hairy; on his wrist was a thin gold watch with a black face.

Mike shook hands. "You play for the Chicago Cubs," he said. "Third base."

"That's right."

"I've seen you play—on TV. I used to have your baseball card."

"Is that right?"

"Yeah . . . Say, what's the matter, anyway? Why can't you guys ever win the pennant?"

Red Parsons's face turned even redder. "I guess I can't answer that." He kept smiling. "But how are *you* doing?"

"Oh, I'm okay. The doctor says I'm going to be all right. . . . Hey, I'm sorry about that—I mean, what I said about winning the pennant. I was just kidding."

"That's all right."

"You're really a good player. I used to play third base too—in Little League. But football's my main sport."

"Is that right?"

"Yeah. I'm an end—was. No speed, though. Pretty good hands but no speed."

Red Parsons held an awkward smile. "Well, good to meet you. Good luck." He shook Mike's hand again, then went to the next bed.

Red Parsons! The same Red Parsons Mike had seen play all those times on television. Red Parsons. One of the greatest glove men in the game. Yet now Mike was someone Red Parsons had come to visit. Mike watched him as he went from bed to bed. He looked so healthy, with his crew cut, his trim, compact body, his muscular arms—too healthy, Mike thought, as though, among the patients with their tubes and bandages, Red Parsons was the one who was abnormal. He must feel uncomfortable, Mike realized. He raised his right arm as Red Parsons waved goodbye from the door.

A voice came from the bed next to Mike's. "Hey, man, you really put it to him." It sounded like croaking, like the voice of someone old. After a moment Mike realized it was meant for him.

"Huh?"

" 'Why don't you guys ever win the pennant!' Man, I almost cracked up, I'm not shittin'."

"Oh."

"You got balls, man, to say somethin' like that. You remind me of my brother. He woulda said somethin' like that too; he's always mouthin' off, he don't care who it is."

Mike lifted himself up and looked over. The patient's jaw was wired and there was a white brace under his black face, like a Santa Claus beard. "It's the truth, man," Mike said, "they never win."

"No lie. I'm a Saint Louis fan myself. Cards all the way."

"They got a team. . . . Who're you with?"

"Air Cav."

"Oh, yeah? I've seen you guys—helicopters like locusts. What'd you have, one for every man?"

"Just about. We go in style. How 'bout you?"

"Marine Corps. We go on foot."

The soldier let out a short, choking sound that Mike took for a laugh. "That's all right. . . . You up north?"

"Uh-huh. Operation Boone."

The soldier whistled softly. "You must've seen some shit, man."

"Enough."

"You said it, man: enough is enough."

"Too much."

The soldier laughed again. "You got it, man. You're all right. Hey, what's your name, anyway?"

"Mike."

"Mike? Reggie. But they call me the Shredder. We all had names in my squad—the Zapper, the Pounder, the Bleeder. I was the Shredder. How 'bout you, man, you have a name?"

Mike hesitated. "Yeah," he said, "we had names too."

"Oh, yeah? What was your name?"

Mike hesitated again. "Crazy Mike."

The Shredder gave out more choking noises. "I like that, man. Crazy Mike. That's you, all right."

Mike smiled at the Shredder's approval and lay back down. The talking had exhausted him. The Shredder became silent again too.

Crazy Mike. When had Longo first called him that? Mike's first day at the Fort. The Fort? But the Fort was gone—did it ever really exist? Did any of those characters—Brutus, the Professor, Captain Blood, the Cisco Kid?

2

CRAZY MIKE

Mike was afraid. But of what? He had been told the helicopter might receive sniper fire, yet as he stared out the window the ground below seemed harmless to him: broad sandy stretches, clumps of trees, tiny houses, watery fields. It was so different from what he had imagined Vietnam to be: thickly wooded mountains full of hiding Vietcong. Here it seemed too open to hide.

The helicopter lurched and Mike became more afraid. This was what scared him—merely being in a helicopter. He didn't like helicopters—whether he was in Vietnam or in the States. He didn't like airplanes either, but he liked helicopters even less. They were too small, too close to the ground; a crash seemed much more likely than when he was too high up to see down. He looked at his watch: eleven o'clock. He was hungry; he'd feel better after he ate.

The helicopter landed on a small sandy hill encircled by barbed wire. Mike grabbed his seabag and rifle and jumped off. From a group of marines standing nearby one came toward him. It was the battalion chaplain, Mike knew; the first sergeant had told Mike that he was the reason the helicopter was coming out, not Mike. Mike saw captain's bars on the chaplain's collar and wondered whether he should salute. He hesitated, then brought his hand up to his head. The chaplain—young, Mike thought—hesitated too, then returned the salute, brushed past Mike, and boarded the helicopter.

Mike turned toward the group of marines. Most of them were barefoot and bareheaded; some wore only shorts. One of them had a camera raised to his eyes, pointed to where the helicopter had gone.

"I'm looking for Captain Matthews," Mike said. One of the marines laughed.

"Over there," another one said, pointing to a tent twenty meters away. Mike thanked him and began to walk, feeling the stares of the marines behind him.

Inside the tent a tall, dark-haired, crewcut marine with a green towel around his neck stood over a small metal desk, staring down at a map. Next to the map was a pair of large black binoculars. Mike looked quickly for a sign of rank on the marine's utilities, but saw none.

"Sir?" he said.

The marine turned, scowling. "What is it?"

"Sir, uh, Private First Class Allison reporting for duty," Mike said, trying to stand at attention while still holding his seabag and rifle. "I'm to report to Captain Matthews, sir."

The marine kept staring. Finally he said, "Rest." Mike let out his breath. "I'm Captain Matthews," the marine said and held out his hand.

Mike shook it. "Put your gear down a sec," the captain said. "Have a seat. What'd you say your name was? Not too good on names." He seemed to be smiling and scowling at the same time.

"Allison, sir. . . . Aye, aye, sir." Mike dropped his seabag and placed his rifle on top of it.

"No—belay that. On second thought, come on over and take a look. You might as well—you're going to get pretty familiar with this area; I want you to know exactly what we're doing."

"Aye, aye, sir."

Mike stared down at the captain's map. It had a clear plastic surface on which were multicolored grease-pencil markings.

"You familiar with Vietnamese history, Allison?"

"Uh, yes, sir."

"Say what?" The captain jerked his head up and lowered his eyebrows, frowning down at Mike. "How's that?"

"I mean—yes, sir, I've done some reading—"

"Oh?" The captain sounded suspicious. "What?"

"Oh, articles, sir—I mean, magazine articles. And some books too—"

"Books? What books?"

Mike felt his face get red. "Uh, one was a collection of essays on Vietnam, it was called *The Vietnam Primer*—"

"I've seen it." He snapped out the words, then peered closely at Mike. "You been to college?"

"Yes, sir; a year and—"

"Where?"

"Where? Uh, I mean, in Virginia, sir; a little school called—"

"I thought so. You sound like the college type. Another one." The captain snorted. "Well, reading books is fine, Allison, but you're going to find that it's a little different over here than what the eggheads say. I wouldn't start out with the attitude that I knew everything there was to know about this war."

"No, sir, I—"

"Don't get me wrong, I think it's a good thing, reading all those books. Shows a good interest. That's what we need over here, could use more of it." He turned back to the map. "Anyway, I was just about to tell you that this particular part of South Vietnam happens to have quite a bit of history to it, but I guess you already know that, from all those books you've read. You know who comes from around here?"

"Uh, no, sir."

"No?" The captain snorted again, "Ho Chi Minh, that's who."

"Really? I mean, really, sir?"

"That is affirmative. From right around here, one of these little vills. And that's exactly what this part of the country is all about: little vills and revolution. It breeds Ho Chi Minhs. The French had a hell of a time when they were here—about wrote it off." He picked up a pack of cigarettes from the desk and tapped on it. "Smoke?"

"I . . . uh, why, yes, thank you, sir." Mike took one from the pack. The captain lit his and handed Mike the lighter. It was heavy, with an inscription. Mike tried to read it as he lit up.

"Filthy little things," the captain said, studying his cigarette. "Always considered them a sign of weakness myself. Wouldn't you agree?"

"Sir? I . . . uh—" Suddenly the captain grinned, showing a row of crooked teeth. "Oh, yes, sir," Mike said, smiling too.

The captain's grin vanished. "Here's where we are now." He tapped on the map with his little finger. There was a black circle about a half inch in diameter; inside it was white. Another half inch to the right, Mike noticed, was the ocean. "Before we moved in the VC had pretty much free use of this area," the captain said. "Our mission is to stop that." He turned to Mike and dragged on his cigarette.

"Yes, sir."

The captain tapped the black circle again. "This knoll we're on used to be only a platoon outpost, not a whole company. Till three months ago. You know what happened then."

"Uh, no, sir."

"Say what?"

"I said, I don't know, sir."

"You mean they didn't tell you at battalion?" The captain glared angrily at Mike. "Okay," he said, "I'll make it short: about three months ago a battalion of main-force VC attacked the place one night and overran it. Almost wiped out the whole works."

"Really? Sir?"

The captain nodded. "That is affirmative." He knocked cigarette ash on the sandy ground and Mike did the same. "You see this village?" The captain pointed to the map again.

"Yes, sir."

"Binh Le." He pronounced it *Bin Lee*. "As you can see, it's right next to the outpost. Hell, when you step outside and look across the wire you're looking right down on it. Well, that's where

Charlie attacked from: a whole battalion of the little fuckers. Of course their battalions aren't as big as ours—maybe five, six hundred men—but still, that's a hell of a lot of VC for one marine platoon. Now how do you suppose they moved a whole goddamn battalion into that little vill without anyone knowing?"

Mike tried to think. This was his father's method, he realized—asking questions as he was explaining. It made Mike nervous. "I don't know, sir."

The captain snorted. "Of course you don't: because the answer is, they didn't. Someone had to know. The villagers did—every last one of them. So the real question is: how could Charlie do it without *us* knowing—I mean, the marines that were here at the time?" Mike opened his mouth, but the captain went on. "A few at a time, that's how. Disguised as villagers." He pointed to the edge of the ocean. "Some of them came in at night, along the beach. Some from the villages west of here. Took them about a week. Meanwhile our patrols were going through the vill and never saw a one: because they were hidden in the villagers' hooches. And all that time not one villager said a word." He glared at Mike.

"Yes, sir."

"And then they attacked. At night. A sapper unit blew its way through the wire and all hell broke loose. No way the lieutenant in charge out here could call in indirect fire. Hell, it was hand-to-hand, the VC were right here in the CP, right the hell where you're standing." He kept glaring, his nostrils puffed out.

"Yes, sir."

The captain snorted again. "But they blew it. For all the smarts they're supposed to have, they made a mistake, a big one." He paused, and Mike tried to think of what the mistake could be. The captain went on: "They picked the wrong night."

"Sir?"

The captain barked a laugh. "That's affirmative. Unfortunately for Charlie—but lucky for the marines who were here—he just happened to pick the time when the platoon up here was being rotated off. So there were two platoons that night; the replacement platoon as well." He turned to Mike. "Funny, isn't it, after all that planning, the night the VC choose to attack just happens to be the one night when the outpost is at double strength?"

"Yes, sir." Mike smiled with the captain at the Vietcong's mistake.

The captain stopped smiling. "Still, those little fuckers pretty near wiped out those two platoons. I guess it worked the other way, too. I mean, nobody up here was expecting an attack *that* night, not at double strength." He dragged on his cigarette, then dropped it in the sand and crushed it with his boot. He shook his head. "It was a hell of a battle—the good old-fashioned kind. Touch and go. Hand-to-hand for a while. But our side fought like hell. Hell, the lieutenant in charge had them singing the goddamn Marine Corps Hymn." He lowered his voice. "He got waxed at the end, the lieutenant. Damn fine marine; up for the Navy Cross." Mike nodded solemnly. "But the troops fought them off. Over seventy percent casualties when it was all over, including twenty KIA. The VC left twenty dead of their own—which is a lot, for Charlie. They're like us: they don't usually leave their dead behind." He stared at Mike.

"Yes, sir."

The captain turned back to the map. "Anyway, that's when regiment decided to keep a company out here. Because they found out some pretty interesting things afterwards from POWs and captured documents—plus they had some intelligence types out here interrogating villagers in Binh Le. And the big question was, why did the VC go to all that trouble—I mean infiltrating an entire battalion into that little village—to attack one marine platoon on a small outpost like this? Hell, the platoon hadn't made a *dent* in the VC activity out here—killed a few cadre, that was about it. Plus the VC knew they'd never to able to hold on to this hill, they know damn well we'll send out whatever's necessary to take it back. So why did they do it?"

Mike furrowed his brow. "I don't know, sir."

"Because they wanted to make that platoon a *symbol,* that's why. They wanted to show the villagers that the big bad Americans could be *beaten*: overrun, wiped out, zapped, completely. That's affirmative. They wanted the villagers to know that any time they chose to, they could put us out of business. Why? So the villagers wouldn't *trust* us, that's why. Because—and I'm sure you've got this from your readings—because the strength of the VC lies in those villagers: the peasantry. That's where Charlie gets his food, his recruits, his intelligence. And what Charlie wanted to show the people in this area was that they could not depend on the United States Marine Corps to protect them." He stopped, out of breath, and stared down at Mike, as though in triumph.

"Yes, sir. I see, sir."

"So that's why we're here: to show the locals that we can be counted on. That we will not desert them. That we will stand up to the VC bullies. And that is what successful counterinsurgency is all about. Look here." He pointed to the map. "You can see how populated this area is—there's vills all over the place. That's why it's so important to the VC: it produces a hell of a lot of rice—*and* recruits. Hell, they're grabbing kids all the time; we know, we've been told. But obviously one company of marines can't keep watch over everyone. So, we started with the obvious." He tapped on the map. "The village of Binh Le."

"Yes, sir."

"Through constant patrolling and various civil-affairs and psy-ops activities we have demonstrated to the people of Binh Le that we mean business, that we're here to stay. The result being that we are now at the point where we have just about completely deprived the VC of their support." He nodded in agreement with himself.

"Really, sir?"

"That is affirmative. But it wasn't easy. It has taken time: time and effort, a hell of a lot of both. Hell, at first Charlie'd beat up anyone who even looked at us, much less talked to us. We suspect they murdered a couple too. Now he doesn't dare even enter the village, day or night. Plus the villagers tell us of any sign of VC activity in or around Binh Le. But the point is this: we have shown them we care, that they can count on us."

"Yes, sir."

"Now eventually, what we'd like to see is some kind of South Vietnamese unit in Binh Le, a PF platoon, for instance, so we can do the same work in other villages. Like Ai Tu." He pointed to a village on the map a half kilometer west of the outpost. "There seems to be a hell of a lot of VC activity in Ai Tu"—*Eye Too*, he pronounced it—"in spite of our work in Binh Le. I suspect there's a deeply rooted VC infrastructure there. That's another reason we need a local unit out here: they're a hell of a lot better than we are at going into a vill and finding out which people are actually VC. I keep telling battalion to send us some Vietnamese types to help us out, but nothing yet.

"But the main thing for us—still—is to make the people understand that we will protect them. It means work. You're out in the field a lot, patrolling, setting ambushes, going through villages, checking I.D.'s, searching hooches. Remember how they infiltrated that battalion the last time? It's an unconventional war and we've got to use unconventional means. We can't sit back and wait for the big battle to happen. Why the hell do you think I'm spending all this time talking to a brand-spanking-new pfc.? Hell, it's a pfc.'s war. I don't give a damn about rank: I want interest, initiative. We're stuck out here where battalion leaves us pretty much on our own, and that's fine with me. Any time you've got an idea for fighting this war you come right in here and let me know. Remember that."

Mike straightened. "Yes, sir. Aye, aye, sir."

"Now we've got about five more months of the hot season coming up and it's going to be tough, damn tough. Forget about sleep. You'll be tired all the time, but you've got to be alert, too, constantly. As soon as you step outside the wire there's the threat of mines and booby traps—not to mention snipers. Snipers—fuck 'em!" An angry look crossed the captain's face. "We've got a couple around here that've been busting our chops. Lost a dozen men in the last month, KIA. Had a memorial service for them this morning, in fact—battalion chaplain was out. Damn fine padre."

"Anyway, you're going to be frustrated as hell. These people are stubborn; you're going to want to give up on them. But you can't. They're good people, and if we show them that we mean it—that we're here to stay, to protect them against VC intimidation and terrorism—then they'll come over to us. I know it. I've seen it happen. It's the only way. Because this really is a battle for the hearts and minds of these people." He stared down at Mike.

"Yes, sir."

"Any questions?"

"Uh . . . no, sir."

"Right. I'm assigning you to first platoon. Sergeant Jefferson's the platoon commander. It's way understrength—hell, the whole company is. We came off Red River two months ago with half our men. And what do they send us? One fucking marine. Not that you're not appreciated, don't get me wrong—er, what was your name again?"

"Allison, sir."

"Allison. I'll get the hang of it. . . . But we'll do with what we've got; that's the marine way. Hell, if the Army was out here they'd have a regiment. . . . Anyway, I hope to get a lieutenant soon for the platoon, but in the meantime Sergeant Jefferson's in charge. Damn fine marine. He'll brief you about what we're doing."

"Yes, sir."

"Good luck, Allison. And remember: the VC attacked here once. They'll try it again. Don't let up!"

"No, sir. Aye, aye, sir!" Mike straightened to attention, stood a moment, then picked up his rifle and seabag and went outside.

He stood, waiting. It was very hot; his shirt was almost completely soaked with sweat. He had been nervous, he knew, talking with the captain; he wondered whether his hand had been wet when they shook hands. Mike had never shaken hands with an officer before—nor taken a cigarette from one, nor even talked with one. He liked the captain, he decided. The captain was gruff, but not the way a sergeant could be. He had spoken to Mike almost as an equal. Mike liked what he had said: about infrastructure, main-force units, cadre, counterinsurgency, unconventional warfare. These were the things Mike had read about.

He turned and gazed out over the barbed wire at the village below. Binh Le. Through the trees he could see houses, villagers moving about; he heard a chicken squawk. What must that night have been like, when the VC attacked? In training nobody had ever said anything about getting overrun: marines were always supposed to overrun the enemy. Why were they singing the Marine Corp Hymn? He yawned. Binh Le seemed such a sleepy, peaceful village. The villagers were probably eating lunch now, he thought. Did villagers eat lunch? What kind of food did they have? What were their *lives* like? Mike remembered one of the books he had read—by a college dropout who had spent a year in Vietnam, visiting different parts of the country. Perhaps, Mike thought, that was what he should be doing.

A marine walked up to him. He was black and wore a green T-shirt and utility trousers and no cover.

"You the new man?"

Mike saw that there was no way of telling this marine's rank either. "Yes, sir," he said. "Pfc. Allison."

"I'm Sergeant Jefferson. Come on with me." He had a soft, high-pitched voice.

"Yes, sir." Mike walked with the sergeant toward a large GP tent.

"You meet the captain?"

Mike nodded. "Yes, sir."

"He give you his speech?"

"Uh—"

"About what we're doing."

"Oh. Yes, sir, he did."

"Then you know what's going on."

"Yes, sir . . . but he, uh, said you'd be giving me a briefing too."

"You'll see how it works. Don't call me sir."

"Yes, uh, Sergeant."

"And no salutin' out here, neither."

Mike followed him into the tent. It was dark and full of smells: of cigarette and cigar smoke, rifle-cleaning oil and burning candles, sweat. Slowly Mike's eyes adjusted to the light. A huge black marine wearing nothing but camouflage-striped shorts was sitting on a poncho liner, taking apart a machine gun. Next to him a marine was curled up, sleeping. Other marines were cleaning rifles, eating out of C-ration cans, reading books; one was cleaning a camera. At the far end of the tent a marine read aloud from a letter; nobody seemed to be listening. Littered all around were C-ration cans, T-shirts, weapons, hand grenades, empty cigarette packs. The place was a mess, Mike thought. What did it have to do with what he had been taught in training, or with the kind of dedication the captain had spoken about?

Sergeant Jefferson shouted in an even higher-pitched voice than before: "Tracy!" A shirtless, suntanned marine, wearing a pair of issue glasses, came forward.

"What is it, Jeff?"

"You've got a new man. Pfc. . . . What d'you say your name was?"

"Allison."

"Allison. . . . This is Tracy—Corporal Johnson—your squad leader."

Mike dropped his seabag and rifle and shook hands. Mike was surprised: Tracy looked his own age. He had expected his squad leader to be a least a few years older—like Sergeant Jefferson. But there was something about Tracy that Mike liked.

Jefferson left the tent and Tracy introduced Mike to his fellow squad and platoon members. Most of them had nicknames: Short-round, Motor, C.C., Rain, Day-train, Ski. The large black marine Mike had first noticed was called Brutus; he was a machine-gunner. The squad radioman, Pogo, was the one who had been sleeping next to him. He was the smallest marine Mike had ever seen. Lance Corporal Blevins, with blond hair and a southern accent and half a cigar in his mouth, was a fire-team leader. Mike liked him, too. Then Tracy introduced him to the marine who had been reading aloud at the end of the tent.

"This is your fire-team leader," Tracy said, "Longo."

The marine smiled broadly and held out his hand. He was shorter than Mike, with high cheekbones and short curly black hair. He too had no shirt on, showing a smooth, hairless, bulging chest and sharply defined stomach muscles. "Hi, Mike," he said. "Welcome to the Fort. I'm Ed."

There were shouts of derision from various directions: *"Ed? . . . You're no fuckin' Ed! . . . You're Longo—fuckin' hippie!"*

"If you're Ed," the marine called Pogo said, "then my name's Roger P. Whipple." He sounded like a ten-year-old. His head seemed huge on his tiny body; his hair stuck out all over.

Longo grinned; he seemed to enjoy the attention. "Hey, looks like we're the Fearsome Foursome again." He spoke to no one in particular. "But that means the squad is no longer the Blind Nine. . . . Let's see, the Terrible Ten? Or how about the Tenacious Ten?" He had a slight lisp, Mike noticed.

"The fucking-what-ten?" It was Short-round. He was very short, with thick black hair and a chunky body.

"Can't wait till we're eleven," Pogo said. "How about the Elevating Eleven? Then we could—"

"Shut up, Pogo," Tracy said. "You don't make any sense."

"Don't make any dollars, neither." Nobody laughed.

"Forget it," Longo said. "The Terrible Ten, that'll do." He turned to Mike. "You meet Captain Blood yet?"

"Huh?"

"The skipper. Captain Matthews."

"Oh. Yeah. I met him."

"Man, he's really into it, isn't he? He give you that stuff about the hearts and minds? . . . Captain Blood—hearts—get it? . . . He was Captain Hook for a while, but Pogo said that that would make this Never-Never Land and he'd rather get older than stay here. Then he was Captain Gallant and we were all Germans and Englishmen run away from the law, changed our names. You ever see *Beau Geste?*"

Mike frowned. "No."

"Great movie. Anyway, Captain Blood's all right; he really gets into it." Longo stopped smiling and brought his eyebrows down; his voice dropped: " 'They're stubborn, but we have to show them that we care.' " He grinned. "Hey, I like him, we have intellectual discussions all the time—"

"Sure you do, Longo." It was the marine called Motor. He spoke without looking up from a magazine he was reading.

Longo spoke to him. "Yeah, we do, I'm not kidding. Like about how to fight the war—serious stuff like that." He turned back to Mike. "I've got this idea, man—"

Motor looked up. "Oh, Christ, not your idea again, Longo."

Short-round laughed hoarsely. "You call that an idea, Longo? That's close."

"But I know it would work." Longo turned from Short-round to Mike, smiling, holding up his hands.

"Hey, Longo," Pogo said, "what's an idea?"

Longo shook his head at him, grinning, then said to Mike, "Captain Blood tell you about his model village, Binh Le?"

Mike hesitated. "Yeah."

"Man, wait'll you see Ai Tu—that's Number Ten City; *beaucoup* VC, as they say out here in the desert. . . . But don't get me wrong, man, the captain's all right, he doesn't hassle us too much—except for his ban on mustaches. But that's only because he can't grow one. Not a decent one, anyway."

Longo stopped talking and stared at Mike, smiling. Mike turned away. Why hadn't he been assigned to Blevins's fire team?

"Where're you from?" Longo asked.

Mike shrugged. "Virginia, now."

"Oh, yeah? I'm from California."

"I've heard of that," Pogo said. "That's in Los Angeles. Never been there but only because I never wanted to. It's probably real nice, or—"

"Goddamnit, Pogo, shut up." Tracy sounded angry.

"I wasn't saying anything. Never do." Pogo lay back down next to Brutus.

Blevins, from where he was sitting, said, "Whereabouts in Virginia, Mike?"

"Western part—Kingston."

Blevins nodded. "I've heard of it. I'm from South Carolina. Spartanburg."

Mike nodded. "Heard of it."

Pogo sat up and spoke again: "What're ya gonna call him, Longo? Ain't ya decided yet?"

Longo gave a sheepish look. "Hey, man, I don't go around giving names. It's more like people name themselves, that's all."

"Watch out," Pogo said to Mike. "Once he gives you a name, you're stuck. We wouldn't have to be here 'ceptin' he's got everything named. You'll see: wait'll you meet Zorro and the Cisco Kid." He blinked his eyes in a painful way as he spoke. Was he retarded? Mike wondered. He had never met anyone who looked or sounded less like a marine than Pogo. Unless it was Longo.

Longo showed Mike where he could put his gear and make himself a place to sleep. It was nothing more than a space in the sand, between Longo and Motor.

"Fosdick used to be here," Longo said. "Fearless Fosdick—remember him? Guy with all the holes in him?" Mike shook his head. "Man, Fosdick was incredible: kept getting these through-and-through wounds. Looked like a piece of Swiss cheese. Finally got hit in the head—gotta get a metal plate put in. Frankenstein, we'll have to call him." Mike said nothing.

Just then Sergeant Jefferson came back into the tent, carrying what looked like a bamboo tray. Flies buzzed over it.

"What the fuck is that?" Short-round asked.

"Food," Jefferson said.

"You're shittin' me."

Mike frowned at Short-round. How could he speak that way to a sergeant?

"It's from the gooks," Jefferson went on. "They sent it up from Binh Le for the captain, on account of we gave them some rice yesterday. Captain don't want it and neither does anyone in second platoon. Whoever wants it can have it."

A chorus of replies greeted his offer: "Give you the shits. . . . Probably poisoned. . . . Get it the fuck out of here!" Longo began to explain to Mike, although Mike hadn't asked him: "The vill took a couple of artillery rounds by mistake last week; some old lady got killed, so the battalion chaplain came out with a few sacks of rice to make amends. . . . Come on—let's take a look."

Longo got up and walked toward the tray. For a moment Mike stayed where he was, then he followed. On a plate were large chunks of what looked like white chicken meat with small green peppers mixed in. Next to that was a bowl of rice. There was also what looked like some kind of green salad. A pair of chopsticks and a paper napkin were on the side.

Longo said, "Damn, I'll bet those peppers are hot. They like them hot over here. I thought I liked them hot till I tasted one of theirs."

Jefferson shrugged and began to leave.

"Wait," Mike said. He hadn't known he was going to speak. "What?"

Mike nodded. "I'll take it. I'm, uh, hungry."

"You got it." He handed the tray to Mike.

Catcalls, protests, warnings, obscenities came at Mike from different parts of the tent. "Man, he's trying to get out of the field already!" someone shouted and others laughed. Mike, wishing now he hadn't spoken, walked back to his space and sat.

"Watch out for those peppers, man." It was a tall, thin, red-haired marine whom Mike hadn't noticed before. Mike smiled at him, but the marine didn't smile back.

Mike examined the food, waiting until he thought nobody was watching. Then he took the chopsticks in his hand and picked up a piece of the white meat.

"Look, he's like Rain—thinks he's a fucking gook!" It was Motor. Mike's face felt hot. He waited again, then saw Motor turn away with a scowl of disgust.

It was chicken. It was good, too. It was very good. Mike took some rice. It was sticky and tasted different from the rice he was used to, but he liked it. He was hungry, he realized. Then he had some salad. It had a taste he had never experienced before, a strong, sharp taste. For a moment he thought of poison. But he liked the taste. He ate more chicken, then picked up one of the peppers with the chopsticks. He bit off half and began to chew.

Just as he was finished telling himself that it wasn't very hot, he began to feel something spread in his mouth. It was heat; it turned into burning. He tried to stop it by eating rice but it seemed only to get worse. He fumbled for his canteen, swished water around in his mouth, and now it really did get worse. He sucked air in and blew it out.

"Hot, huh, man?" It was Longo. Mike realized he had been watching.

"Shit."

"Hot?"

"Yeah." Mike took more gulps of water. He swore again. "It's burning." He drank the last of his water.

Some of the marines were laughing now. "Sucker!" Sweat rolled down Mike's face. "Ho Chi Minh's revenge!"

The tall, thin marine who had spoken before came over and knelt by Mike. "Don't drink water," he said, "it'll only make it worse. Go on, eat some more rice."

Mike did. Someone shouted. "You gonna give him a Heart, Crane?"

"Shut up!" The marine sounded angry. "I've seen people put in a hospital they were burned so bad. Anybody got a biscuit?"

"Here." Longo handed Mike a C-ration biscuit.

"Thanks," Mike said. He stuffed it in his mouth, but the burning kept on. How was he going to stand this any longer? It felt as though his skin were peeling off. The thought of going to a hospital—getting out of this place—crossed his mind.

Crane, kneeling by Mike, said, "I told you not to eat that pepper. You're crazy!"

Suddenly Longo shouted, "That's it! That's who he is—he's crazy! When he first came in here, I knew it. He had that look.

Crazy Mike—that's his name—Crazy Mike!" He grinned excitedly.

Mike, sucking in and blowing out air, heard Pogo speak: "Too bad for him. I wish Longo'd go back to California. Then we wouldn't have to be here. He's made this whole thing up."

"Shut up, Pogo," Tracy said.

Mike, his head down, continued to puff and eat rice.

That night Mike went on his first ambush patrol.

"Hot dog," Crane said after Longo's briefing in the tent, "a Binh Le ambush. That means sack time. Not even Zorro comes around Binh Le."

At 2300 the five members of the ambush patrol—the four-man fire team plus Crane, who Mike had learned was the platoon corpsman—went through an opening in the barbed wire; a few seconds later they were in the village. There was no moon and the marines had to walk inches behind one another. Once, Short-round, the point man, stopped, and Mike, his cover, bumped into him.

"Watch where the fuck you're going," Short-round growled.

"I'm sorry—"

"Shut up, you guys," came Crane's even louder voice from behind.

They set up on a trail that ran around the outside of the village. Nobody seemed to expect to see or hear anything; nobody was concerned with cover. Only one man stayed up at a time while the rest slept. Mike, standing his watch, stared into the blackness in front of him and tried to stay awake. It was so dark around him it seemed as if his eyes were closed. He began to get afraid—not of the enemy, he couldn't imagine they were in any danger—but simply of being alone. Scenes from his past came into his mind: first days of school, of boot camp, when he had wanted to run away and never come back. What was he doing here?

He shook his head. Suddenly he heard something. A snore. What kind of ambush was this, anyway? He thought of one of those books he had read—a novel about a CIA agent working with mountain tribespeople, in love with the chieftain's daughter. On his ambushes everyone was always awake—and they always got two or three VC, captured or killed. What did this ambush have to do with what the captain had talked about, with what Mike had come to Vietnam for? He found himself wishing he were back in the captain's tent, standing over the grease-penciled map, discussing history and strategy. He tried to think of an idea for fighting the war.

When it became light the patrol moved back through the village. It, too, was different from what Mike had expected. It was dusty and smelled of animal dung; the villagers' clothes looked dirty. Old men and women squatted together, talking, as if the marines weren't there. On the ground, scattered like litter, were pieces of paper with Vietnamese writing.

Suddenly a group of small children rushed up to the patrol, holding out their hands and chanting, "Marine number one, marine number one. . . . You got cigarette? You got cigarette? . . . Marine number one."

"Lying bastards," Motor mumbled, making a threatening gesture.

One of the children followed Short-round. "You got money?"

"That's close," Short-round said, shoving him away.

Then they surrounded Longo. Some of them knew his name: "Long-o! Long-o!"

Longo was smiling. "Hey, look what we have here: the Binh Le Street Players." He picked one of them up and held him next to his face. "Didn't your mommy ever tell you you're too young to smoke? Huh? Hey, you want a lollipop? Too bad, I don't have any. Here . . ." He took out cans of C rations from his trouser pockets and handed them out. "Don't grab, don't grab. Be cool."

Motor, standing next to Mike, said, "At least with Longo around the dirty fuckers won't bother you as much." He laughed dryly. "He's like flypaper."

Then a wrinkled old man with a beard like Ho Chi Minh's and dressed in what looked like pajamas came up to Longo, shooing the children away. He began talking very fast.

Longo nodded. "Yeah, yeah, that's cool, man, that's cool." He said to Mike, "Hey, can I bum one of your cigarettes?" Mike gave him one and Longo handed it to the old man. "Here, papa-*san*, here's a little present from Crazy Mike. . . . You say you've never met Crazy Mike? Allow me. Crazy Mike, meet Rip van Winkle. . . . Don't talk too loud, he just woke up. . . . Didn't you, papa-*san?* Hey, Rip, Crazy Mike here really likes your chow—you know, chop-chop? Crazy Mike ate it all up." Longo gestured with his fingers up to his lips and pointed at Mike.

The old man turned to Mike, talking excitedly. His teeth were yellow and his skin was blotched. Longo said, "That's right, Rip—Crazy Mike here. He ate it all up." The old man stopped talking and smiled. He had a nice smile, Mike thought; a kind face.

"Rip says to come over for dinner sometime—right, papa-*san?*" The old man bobbed his head. Longo, still grinning, told him goodbye, that they'd be back sometime to have a meal.

When they started back to the Fort Mike said, "You speak Vietnamese, Longo?"

"Hell, no. You kidding? I got a hard enough time with English."

"Then how did you know what the old man was saying?"

Longo threw out his arms. "I could tell, man. You don't need to know the language to communicate. The old guy just wanted to, like, *express* himself—you know? Be seen by his neighbors talking with the big Number Ones—you dig? It's cool, man."

"Is he the village chief or something?"

"Sure, man—something. If he isn't he wants to be. He's all right. He likes you."

When they got back to the Fort, Mike heard that another ambush, from the third platoon, set up on the far side of Ai Tu, had been hit. Two marines had been wounded, one in the stomach and the other in the leg. Both had had to be medevacked. It was the work of Zorro, everyone said.

*   *   *

The next day Mike went on his first daylight patrol. There were seven of them: the fire team, Crane, plus a two-man machine-gun team—Brutus and his assistant, C.C., the marine who always seemed to be taking pictures or cleaning his camera. In training Mike had enjoyed patrolling, with the marines silently and warily passing through wooded areas, communicating by hand signals. Now he found himself clumsily moving across rice paddies in full view of villagers working on their crop. The marines in the column talked out loud and smoked cigarettes; when they stopped for chow they left empty C-ration tins behind. It was a sunny, hot day and Mike sweated heavily. He had thought he was in shape, but halfway through the patrol he had drunk both his canteens and he was still thirsty. How hot was it? It must be over a hundred degrees. Mike's back, under his flak jacket, began to ache; his legs felt weak. What if they made contact with the enemy? Mike didn't want to think about it; he just wanted to get back to the Fort where he could drink water. Never had he been this thirsty, had his legs felt so weak.

They entered a village.

"Welcome to Ai Tu," Longo, smiling, said to Mike. "Ever read *Julius Caesar?*" Longo seemed to be hardly tired or thirsty at all.

"What? Oh, yeah."

"This vill is what he was talking about, man. *Ai Tu, Bruté?* Just don't turn your back."

Behind Longo, Crane laughed raucously. "That is about the worst I ever heard, Longo," he said.

The village seemed even dustier than Binh Le. There weren't as many people visible; only two or three children begged for money and cigarettes. The same pieces of paper with Vietnamese writing were littered all around.

Longo stopped by a wrinkled old woman squatting next to a large cooking pot in front of a house. "Hey, Ma Barker," he said, "you hiding any VC in that pot? How about Zorro—he in there? You haven't seen the Cisco Kid around, have you?"

The woman spoke back in a harsh, unfriendly voice.

"I know, I know," Longo said, "you're pissed off at me 'cause I didn't bring you that picture of Lyndon Johnson I promised. But it's coming, soon." She spoke some more. Longo said, "Hey, everything's cool. You want to be in the movies or not?" He turned around. "Motor, Short-round, search the hooch. Crazy Mike, you cover. Don't take too long."

Motor and Short-round went into the house. Mike said to Longo, "What are they looking for?"

Longo shrugged. "Who knows? Autographed copies of Ho Chi Minh. They won't find anything. Ma Barker's too smart for that. This just lets her know that we know she's VC."

"How do you know that?"

Longo smiled. "Man, everyone in this vill is VC. Besides"—he pointed with his M-16 at the pot over the fire—"that's a pretty big pot of rice just for herself. I'd say she's expecting some company—sometime." Mike nodded. "Plus," Longo said, gesturing in back of him, "*he* might be watching."

"Huh? Who?"

"Captain Blood. You know, with those binoculars of his: he's always looking out. Big Brother, we almost called him."

Mike turned but he could see nothing of the Fort through the trees of Ai Tu. He turned back to Longo. "Say, who is this Zorro guy, anyway?"

Longo grinned. "Watch out for him, man—he's Number Ten. Him and the Cisco Kid—one at night, the other by day. You bag one of them and Captain Blood'll love you forever."

Motor came out of the house. "Nothing," he said. He turned. "Hey, mama-*san*, watch this." He coughed up phlegm and spit it into the pot. The old lady rattled out words. "Shut the fuck up," Motor said, "or I'll punch your teeth in."

Short-round, coming out of the hooch, laughed huskily. "That's right, Motor—that's brave." Motor swore again.

"Okay?" Longo shouted. "Let's get this over with. As soon as you don't find anything in the rest of these hooches, we'll go."

When they got back to the Fort, Mike drank almost two canteens full of water.

*   *   *

Mike went on more patrols in the following days and it seemed that his problems weren't getting any better: always the enormous thirst and the pain in his back and the drained, weak feeling in his legs. What if they found any VC—or any VC found them? It was obvious to Mike that the marines were a much more visible target than their enemy. Other patrols in the company were making contact. In the week after Mike arrived four marines were wounded and one killed, all from the second and third platoons. The woundings were the work of the Cisco Kid, everyone said; the KIA belonged to Zorro. Zorro had a captured grenade launcher and the Cisco Kid an M-1 rifle; between them they were responsible for over half of the company's casualties. How many more VC were there? Nobody Mike talked to seemed to know. Some thought that all the villagers were VC, others that they came and went, only a few remained in the area permanently.

In all the villages—except Binh Le—were booby traps and mines that added to the marines' casualties. Also in the villages, scattered everywhere, were those pieces of paper with Vietnamese writing Mike had noticed on his first patrols: leaflets, he soon learned, calling on the VC to defect. Rain, the squad grenadier, who was on his second tour in-country and was teaching himself Vietnamese, would bring back samples of the leaflets to translate. Sometimes marines brought back other things, too: cups and plates and sticks of incense and candles, taken from villagers' homes. Once Day-train brought back a puppy, stuffed inside his flak jacket. Snoopy, Longo immediately named it, and C.C. snapped picture after picture. But when the captain found out he made Day-train return it—because of possible rabies; besides, he said, marines shouldn't take things from villagers.

When he wasn't patrolling, much of Mike's time was spent cleaning his rifle and gear. In boot camp he had disliked rifle cleaning and now he grew to hate it: over and over, the same messy task, fumbling with the parts in the sand by insufficient light. Why keep it clean? He had yet to use it. As he sat in the tent doing his chores, he would listen to the talk around him. The

marines spoke of where they came from and what they were going
go do when they went back. Motor was from a suburb of Detroit
and talked of cars all the time. "Tracy" was short for "Dick
Tracy"—because he wanted to be a cop when he got out of the
Corps. There was talk of Vietnam, too: about fire fights and casualties and VC KIA, Operation Red River and before that; about
how long each marine had been in-country and how long he had
to go.

Once, a few days after Mike arrived, he found himself sitting
next to Longo during a break in one of their patrols. They were in
a shady area on the edge of a rice paddy. To Mike's right, Motor
was sleeping; Short-round was eating C rations; Pogo was asleep
too.

"Hey, man, where'd you learn to eat with chopsticks like that,
like you did that time in the tent? You looked pretty good."

Mike shrugged. "When I lived up North."

"Oh, yeah?"

"Yeah." He drank the rest of his water and put away his canteen. He was still very thirsty. Longo took out one of his, swished
water around in his mouth, then spit it out.

"Want some of mine?" he said.

"No . . . I mean—yeah; maybe. A little."

Mike swished water around too but then swallowed it. He took
another large gulp. "I, uh, guess I am pretty thirsty."

"That's all right, man; go ahead, take some more." Mike hesitated, then did so. "You'll get used to it," Longo said. "I was like
that too, when I first came over."

"Really?" Mike handed back the canteen. He lit a cigarette,
then offered one to Longo.

"Thanks. . . . So where'd you live up North?"

"New York."

"City?"

"Yeah, when I was little."

"Really? Wow, that place scares me. I mean, like, I've always
wanted to go there, but I'm afraid of it too. You know what I
mean?"

Mike nodded. He was staring across the rice paddy toward the tree line opposite, pretending to look for VC. He was still thirsty.

Longo was talking again: "So where'd you go to high school—in Virginia?"

"Yeah."

"And then you went in the Crotch?"

Mike shook his head. "College first."

"No shit? You went to college?"

"Yeah. For a while."

"Hey, I didn't mean it like that; it's just that not too many grunts have been to college. You graduate?"

Mike shook his head. "Quit."

"You quit? Me, too, man, I quit too."

Mike turned. "Really? You went to college?"

Longo smiled. "Yeah, like I said, it's pretty unusual. Didn't last very long, though. Where'd you go?"

"Little school in Virginia you've probably never heard of. Henry and Lee."

'That's right, I haven't. I went to one you probably never heard of either. Monte Rio."

"In California."

"That's right. How'd you know that?"

"They play football. I've seen their scores."

"No shit. So you dig football, huh? You ought to meet my brothers, man; they're the same way: talking about some school nobody's heard of, Northwestern South Dakota State, just because they saw it mentioned once in the sports pages, maybe it played in the Cornflake Bowl one year, something like that. Man, if you could make money from knowing stuff like that, my brothers'd be rich. . . . So why'd you quit, anyway?"

Mike shrugged. Why were they sitting here? Was it safe? He wanted to get back to the Fort, to the water bag hanging by the platoon tent where he could drink as much as he wanted.

"Didn't like it."

The answer seemed to excite Longo. "You too? The same with me, man. I mean, like, I didn't dig it at all. All those people were so *serious*—you know what I mean? I mean, I don't know what it was like where you went, but Monte Rio . . . how can I describe it?" He brought up his shoulders and raised his arms. "It's like this real small private college in northern California full of rich kids who couldn't get into anyplace better. Except me, of course—I was on scholarship, full one." He shook his head. "But these other kids, they were really something: all of them pretending they were at Stanford or Yale or someplace like that, wearing these real preppy clothes, taking themselves so *seriously*. I felt sorry for them, I really did." He became thoughtful. "And then, when I quit, everybody wanted to know why—the dean, the professors, even the president. Why? Why? What happened?" He smiled. "How could I tell them? I quit because I quit." He paused. "Actually, I think I was about to flunk out, anyway. I had a real problem with classes—just couldn't sit still—you know what I mean?"

Mike nodded. Longo seemed unable to speak without moving—waving his arms, squirming, gesturing with his hands. Mike sat very still.

"So what was your major, anyway?" Longo asked. "What were you studying?"

Mike hesitated. "Business."

"*Business?* No wonder you quit."

"Yeah . . . well, actually, I got into a little trouble too."

"Oh? Like what?"

Mike gestured impatiently. "Nothing much. Booze in the room—stuff like that."

"Oh, yeah?" Longo became excited again. "Man, this *is* like the French Foreign Legion—you know?—how all those German and French guys get in trouble with the law and then join up to get away, change their names. Pogo was in trouble too"—he nodded toward him—"knocked up some girl who was going to bring a paternity suit. You know C.C.—machine gunner, guy who's always taking pictures? He got in some big brawl back in Memphis and the judge made him join the Crotch—or go to jail. C.C.'s a brawler—was in a big one in Okinawa too, on his way over, got busted. And Rain"—Longo lowered his voice—"Rain got caught bringing back some big load of grass from Mexico—Tijuana." Longo shook his head. "Man, I wish we had some over here—after all that stuff you read about back in the States, how it's all over Vietnam. The Crotch don't have nothing: no bennies at all."

Mike said, "Oh, yeah?"

"Look at the Army," Longo went on, "they've got everything. I got this cousin who was over here, stationed in Saigon—man, the way he talked about it, it sounded like one big R and R. I mean, he comes over the house with all these pictures to show us—like, I thought it was going to be all this gory stuff—but no, it's his girl friends! I mean, they were *pictures*, man: like, the Vietnamese version of *Playboy* or something. My mother almost hit him over the head. . . . So when I got drafted I figured, well, at least there's all this other stuff going on. But no way, man, not in the Crotch."

Mike blew out smoke. "So," he said, "you got drafted?"

"Shit, you don't think I'd *ask* to join the Marine Corps, do you?" He swore again. "Like, I never thought *they* would take *me*. I mean, I was working in a dance company at the time—"

"A *dance* company?"

Longo grinned. "Sure, why not? I mean, I really go for that stuff, you know? Like, those were the only courses I really liked in college—dance, drama, stuff like that. I used to do everything—act, direct, stagehand, sell tickets—you name it. Hell, I would've stayed there if I could've just done that all the time." He turned toward Mike. "You ever do any theater—drama club or anything like that?"

"Huh? Me? No."

"No? You've got a good voice for it."

"So, uh, what happened?" Mike asked. "I mean, you said you were a *dancer*—when you got drafted?"

Longo smiled sheepishly. "Yeah, I was with this group called the Brooklyn Dodger Dance Collective—"

"In New York? I thought you said you were never in the city—"

"I wasn't, man—never near the place. This was in L.A. That's where I'm from—outside it, place called Compton. But these

people who started the dance company were from New York—
some of them, anyway—and one of them was this big baseball nut
who wanted everybody in L.A. to know that the Dodgers—but
what does that matter? You can call something anything you
want. I mean, like, it's all in the *mind*, you know? Like, we were
the Brooklyn Dodgers of this guy's mind."

"But—you were really a *dancer*? A professional?"

"Sure." Longo looked pleased. "I was a dancer because I called
myself one—same thing. I mean, I had taken some classes—jazz,
tap, ballet—"

"*Ballet?* You took ballet lessons?"

Longo laughed. "Classes, man. But the way you just looked—
that's *exactly* how I wanted the draft board to react. I mean, like, I
was really putting it on." He flapped his wrist. "I mean, for 'main
occupation' I had written down *ballet dancer*—even though I
wasn't even getting paid at the time." Longo shook his head and
swore. Suddenly Mike laughed. "But they didn't bat an eyelash. I
mean, they didn't say a *word*! What kind of draft board was that,
anyway?" He flapped his wrist again. "I should've gone in tights,
man—I knew I should have. I'd be back in California right
now. . . ."

Mike shook his head, grinning. "That's something, Longo, that
really is."

Longo smiled back. He said, "So how about you—you get
drafted too?"

Mike shook his head. "Negative."

"You mean you *enlisted*?"

"Uh-huh."

"What did you do that for?"

Mike could feel Longo's stare. "Why the hell not?" he said.
"There was a war going on—you know?"

"Man, you really *are* crazy."

Mike thought of saying something more. He flicked away his
cigarette.

Longo looked at his watch—a Mickey Mouse watch, Mike noticed. Longo said, "Well, guess we'd better get on back. Don't want Captain Blood to think we're winning too many hearts and minds. . . . Hey, Short-round, wake up Pogo."

"Uh-uh," Short-round said. "I ain't waking up nobody. Last time I did that out on patrol fucking guy tried to kill me. Ski. Said I woke him right in the middle of a fire fight—in his dream!"

Mike and Longo laughed. "Hey, Pogo," Longo called out, "wake up!"

"Fuckin' guy sleeps more'n anybody I know." It was Motor, now awake himself.

Pogo opened his eyes, rubbed them, then stretched. He looked like some kind of small furry animal.

"Time to go home?" he asked.

"Back to the Fort."

"Oh. I thought maybe the war was over or something." He put on his helmet and stretched again. He really did look like a comic-strip character, Mike thought.

Longo said, "What were you dreaming about, anyway, Pogo?" He turned to Mike. "Pogo has the greatest dreams, man. He'd be great making movies, he really would—"

"Oh, God," Pogo said, "now I remember. A terrible dream. No, please, I beg of you, don't make me repeat it."

Short-round said, "Bullshit, Pogo. Go on, tell us. What was the dream?"

"Yeah, Pogo," Motor said, "let's hear it."

"Well . . ." Pogo sat down and screwed up his face. "It was like this. I was back home in Nebraska, out in this field. It was spring. A real nice spring day. Not too cool, not too hot. Just perfect. A little bit of a breeze—"

"Enough with the weather report," Short-round said. "What happened?"

"Well." Pogo spoke as though he had difficulty controlling the muscles of his mouth. "I was lying down, right by a brook. Overhead there was a big old oak tree making lots of shade for me. And then suddenly there were all these girls: all around me, all of them just wanted to do whatever I wanted them to do. And they were all really beautiful, too. Plus, none of them had anything on. . . . Come to think of it, I didn't either."

Mike, grinning, said, "Sounds like a pretty good dream to me."

"Oh, no," Pogo said, "it was horrible. Just listen to what happened. Then I fell asleep. And I had a dream. I dreamt I was in a strange country, far away, halfway around the world. There was a war going on. I had to go on patrol all the time, eat my food out of little cans. There were people called Short-round and Motor—"

"Oh, go fuck yourself, Pogo," Short-round said. "You didn't have no dream like that."

Pogo raised his eyebrows. "Oh, but I did. You can ask Longo—he was there. Go on, tell them, Longo, how you woke me."

Motor shook his head. "This whole squad is crazy—nuts, bananas."

"Yeah, right," Short-round said, "everyone but you, right Motor? That's close." He laughed throatily.

"Come on," Longo said, "let's go, you guys. Saddle up. It's getting late. Captain Blood's gonna wonder where we are. He's probably up there right now scopin' us out with those bug-eyes of his. He sees all, man."

"Then he'll tell you," Pogo said, "about my dream."

When they got back to the Fort, Mike went to the water bag and drank until he felt he was going to burst.

One evening a tank on its way out to the Fort hit a mine and got stuck. Nobody was hurt, but Mike's platoon had to go out and set up a perimeter defense around the tank while the crew repaired it. Motor was happy; he hung around the crew, asking questions about the engine. But when it became dark the rumor spread that the VC were going to attack. For hours a helicopter dropped flare after flare, keeping the area light, while Crane, the corpsman, cursed the captain for leaving them so exposed. The marines collected the small parachutes from the flares to take back to the Fort and decorate their tiny makeshift mess hall—the

MGM Commissary, Longo had named it, run by a marine he called Prince Mike Romanoff. Finally, at three in the morning, the tank got moving and the platoon went back. There was no attack.

Another night Mike, standing watch at the Fort at two in the morning, found himself unable to stay awake. Time after time he'd rouse from his drowsiness as his head fell forward. He'd open his eyes wide and stare out at the moonlit night, then begin to fall asleep again. How could this be happening? he wondered, in between nods of his head. In training it had happened, but now he was in a war. But was it really war? Sitting atop the sandbagged bunker, fully exposed in the moonlight, Mike could not imagine that he was in any danger. If only he could sleep!

Suddenly he heard a sound behind him. For a moment he thought he was too tired to turn around. But he did.

"Who is it?"

He was answered by a low, gruff voice: "Who's on watch?"

"I am, sir. I mean, Allison. Pfc. Allison, sir." Mike stood up. Now he could see the captain's face, dotted with sweat. Around his neck were a pair of binoculars and a green towel.

"Hell, don't look at me, marine. You're on watch." He gestured toward the wire. "Anything out there?"

Mike spun around. "No, sir. I haven't seen a thing, sir." He smelled tobacco on the captain's breath behind him; a strong, foul odor.

"What time is your watch?"

"Two to four, sir. I mean, zero two hundred to four hundred. Sir."

"And who succeeds you?"

"Sir? Oh, uh, Short-round, sir."

"Short-round?"

"Uh, yes, sir." Mike realized he didn't know Short-round's real name.

"That another one of Longo's labels?"

"Uh, I guess so, sir."

"And what name does he have for me, Allison?"

"Sir?" Mike felt his face get hot. "I, uh . . ."

"That's all right, marine." Mike could tell the captain was smiling. "I know all about Longo. He tell you his plan yet—the one he's got for ending the war?"

"Sir? I, uh, don't think—"

"Wish to hell we could use it." He laughed drily. Then his voice became serious again. "Allison," he said, as though to himself. "Aren't you the one who's read all those books about how to fight this war?"

"I, uh, I've read a couple of books, yes—"

"And so what do you think now, Allison, now that you've had a little taste of it—firsthand, so to speak? Any ideas?"

"I, uh, I'm not sure—"

"It's a little different when you're right in the middle of it; those professors don't have all the answers."

"Yes—uh, no, sir."

The captain snorted. They stood for a few moments in silence. "Tired, Allison?" the captain asked.

"Uh, yes, sir, a little."

"I'll bet you are." The captain's voice became louder. "I'll bet you're tired as hell. And you're going to get a lot more tired, too. Because the truth is, there's no easy answer to this war. Charlie's trying to wear us down and we're trying to do the same to him. And the first one that falls asleep, gets it: zap. Don't be fooled, Allison. They're out there—they're out there and they're watching." He raised the binoculars to his eyes.

"Yes, sir."

"Damn, even with this moon I can't see a thing." He lowered his glasses and shook his head. "They say Charlie can see in the dark better than we can, but that's a lot of crap. I know, Allison, I've read what the experts say, and it isn't true. Don't believe it."

"No, sir."

The next morning, eating a C-ration breakfast in the tent, Mike told his fellow marines about his talk with the captain.

"You're shittin' me," Short-round said. "He didn't ask you that, did he? About what Longo calls him?"

"He really did."

Short-round threw his head back and laughed. "And what'd you tell him—that we call him Captain Blood? You probably did, you crazy bastard."

Mike grinned and said nothing. Pogo said, "You ought to tell him we call him Zorro."

"Zorro?" Mike said. "What are you talking about, Pogo?"

"Ignore him," Tracy said. "He's stupid. He doesn't know what he's talking about. . . . Shut up, Pogo."

"But I'm serious," Pogo said, scratching his head and stretching. "That's who Zorro really is—the captain. I finally found out. Last night. I saw him sneaking back through the wire on my watch—right before Crazy Mike. Didn't that ambush from third platoon get hit by Zorro right about that time?"

"That's right," Mike said, "I remember now—he was all sweated up when I saw him. Captain Blood, I mean."

"See?"

"That's great," Longo said, excited. "Good work, Pogo. So it was Captain Blood all along. Now we've got to catch him in the act. . . . But who's going to fight the big sword duel with him at the end?"

"You mean then we get to go home, Longo?"

"Jesus," Motor said, "what a squad full of idiots."

The next day the whole squad went out on patrol. Longo's fire team was first in the column, with Short-round point and Mike cover; Longo was behind Mike and Tracy behind him. They were just entering the village of Ai Tu late in the afternoon when suddenly Longo said, "Hold it."

Immediately Short-round stopped. Without turning around, he said, "What is it?" He seemed to have become even shorter, standing with his knees slightly bent, his rifle at the ready.

"Something's wrong."

What could be wrong? Mike thought. He was out of water; he had a sharp pain in his back and his legs were tired. He wanted to get back to the Fort.

Tracy asked, "What is it, Longo?"

Longo frowned. "There's no people, man. Where is everybody?"

Mike looked again at the few hooches he could see. Longo was right.

Tracy said, "But—maybe so, but we're supposed to go through and search."

"Something's going on," Longo said.

Tracy said nothing; he pushed his glasses back up on his nose. Ahead on the trail Short-round was on one knee, staring ahead, as still as a rock. Mike shifted his weight from one leg to the other.

Tracy said, "Maybe we should radio the Fort."

"You know what they'll say, man—all the more reason to go through."

Tracy kept staring ahead, frowning. Now he was biting his lips.

"You could say we got lost." It was Pogo, right behind Tracy.

"Shut up, Pogo."

"But it's true: I am lost. Have been ever since I got here. Where are we, anyway?"

"I said *shut up.*"

There was silence. Then Longo said, "Maybe we should go back and go around."

"But we're supposed to go through." Tracy sounded like a little boy. "It's the patrol route. What if the captain is watching with those goddamn glasses of his? If we go around he'll see when we're coming in. . . . Besides, that's not the point. We're supposed to go through." Nobody said anything. "All right, go ahead, Short-round." Tracy sounded as if he were making a compromise. "But be real careful."

Short-round, still with his back turned, said, "I wasn't about to go rushing through."

"Move through on the right," Longo said. "Get off the trail."

Short-round, with Mike following, stepped slowly through bushes into a small yard. He went to the door of the house, looked in, then proceeded to the next hedgerow. He inspected it, then carefully picked his way through. Mike did the same. Now he wished they had gone back and around, as Longo had said; it would have been much faster than this. He hoped one of the hooches would have water.

There was a shot, then more shots, then a burst of fire. Was it Short-round who fired? He was down; Mike could no longer see him. "Oh, fuck!" someone shouted. Short-round? The dirt to the right of Mike's feet kicked up. Now there was so much firing it sounded like the machine-gun range at Camp Lejeune. Something hit Mike in the back, hard. He went down.

"Get *down*, man!" It was Longo, half covering Mike with his body. It was he who had hit him in the back, Mike realized. The two of them crawled to a tree, five feet off to their right. Longo kneeled and fired a burst from his M-16, then got down again, but with his head up, observing.

"What is it?" Mike said. "Where are they?"

Longo ignored him. "*Short-round!*" he yelled. "You all right, man?"

A muffled voice answered: "That's fucking close!"

"You hit?"

"No shit!" Mike cringed; it sounded as though Short-round was crying.

Longo turned and shouted back: "*Crane!*"

The firing went on. Mike raised his rifle and put it on automatic. But where should he fire? What was going on?

"See that tree?" Longo said, as if reading Mike's thoughts. He pointed ahead and Mike nodded. "When I say *go*, fire a burst at the top of it. He's gone, I know. I just want to make sure." He raised up on his haunches. "All right? . . . Go! . . . *Fire!*"

Mike fired. Longo rushed ahead out of sight. It occurred to Mike that he had never seen anyone move as fast.

Tracy and Crane, the corpsman, came up next to him. "What's happening?" Tracy said. Mike hesitated, began to answer, but Tracy spoke again: "Where's Longo?"

Mike nodded. "Up there. He told me to stay here."

"He hit?"

Mike shook his head. "But Short-round is. I mean, I think he is."

Crane swore. Tracy looked behind him, then ahead again. "*Longo!*"

Longo's voice came back: "Yeah, it's okay! Hold your fire. He's beat it. Get Crane up here—fast!"

As Tracy shouted back—"Hold your fire! Hold your fire!"— Crane loped ahead. Mike thought for a moment, then went up too.

Crane was kneeling next to Short-round, studying his eyes; Longo stood a few feet ahead. Short-round's right thigh was bright red and his face was very pale. Mike joined Longo and stood as he was standing, looking out, his rifle ready.

"What's your name?" Mike could hear Crane saying. "Tell me your goddamn name!"

Short-round swore. "You know it!"

"Tell me!"

Short-round swore again. "It's . . . Short-round!"

Suddenly Tracy, Pogo, and Motor came up to the position. Motor looked quickly at Short-round's leg, swore, then went and stood by Longo and Mike, facing away from Short-round. His face was pale, too.

"You're okay, Short-round," Crane said and stuck a needle into Short-round's arm.

"Fucking close," Short-round said. "I'm gonna lose it, aren't I, Crane?"

"Shut up! You're not going to lose nothing!" Crane swore. "Just take it easy—don't panic! Goddamnit, I've seen worse legs on Navy nurses." He took out a bandage and began to wrap it around Short-round's thigh. Then he took out another. Meanwhile Tracy shouted back at Blevins to bring up his fire team, along with the machine gun. Mike turned toward the front again and breathed deeply.

"That fucker," Crane said, still working on Short-round. "He's laughing his ass off right now."

Mike asked Longo, "Who?"

"The Cisco Kid," Crane answered. "Who else?"

"Really? Are you sure?"

Crane swore again. "I said so, didn't I? I'd know that goddamn rifle anywhere. M-1. Damn good weapon. I'd love to know how he got his hands on it. I'd court-martial the fucking marine who let it go."

Mike looked toward Longo, who nodded. "This is about the twentieth time the Kid's hit someone since we've been out here." He shrugged. "I figured something like this was going to happen." Mike glanced quickly at Tracy but Tracy, staring down at Short-round, said nothing.

Blevins came into the clearing along with his fire team and Brutus, C.C., and Rain.

"Goddamn," Blevins said, slowly drawing it out. He took a half cigar out of his mouth and stared down at Short-round.

"Shut up and set up your team, Blevins," Tracy said. "Over there—on the right. Longo, set your men up on the left. Rain, up there by the tree. Brutus, over there." Rain, the grenadier, moved swiftly and quietly into position. Brutus moved quickly too, but C.C. lingered by Short-round.

"Get the hell out of here, C.C.," Short-round said. "You try to take a picture of my leg and I'll shoot you, I swear I will." C.C. ran the few feet over to Brutus.

Pogo finished calling in the medevac report and then said to Tracy, "They'll be right here." He sounded as if he were talking about a take-out food order.

"That's close," Short-round said. "Watch, they'll have a flat rotor, or whatever it is fucking choppers get. Just my luck. Lose a fucking leg."

"Goddamnit—shut up!" Crane shouted it. "I told you, you're not going to lose it! You're going to be all right!" Looming over Short-round, he looked as if he might hit him.

Blevins, edging back toward the center of the clearing, said, "Don't worry, Short-round, we'll get that bastard. That's a promise."

"That's fucking close too." Short-round lashed the words out at Blevins. "You're so fucking slow you couldn't catch that tree. And stop eye-balling my goddamn leg!" Blevins puffed on his cigar and stared blankly away.

In a few moments the chopper appeared. Pogo threw a red smoke grenade, and it came down, its rotors whirring, filling the small yard with wind and noise. Mike helped carry Short-round. When the helicopter left, the marines stared after it, silent, then started back to the Fort.

That evening in the Commissary, over a B-ration meal of canned scrambled eggs, there was much talk among the marines about the Cisco Kid.

"Now I don't normally get violent," C.C. said, "but I personally serve notice I'm gonna kill that cowardly little motherfucker. And then after I get through taking his ears and toes off, I'm gonna shove a grenade down his throat, just for the hell of it."

"No, you don't get violent like it don't get hot over here," Brutus said. "It's a good thing you're over here, anywhere else you'd be in jail. But I do hope you get him—I hope someone does. I believe he's done enough damage." Brutus's soft, muffled voice sounded strange coming from someone so big.

"Has anyone ever seen the Kid?" Mike asked.

Rain shook his head. "He's good; he's real good. Sometimes I wonder if he's even trying to kill us. He's only zapped a couple so far—"

"Not like that goddamn Zorro," Blevins said.

"Just about every time it's a wound," Rain went on, "a bad wound, usually." He turned to Longo. "Remember Shadow? Shattered his elbow. And Fibber—right in the knee." He and others continued the list, naming marines Mike had never met: Thunder, Hornet, Fearless Fosdick. "It's like he's teasing us," Rain said. "It's like he knows it costs the government a hell of a lot more to nurse a guy for six months than to bury him." Mike nodded in agreement. He liked listening to Rain. Rain rarely said anything, but when he did it was always worthwhile.

"We'll get that bastard," Blevins said, looking at Mike. "You wait."

"Bullshit." It was Crane.

Blevins seemed taken aback. "Huh?"

"I mean we're never going to get him—we're never going to get anyone. This whole thing is stupid. Go out, get wounded, call in the chopper, come back. For Christ's sake . . ." Crane lowered his head. " 'Captain Blood' is right—all the goddamn officers—make them go out on patrol, patch up the wounded, see how they like it."

Blevins laughed for a moment. "Goddamn, Ichabod, I believe you're angry." He glanced around the table, but nobody said anything. Suddenly Crane got up and walked back toward the platoon tent.

After Longo finished eating he said to Mike, "Hey, man, can I have a word with you?"

"Sure."

They were sitting across from one another at the table; everyone else had left. It was almost dark; the hanging parachutes cast vague shadows against the Commissary's walls. Longo smiled in a hesitant way. "Well, I guess you've probably figured out what I'm going to say. . . ."

Mike gave him a puzzled look. "I'm not sure."

"I mean, with Short-round getting hit. That means the fire team needs a new point."

"Oh." Mike felt a sudden hollowness inside. He tried to think. Why was he so slow to figure things out?

Longo went on, "Now, I know you've only been here—how long?"

"Two weeks," Mike said, "with the platoon. Actually, a little less."

"Two weeks. Man, time goes awful slow over here. Thirteen months is like forever." Longo was thoughtful. Then he said, "Yeah, I know that's not very long—but it happens in less time. I've heard about some units up north where they put a guy on point right away, like, first day. He makes it or he doesn't." He shook his head. "But I don't believe in that—not if you don't have to. But it's like I don't really have much choice, seeing as how there's only three of us and I'm the team leader and Motor's already been point. I mean, I could make Motor point again, but I really don't want to. He's pretty shook up—he and Short-round were close. . . . Besides, I think he's starting to lose it."

Mike nodded. His stomach felt a little sick, as if he had eaten too much. From across the wire down in Binh Le he could hear villagers talking. He wished he were down there too, a simple villager. "The Three Blind Mice again," he said, trying to smile.

Longo grinned. "Right, man. . . . But the thing is, point is not really that big a deal—that's what you've got to remember. I know, back in the States, you hear a lot about how bad it is. But a lot of that is smoke. I mean, if Charlie is really serious about putting a hurt on us—like, if there's a main-force unit out there— then it's really not gonna matter whether you're point or not; in fact, Charlie's probably gonna let the point man go by before he opens up. So don't let that stuff rattle you." Mike nodded. "And if it's a sniper—like today with Short-round—actually I was surprised the Kid went after him because usually he tries for the patrol leader or radioman or machine gunner—like, something that takes a little training or more experience. Like Rain says, he's not stupid. But the main thing is not to walk into it—like we did today. I mean, I *knew* something was going to happen."

Mike nodded. "Yeah."

"So don't be afraid to take your time. Survive, that's the main thing. You've seen how Short-round does it, watches where he steps and all that. If you want to stop and look around, that's cool, go ahead and do it. And if you want to go back, try another way, that's all right too. When you're point it's your show: you decide where to put your feet."

"Uh-huh."

"I mean, if it was up to me, we'd never even walk through a vill like Ai Tu anyway. What's the use? We know the gooks don't like us, we know there's gonna be at least a booby trap or two. So why the hell go through?" He held out his arms and smiled wistfully. "If they'd only listen to me—my plan. . . . Anyway, there haven't been any big VC units around here for a while; I just hope it stays that way. Because they could wipe out any of our patrols any time they wanted to." He laughed. "It would be no contest—seven, eight guys against a company or even a platoon? Sometimes I wonder why they don't do it. Maybe they figure they made their point—the time they overran the place."

"But I thought they—I mean, the captain said they didn't, like, succeed. In wiping it out, I mean. That they were driven back."

"Succeed?" Longo raised his shoulders and smiled; his high cheekbones stuck out. "Man, what do you want them to do? Whenever they get through the wire that's a victory. Word gets out and guys start thinking twice—you know, about all that invincible stuff we've been fed about the Crotch. Man, I know a couple of dudes who were here—that night. They said it was bad, man, real bad. Like nobody knew *what* was going on. The gooks were running around, shouting stuff in English; guys were shooting each other—"

"Really? But—they did fight them off."

"Or the gooks decided to leave. Like I said, maybe they figured they had made their point." Longo shook his head.

Mike nodded and thought about asking a question. But Longo went on: "Not that I'm complaining. I mean, things could be a lot worse. Like, I wouldn't want to be up north, up by the Z."

"I hear that's pretty bad."

Longo opened his eyes wide. "Bad? Shit! They get overrun up there for breakfast. I've got a cousin who's up there and you should read his letters. Like, those guys go without food and water, sometimes. And man, they're not fighting Zorro and the Cisco Kid; they're not even fighting platoons or battalions. They've got fucking *divisions* up there, NVA divisions. Man, this one time my cousin was out with his company and he saw a *tank*. Can you believe it?"

Mike frowned. "But we've got them here—"

"No, this wasn't ours. This one said NVA."

"Oh . . . really? No shit."

Longo smiled good-naturedly. "I couldn't believe it either; things are really rough up there. I mean, I'm not saying it doesn't get bad here—like, I hate to see a guy like Short-round get hit. But it's a hell of a lot better than some other places I've heard about. And it beats going on operations, too. At least here we can figure out some ways of avoiding casualties."

There was a pause. Mike asked, "Were you on Red River?"

Longo nodded. His voice dropped. "It was the shits. I mean, I hate to sound like Motor, but it really was. It sucked. We were supposed to be the blocking force—some battalion from Fifth Marines was going to drive this big VC unit right into us, our battalion; that was the plan. But the only thing we ever saw was a bunch of farmers, scared shitless. And then we ran into this minefield. It was bad, really bad. Like, guys without arms and legs, bleeding to death. . . . And then the snipers started. Man, it was like being stuck in quicksand with a nest of bees over your head." He looked down at the table and slowly shook his head. Mike lit a cigarette, cupping it in the darkness. "And all because some colonel from division made us go on. I mean, it was *obvious* we were going to hit more mines—after the first ones. But no, we had to get into place. So we could kill all these VC they were going to drive into us. . . . I guess that's the one thing that really gets me, when they start acting *stupid* like that—I mean, the guys who are in charge. When they start that stuff about how you have to do something because you have to do it, an order is an order and all that."

Longo paused again, then looked up and smiled. "Man, the military is really something, isn't it? I mean, like, it's so *absurd*, you know what I mean? Like boot camp—wasn't that something, all that yelling and stuff, the way those D.I.'s tried to come over as being so *bad*, like, *mean*. Man, sometimes I really had to control myself—from laughing—you know?" He smiled wistfully, then said, "Where'd you go to boot camp, anyway? P.I.?" Mike nodded. "I went to San Diego. Man, that was one thing I was glad about: I can't *stand* the cold. As long as it's warm, I'm okay. When'd you go through—what months?"

"January, February."

"Shit. Didn't it get to you? The cold?"

"Not too much."

Longo shivered. "Man, just thinking about it . . . "

Mike said, "I guess this heat gets to me sometimes. I mean, I get so thirsty. Like, out on patrol; sometimes it's hard to concentrate—because I get so thirsty. I've got this pain in my back, too, when I carry my rifle. I don't know what it is; but it seems to be getting worse. . . ."

Longo smiled good-naturedly. "Yeah, when I first got here I had all kinds of things wrong with me too."

"No, I didn't mean—"

"But you get used to things." Mike opened his mouth, then decided to close it. "Anyway, you got any questions?"

"I—guess not."

"Then I guess that's it."

"Oh, one thing."

"What's that?"

"I . . . I mean—I guess I forgot to tell you—before. Sometimes I'm a little slow. . . . But thanks. I mean, for this afternoon—knocking me down like that."

Longo grinned. "Forget it. I hope I didn't hurt your back. Man, I couldn't believe it—you standing up like that, right in the open. You're crazy, all right. Just don't do that when you're point. Get down. It's good not to be afraid, but don't be foolish."

"Right," Mike said.

That night, sitting cross-legged in the platoon tent by the light of a candle, Mike wrote a letter to his parents. It was short; he told them the food wasn't as bad as he had expected but the mosquitoes were worse. Then he wrote to one of his buddies from boot camp who was still in the States.

Dear Smitty,

I meant to write you sooner, but I have been busy as hell—patrols in the day, ambushes at night, digging ditches, cleaning your weapons, standing watch on the lines—I'm tired all the time. It is hot as hell, too.

Things are really different over here from training. Only three men now in my fire team and ten in the whole squad. I am on a company-sized outpost in the heart of VC country—Ho Chi Minh came from around here. A couple of platoons almost got overrun on this same outpost not too long ago.

The guys I am with are really something—it's like the French Foreign Legion; some of them had to come over here or go to jail. My squad leader seems pretty solid although he is young, about my age. My fire-team leader is a real character—was a *dancer* when he got drafted! But he is really good in the field and seems to have a sense for when something is going to happen.

Like today—made my first contact. It was on a patrol. A sniper hit our point man while we were going through a village. I was right in back of him—cover—and nearly got hit myself. The point—guy named Short-round (everybody here has nicknames; they call me Crazy Mike)—was wounded in the leg pretty bad— he might lose it—and had to be taken out by medevac. There's a shitload of mines and booby traps around too.

Well, tonight I got the word from my fire-team leader. I am the new point man. It is kind of scary, I have to admit. But what the hell—you get used to things over here.

Take care, and have a few cold ones for me.

Mike

A few days later six new marines came out by amtrack to join the company. One was assigned to Mike's fire team—Willie Black, a pfc. right out of Lejeune. He was shorter than Mike but had broad shoulders and a narrow waist. When Longo asked where he was from he said Fort Lauderdale, Florida.

"*Fort Lauderdale?*" Motor sneered. "Isn't that where the boys are?"

"It's where the girls are, man," Black said, "lots of girls, all over the place. Wish I was back there right now, I'll tell you that."

"Yeah, actually, I'd like to go down there myself sometime,"

Motor said. "That was a pretty good movie. . . . Hey, Longo, what're you gonna call him? Who was in that movie?"

Longo shrugged; he looked sheepish.

Mike asked, "You play football?"

Black nodded. "Halfback, man. Ran track too. Dash man."

"You look like a halfback," Mike said. "I'll bet you're fast."

"Man," Longo said, smiling, "you're black all right. You're about the blackest dude I've ever seen."

Black grinned. His teeth were like lights in the darkened tent. "That's me," he said, "black and fast. Just wait till those Vietcongs start shooting, you'll just see how fast: you ain't gonna see nothin' but a black *streak.*"

"That's it!" Longo, excited, turned to Mike. "His name: the Black Streak! That's who he is."

Black seemed pleased. "The Black Streak," he repeated, "that's me, all right. The Black Streak."

The next day Jefferson came into the tent. "Swim call! Anybody who wants it, outside in five minutes."

"*Swim* call?" The Black Streak smiled broadly. "That's more like it—that's just like back home. Hey, maybe it ain't so bad over here after all."

Mike smiled at the Black Streak's talk. He seemed to have no inhibitions about speaking up, even though he was the newest member of the squad.

Mike turned to Longo and asked quietly, "Swim call? What's that about?"

"Sure. Hey, didn't you know? That you're right next to the Malibu of Southeast Asia? Wax down your board, man, it's surfin' Vietnam. Shit, what did you come over here for, anyway? Didn't your recruiting sergeant tell you?"

Motor swore. "Yeah, get your fucking balls shot off, riding some fucking wave. No way." Motor seemed to be swearing and complaining even more than usual.

Mike glanced around the tent to see what the others were going to do. *Swim call?* It seemed to him that that wasn't something he had come to Vietnam for. Besides, he still had his rifle to clean.

"Come on, man," Longo said, "the water's great, it really is."

"Really?" Mike shrugged and joined Longo and the rest of the marines who wanted to go, about half the company, assembling outside. Captain Blood led them through the wire.

When they got to the beach half the marines stripped while the others took up defensive positions along the tree line at the sand's edge, a machine-gun position at each end. Mike was part of the first shift to swim.

Longo was right, Mike thought, it was a beautiful beach. The sand was clean and white, the water a deep greenish-blue, the breakers high and regular. Longo jumped up and down in the shallow part, shouting, like a child afraid to get wet. He had a tiny waist, Mike noticed, and legs like Mike had never seen, huge in the thighs, then tapering quickly. Suddenly he dove through a breaker and began to swim. "Come on, Crazy Mike," he shouted back, "let's get the hell out of here! Come on!"

Mike followed, swimming breaststroke. After a while he stopped and treaded water, but Longo kept swimming, straight out. Mike looked back; everybody else was grouped together near the shore. He stayed where he was, treading water, watching Longo swim farther and farther away.

"*Long-o!*" It was the captain, standing on shore, his hands up to his mouth. "*Come back, Longo!*"

Mike watched as Longo swam back. Then he treaded next to Mike. "Shit," he said, gasping for breath, spitting water, "he spotted me. . . . I figured this time I'd get away."

Mike laughed. "Where were you going?"

"Sweden."

"*Sweden?*"

"Yeah. . . . You ever read *Catch-22?*"

"No."

"Oh, man, you got to. You'd love it . . . all about World War II—the real story. . . . This guy Yossarian—he's crazy too—takes off at the end for Sweden, all these beautiful women there. Only he had a raft or something. That's what I got to get."

They swam in to where Mike could stand.

"You ride the waves?" Longo asked.

Mike nodded. "That I can do. Bet I beat you."

They waited and caught the next wave. As he felt the power of it seize his body, Mike became afraid. But he kept his head down, his arms stretched in front of him. When he stopped and lifted his head he was on sand. He turned and saw Longo ten feet behind.

"Beat you, man!"

Longo shook his head, smiling. "That's not the object," he said. "You should ride them like this, so you can see where you're going." He craned his head back and put his arms to his sides. "California-style."

"Negative," Mike said. "You go farther my way. East Coast–style."

They rode more waves and for a few minutes Mike forgot where he was. Then the captain called in their shift and Mike and Longo dressed and took the positions of Crane and the Black Streak, who stripped and went in. Longo sat down cross-legged, his rifle in his lap, his body half turned toward the water. Mike could smell the salt on his body; he felt cleaner than he had in a long time.

"Man," Longo said, gesturing toward the water, "look at this place. . . . I *know* my plan would work. It'd be perfect for it."

Mike hesitated. He was sitting down too, looking out toward the tree line. "What plan?" he finally said.

For a moment Longo looked sheepish. "It's simple," he said, "when you think of it." His shoulders went up. "It came to me one night while I was standing watch. There I was, about half asleep, looking for all these VC that're supposed to be out there, wondering how much longer it's going to go on. The war, I mean. Thinking about how when it does get over there's going to be all these movies coming out—because there always is, after any war.

And it occurred to me that that's really the best thing that comes out of a war—the movies, I mean. I mean, what would it be like to grow up without them? What would the movie business be like? I mean, can you imagine John Wayne without war movies?" He stared expectantly at Mike and Mike gave a tentative smile. Longo went on. "And then I got to thinking about C.C. About how he's such a violent guy but how there's this other side of him too—you know?—like, with his camera. How he gets so *into* it—taking pictures, I mean. Sometimes it seems like that's all the war is here for—for him—so he can take these great pictures of it. . . . And then suddenly it hits me, my idea. The answer to the whole thing." He smiled broadly at Mike.

"Well, what is it?"

Longo spread out his arms. "We just skip a few steps, man." His voice rose with excitement. "Like, instead of waiting for the war to end, we just go ahead and start making movies right now. Like, turn this whole thing—this war, this country, this whole *scene*—turn it all into one big movie!"

Mike turned back toward the tree line. He could feel sweat dripping from his armpit. He said, "You mean a documentary?"

"No, man, not a documentary. A *movie*: a real movie. . . . Wait, hear me out." Longo was talking fast. "I've thought about this a lot since then, I really have. I know it would work. I mean, look at this place"—he waved his arms—"this beach—it's better than Southern California; and the country is full of beaches like this. And that's the basic idea: turn the whole place into another California: Hollywood, Disneyland, the whole works. Man, you know how many people visit Disneyland every month?" Mike shook his head. "You ever been to Hollywood?" Mike shook his head again. "Man, you don't know—I mean, what it's like. Like, I had an uncle—Uncle Freddie—he was a sound technician for MGM and he used to take me to the studio all the time when I was little. It's, like, *everybody* wants to be in the movies—you know, be part of the scene, one way or another. Or go to someplace like Disneyland. Oh, man"—Longo's eyes widened; his arms were up in the air—"the gooks'd just *love* Disneyland. It's like a fever—Hollywood, Disneyland, that whole scene—all you got to do is be around it, you catch it. Even people who never think about it—all of a sudden they want to be in the movies too. Look at Motor—*Where the Boys Are*—even he gets excited."

Mike nodded. Longo continued: "Think of it, turn this war into one big Hollywood set. With everything: commissaries, cameramen, directors, p.a.'s, stuntmen, wardrobe people, makeup, fan clubs—all that stuff. Man, you don't even have to tell the other side what you're doing: they'll know, once you start shooting. And then everybody'll want to get in on it. And wages, too—*union* wages. Man, you start paying the VC union wages to be in this big Hollywood spectacular and just *see* how fast they'd join up. Shit, all this money we're spending over here—helicopters, jets, napalm—you could really make a good movie—all kinds of special effects."

Mike smiled at Longo's excitement. "But how would it end?"

"End? Who needs to end it? You just keep making more movies. Like, we make ones with us winning, to show back in the States—and they make ones with them winning, to show in Russia and China. That's all right, man, that's cool: it's only movies. And they don't all have to be war movies, either—that's just to take care of the people who've got to have a war. You could make romantic movies, musical comedies, anything. Like, look at this set, for instance—think of what you could do with it. *Beach Blanket Bingo, Vietnam*, with Annette Funicello and Frankie Avalon—remember them?—just an example. *Where the Boys Are*. . . . Yeah"—Longo squirmed around where he sat—"and then get some car dealers over here. Man, you ever see car lots in L.A.? They're as big as cities, I'm not kidding. The bases here'd be perfect for them. Put in some freeways. . . . That's what people want—movies, cars, beaches, freeways, Disneyland. There wouldn't be any fighting. . . ." He frowned. "Except for the gang wars that would spring up."

Mike laughed. "Right," he said. "See? You'd still have violence."

Longo regained his excitement: "But they could be in the

movies too! I'm not kidding: I had the same idea for dealing with the gangs in L.A.—just put them in the movies. It would work, I know it would. Like, I knew this one dude in Compton—Ray the Blade—who was really bad, man. I mean, *mean*. Like, he'd as soon kill you as look at you. But all of a sudden he gets a job in a movie—playing a gang leader, of course—and suddenly he's this big responsible citizen, union member, all that. Just wants to be in more movies, doesn't want to kill people anymore—except on the screen. That's what I mean, that's what the movies'll do to you."

"Really?"

"Really."

"No, I mean—you knew someone like that?"

"Oh, yeah: I knew lots of guys in gangs—where I grew up." Mike nodded.

"But I know it would work. Everybody thinks I'm just shitting, but I'm not. I even told Captain Blood about it. Man, I'd tell General Westmoreland—LBJ, himself."

Mike smiled. "I know," he said, nodding. "Captain Blood told me."

Longo opened his eyes wide. "What? He did?"

"Uh-huh. That night he talked to me when I was standing lines—when he asked about what his name was. He also asked if you had told me about your plan for ending the war. He said it was a good one."

"So he thinks so too! I was wondering what he thought." Longo sounded happy. "Yeah," he said, "that first night I thought of it, that's when I told him. Here he comes, checking the lines, wearing those binoculars of his—what does he think he's going to see with them, anyway? And then he says"—Longo dropped his voice—" 'Well, you've been to college, Longo, so you should have some good ideas for fighting this war'—with that look of his that *he* probably got from some war movie himself when he was little. No shit! I almost said. But instead I said, 'Yes, sir, as a matter of fact I do, I just thought of a great idea.' And then I tell him all about it—in detail, showing him just how it could actually work. And then when I finish he looks at me like

I'm some kind of mental case—which wouldn't be so bad either, maybe he'll take me out of the field. But he says, 'Yes, well, that may be a little hard to put into effect; but I'll think about it'—or something like that—like he doesn't know what to think—and then goes on to the next position."

Mike laughed, imagining the look on Captain Blood's face. "That's great," he said.

"Really? You think it would work?"

"Huh?"

"The *plan*," Longo said. "You think it would work?"

"Oh . . . yeah, sure. Why not?"

"That's great." Longo beamed. "That's two of us. Now all we got to do is convince everyone else."

Mike laughed. "Right. That's all."

The marines came out of the water and dressed and then they all went back to the Fort. A few days later there was another swim call and the same thing happened: Longo jumped around in the shallow part like a little kid, then dove through a breaker and swam straight out. "*Long-o!*" Captain Blood called out, and Longo swam back. "Shit," he said to Mike, "spotted me again. Next time." And then he and Mike rode the waves, Mike winning.

Mike had to walk point on patrol for the first time. There were nine of them going out—the fire team, Brutus and C.C., Rain, Crane, and Pogo. The plan was to leave the Fort at 0500, go west and south, avoiding Ai Tu and skirting some other villages, and then search a village Mike had never been in before. Frontierland, Longo called it.

Mike woke at four in the morning, ate, and got himself ready.

"You okay, man?" Longo asked as they waited by the barbed wire in the semidarkness.

"Sure."

Longo grabbed Mike's shoulders and shook him. Mike could smell coffee on Longo's breath. "Okay, nothing rattling—only your brains." Mike tried to smile. "Just remember what I told you: take your time. You want to stop and go back, do it. We've got all day."

Mike nodded. He was sure the others in the patrol could hear them. He glanced back and saw the whites of Streak's eyes. "No sweat," he said. His heart was racing.

Longo checked the others, then came back to Mike. "Look," he said, "I'm going to be behind you—cover; on the way out, anyway. It's not that I don't trust you; it's just that I know you've never been down to Frontierland before."

Mike nodded. "Sure."

Longo stood close and held Mike's eyes a moment, then stepped back and turned to the rest of the patrol. "Okay," he whispered, "lock and load." There was a series of soft clicks. Longo came back to Mike. "Keep your safety off—just don't tell anyone I told you to do it."

"Right."

Mike brought a magazine up to his rifle. His hand was trembling. Could anyone see? He held the lever back and slid the magazine in. Then he drew back the receiver and chambered a round. The soft clicking into place seemed to soothe him. Silently he switched the safety off.

"Okay, Crazy Mike," Longo whispered, "let's go."

Mike began walking, softly and quietly, through the opening in the barbed wire. Then he was outside. In front of him was a stretch of sandy, uneven terrain, scattered with dark depressions. He looked straight down, at where he was stepping. What was he doing that for? There wouldn't be any mines or booby traps here—it was too close to the Fort. But what if the VC had snuck up at night and planted some? He wished he had kept better watch at night. He would in the future, he told himself. Was he moving in a straight line? Suddenly he remembered a tip he had learned in training: pick an object ahead to walk toward, then pick another. But it was too dark for him to see anything—why couldn't they have started later? His eyes found a bush.

Wait, he told himself, he was moving too fast. He slowed. He wanted to turn around. Why? He wanted to *see* someone. That was it, that was what made this so different from other patrols: there was no one in front of him. Were the others really behind? The thought seized him that maybe he had left too soon; Longo was still back at the Fort. No, he told himself, that was ridiculous. He turned to his right, as if listening for something he might have heard. There was Longo in the corner of his vision. He turned back to the front.

"*Slow down.*" It was Longo, whispering. Mike nodded.

He was at the bush. He picked another object: a tree. They were approaching a tree line. Shouldn't he be looking for snipers? No, that was Longo's job—cover. Then what was Mike supposed to do? For a moment panic grabbed at him: he was here only as a target, waiting to get hit. Rushing—he knew—he reached the tree line and stopped. He looked around, then behind. Everyone else had stopped too. Then Mike realized they had stopped because of him. He began to move again.

"*Slow down, man.*"

He was in a rice paddy in a dike, walking very carefully. But the dike must be safe—otherwise Longo would've told him not to take it. But what if Zorro or the Cisco Kid was waiting in the next tree line? Panic began to tug at Mike again. What would it be like—suddenly to get hit in the thigh, like Short-round? At least he'd get out of it. He told himself not to think that way—not to think at all. What should he look at, the tree line or the ground? To the right or the left? He realized he was speeding up again; he told himself to go slower.

There was movement to his right. What was it? What should he do? Stop? Get down? But then he'd get wet. But so what? Shoot? Maybe he should have shot already. Thoughts crowded his head as he tried to see. His heart was beating fast again.

"It's all right"—Longo's whisper from behind—"it's only some farmer."

Mike nodded. Now he could see the old man in his rolled-up pants and conical hat. He was crouching at the edge of the paddy, doing something with his hands in the water. Mike smiled. He felt a kinship with the old man, both of them going about their business in the early morning.

Off to the left the sky became bright. Mike began to sweat. But he wasn't thirsty—that was good, he told himself, he must be getting used to patrolling. Maybe he wouldn't drink up all his water today. He felt a little drowsy. He turned and saw the marines behind him. Motor tripped and swore out loud. Brutus, his huge bare arms bulging out of his flak jacket, looked lost in thought. The Black Streak was frowning. Crane was smoking a cigarette. Only Longo seemed to be constantly searching with his eyes to the right and left. Mike turned back and peered ahead.

The sun came up. Mike rolled up his sleeves and took a little water from one of his canteens. He was sweating. Now he thought he liked it better when it was dark.

They came close to a village and Longo told Mike to stop. He came up to Mike's position and stared ahead. A few thin curls of smoke came up from some hooches. Mike turned to Longo. There were small beads of sweat on his upper lip.

"Hui Trong," Longo said. "Bad place. Number Ten City. *Beaucoup* booby traps. Patrol from third platoon lost three men in there couple of days ago. Another guy from third squad—Beaver—stepped on a *punji* stake, might lose a foot. Let's go this way." He pointed to the right, across a rice paddy to a tree line. Mike nodded and quickly took another drink of water. Longo turned around: "Machine gun up!"

Brutus and C.C. double-timed to the head of the column, flak jackets and bandoliers bouncing and clattering. Longo showed them where to set up and they got down and trained their gun on the village. Then Mike began to move slowly across the paddy on a dike to the right. "Faster, man," Longo said, "let's get the fuck across." Mike went into a crouch and took long strides, nearly running.

He got to the opposite tree line, stood beside a tree, and pointed his rifle at the village. Longo, across now too, got down on the ground in a slight hollow. The others came over, then

Longo called for the gun team. Brutus and C.C. double-timed again. When they reached the tree line they were gasping for breath.

"You ought to get in shape, man," C.C. said.

Brutus swore. "Don't you talk to me, C.C. I'll outrun you anytime."

Longo said, "Gimme your camera, C.C. I got to get a picture of both of you, huffin' and puffin'." C.C. shook his head, panting. Mike smiled, drinking water, then Longo signaled him to continue.

A half hour later Longo called another halt.

"Okay," he announced, "come on around and listen up—but not too close." The marines gathered in a small clearing in a wooded area. "Now, according to Tracy," Longo said, "who got it from Jeff, who got it from Captain Blood, there's a big intelligence report from battalion about Frontierland. This is it: there are VC sympathizers living here. Can you believe it? So here's what we're supposed to do: Tracy says we have to go through and search for VC sympathizers. That's it. So here's the plan: as we go through, if you happen to see any likely looking VC sympathizers, then we'll stop and conduct searches and probably set off some booby traps and maybe a few mines. Bit if you *don't* see anybody who looks like a VC sympathizer, then we don't stop—until we're all the way through and it's time for chow. Any questions?" Mike heard Crane, next to him, chuckling. He turned and saw the Black Streak, smiling. "Okay," Longo said, "let's go."

They started through the village. A wide dirt trail led from one end to the other. There were trees all along it; Mike appreciated the shade. He tried to keep his attention on the path in front of him, but his eyes wandered. There were villagers out in yards, children running around, chickens. It was nice here, Mike thought, nicer than Ai Tu or Binh Le: shadier, cleaner. Then he realized there were no leaflets on the ground. Suddenly something caught Mike's attention: the long, shiny black hair of a girl standing in a courtyard. She turned and Mike saw that she was beautiful. Then she disappeared into a house. How old was she? Had she seen him staring? Mike wondered whether she was really as beautiful as she seemed.

They stopped for chow at the edge of a rice paddy by a dirt road.

"Keep it spread out," Longo said. "Don't bunch up. And keep an eye out while you're eating."

Mike opened his first canteen; empty. As he opened his second he told himself not to drink too much, but he put it to his lips and drank at least half. Then he opened a C-ration can of sliced peaches and drank all the syrup. Sitting next to him, Crane was eating cheese and crackers. Just watching Crane eat the dry crackers made Mike thirsty and he drank more water.

"Goddamn, you sweat a lot," Crane said. He was sitting cross-legged, his bony knees sticking out.

"Yeah," Mike said, "I know."

"You always sweat that much?"

Mike nodded. "Playing football, I used to sweat like this."

"Your father sweat like that too?"

"Huh? . . . Yeah, I guess he does."

"I figured," Crane said. "Make sure you take your salt pills; you can dehydrate, sweating like that. That's no way to get out of the field—heatstroke can kill you."

"I take 'em."

Crane spread cheese on another cracker. Suddenly he laughed: "Goddamn, that Longo is something, isn't he? I wish he led *all* our patrols. He *never* makes contact."

"Is that right?"

"Hell, I'm telling you." He gestured with his cracker toward Mike's face. "I know: I go out with everybody—in the platoon. Longo's good. Hellfire, he could be running this company. I wish he was. He'd put me out of business."

Mike nodded. "Is that right?"

"Hell, yes, it's right: I'm telling you. Longo's great: he's made for this war." He took off his helmet and ran his fingers through his hair. His thinning reddish hair made him look older than the others.

Mike nodded. "Let me ask you something, Crane," he said. "Shoot."

"It's this. Should I try to drink less water or should I just go ahead and drink when I get thirsty? I mean, keep trying to fill my canteens?"

Crane rubbed his chin. "Hell, I've heard it said both ways. I'll tell you this, though: if you're thirsty, you'd better drink. That's the way they're teaching now. They used to teach you should try and get along without. But as long as you drink and take your salt tablets, you're not gonna dehydrate. That's the main thing."

"I'm really thirsty," Mike said. He smiled at Crane. "How about paddy water? I mean, if you put those pills in it. Isn't it okay to drink?"

"Hell, I wouldn't. Those pills aren't that strong. Besides, you'd have to use too many of them—the water'd taste like shit. I hate that taste."

"I don't mind it."

"I'm telling you: stay away from paddy water. Unless you want to get sick. I've seen that. I've seen guys do all sorts of things to themselves, to get out of the field. They're coming up to me all the time with new ideas. One guy, Catman—this was before you were here—he got the rot so bad he's probably gonna lose his feet. But that's what he wanted: just to get out."

"Really?"

"I told you, man: I saw it. I've seen all kinds of shit over here, what some guys will do. And I don't blame them, neither. You can take only so much of this shit. But I'll tell you one thing: I wouldn't do it by drinking bad water and fucking up my guts. There's a lot simpler ways than that." Suddenly he laughed: a dry, hoarse laugh.

Mike smiled. "Don't worry, Crane, I wouldn't do that."

"Oh, yeah?" Crane frowned. "Hell, you got no idea what you'd do. Wait'll you been over here a while, you'll find out."

Mike stopped smiling. He opened a can of pork and beans. "Where're you from, Crane? Down South somewhere? Virginia, Tennessee?"

Crane nodded. "Kentucky."

"I figured—the way you talk. I live in Virginia—I mean, my folks do. Western part. Kingston. Near Tennessee. Not too far from Kentucky."

"Uh-huh. Where'd you grow up?"

"New York."

"I figured. You don't sound like no Tennessee. New York City?"

"For a while."

"Hellfire, that's where I'm gonna go—if I ever get out of this shit. New York City. Gonna have me a ball." He lit a cigarette with his long bony fingers.

Mike smiled. "That's the place all right—"

There were shots.

"Get *down!*" Crane yelled. He had already moved, down to the ground. Mike slid down beside him. He felt a pain slash at his left arm just above his wrist. What had happened? The sound of rifle fire was deafening now; even Crane was firing with his .45. Telling himself not to think, just to react, Mike raised his rifle and fired a round on semiautomatic toward where the others were firing, across the rice paddy at a clump of trees on the side of a ridge, a hundred meters away. Questions crowded into his mind: what were they firing at? And where? What was that pain in his arm? Then he remembered something: dirt kicking up on either side of him. So, he thought, this was what it was like to be wounded. Was he bleeding? Badly? Was he going to get out of it?

"Hold your fire!" It was Longo. He was on one knee, staring across the rice paddy. "Anybody hurt?"

Nobody said anything. Then Crane yelled, close to Mike's ear: "It was the Kid, the goddamn Cisco Kid! I'd know that rifle anywhere. I dream about it!" He swore angrily. "We're never gonna get him."

Longo swore too: "I *told* you guys not to bunch up!" Mike could hear his lisp.

There was silence, followed by comments: "That fucking Kid. . . . Goddamn M-1—where'd he get it, anyway? . . . Cocky bastard. . . . Made me spill my fucking chow. . . . We're lucky, though."

The Black Streak said, "What the hell he do that for, anyway? I never did nothin' to him."

Pogo nodded. "Yes, you did."

"Huh?" The Streak's eyes opened wide. "What'd I do?"

"You didn't invite him to lunch."

"Damn, I'd like him to eat this stuff—he wouldn't be shootin' at us—just let this stuff do the work." A few marines laughed.

Longo seemed thoughtful. He stared toward where the shots had come from. "Maybe he thought we did a big search or something. . . ." Mike kept glancing down at his arm. There was blood all over his wrist.

Suddenly Crane shouted, "Goddamn! You're hit, man—you're *hit!* Just stay right there. Don't move. Don't do a thing!" He grabbed his medical kit.

"I won't," Mike said.

"Longo," Crane said, "make sure that fucker doesn't start shooting again! This crazy bastard's hit—doesn't say a goddamn word. We got a casualty. . . . Christ, man, I told you to get the fuck down!"

Longo swore again, angry. "I *told* you guys not to bunch up!" He came over to Mike and the other marines began to too. "Stay down, damn it! Keep it spread out. . . . That's just what he wants—one guy gets hit, everybody crowds around. Come on, spread out!" The marines retreated.

Crane said, "Looks like you got a Heart, man."

"*Ouch!*"

"Take it easy, take it easy, it's not that bad. Don't think you're gonna get a medevac out of this. You might pull light duty a few days, that's about it."

Mike began to reply, then kept silent. He stared down past his wrist and saw something on the ground.

"How bad is it, Crane?" Longo asked.

"Not too bad." Crane wrapped a battle dressing around the wound; his fingers were trembling, Mike noticed. But they gripped his arm firmly. "Looks like a flesh wound; bleeding's not too bad. Just missed the damn vein—lucky as hell. Could've shattered his wrist."

"Lucky is right," Longo said to Mike. "He hit all around you, man."

Mike nodded. "Oh, yeah?" Suddenly he smiled embarrassedly. "Wait," he said, "I mean—Longo, Crane, I, uh, don't think I was hit."

Crane said, "What the fuck are you talking about?"

"I think I cut it. On that. When I got down." Mike nodded downward. Longo picked up an empty C-ration can.

"It could've been a wound," Crane said. "I've seen a lot of them like this—flesh wound."

"No," Mike said, "I remember. I felt it just when I got down—when my hand hit something. It couldn't've been a round. My hand was behind cover when I felt the pain. I remember."

"Fuck it. You don't know that."

Mike withdrew his bandaged hand and got down to demonstrate. "See?"

"Don't get it dirty!" Crane yelled. Then he said, "I'll write you up, anyway. You'll get your Purple Heart, don't worry."

"But . . . I didn't get hit."

"So what? You might as well have."

"Huh?"

"Look, man, officers back in the rear do it all the time. They stub their fucking toes getting out of bed, drunk, and make a corpsman write them up for a Heart. I've heard all kinds of stories."

Longo stared across the paddy, then glanced at the other marines. "We've got to call this in," he said. He looked at Mike.

"I'm not shitting you, man," Crane said. "I'll write you up. Two more and you're out of the field. Don't be a fool."

Mike turned away. "That's okay, Crane. Just forget it. . . . Thanks, anyway. And thanks for the bandaging."

"Man, are you crazy? Two more and you're out of the field!"

Pogo said, "Why don't you compromise? Say the Kid hit you with a C-ration can."

Mike smiled. "Good idea, Pogo."

Crane said, "I still say you're crazy."

"Sure, he's crazy," Longo said, "he's Crazy Mike.... Go ahead, Pogo, call it in. Tell them no casualties."

They started back. Their route was straighter now, parallel to the shoreline about a hundred meters away from it. As Mike walked he kept going over what had happened in his mind. Why did he always react so slowly. He had to work on that, he told himself. And how did everyone else know right away where the firing was from and what kind of weapon it was?

"Hey, slow down, man—we'll get there."

Mike turned and nodded to Longo. If only he didn't have this thirst! He gazed at the rice paddy water around him. *Water, water, everywhere, nor any drop to drink.* He remembered how he used to hate memorization. If only he could be back in Mrs. Adams's class now! But no, that wasn't how he should be thinking. Hadn't he thought the same way at the beginning of boot camp? But he had adjusted. But would he ever adjust to this thirst? Maybe he should fill up with rice paddy water. He'd be all right. Who cared what Crane thought? There was something strange about Crane, Mike decided. Did officers in the rear really do what Crane said they did? Mike didn't think so. Crane was exaggerating; he liked to shock other people.

Mike's back began to ache. Why was that happening so much? Was it the way he carried his rifle? But he had always carried his rifle like this in training. Was it his posture? He straightened his back and looked to the right and left. But he had good posture. He had learned it in boot camp.

For no good reason he stopped, stared at a farmer working in a rice paddy, then continued. What had he been thinking about? Boot camp. It was strange, he thought, the way boot camp was so different from what he had imagined it would be: being out in the woods by himself, learning to become independent, fearless. Instead all they seemed to do was polish their boots, clean their rifles, and march—getting screamed at all the while, sometimes punched and kicked. How Mike had hated that screaming! He had hated all of it. What did marching have to do with fighting a war? But as boot camp went on Mike began to sense changes in their marching: the way forty people, strangers at first, began to move as one unit, making *one* sound—not forty—as their heels came down on the pavement, with nobody swaying, everybody's shoulders still, arms swinging together. He began to feel part of that unit. Then he understood what marching was all about.

"Hey, man, slow down! Take it easy. Where you going to, a dance?"

Mike half turned around. "Sorry." He realized he hadn't been watching very carefully. He had been thinking too much. He scanned the tree line ahead, the hedgerow to his side, the ground in front. He swallowed. God, he was thirsty! Would he ever forget this? No, never—never again would he take for granted the simple act of having a glass of water. When he got back. If he got back. Maybe he should ask Longo for some water. No, he shouldn't do that. Maybe the Kid would fire at them again and then he could dive in the rice paddy and swallow some. No.

It was the middle of the afternoon when they approached the wire outside the Fort. Another patrol was coming out and Mike stopped and waited. It was a big patrol; it looked like a whole platoon. Mike recognized some of the marines. He nodded toward the other point man.

"Any contact?" the point man asked.

Mike shrugged. "Sniper."

"Cisco Kid?"

"Affirmative."

The point man swore. "You get hit?"

Mike glanced down at his bandaged wrist. "Yeah," he said. He smiled. "By a C-rat can."

"Huh?"

"The Kid threw it at me."

The other point man shook his head.

"Get some," Mike said, and the other patrol went on its way.

Several days later the company was scheduled to conduct a med-cap in Binh Le.

"Fantasyland," Longo announced. "Easy duty—except for Crane. This is his day." Crane, sitting in the platoon tent, looked up from his medical kit and smiled.

"I don't know how you do it, Crane," Motor said, "treat all those filthy bastards."

An amtrack and tank brought out a battalion surgeon along with food and medical supplies from battalion headquarters. A marine psy-ops team came out as well, with three Vietcong defectors. At 1000 hours the party, with Captain Blood leading the way, accompanied by the first platoon for security, proceeded through the barbed wire into Binh Le.

As soon as they entered, villagers flocked around the captain, talking noisily to him and to each other. "Look at that," Longo said to Mike, "looks like he's running for mayor. This is it, man, this is his scene: the hearts and minds. He really gets into it." Mike agreed; the captain seemed to thrive on the attention, dropping his customary scowl and grinning openly.

Mike's platoon set up in two-man positions around the center of the village. From where they were standing, Mike and Longo had a good view of the goings-on. Now the villagers lined up in front of the doctor and corpsmen. Each villager, as he came to the head of the line, opened his mouth wide for inspection.

"Man," Longo said, shaking his head, "looks like they're checking horses. What is this, socialized medicine? I thought that's what we're fighting against." Mike laughed. "Hey, you ever been to the track?"

"Huh?"

"You know—the race track—horses."

"Oh. No."

"No? I used to go all the time," Longo said. "Had an uncle who was a groom at Santa Anita. He was really good with horses, man—like Crane with these people. You can tell when someone is really into what he's doing—has a feel for it, you know?" Mike nodded. The VC defectors were giving speeches through a portable loudspeaker and handing out leaflets to villagers who had already been examined and received their medicine. "Wow," Longo said, "more leaflets? If only that was money!" In another area marines under Prince Mike's supervision were passing out food. Meanwhile C.C. roamed around the activities, taking pictures.

"Man," Longo said again, "can you imagine what a McDonald's would do over here?"

"Right," Mike said, "open 'em up all over."

"You got it—that's part of the plan too. A McDonald's in every village. Trade a rifle for a year's supply of burgers. Bring in a leaflet for a free shake. For the kids, candy cigarettes and Monopoly money—they wouldn't know the difference. Man, the people would love it. Who would want to fight?"

"Right," Mike said.

After a while the children of the village began to congregate around Longo, chanting his name and holding out their hands, begging.

"Hey, hey, look what we got here—the Binh Le Street Dancers. Come on, how about it, kids—a little dance? That's the way to make some money." Longo shuffled his booted feet on the hard-packed dirt. The children squealed, jumping up and down around him.

Mike grinned. "That's great, Longo—you can really tap-dance."

"This is nothing. I had an uncle who could *really* do it." Longo spoke as his feet were moving. "Uncle Oliver. He's the one who taught me."

"Hey, how many uncles do you have, anyway?"

"Man, I got more—"

"That's it!" Mike interrupted, excited. "It just came to me!"

"Huh?"

"Who you remind me of—with all that stuff about your relatives."

"Who's that?" Longo stopped dancing; he was smiling at Mike.

"Gracie Allen—you know, on the old 'Burns and Allen Show,' on TV? The way she'd always talk about her relatives at the end of the show, with George. Never the same one. You ever watch it?"

Longo's face lit up. "Man, I used to watch reruns all the time. I *loved* it. Remember when George would go up to his study and watch the show too, on his own television? And then Henry Bon Zell or whatever his name was would come up and George would know exactly what he was going to say? Man, that was really, like, *absurd*."

"Yeah," Mike said. "Yeah, that's right."

In the middle of the afternoon the med-cap came to an end. As Longo and Mike began to walk back toward the Fort, one of the villagers rushed up to Mike, speaking in a hurried way. Mike stopped. It was an old man. After a moment Mike recognized him.

"Look, Longo," he said, "it's Rip van Winkle. What's he saying?"

"Don't ask me, man. He's talking to you." Longo was grinning. "Go on, talk to him."

"But I can't."

"Sure, you can. Go on—use your hands, anything. Ask him what he wants."

Mike stared at the old man, who was still speaking rapidly. His eyes opened wide and closed again as he talked. It seemed to Mike that he might be upset.

"Longo, what's he saying?"

Longo walked up to him. "Hey, Rip, when'd you wake up? What's the fuss, man? What you trying to tell Crazy Mike?"

As though he understood every word, the old man turned to Longo and spouted his words at him. Longo nodded. "Yeah,

yeah, that's cool, that's cool." The old man brought his fingers to his lips and spoke some more.

"Hey, he's trying to invite you over for chow, right? A little chop-chop? Okay? Number one chop-chop for Crazy Duncan Hines Mike here, over at the Café van Winkle, right? . . . That's it, man, he must know you dig the local chow." He pointed at Mike's bandaged wrist. "He thinks you're a big hero."

The old man was quiet. He stood and gazed at Mike, blinking.

"What should I do, Longo? How can I tell him I can't go?"

"Why not?"

"But—don't we have to get back?"

"We'll get back, man."

"No, but I mean . . ."

"Hey, this place is as safe as Oceanside, California." Longo turned. "Motor, Streak—you guys go on back. We'll be there in a few minutes." He said to Mike, "We can't let the old guy down."

"But . . ." Mike thought of his rifle. Didn't he have to clean it?

"Come on, man," Longo said, beginning to walk.

They followed the old man down a path off the main trail, Mike carrying his rifle as if he were on patrol, Longo talking to the children still tugging at his pants. Once, the old man stopped and yelled at them and they scattered. Then he went into a small house off the path.

Mike said, "Hey, Longo, I can't believe we're doing this. You sure it's okay?"

"Hey, Rip's not gonna hurt us."

"No, I mean—what about at the Fort? Aren't they gonna miss us?"

"Shit. Who's going to miss us? We got no patrols, it's an afternoon off. Hey, look, we'll tell them the old man's Ho Chi Minh's brother; he's got some hot intelligence for us. This is what Captain Blood wants, isn't it—get to know the people?" Mike stared at him. "It's cool, man. What can they do, anyway—send us to Nam? Come on: you're Crazy Mike, remember?"

Mike smiled. "Right."

They went inside. Immediately Mike noticed a strange smell. He glanced around the room. The floor was hard-packed dirt, yet the room seemed neat. In one corner was a thin bamboo mat; on a wall was a red-and-yellow scroll with Chinese characters, beneath it a picture of an old man with a full white beard. On a small wooden counter a stick of incense was burning.

"Hey, Longo, what's all that stuff?"

"Some religious stuff," Longo said. "You see it a lot over here. Chinese, I think. Buddhist or something like that. That's probably his ancestor. They're big on ancestors."

"Yeah," Mike said, "I read about that. They go for Confucius. Maybe that's him."

The old man motioned for them to sit at a small wooden table. He went to the rear of the house, then came back with plates of food. Cold chicken again with the same green peppers and soup and rice.

"Man, he must really like you," Longo said. "I mean, I don't think these people eat much meat."

"Really?"

Mike took a piece of chicken in his chopsticks and chewed. It was good, he thought—although not as good as the time before; it tasted a little old. The old man hovered over them like a mother, chattering as if Mike and Longo could understand.

Longo said, "I think he really digs you eating with the chopsticks."

"You, too," Mike said.

"Nah, I'm not as good as you are. Hey, you gonna try a pepper again?"

"No way."

Longo bit into one. "*Phew*—that is *hot.*" Mike watched him but he didn't sweat. He finished the whole thing.

"Hey," Mike said, "how do you ask for water?"

"Just go ahead and ask him."

"But—"

"Go ahead, you can do it."

Mike looked up. "Hey, Rip van Winkle—I mean, sir . . .

Ong—can I have some water?... Water? ... Drink?... Thirsty?" He pulled out his canteen and pointed to it, then he made drinking motions. "See?... Thirsty." He stuck out his tongue.

The old man spoke excitedly, then went out the back.

Longo said, "See, it's easy."

Mike nodded, finished his soup, and took another piece of chicken, brushing away flies. "Man, I'm thirsty," he said, "and we didn't even go on patrol today." He looked up from the food and saw Longo staring at him. "What is it?"

Longo smiled. "Nothing, I was just watching you, that's all. I mean, the way you handle the chopsticks and stuff. You've really got something for food, don't you?"

"Huh?"

"I mean, you really dig it.... You like to cook?"

"Yeah, a little."

"Hey, that's great. I'll bet you're good, too, How'd you start cooking?"

Mike took another piece of chicken. "I don't know. When I was little. My mother taught me. Scrambled eggs. Pancakes." He shrugged. "Then I started adding stuff to the eggs."

"Just like my brother Ron—he loves to cook. Says he is *creating*. Put him in a kitchen and he could stay for hours. Makes a mess, too—pots and pans all over the place. You call that creating? my mother says.... Man, you'd really like my mom. I know it, man. She *loves* to cook. Some weekends—when something's going on, like a birthday or something—she'll be in the kitchen *all* the time. No shit, like, all weekend long: it's like the whole weekend is one big meal. People coming and going—aunts, uncles, neighbors, girl friends; the TV is on in the living room; there's a stereo in one of the bedrooms; discussions, fights; someone's throwing a football around; a card game is going on; someone else is telling jokes. And right in the middle of it my old man is taking a nap." He snorted. "It's like this big circus going on all over the house—you know what I mean? And meanwhile my mom is putting out all this food, like, nonstop." He shook his head. "Man, when she puts out her fried chicken, that stops everything. Even my old man gets up for that."

"I love fried chicken."

"You *got* to come and visit. Christ"—Longo rolled his eyes—"I keep forgetting where I am. But when we get out of this shit." He rapped on the table. "You ever been to L.A.?"

"Negative. Only time I was ever in California was on the way over here. One day."

"Oh, man, you *got* to come. You can stay at our house—there's always a spare bed, somewhere, or a couch, or *some*thing. I'll show you *all* around. It's crazy, I'm not kidding you—L.A., I mean; I mean, you'd fit right in, believe me. The thing is, you just can't take it too serious, that's all. But you'd love it—I guarantee it."

Mike smiled. "Hey, Longo," he said, "I've been meaning to ask you: you play any sports?"

"Did I play any sports? Shit, man: I *had* to."

"What do you mean?"

"I had no choice: my brothers *made* me." Longo grinned.

"Really? How many brothers you got, anyway?"

"Five."

"Five?"

"Uh-huh. All older, too. How about you?"

Mike shrugged. "Just me. . . . So what'd you play, anyway?"

Longo rolled his eyes. "You name it—football, basketball, baseball. Like, I was always the sixth man—you know? My brothers could never play three against two: they always needed *me*, even when I was little. And come down on me if I fucked up"—his voice rose—"man, I *had* to be good." Mike smiled. "And then the same thing in high school: the coaches would say, 'Oh, another Longo? Good, suit him up.' Because they all knew my brothers—so I had to play for them too."

Mike laughed. "Really?"

Longo nodded. "But I really didn't dig it, man. I mean, I like sports all right—the exercise, the movement. But not like my *brothers.*" He made a face. "They'd take it so *seriously.* Even games on TV—you know?—arguing about who's better: 'Bill Russell—no, Wilt Chamberlain; Mickey Mantle—no, Willie Mays.' I mean, getting into *fights* about it." He shook his head. "It was, like, I never cared that much about the games themselves. I mean, you win—so what? You know what I mean?"

Mike stared at the food in front of him. "Yeah," he said slowly, "yeah, I guess I do. I mean, something like that happened to me with football." He looked up at Longo. "I quit the team, my senior year."

"Oh, yeah? What were you, the star or something?"

Mike snorted. "Nah. Wasn't even first team. Wasn't really fast or big enough."

"Halfback?"

Mike shook his head. "End. Ever since I was little—always liked to make catches. Dive after the ball and get it right on my fingertips—stuff like that. . . . But then, I don't know, I guess I just didn't really like all that rah-rah stuff about being on a team. It wasn't *real.*"

"Yeah, that's exactly how I felt." Longo spoke excitedly. "And then I started to get into *acting*—I mean, theater, dance—all that stuff. And a lot of it was the same as sports: like, *movement.* And it was all a game too, but it just seemed so much more *real* to me—"

Suddenly Longo grabbed Mike's arm. "Holy shit," he said, "look what he got for you!" Rip van Winkle was standing before them, holding two brown bottles.

"What?"

"Tiger beer."

"Tiger beer? What's that?"

"It's *beer,* man, that's what it is."

"Beer?" Mike said. "Real beer? You mean they've got beer over here?"

"Sure. Guys from the company buy it down here sometimes. Crane does, I know."

The old man set the bottles on the table and began to open them.

"Hey, look at that, Longo. He's got a regular church key."

"Sure, what do you think? That they only have can openers in the States?"

Mike grinned. "I didn't know—I mean, out here in the boondocks."

The old man spoke to him.

"Thank you," Mike said, still grinning. "Thank you very much." He took one of the bottles. "You think it's all right, Longo?" He couldn't stop grinning.

"I guess we'll find out."

Mike put the bottle to his lips and drank. "Hey, it's not bad at all. It tastes good. I mean, it tastes like beer."

Longo took a sip and grimaced. "Man, what kind of beer you been drinking? It's so warm!"

Mike laughed. "Any kind. I like beer. Warm or cold, I don't care." He turned to the old man. "It's good," he said, "very good. Thank you . . . . What's the word for *thank you*, Longo?"

"*Cam on.*"

"That's right, I knew that. . . . *Cam on, cam on.* Tiger beer number one. Number one."

The old man bowed and spoke.

"What's he saying, Longo?"

"How do I know?"

"You think he's got any more?"

"Hey, we haven't drunk this yet."

"We will. I'm thirsty. You think he'd get some more if I gave him some money?"

"Who knows? Ask him."

"How much should I give him?"

"Up to you."

Mike felt strange pulling out his wallet—as though he were back in the States. He had wondered why he carried it, why everyone carried wallets, even in the field. Now he was glad he did. He took out some MPC's.

"How about five dollars?" Longo shrugged. "Hell," Mike said, "can't spend it anywhere else. . . . Here. Thank you very much.

Cam on, cam on. You have more beer? More Tiger beer? Beer very good—number one. Want more. Understand?" He pointed to the bottle and pretended to raise it to his lips—several times. The old man nodded, took the money and left.

"Jesus," Longo said, "you don't need any help with the language."

"Really? You think he understood?"

Mike and Longo got back to the Fort just as the sun was going down, both of them with bottles of Tiger beer stuffed into their trouser pockets. A swim would be nice before chow, Mike thought. He wanted to take off his boots and feel the sand on his feet.

He saw Motor by the water buffalo. "Hey, *Motor!*"

He spun around. "Yeah?"

"Guess what we've got, you fucking *Motor!*" Mike quickly pulled out a bottle of beer and put it back. He giggled.

"You're crazy, man," Motor said, scowling. "I wouldn't drink that piss if you paid me."

Mike grinned. "It's good, Motor, it'll make you happy. Don't you want to be happy, Motor?" He gave Mike a dark look and turned away.

Longo said, "Come on, Crazy Mike, let's go. Chow time."

"Wait!" Mike stopped abruptly. "Shouldn't we clean our rifles?"

Longo laughed. "They are clean, man. Let's go eat."

"Chow time!" Mike shouted. He cupped his hands and shouted again. "Hey, Prince! Where's the fucking *chow!*"

In the Commissary Mike ate greedily. His serving of pork and beans disappeared in a few seconds. "We want more! We want more!" he yelled, banging on the table.

C.C. laughed. "Ol' Crazy Mike's feeling pretty good, aren't you, Crazy Mike?"

"Hey, Longo," Mike said, "where's Captain Blood? He put on his Zorro uniform yet? Let's go tell him we found out who he really is."

Longo shrugged toward the others. "What can I say? He's Crazy Mike."

The Black Streak, on the other side of Longo, said, "Huh? You mean to tell me that this Zorro dude is really Captain Blood?"

"You got it!" Mike shouted. "You're with it, Streak—all the way. You want to help me unmask him? You can fight the big duel."

"What duel?"

"At the end of the movie."

The Black Streak glanced around the table, frowning. "Man, what's he talking about, anyway?"

C.C. laughed again. "God*damn*," he said, "I'd sure like to go out raisin' hell with you some time, Crazy Mike. Wish we was in Okinawa right now— we'd show them some craziness."

Brutus said, "You two in Okinawa together is about the only thing that'd make me want to stay in the Nam."

"What'd you do in Okinawa, C.C.?" Mike asked. "I heard you raised some hell over there."

"Raised some hell?" Ski broke in. "Ol' C.C. 'bout took on a whole company of M.P.'s just 'cause some hooker stole some money from him—what was it, five dollars, C.C.?"

"That right, C.C.?"

"Hell, it wasn't that," C.C. said. "She tried to steal my camera."

"Uh-oh," Brutus said, "don't do that to ol' C.C."

"What was that, anyway," Ski said, "the second or third time you been busted?"

"Aw, hell," C.C. said, "who keeps count? Hey, who's talking, anyway, Ski. How about the time you got busted for taking on a whole bar one night?"

"Oh, yeah?" Mike said. "Where was that?"

"Okinawa," C.C. said. "Ski wanders into some big Air Force hangout and starts shooting his mouth off, then tries to fight everyone in the place 'cause one of the airedales makes some crack about the Crotch."

"That right?"

"Hey, that's nothing," Ski said. "How about the time you got busted for taking potshots at choppers at Memphis Naval Air Station?"

"Really?" Mike said, grinning again, turning back to C.C.

"While he was standing guard duty, too," Brutus said. "Shot at them with his forty-five."

Pogo said, "Maybe they was VC helicopters."

"You did that, C.C.?"

C.C. bowed his head. "Aw, hell, I thought they was doves—wanted to do a little hunting, that's all."

The marines at the table laughed. Brutus said, "Bullshit, C.C. You were trying to get thrown in the brig and get out of going to Nam."

C.C. said, "Well, even if I was, it didn't work. They threw my ass over here." The marines laughed again.

Mike said, "How come they call you Ski, anyway, Ski? You like to ski or something?" Suddenly the whole table erupted in laughter. Mike smiled. He felt a warm glow within him. It was all right for them to laugh at him, he thought. He had known them for only weeks, yet they were the best friends he had ever had.

Blevins, sitting at the end of the table, said, "Hell, no. What's your real name, Ski? O-gal-agew-ski?"

"Owlakowski," Ski said, "and you're the only one who's ever had trouble with it, Blevins."

Blevins puffed on half a cigar. "Not too many of those where I come from."

"Well, there's a lot of them where I come from."

"Where's that, Ski?" Mike asked.

"Wilkes-Barre, Pennsylvania."

Mike nodded. "How about you, C.C.? Are those really your initials?"

The table laughed again. Brutus said, "Didn't you know? He's Candid Camera."

Mike laughed. "That's perfect. Candid Camera—C.C." He looked around the table. "Where's Day-train? How'd he get his name?"

"Forget it," Ski said. "That one takes about an hour. Longo really had to work for that one."

Mike leaned over. "How come you don't have a nickname, Blevins?"

"He does," Ski said, "it's—"

"Easy, Ski," Blevins said. "I told you—you know what to call me."

"Oh hell, take it easy, for Christ's sake."

Rain spoke for the first time: "I know what it is. It's *Lightning*."

Blevins chewed on his cigar. "I told you guys—"

Rain said, "But it's perfect, Blevins. You're so goddamn fast."

Ski laughed quickly. Blevins's face turned red. He had a cowlick sticking up on the back of his head that gave him a comical look. "You know what my name is, Rain," he said.

"Sure, I do," Rain said, expressionless.

Mike turned the other way at the table. "Hey, Crane—Ichabod—guess what me and Longo found in Binh Le today?"

Crane spoke with his face down close to his food. "Can't guess."

"You know, man. I heard you got a regular supply down there. Isn't that right, Crane?"

"If you say so."

"Hey, it's okay, man. I like the stuff too. You're all right, Crane, you're a damn good corpsman. Damn good. I heard about you on Red River. Tell me, was that bad or not? Huh? Was it bad?"

Crane swore, picked up his metal tray, and went to the trash.

"Hey, man . . . Hey, Longo . . ."

"It's all right, man," Longo said.

Mike looked around. It was almost dark. "Hey, Longo," he said, "let's go for a swim!"

C.C. laughed. "He's crazy, all right."

After chow Mike and Longo went to the tent and sat down with their beers. "I'm okay," Mike said, opening another, "I'm feeling good, that's all."

"You sure are."

"Man, this beer must be strong—went right to my head. But I'm all right now." Mike lit another cigarette. A group of marines from the second squad filed out to go on an ambush. Mike saw Crane's tall, angular figure leave with them. A second ambush, from the third squad, had already left. In the half-empty tent a few marines wrote letters or read by candlelight; others slept. Mike and Longo sat facing each other, cross-legged, a candle stuck in the sand between them.

"Hey, Longo, you think Crane's all right? I mean, I didn't mean anything. Really. I was just a little drunk—you know?"

"It's all right. Crane gets a little touchy sometimes, that's all. He gets angry."

Mike blew out smoke. "Yeah, I noticed."

"Forget it." Longo yawned.

Mike took a long swig of beer. Suddenly he said, "Hey, Longo, listen to this."

"What's that?"

"Listen." Mike sat up straight, took a deep breath, and cleared his throat. "Ready? . . . All right." He cleared his throat again and spoke in a grave tone: *"To be, or not to be—that is the question: whether 'tis nobler in the mind to suffer the slings and arrows of outrageous fortune, or to take arms against a sea of troubles, and by opposing . . . end them."* He cleared his throat.

"Hey, that's good, man."

"Wait. . . . *To die, to sleep—no more . . . and by a sleep to say . . . we end . . .* something about the thousand natural shocks— and then a consummation—yes! . . . *To sleep! Perchance to dream—ay, there's the rub.* . . . I used to know more, man."

"That's real good—"

"Wait, listen to this." He coughed, then composed himself. *"Tomorrow and tomorrow and tomorrow, creeps in this petty pace from day to day—"*

"That's this place, all right—"

" *'Til the last syllable of recorded time. . . . And all our yesterdays have lighted, fools, the way to dusty death—"*

"That's Nam in a nutshell—"

"*Out, out!—brief candle. . . . Life is but a walking shadow, a poor player who struts and frets his hour upon the stage and then is heard no more. It is a tale told by an idiot, full of sound and fury, signifying . . . nothing!*" He whispered the last word.

"Hey, that's really good," Longo said. "Where's that from?"

"*Macbeth.*"

"Oh, yeah? I thought you said you weren't into theater."

"I wasn't, really. Freshman English. Mrs. Adams—she made us memorize them. Some other stuff, too. Actually, she wanted me to go out for the school theater. She said I'd be good."

"You would be, man. You've got a good voice."

"Really?"

"Yeah."

"Thank you. That's what she said, too."

"Ever read *Othello?*"

"No."

"That's my favorite—"

"Oh, yeah? . . . Hey, Longo, my mother—I meant to tell you—she used to be in the theater."

"Oh, yeah? She was an actor?"

"An actor? No, a singer. Musical stuff. She was in a few things in New York City—where she grew up. Not big things—I really don't know too much about it—that was before I was on the scene. But she's got a good voice; everybody says that. When she sings. But she doesn't sing anymore. Just once in a while at a party or something."

"Oh, yeah? What does your dad do?"

"Businessman. In charge of a factory."

"Oh."

Mike held up his bottle and checked the level. Empty. Longo yawned. "Maybe we should sack, man. We got a long hump tomorrow."

"Negative," Mike said. "I got an idea. Let's go down to Binh Le and get some more beer."

Longo grinned. "You really *are* crazy."

Mike opened the last bottle and drank. Then he stood up. "Don't go away. I'll be right back."

Outside, standing over the pisstube, Mike breathed deeply, trying to clear his lungs of smoke. He looked toward the barbed wire and saw a figure standing by a pile of sandbags. Later, Mike knew, he would have to stand watch himself. He didn't care. He remembered a novel he had read about the French in Indochina; the Foreign Legion used to get drunk all the time. Why not? Was he really here, in Vietnam? He felt like laughing.

He went back into the tent. "Hey, Longo," he whispered, sitting down. "Tell me something."

"Sure, man, what's that?"

"Tell me: how did I do—I mean, the other day? You know, on patrol."

"Huh?"

"As point."

"Oh . . . you did great."

"Really?"

"*Really?*" Longo's eyes opened wide. "Would I shit you? Hey, John Wayne himself couldn't've done any better. Nobody could."

Mike grinned. "Don't blow any smoke, man."

"I'm not blowing smoke. Man, you were like—like a combination of Robert Mitchum, Gary Cooper—"

"Cut it out, Longo—"

"No, man, you really looked *good* up there. Hey, I had to keep reminding myself I wasn't watching some movie. No wonder we didn't make any more contact. The gooks took one look at you and said, 'Uh-uh, it's Crazy Mike.'"

"Fuck you, Longo." Mike was still grinning.

"Really. . . . You ever do any hunting?"

"Negative."

"Hey, what's all this 'negative' shit, anyway? You think you're in the Marine Corps or something?"

"Shut *up*, you guys!"

Mike ducked his head, looked toward Tracy, then put a finger to his lips and laughed silently. "No," he whispered to Longo, "no hunting."

"You ought to," Longo whispered back, "no shit—you'd be good. My Uncle Howie—he used to hunt a lot—"

"*Another* uncle?"

Longo looked sheepish. "Yeah, well, I come from a pretty big family. . . . Anyway, he took me out a few times—when I was little—up in the mountains, east of L.A. He was really good. You know: smell the air and study the ground, stuff like that."

"Oh, yeah? Do you like that, hunting?"

Longo shook his head. "Not really—too much like this. Besides, I don't like to walk. I like to fly. That's my thing, man."

"Really? What do you mean—like, be a pilot?"

"You got it."

"Really? . . . How come?" Mike drank more beer and lit a cigarette. He listened carefully: everyone else seemed asleep now.

"How come?" Longo smiled, raising his shoulders. "*Because*, man . . . I don't know *why*. Because I've always been that way. Ever since I was little, I wanted to fly, be a pilot."

"Really? But . . . I thought you wanted to be an actor or a dancer or something like that."

Longo smiled good-naturedly. "No, that's just something I *do*. Like, you've got to do *something*—you know? And that stuff—well, I'd just rather be doing it than some other stuff—like studying, or playing on some team, or going to boot camp. . . ." Mike nodded. "But *flying*"—Longo's smile faded a little—"that's something else: that's my *dream*. . . . Man, I can remember"—his voice became excited again—"when I was little, my Uncle Charlie, he used to be a baggage handler at L.A. International—"

"Another—!"

"*Shhh!* Anyway, he used to take me to the airport, sometimes—like, back when I was eight, nine years old—and, man, I was never so excited in my life. Just sitting there, watching those planes come in and take off. And it was like I knew, right then, what I wanted to do. I *knew*. You know what I mean?" Mike sipped beer and nodded. "And I can still do that—I mean, spend a whole day at an airport, just watching planes coming in and out. I feel ... I don't know how to say it. . . . It's like—it's not the planes themselves, it's the way they move through the air, the curves. . . . To be able to move like that—it's like a *miracle*, you know what I mean? I mean, even though it can all be explained scientifically and all that—cause and effect—still, every time I see it I get the same feeling: like, chills all over. . . . I don't know." He stared down.

Mike said, "So have you ever flown—taken flying lessons?" Longo shook his head. "No? Why not?"

Longo shrugged. "That takes bread, man."

"Oh."

Longo smiled. "That's why I tried to get into OCS."

"You *what?*"

"*Shhh.* . . . Yeah, when I was in boot camp—I applied."

"You wanted to be an *officer?*"

"I didn't care about that. I was just trying to get into flight school. You've got to be an officer for that."

"Oh."

"I mean, I figured as long as I had to be in the Crotch, I might as well get them to teach me how to fly."

"So what happened—with OCS?"

Longo shrugged. "Don't ask me, man. Ask them. I mean, they were taking guys for OCS out of boot camp with less time in college than I had. I passed all the physical tests: eyesight, reflexes, all that stuff."

"Oh, yeah? Maybe they didn't want any *ballet dantherth.*" Mike flapped his wrist. Longo smiled and nodded. "Anyway," Mike said, "maybe it's just as well—I mean, that's dangerous; those guys are getting shot down all the time over North Vietnam."

Longo shook his head with an expression of disbelief. "Man, what do you call this—*safe?* What's the difference, getting zapped in the air or on the ground? I mean, if you've gotta go, I think I'd rather be up there. Hey, you ever see those old World War I flying movies—?"

"*Would you guys shut the—*"

"Yeah, yeah, yeah"—Mike spun around toward Tracy—"we will, we will. Right now."

Longo whispered. "Maybe we should sack, man."

"Wait." Mike got up. "I'll be right back. There's something I got to tell you." He went outside. When he came back he whispered, "Hey, Longo."

"What's that?"

Mike crushed his empty pack of cigarettes, then picked a long butt out of the sand and lit it. "I just wanted to tell you . . ."

"What?"

"Well . . ." Mike blew out smoke. "Remember when I first joined the company?"

"Sure."

"Well, I . . . just wanted to tell you." He grinned. "I didn't like you. Then. I didn't like you at all."

Longo's eyes opened wide. He hissed, "*No shit!*"

"Really? You could tell?"

"Could I tell?" His whisper was high-pitched. "You acted like I had killed your mother or something. And I'm thinking to myself, 'What did I do to this guy, anyway? Or is he just mean?' "

"No—it wasn't that obvious, was it?"

"Man, you had *icicles* coming out of your eyes. Shit. I thought Jeff was coming in here with an air conditioner—temperature dropped about twenty degrees; I had to put my shirt on."

"Come on"—Mike was laughing—"it wasn't like that."

"And I'm thinking, 'And I've got to have this guy in my fire team? Man,' I thought, 'at least we'll be cool out on patrol.' *Hickey*, I was ready to call you."

"Huh?"

"From *The Iceman Cometh*. A play."

"Right. I've heard of it."

"But then I saw the way you were looking at that food. And the way you asked for it—real sudden, like; just when everyone else was putting it down. And I could see that you were a little crazy." Mike grinned. Longo asked, "So what did you have against me, anyway?"

"Nothing," Mike said. "Nothing. I mean, I just thought you were a loudmouth, that's all."

"Man! What are we supposed to do—shut up for thirteen months? You don't talk over here, you'll go insane!"

"Anyway, I just wanted to tell you. Like, I think you're all right."

"Hey, thanks, man. You're all right too."

"*If you guys don't shut the fuck up right now—*"

"*Shhhh!*" Mike hissed at Longo. "It's late. We better sack." He raised the beer bottle to his lips and drank the rest of it.

Longo whispered, "You *are* crazy."

Mike brought the bottle down and stared for a moment at Longo. The flame from the short piece of candle jumped high, and suddenly in the flickering shadows Longo's face looked different, like the face of someone Mike had never met. Something was wrong with the eyes, Mike thought: the shadows from his cheekbones. He shook his head. He was tired, he realized; very tired. He stuffed his cigarette into the sand as Longo blew out the candle; then he lay down and went to sleep.

Someone was shaking his shoulder. Mike wished the person would stop. He didn't. If Mike kept pretending he was asleep, he vaguely thought, maybe the person would go away.

He didn't. "Come on, man, get up! It's your watch."

What was he talking about? Mike pretended not to hear. The shaking became stronger.

"Get the fuck *up! Now!*"

Mike opened his eyes. It was dark. His shoulder hurt. "Huh?"
"Wake *up!*"

He realized who it was: Tracy. Who was Tracy? The Fort: he was in Vietnam.

"Huh?" he said again, and jumped to his feet. That was right:

Vietnam. He realized he had been thinking he was somewhere else. But where? It was in the dream.

"Yeah," he said, "sorry. . . . What time is it? Oh, yeah." His watch said just past three. "Yeah, sorry. I'm up. It's all right." He swallowed and felt sick.

"It's not all right." Tracy was angry. "You're late. Get the hell out there. Now, goddamnit!"

Mike grabbed his rifle. "Yes, sir—I mean, I'm going. Sorry." Tracy swore again.

Mike rushed outside the tent. It was light out here and cool. He found the pisstube and peed into it. Now he remembered: the beer. Why had he done it? He found his way to number five bunker. There was no one here. Where was the person on watch? Of course: it had been Tracy. No wonder he was angry!

Mike yawned and rubbed his face. How could he have done this—gotten a hangover over here? He might as well be back in college.

He sat on the sandbags and looked at his watch. Five minutes had passed. Five minutes! How was he ever going to do this—sit here and stay awake for the next two hours? And not only that: then go on a two-day patrol. It seemed inconceivable to him. He gulped down some water from his canteen. His lungs hurt. Why had he smoked so much? Why had he drunk all that beer? Why? Why? What did it matter, why?

Suddenly he remembered his talk with Longo. Uh-oh, he thought, what had he said? He went over it in his mind. It was all right—Longo had done most of the talking. Mike had listened. Except for the Shakespeare stuff. And then the part about not liking Longo. Mike felt his face get red. Had anyone heard? No, they were whispering. Tracy: now Mike remembered Tracy swearing at them. No wonder he had been angry! Who else had been listening? Nobody; just Tracy, and Tracy wouldn't think anything. Tracy didn't think. Become a cop was right—no imagination. No, that wasn't right. Tracy was all right. But what was there to think, anyway? It was just talk. Mike could apologize to Tracy; tell him it wouldn't happen again. And it wouldn't, either.

He heard a sound behind him.

"Who's on watch?"

"Me. I mean, Allison."

The person moved closer. "Who?"

"Allison—oh, hello, sir—I mean, this is Pfc. Allison. Sir." Mike realized he had almost said Captain Blood.

"What position is this?"

"Sir?"

"What number?"

"Number five, sir."

"Who did you relieve?"

"Uh, Tracy, sir—I mean, Corporal Johnson."

"And who relieves you?"

"I . . . I don't know, sir—wait, no one does, sir. We leave on patrol zero five hundred."

The captain nodded. "All right, Allison. All right." He pointed at Mike's wrist. "What happened there?"

"Oh, just a little accident, sir."

"What accident?"

"I, uh, cut it on a C-ration can. A few days ago. Sir. When the Cisco Kid started shooting at us out on patrol." Down in Frontierland, he wanted to say.

"Had a close call, eh?"

"Yes, sir."

"How'd you know it was the Kid?"

"Well, he was firing an M-1, sir."

"We're gonna get that bastard, one of these days, Allison."

"Yes, sir."

The captain looked closely at Mike. Mike turned toward the wire. He tried not to breathe—his breath must smell terrible, he thought.

The captain said, "What did you think of that village you checked out down there, Allison?"

"It, uh, seemed like a nice village, sir."

"Oh? What do you mean by that?" The captain's voice was sharp.

"I mean, we didn't see anything—suspicious. It just seemed like a nice village. Maybe the VC haven't made any real inroads there yet. The people seemed real nice." *Plus there was a nice piece of ass,* he thought.

The captain nodded. "Sounds like you're getting a real feel for things over here, Allison."

"Yes, sir." *That's close.*

"That's good. We need more men like that. You're the one who's read all those books, aren't you?"

"Uh, well, yes, a few, sir."

"That's good, but it's no substitute for the real thing, Allison. Those professors don't know everything. This is a tough war— maybe the toughest we've ever fought. Do you know why?"

No, do you? "Uh . . ."

"It's because of the *people,* that's why. We've never fought a war like this before—not a big war; where we're around the people all the time. The normal rules of warfare just don't apply. You catch my drift?"

Drift? Snowdrift? Yes, sir, they're all over. The Iceman Cometh. "Yes, sir." He spoke low so his breath wouldn't carry. No more questions, please, he thought. He kept staring over the wire.

The captain was silent. Then he said, "I'd like to see them try it." His voice had changed; it sounded grim, determined.

"Sir?"

"Attack this place—like they did that night. Those fuckers . . . they'll find out what marines are made of. You'd see some blood then."

Oh, boy, Captain Blood is right. "Yes, sir."

"There's been a report, Allison: the VC may be up to something. So keep a close watch." Mike began to reply, but the captain was gone.

Mike shook his head. What was happening to his mind? As if he were back in college. Oh, that he were—how he'd like to sleep late this morning! Why did he ever quit and do this? He looked out over the barbed wire. No, he wasn't in college, and it wasn't a movie. He was in Vietnam. There were VC out there; they wanted to kill him. They might be out there right now, sneaking up to the Fort. The Fort? What Fort? *Hey, Longo, guess what I told Captain Blood—that there are snowdrifts out there, we're gonna perform* The Iceman Cometh. Mike smiled.

The platoon left the Fort at 0500, with Mike's squad second in the column. Thank God, he thought, he didn't have to walk point. They went west, passing through rice paddies and villages, some of them deserted, then changed course to northeast. The marines checked I.D. cards and searched hooches. They moved slowly; it was a two-day patrol with much time allotted to reach their checkpoints. Mike kept refilling his canteens from villagers' crocks, but no matter how much he drank he was still thirsty. Never before had he felt so hot. Soon the pain in his back began and then it became worse. It was as though there were a connection between the thirst in his throat and the pain in his back. If only he could put one of them out, it seemed, the other would go away too.

At one village there was a commotion up ahead in the column. As marines went up to look, Sergeant Jefferson yelled at them in his high-pitched voice not to crowd around. Mike went up too, pushing his way forward so he could see. Sticking up from a wide, deep hole in the ground, like the teeth of some deadly fish, were sharp-pointed sticks. *Punji* pit, someone said. Nobody was hurt: the point man had seen the camouflaged bamboo cover just in time. Marines blew the pit with TNT and moved on.

At the next village Rain stopped suddenly and picked up a leaflet. "It's in English," he said. "VC."

Other marines bent to pick up copies. "Careful!" Jeff shouted, "they could be booby-trapped." But the marines kept picking them up, and Mike did too.

On the paper was a black-and-white drawing of an upraised arm with a clenched fist. *Dear Black Marine,* the text read, *Why are you here? The National Liberation Front of South Vietnam has no fight with you. You are exploitd by the Imperialist Masters of your Own Country. Our strugle is your strugle too. Go home! You do not want to die in our land, so far from your lovd ones. Go home while you are still alive and join in the strugle against oppresion.*

The Black Streak seemed excited: "Hey, Longo, how about this, man!"

"I've seen 'em before," Longo said. "I think it's a great idea."

"Huh?" The Black Streak looked wary.

"Sure," Longo said, "let 'em fight the war like this—with leaflets. See who can write the best ones."

"Oh." The Streak turned back to the leaflet, studying it. "Man," he said, shaking his head, "this is really something; I ain't never seen anything like this. . . . What do they think, anyway? We can just pack up and go home? Man, are they stupid!" He picked up two more. "I'm gonna send these home to Florida. Wait'll they see them back there!" He was smiling.

Motor said, "Cheap bastards."

"What's that, man?"

"Hell, I'd be insulted if I was you, Streak. When we tell them to stop fighting at least we offer them some money."

"No shit?" Streak frowned. "Yeah—what kind of deal is this, anyway? They want me to go up for court-martial and they don't even offer me any money? Man! Who's going to pay my lawyer?"

Mike laughed. "Hey, look here, Streak, you're right, they really are stupid: they can't even spell."

"Huh?"

"See?" Mike held a copy up to him. "*Exploited* and *struggle* are both spelled wrong. *Loved*, too."

Streak looked at Mike with suspicion. He said, "What do you think this is—school or something?"

Tracy shouted, "All right, all right, break it up! Spread it out. Start checking out these hooches. These leaflets look fresh—Charlie's around here somewhere. Longo, take your team over to the right. Blevins, you're on the left. Come on, move it! And search those hooches good!"

Streak and Mike began to move. Streak spoke in a low voice: "Hey, Crazy Mike, you think he's right? You really think the VC is around here?"

Mike shrugged. "Could be, Streak."

Streak glanced around. "But listen here, you're smart. Tell me: you think this is right, what I'm thinking?"

"What's that?"

"That maybe they won't shoot me, they see I'm black?"

Mike smiled. The Streak's face, beaded with sweat, was the picture of seriousness. For a moment it seemed to Mike as if they really were in a movie. "Sure, Streak," he said, "sure."

They went on and on, past village after village, farther from the Fort than Mike had ever been. As he gazed out over the flat countryside, at the palm trees and wisps of smoke rising from hooches, the vast, far-reaching sky, a strange feeling came over him: as though he and the other marines were on a mysterious, faraway quest, unbeknownst to the villagers they were passing, working in the fields, the begging children: as if the heat and their thirst were leading them to a place no one had ever been before, an enchanted land, where time ceased to exist.

In the late afternoon they came to the shoreline. Jefferson halted the patrol.

"This is what I was hoping for," Longo said to Mike. "Jeff did it the last time we were out with the whole platoon. It's great."

"What's that?"

"Set up on the beach, for the night."

"Oh, yeah? We get to go swimming?" Mike eyed the ocean thirstily.

Longo laughed. "Man, you got swimming on your brain. You wanted to go last night, remember?"

"Yeah, I remember." Mike looked away. "What's so good about it, then—setting up on the beach?"

"Because if we set up here, then we don't have to do a three-sixty. Only a one-eighty. Charlie's not going to attack us from the ocean."

Mike stared at the waves rolling in. He would like to go swimming, he thought—if only he could drink that water. "So?" he said.

"So that means more sack time." Longo smiled. "Five, six men to a position, instead of three. At least."

"Oh." Mike shook his head. His brain was certainly working slowly.

Longo was right: the platoon did set up a 180 degree perimeter, and Tracy's squad with its attachments had only two fighting holes: seven men per position, one hour of watch per man.

After the marines assumed their positions they ate. Mike made a little stove with one of his C-ration cans and a heat tab and warmed up a can of beef and potatoes. Around him he could see tiny glows from other C-ration stoves.

"Hey, Longo."

"What is it?"

"Look at this scene."

Longo gazed toward where Mike gestured. "Yeah?"

"You ever read *The Iliad?*"

"No."

"It's like the Greeks in the Trojan War, man, camping out on the beach. See the fires?"

"Oh, yeah? They set up on the beach like this too?"

"Yeah. And cooked lamb and drank lots of wine. You got any wine?"

"Oh, Christ, that's just what we need."

"Right. . . . So what do you think?"

"Huh?"

"Can we use it in the movie?"

"Of course, man." Longo grinned. "The Trojan War . . . that was all about some broad, wasn't it—how it started?"

"Helen of Troy. The most beautiful woman in the world. How about Ma Barker for the part?"

Longo laughed. "You've got it, man. You've got it."

C.C., a few feet away, said, "Damn, you college guys, you're too much for me."

"You can be in the movie too, C.C.," Mike said. "You can be cameraman—right, Longo?"

"Really?" C.C. beamed.

Mike made a bed for himself in the sand, smoothing it out and building up a pillow. It was only 2100 and he had drawn last watch: he could sleep eight hours straight. Eight hours! When was the last time he had slept eight hours?

He stared at the stars and listened to the surf. The smell of the night air reminded him of someplace he had been. Florida—once with his parents on a spring vacation. He remembered how much he had liked it. This was where he was meant to live, he thought, near the ocean. He imagined himself staying in Vietnam until the war was over—extending his tour, then extending again, however long it took. He would have some kind of job working with the people, speaking their language, eating their food, living among them.

His back began to ache and so he turned to the side. That girl he had seen in Frontierland, the beautiful one—perhaps he would meet her; they would talk, fall in love, live together in a little hooch by the ocean. . . .

And then what—when the war was over? Back in the States he would be a different person: scarred, gaunt, silent; unable to smile; eating only rice. He'd have to live by the sea. But where? California, he suddenly thought: he'd visit Longo. He pictured Longo's mother in his mind, a big woman cooking away in the kitchen, accepting Mike as a son. . . .

His hip was hurting; he turned to his other side. He looked at his watch. Almost ten. Hadn't he better sleep? But he had plenty of time to sleep. Still over seven hours.

But what would he do in California? Longo would be working in Hollywood—something to do with the movies, sending himself through flying school on the side. He'd introduce Mike to actresses; they'd fall in love with him. . . . He'd go hunting, too. He had never been hunting, but Mike now saw that Longo was right: Mike had the hunter in him. Sometimes he would disappear for days up in the mountains, all by himself. His girl friends wouldn't understand this need to get away. . . .

Mike turned again. Now both hips ached. Eventually, though, he thought, he would leave: California wouldn't be right for him. No place would: he'd feel like an outcast, different from normal people, with feelings they couldn't understand; sometimes with no feelings.

Where would he go? He knew: to the only place where he could really feel at home. He imagined his return: a hero's welcome in Binh Le: villagers cooking big meals for him. The girl from Frontierland would be waiting; they'd move back into their hooch by the ocean. . . . But then something would happen: the VC would come back, begin the war again. Mike and his wife would be their first targets. . . .

No, that wasn't a good ending. Mike tried to backtrack in his fantasies—to his arrival in California, Longo's mother in the kitchen. But all that seemed stale now. He wished he hadn't thought at all, that he had gone to sleep right away. What time was it? He didn't want to look.

His hips kept aching and he woke several times during the night. When Longo roused him in the morning he felt as if he hadn't slept. He was exhausted. He stood his hour of watch, yawning, cursing himself for not sleeping more.

The next day the platoon continued its patrol. Late in the morning the lead squad received sniper fire. The Cisco Kid, everyone said. Mike agreed: he thought he could recognize the deep crack of the Kid's M-1. One marine was hit in the arm. Then in the afternoon, as the fanned-out platoon was searching through a village, two marines from the third squad tripped booby traps, both of them hand grenades rigged with wire. Four men were wounded and had to be medevacked. Crane said that one of them might lose an eye. It was late in the evening when the platoon made it back to the Fort.

Before every patrol on which he was point, Mike would get the same feeling, a mounting fear in his stomach and chest as he imagined that this was going to be his time to get hit. Then he'd load his rifle and walk through the wire and the fear would pass; instead he'd have a very different feeling: of being able to do anything he wanted, go anywhere he wanted to go, with no one in front of him and a loaded rifle in his hands. He came to savor these moments of power in the early morning. Later, after the sun came up, the marines would talk, Mike's back would ache, he'd get thirsty, and his mind would wander; and then he'd have to force himself to concentrate on the path in front of him.

He was getting better at walking point, he knew. He learned to go slow and when to take the long way around, when to stop and let the machine gun set up, when to go fast. His legs became stronger; they no longer felt they would give out halfway through the patrol. Twice he spotted booby traps. The first was one of the marines' own grenades rigged to a small tree that had fallen across a path; the second was a 60mm mortar round—also one of theirs—set to go off by a gate, right in the middle of Ai Tu. "That would've killed you, sure," Crane said. Another time in Ai Tu he stopped abruptly when he noticed what looked like freshly packed earth in front of him. Longo knelt and probed into the ground with his bayonet. It was a *punji* pit—a tiny one, about a foot and a half square and deep. Only two small stakes were inside it, but each had a cartridge tied to its tip. Crane told Mike he would have lost a foot. Another time, as the patrol was approaching Ai Tu, a sniper opened fire and sand kicked up a few inches in front of Mike. He dove behind a tree while Longo, behind him, returned fire. It was the Cisco Kid. Afterward Longo said, "Jesus, Crazy Mike, you're really having a time, aren't you?" And there were more meals in Binh Le, too. Twice he and Longo ate at Rip van Winkle's following early morning ambush patrols. They were simple meals—rice and a potatolike vegetable Mike had never eaten before. The old man expressed gratitude to Mike and Longo for making his village safe.

And then came Mike's first real fire fight, after nearly two months at the Fort.

It began one afternoon, late, just before the sun went down.

Mike had come in from a patrol and had cleaned his rifle, then lain down in the tent with one of Rain's Vietnamese-English phrase books. After looking at a page or two Mike nodded off to sleep. Vaguely, now, he became aware of a commotion outside. Firing was going on, people were shouting. But the firing seemed quite distant, and Mike tried to sink back into sleep. The shouts became louder. Someone would wake him, he told himself, if it was anything important. But what was going on? Finally Mike realized he couldn't sleep and he got up.

He walked outside, barefoot, toward a group of marines shouting and talking excitedly near the wire on the Ai Tu side of the Fort. Captain Blood, binoculars up to his eyes, towel around his neck, stood in the middle of them, like a coach on the sidelines surrounded by players. "Maybe it's just snipers," a marine said. "Shit it is," another answered. "Them's automatic weapons."

Mike saw Longo on the fringe of the others and went over to him. "What's going on?"

Longo kept staring over the wire as he spoke. "It's trouble; sounds like a squad, at least. It's a fire fight."

"Really? Who's out there—I mean, for us?"

"Patrol from second squad—the whole squad, I think. They're pinned down, can't move."

"Where are the gooks?"

"In the vill."

"But . . ." Mike frowned. It didn't make sense to him. Where was the pinned-down squad? He squinted, trying to see for himself, but he could make out no figures. There was the village, and there the sandy expanse of land between it and the Fort. Firing was going on, Mike could hear that—but where were the marines? What cover could there be out there? The land looked flat to him. A fire fight, he thought: a real fire fight. He yawned. He was still sleepy.

The captain lowered his binoculars and shouted at one of his radiomen, "Goddamnit! What's holding the mortars up?" Mike moved closer to the center of the group. Now he could hear a voice coming over one of the radios: *"Can't move. . . . We've got casualties. . . . One of them's hurt bad—he may be dead!"* There was panic in the voice, Mike could tell. It seemed strange to him to be able to hear it but not see the marine. Mike yawned again and shook his head; he couldn't get rid of his drowsiness. The sun was just going down past the village. In another hour it would be dark. He looked around and saw that Longo was no longer there.

The captain took the handset from his radioman and shouted into it, "You're doing all right, One Bravo Alpha, you're doing all right! We'll get you out of there!" He shouted to another radioman, "I want a fire mission—*now!* Those men are in trouble!"

Suddenly there was the sound of mortars going out from the south end of the Fort, and Mike could see gray clouds in the village. The marines standing around Mike cheered, but the firing went on. The captain raised his binoculars to his eyes again as if he might see something new. Then he turned to his side. "Sergeant Jefferson, get a squad ready! Looks like they're going to need help."

"Aye, aye, sir." Jeff's high-pitched voice sounded ineffectual compared to the captain's.

"Who are you going to send?"

Jeff hesitated. "Corporal Johnson," he said. It sounded like a question.

"Good," the captain said.

"Sir?"

"What is it?"

"Shouldn't I take my other squad too?"

There was a moment's hesitation. "Negative," the captain said. "I know you want to go yourself, Sergeant Jefferson, but you'll go when I tell you to."

"Aye, aye, sir."

Jeff turned. "Corporal Johnson!" It sounded as if his voice might break. "Saddle your men up and get out there! Come on, get *moving!*"

Tracy started toward the tent. He saw Mike. "Come on, Allison, goddamnit! Let's *go!*"

Suddenly Mike moved. "Yeah, sorry. I'm coming."

"Don't talk, *move* it!"

Mike cursed himself as he ran toward the tent. What was *wrong* with him? He had heard the captain and Jefferson. Didn't he realize they were talking about his squad? What did he think—just because he had been on one patrol today, he didn't have to go on another? Now he knew where Longo had gone—to get ready, just in case. Why hadn't Mike done the same? He started to put on a sock, then threw it aside, pulled on his boots and tied them. His fingers were trembling, he noticed; his heart was pounding. A fire fight: he was finally going to be in a fire fight. Why did it have to be now when he was still half asleep?

Brutus rushed in and grabbed his flak jacket and machine gun. "Goddamnit, C.C., move your ass!" C.C. swore and rushed outside.

Mike went out too, where Tracy yelled at the squad to get ready. Why all the shouting? Mike wondered. What was this, boot camp? He thought again of the novel he had read about the CIA agent working with Montagnards: they had always fought in silence.

The Black Streak was next to him. "Hey, Crazy Mike," he said, "you think it's only snipers?" Mike stared at him. There was something strange in his voice.

"I hope so, Streak," he said, "I hope so."

Streak swore. "I don't want to be in no fire fight," he said. Suddenly Mike realized that the Streak was afraid. For some reason the knowledge made him feel calmer.

He shrugged. "What the hell."

They began to move, Blevins's fire team leading the way. Once they were outside the wire Tracy called out, "Double-time!" and Mike swore as he began to jog. He felt clumsy running in the sand, his ankles weak. His helmet bounced on his head and he wondered why he wasn't in better shape. Quickly he was out of breath.

The firing became louder. The sun had set, but it was still light; in the curves of the sandy ground were hints of darkness.

"Spread out—on line!" Tracy yelled, and they stopped their

jogging and walked forward, in a line, crouched low. Mike heard a *ping* near his head, then three *pings* right in a row.

"*Get down!*" Tracy yelled.

They did. There were more *pings*. It occurred to Mike that he was getting shot at. He flattened his body against the earth behind a small mound.

"Longo, move your men up!"

Longo, to the left of Mike, stuck his head up, glanced around, then shouted, "Okay—move—*now!*" He got to his feet and rushed forward. Mike forced his body to move. Why couldn't he move like Longo?

He got down behind another sandy mound, ten feet to the right of Longo. *Ping, ping,* he heard over his head. Now he understood about finding cover in this ground: it did exist. He heard shouts around him—Motor's voice, and C.C.'s: "Mother fucker! Motherfucker!" Then he heard Longo—"Fire!"—and Mike realized that the marines around him were already firing; that he should do the same. But at what? He switched off his safety and fired single shots toward the village in front of him, two hundred meters away. Longo shouted and they rushed forward again.

Suddenly Mike turned around. He saw the Fort: a cluster of figures behind barbed wire. He imagined Captain Blood standing in the middle of them, green towel around his neck, binoculars to his eyes. Could the captain see him? Mike turned back and aimed and fired, as if he knew where he was shooting. Then he rushed forward.

By fire-team rushes the squad moved closer to the village, and the *pings* became more frequent. Mike fired with purpose; his body no longer felt tired; it seemed to move by itself. Finally he heard new sounds: the shouts from the marines up ahead. They were more like cries than Motor's and C.C.'s angry swearing.

"Keep firing!" Tracy yelled out. "Keep firing!"

Mike put his head up for a second and fired. *Whup*—the sand leaped up from the top of the mound a few inches to the front and side of him. That was close, he thought. He smiled. He was all right. He raised up and fired again. "Fuckers!" he yelled. "You fuckers!"

He saw two marines come running back from up ahead. Just as they were diving to the ground one of them yelled, "*I'm hit!*" Then Mike heard another voice: "Goddamnit! Fire! I need *cover*, goddamnit!" It was Crane. He sounded angry. But why should he be angry? Mike had thought they were doing well.

"Cover, goddamnit!" Crane yelled. Mike raised his head and fired at the shape of hooches and trees up ahead. He took out an empty magazine and inserted a full one.

Tracy's voice again: "Longo, move your men up!"

"Right!"

Mike thought: up farther? Then Longo's voice: "Crazy Mike! Streak! Up on the right—now! Motor, move it on the left!"

Mike heard the steady *rat-tat-tat* of Brutus's machine gun off to his left and something within him suddenly made him move, and then a second or so later made him get down. He hugged the ground and sand flew up next to him. He raised his rifle and fired.

"*Fuckers!*"

Crane was still swearing. "I can't go up there," he shouted. He sounded hysterical. "I can't! I can't!" But suddenly Mike saw him dash forward, a few meters ahead and to the left. A comical figure, Mike thought—C.C. should get a picture.

Longo shouted, "Mike, Streak, Motor—you okay?"

"Okay!" Mike yelled. His voice sounded good to him, reassuring.

"Yeah!" Motor's voice, still cynical.

"Streak?" Longo shouted. There was no answer. "*Streak?*"

Mike fired again. He was breathing hard. Where was Streak? A picture appeared in his mind of Streak dashing back to the Fort, uncontrollably afraid. No, he told himself, Streak wouldn't do that.

Suddenly Longo was next to him. "You see Streak, man?"

"No. I mean, I did before. He was over there, to my right."

"Fuck." Longo looked ahead. "Fuck." Explosions, louder than

before, sounded from the edge of Ai Tu. "Arty." Mike nodded. "One-oh-five's. Looks like they're on target." Mike nodded again. How did Longo know? He felt afraid of the noise, yet protected by it.

"Cover me," Longo said and Mike, grateful to be staying where he was, raised his rifle. Then Longo was gone. How could he move so fast?

"Doc! Crane!" For a moment Mike didn't recognize Longo's voice. "I need *help!"*

"Can't!" Crane shouted back, quickly, from somewhere to Mike's left. "I'm *working!"*

"It's Streak! He's hit—bad! I need help!"

"I can't!" Something in Crane's voice made Mike shiver. As if to get over it, he fired his rifle toward Ai Tu.

Suddenly there was a sharp pain in his leg. "Ouch!" He turned his head and saw Crane diving to the ground, where Longo had gone. He had stepped on Mike's leg, that was all.

Tracy shouted, *"Hold your fire! Hold your fire!"*

But why? Mike tried to listen. The firing gradually stopped. There were still explosions up ahead; now Mike could hear the whistling of the arty and mortars as they came in. He felt safe where he lay. He wanted not to move.

"Hey, Tracy!" It sounded like Jeff's high-pitched voice.

"Yeah!" Tracy sounded angry. "Over here!" Mike turned part-way around. In the semidarkness he could see Jeff and the rest of the platoon advancing slowly over the sand, bent over, like crabs.

"Forget it," Tracy said, "they've beat it. We've got some men hit. We're gonna need medevacs."

"Any KIA?"

"I don't think so—"

Crane's voice interrupted from the right: "Streak's dead! Fuck it! He's dead!"

Mike lay still, staring ahead at the village in the last light of the western sky. *I'll just stay right here,* he thought. *I'm not going to move until somebody tells me to.* He put a fresh magazine in his rifle and pointed it ahead toward Ai Tu.

The artillery fire ceased, and there was quiet. Longo joined Mike.

"Watch it, man," Longo said, "this could be a setup. That's what Charlie likes to do—wound a few, then lay back and wait for the choppers to come in. They know how much a chopper costs." He seemed about to say something more, then stopped himself, put his head down and swore.

The first chopper came down, breaking the quiet; it took out two wounded marines from the second squad. Then another appeared. Mike tensed as it came down, pressing his cheek against his rifle butt, aiming at Ai Tu.

The helicopter took off. There was no enemy fire. The platoon got up and went back to the Fort.

Prince Mike Romanoff had a special meal that night in the Commissary for the first platoon: franks and beans. "I've been saving these dogs," he said. "You guys need them." The marines ate hurriedly and quietly, then went back to the tent to clean their weapons.

Talk began of what had happened. There were speculations about how many VC there had been, opinions as to what should have been done.

"Shit," C.C. said, "I don't go for this stuff—comin' back and lickin' our wounds, like a dog. We backed down, that's exactly what we did. We fuckin' backed down, and that's not the way I was brought up. We shoulda kept going—night or no night. Charged those motherfuckers. I thought that was what the fuckin' Crotch was all about." A few quietly spoken words of agreement arose from different parts of the tent.

Brutus, bent over his disassembled machine gun next to C.C., said, "But we didn't know how many there were, C.C. I agree with you, we shouldn't back down. But it might have been a trap—you don't know." He was right, Mike thought. He liked the sound of Brutus's gentle yet forceful voice.

C.C. swore sullenly. "Who the hell cares."

"You'da cared," Brutus answered, "if we charged into that vill and there was a company of VC waiting to ambush us. You'da cared plenty." C.C. growled something Mike couldn't hear.

Blevins said, "Hellfire, they should've called in close air and bombed the place. That's what they should've done."

"No shit. That's what they should do with this whole fucking country." It was Motor. "Blast it the fuck away. It ain't worth it."

There were more words of assent and then silence. Suddenly Crane erupted: "What the fuck, man, you can't wipe out a whole goddamn vill just 'cause of that!"

Mike glanced at Motor. He seemed about to say something, then shrugged, giving off a disgusted look.

"Where the hell was he, anyway?" Crane went on, angrily.

"Who, Crane?" Blevins asked.

"Captain fucking Blood, that's who. Standing up there with his goddamn bug-eyes—like it's a goddamn opera! Why the hell wasn't he out there?" He lifted a small brown bottle to his lips and tipped it back. "If he had any guts, he would've been out there—with the whole company, too. Instead he sends one squad. . . . For Christ's sake, no wonder Streak got killed. Lucky we all didn't. What the hell is one squad? For Christ's sake!" He sounded as if he might get up and run outside to the captain's tent. Instead, he drank again. Where did he get the whiskey? Mike wondered.

There was silence. Mike bent to his rifle cleaning. Then Blevins spoke again. "I respect what you're saying, Crane, but I don't agree with you." He had a subdued, reasonable tone.

"Oh, yeah?" Crane said. "What the fuck do you know?"

Blevins frowned, taking the cigar out of his mouth. "I believe the cap'n did the right thing," he went on. "I believe I know why he did it, too." He glanced around the tent as if looking for support. When he met Mike's eyes, Mike gave him a questioning look. "I believe this was some kind of test," he said, "or maybe a trap—like Brutus said. To see how we'd react." He stopped again.

Mike said, "How do you mean, Blevins?"

Blevins seemed encouraged. "Well, it looks to me that there's some kind of attack coming up—a big attack, maybe, like they did the last time, when they overrun the whole damn place. That's what I think. That's what they're getting ready for and I think that tonight was part of it. Maybe they would've done it, too, right now—if the cap'n went out there with the whole company. Come up on the other side, through Binh Le—a whole battalion of 'em, at least—maybe even more, since a battalion wasn't enough last time." His voice seemed to pick up conviction as he went along. "Anyway, that's what I think they're getting ready to do. And I believe it's gonna happen soon, too. D.J., cap'n's radioman, says he thinks so too." Blevins nodded as if clinching his argument.

"Bullshit." Crane sounded unimpressed.

Suddenly Mike spoke: "He might be right. It could've been a probe."

"That's right—a probe." Blevins nodded at him with appreciation, and Mike went back to his rifle.

Rain, peering through the barrel of his grenade launcher, said, "I don't know about all that, but I'll tell you one thing: I know what the South Koreans would've done."

"What's that?" Mike asked.

"All they need is one sniper round from a vill and that's it: they burn the whole place down. Don't matter whether the sniper hits anyone or not, either. And you know what happens after that? They don't get any more sniper rounds from that vill. Not from the vill next to it either and not from the one next to it." His tone was matter-of-fact.

"That's right," C.C. said, excited again, "hell, that's what Charlie does too. Man, even the ARVN are tougher than we are. They would've gone in there and burned that vill down, I bet you. That's the trouble: we try to be too nice. You think these people respect that? Us bringing some little puppy back. 'Oh, we're sorry, we won't do it again.' Bullshit. Only one way to get respect."

"That's the truth," Motor said, "that's basic."

Longo, to the right of Mike, spoke for the first time: "Sure, but why mess with the vill in the first place? Just leave it alone, that's what I say—don't go near it." His voice sounded as if it might break.

"That's right," Crane agreed, throwing glares around the tent. "Longo's right. You want to stay in one piece or not?"

For a few moments nobody said anything. Then Pogo spoke: "Why don't we just pretend it isn't there? We could erase it from all our maps and battalion's and regiment's maps too. That way we wouldn't have to bomb it or nothing—"

"Shut up, Pogo," Tracy said. He sounded exhausted. "Shut up or I'll beat your ass."

"As long as you don't beat my face. Then you'd be in trouble. There's all these girls I know back in Nebraska—"

"Shut *up!*"

There were a couple of dry giggles and then the tent became silent again. As he reassembled his rifle Mike became conscious of the empty space next to him. It was as if the Streak had never been there. Had the Vietcong whose bullet had killed him known what he had done? Had any of Mike's rounds hit one of them? He checked each piece of his rifle carefully, more carefully than he ever had before. *So that's what it's like*, he thought, *to be in a fire fight.* He watched his hands as they worked. There was no trembling. Why should there be? He had done all right, he decided—in spite of his grogginess, in spite of not knowing what he was shooting at.

But what if they had kept going—the way C.C. said they should have? Would Mike have been able to do that? The final assault, as he had learned it in training: stand up on line and walk toward the enemy, firing from the hip. Such an assault was supposed to frighten the enemy so badly they would break and run. The French Foreign Legion, according to one book Mike had read, used to do it all the time.

And what if the VC launched an attack of their own against the Fort, as Blevins said they were going to do? How would Mike do then?

* * *

Early the next morning two squads from the second platoon surrounded Ai Tu while the remaining squad searched through it. Afterward Mike spoke with Parrot, one of the marines who had done the searching. No VC or weapons had been found, Parrot said, but four villagers had been killed by the marines' artillery. Parrot, who had been to language school and could speak some Vietnamese, said he kept getting different answers when he questioned the villagers. Some said a great many VC had been there, others said only a few. One old man told him that the VC had beaten several villagers who wanted to move to Binh Le. The VC told the villagers that they were soon going to wipe out the Fort.

Two days later the battalion chaplain came out to the Fort and held a memorial service for all the marines who had died since the last time he had been out, two months before. *Two months*, Mike thought, as he sat with the rest of the company on the top of the sandy hill: could it be only two months? Mike remembered how scared he had been that day on his helicopter flight out, how self-conscious in front of the other marines when he landed. So much had happened since then!

After the service Mike joined his fellow squad members standing around the water bag, smoking cigarettes, drinking water, softly talking. Longo's eyes were red, Mike noticed. He went over next to him and the two of them stood silently and closely together, listening to the other marines talk. It was of the dead, what good men they had been. Standing like this, Mike felt a calmness come over him. It occurred to him that this was the real service, this quiet sharing of feelings with his fellow marines.

That night he made a decision. In a letter to his parents he wrote:

. . . I know I haven't told you much about what I am doing over here, but I feel that it is time that you know. There is no sense hiding it anymore, and you probably have guessed already. I am in combat—"in the field," as they say over here. It gets pretty scary sometimes, but don't worry, I am doing all right. It is a tough war but we are doing the best we can and I believe we are going to win. I have met several Vietnamese—I've even eaten meals at one of their homes—and I know how bad the Vietcong can treat them.

Thank you for your letters; I appreciate them very much.

Love,
Michael

3

HOME

There was a commotion in the hall. Mike raised himself up and saw a line being formed of patients on stretchers. Two orderlies came into his room and checked the names at the ends of beds.

"Allison," one of them said, pointing at Mike's bed.

"That's it."

Without another word they lifted Mike onto a stretcher and strapped him in, then carried him to the corridor and got on line.

They waited. In a few minutes they picked him up again, traveled a few feet, put him back down. Mike felt a small pain in the middle of his back, just to the left of his spine. He tried to shift position but couldn't.

The orderlies began to talk: ". . . Made a down payment on that new Charger I bought. Man, it's gonna break me. That last promotion I got wasn't shit in my pocket. . . . Know what you mean, man, I'm broke all the time. . . . Hey, how're you and Sally getting on? . . . She can go fuck herself, man, she really pissed me off last night. . . . There ain't no decent women here, they're all dogs. . . . Man, this place sucks." They sounded like Motor, Mike thought; in fact, one of them even looked like him.

They moved again, to the head of a flight of stairs, and stopped.

The pain in Mike's back increased; it seemed to spread from the original point up and down his spine. It was because he was lying on his back, he knew; he needed to turn onto his side. He thought of asking the orderlies to unstrap him—just for a second. But they were still talking.

It was more of the same. Nothing seemed to suit them. Whatever they spoke of—their jobs, their girl friends, the country— they complained about, sneered at, derided. Not once did they mention the fact that they were carrying a seriously injured marine. Was this what it was going to be like back in the States? Mike wondered. Suddenly it seemed to him that he didn't want to go. He wanted to go the other way, back to where he had been: where there was a common enemy, where people looked out for each other—even someone like Motor—where there were respect and order.

A thought occurred to Mike: what if they should drop him? Yes, why not? They had seen so many like him, were so bored by it all. They could get away with it—easy, say it was a mistake. It was bound to happen once in a while: the laws of statistics. Drop him right down the stairs, where it would really do some harm. For kicks, just to break the monotony. Kill him.

Mike's heart pounded as they lifted him again. *Please, please,* he begged silently, *don't drop me.*

But of course they didn't. They carried him down the stairs and then outside. It was hot. Why did he get so afraid? He didn't used to be like that. It must have to do with the injury, the shock of getting hit. Mike told himself that he should stop imagining such things: it wasn't good for him. It wasn't healthy.

It was a big plane, a C-141. Mike had never been in one before. It was fitted especially for litters, four rows across, each row four litters high. Two attendants lifted Mike to his position—second from the top near the rear of the airplane. One of them loosened his strap and Mike shifted to his side; immediately his back felt better. He tried to look around. Tubes and pouches hung all over. No one spoke. There was a loud hum from the engines and a subtle vibration throughout.

The plane began its takeoff and suddenly Mike became afraid. Were they going to crash? What chance would he have to survive? Then he felt the plane rise in the air and he breathed easier. He would be all right, he told himself. He was going home. He heard a voice:

"This is your pilot speaking. Welcome aboard MAC Medevac flight 051 bound for Andrews Air Force Base, Washington, D.C., with intermediate stops at Yokota Air Base, Japan, and Elmendorf Air Force Base, Alaska. Approximate flying time to Japan, two and a half hours. We should be touching down at Andrews about twenty-four hours from now, if all goes well. On behalf of your crew I'd like to say that we all hope you enjoy your flight, and please let us know if there's anything we can do. Thank you."

Twenty-four hours? But of course—what did Mike expect? A flight like this took time; he would just have to wait. But what was he going to do for twenty-four hours? And what did the pilot mean by "if all goes well"? Mike lay still and listened carefully to the hum of the engines. Twenty-four hours!

He slept. When he woke it was cold and he slept again. He realized, vaguely, that they were landing. "Japan," a voice said. His hip aching, Mike turned onto his back. The airplane taxied and stopped; there were sounds of doors opening and vehicles pulling up outside. How long did they have to stay here? Now that they weren't moving the slowness of time seemed almost unbearable to him. He thought of Christmases when he was little, of trying to get to sleep the night before. How could the next twenty hours ever pass? There was a slight pain in his back. It became worse and finally he moved onto his side again.

Mike woke. They were in the air again, he knew. He had to go to the bathroom. What was he going to do? He searched for a button to push and found one, then hesitated. He peered over the side of his stretcher. He wasn't that far up. What was to stop him? Watching out for the tubes and bottles underneath, he slowly let himself down.

He walked up the aisle. Forward of the litters was a section of seats that looked like regular airline seats. In the last row sat two attendants. He asked one of them where the head was, then walked up to it, past the seats.

It was easier to pee now; it stung much less. He stared in the mirror. The bandages around his head and jaw were dirty and bloodstained, giving him a battlefield look. His expression was miserable. He looked the way he did in pictures taken when he was little. It must be because his head was hurting, he thought.

When he came out he noticed a woman sitting in one of the seats, her head down, reading a magazine. Had she been there before? She had graying hair and wore a USO armband. Was it the same woman he had met in Da Nang? Yes, it was. What was her name? He went over.

"Excuse me."

She lifted her head. "Yes?"

"Oh . . . I'm sorry."

"Would you like to sit down?"

"Uh, no—yes, I guess so. Thanks."

She got up and let Mike go by. He sat down a seat away from her.

"Aren't you cold?"

"I'm all right." He was shivering.

"Here." She took a blanket from under her seat and put it over him.

"Thank you."

No, it wasn't the same woman. This one was older, with a plain face; nice, but without that special quality the other woman had had.

"Sure you're all right?"

"Yes, thank you; really."

She hesitated, then sighed. "I'll bet you're glad to be going home."

"Yes." Mike knew his look was miserable but felt he couldn't change it, or didn't want to.

"I'll bet your parents are glad too."

"I'll bet."

"It must have been terrible." Mike said nothing. She kept looking at him. "Where are you going?"

"What?"

"Where do you live?"

"Virginia."

"Then I'll bet they send you to Bethesda." She spoke matter-of-factly. "Bethesda Naval Hospital. That's in Maryland, but it's right next to Virginia. Right outside of Washington. It's a very good hospital; one of the best."

"Is that right?"

"Or they might send you to Portsmouth. That's a good hospital too."

"I see."

She smiled. "Don't worry, they'll take care of you." Did he look as if he was worried? When he said no more she turned back to her magazine.

His back began to ache a little so he sat up straighter. He wished he had something to read. What was he going to do—just sit for twenty hours? Or go back and lie down? Which was worse? No, it must be less than twenty hours now. The woman next to him was wearing a watch, but he decided not to ask her the time. She was nice but he didn't want any more of her questions.

He leaned back and tried to sleep. If only his head didn't ache so much! Suddenly he got up, walked back down the aisle, and climbed up to his stretcher. The pain began again in his back and so he turned to his side. He closed his eyes and finally slept.

Mike woke. Something was wrong. Had he dreamt? No. He was in an airplane; it was shaking; there was the tinkle of breaking glass. What was going on? A *disturbance*, he told himself, that was all; nothing to worry about: they were flying through a distur-bance. It was a big plane; there was no danger. The plane bounced—two, three times—the tinkling sound again, louder; Mike's heart pounded. So, he thought, this was what it had all come down to: after making it this far he was going to die in some senseless plane crash, like a kind of joke. *Oh, no, please,* he thought. *Don't crash.*

The flight became smooth again and Mike ceased his pleas. Why had he become so scared? It was because he was in an airplane, he told himself. He remembered the flight to Vietnam. It had been very different from this one: a regular civilian airplane—Continental Airlines, a 707—with brightly dressed stewardesses. There had been turbulence then too, but Mike had ignored his fears as he joked with his fellow marines about getting killed before they even got to the war.

He closed his eyes and slept again.

The airplane landed. "Alaska," the voice announced; "forty-four degrees." Not very cold, Mike thought; he had expected Alaska to be much colder. It was November. He thought of Rain. Rain had been to Alaska—one summer, he once told Mike, working construction and having all kinds of adventures: drinking, fighting, whoring. Maybe Mike would do that too. When he got better he would do anything he wanted.

The plane took off. Mike climbed down again and went forward. The USO woman was gone. He went to the bathroom, then sat down where he had been sitting before. Next to him was a *Time* magazine. *Time* magazine! How long since he had seen a *Time* magazine? He picked it up, examining the familiar format. On the cover was a movie star. Quickly he turned to the news of Vietnam. Heavy fighting around Dak To. There were pictures of exhausted soldiers during and after battle. Mike studied what he could see of their weapons and faces. One of the wounded had a bandage like his.

He searched for more news about the war—about Operation Boone, the mortar attack in Da Nang—but there was none. He looked again at the cover and saw that the magazine was a week old. Then he turned to *Sport.* O. J. Simpson was having an incredible year for Southern California. Mike put the magazine down. His head ached; reading seemed to make it worse.

He was hungry, he decided. He got up and asked one of the attendants whether there was anything to eat. The attendant gave him a small white cardboard box that Mike took back to his seat. Inside were a sandwich, an apple, and a container of milk. Mike unwrapped the sandwich. It was tuna salad. He ate half of a half, then drank the milk. His stomach felt a little upset. He felt cold. He went back to his stretcher and slept.

Hours later a voice sounded: "We are now starting our descent for Andrews Air Force Base and the Washington, D.C., area. Our expected arrival time is 2205. It is now 2115. Ground temperature is twenty-nine degrees. Speaking for the crew of flight number 051, we hope you have enjoyed your flight and we wish you the best of luck."

Mike lay still. He remembered how the marines had responded to the pilot's announcement before they had landed at Da Nang: with catcalls, jeers, boos, hisses, laughter. Now there was silence. It was as though they were all asleep—or didn't care. But who were they? Mike realized he had not met even one of his fellow patients, did not even know what one of them looked like. For a moment he had the eerie feeling that they were all dead.

The humming in the airplane changed pitch. Mike felt pressure in his ears. He worked his jaws. They were sore. The plane shook. Turbulence again, he thought. *I'll be all right, just a little turbulence. Please,* he whispered, *please, let us make it.*

He held his breath. The wheels touched. He listened. Not a sound. Like a plane full of corpses. Now the hum was louder—louder and louder, becoming a screech. What was happening? The screech subsided. A voice said, "We are now at Andrews Air Force Base, Washington, D.C."

Mike let out his breath. He was really here. He felt an unfamiliar swelling within him; it was pleasant. His eyes became moist. He blinked; a tear fell onto his cheek.

He was crying. Why not? It was fitting, wasn't it? Even if it was only one or two tears.

PART
TWO

4

REUNION

Mike, walking out of the bathroom into the corridor, stopped. A woman was standing by the nurses' station, a civilian, dark-haired, wearing a hat, coat, and high heels. In front of her, speaking to the nurse supervisor, was another civilian, a man, also wearing a dark winter's coat, but holding his hat in his hands along with a brown paper bag and newspaper. The woman was leaning slightly forward, blinking rapidly, saying nothing. There was a hint of impatience in her stance, whereas the man, gesturing now with his right arm, seemed at ease. Mike began to walk again, very slowly, holding his head erect as though it might fall off.

"Mother."

She turned. "Oh, there he is, Ernest." Then to Mike: "You can walk!"

The man turned too. "There he is," he said to the nurse supervisor. "There's our Michael."

"Hi, Dad."

"I didn't know you could walk," Mike's mother said.

"Yes, Mother. But I have to be very careful." As if to prove it, he moved even more slowly. When he reached his mother he put his arms around her and, bending his legs and still keeping his head erect, kissed her on the cheek. Her face felt very cold; her coat was cold too. Then he hugged and kissed his father. His cheek was rough with whiskers.

"Good to have you back, big boy," he said, smiling.

Mike turned to the nurse supervisor. "These are my parents, Commander Otis."

"I was just meeting them." She spoke in a crisp, businesslike voice. "Nice to meet you, Mr. and Mrs. Allison." She sat down and picked up some papers on her desk.

"The same, I'm sure," Mike's father said, nodding, smiling graciously, as if he still had her attention. He cleared his throat. "I can see you're taking fine care of Michael here—"

"I'd better get back to bed, Mom." Mike began walking again, faster now. "You and Dad can come in."

Inside the ward he went to the first bed on the right, then very carefully lay back, easing his head to the pillow with his right arm. He smiled weakly at his parents, standing at the foot of the bed, several feet apart, and said, "It's good to see you."

"It's good to see you, big boy," his father said. "Welcome back." His cheeks were red; he looked robust. He looked the way he used to, Mike remembered, when he'd come home from work on a winter's evening and visit Mike when he was sick in bed. It was evening now too. Outside it was dark. It was quiet in Mike's corner of the ward. The bed next to his was ruffled and empty.

"Isn't it, Nancy?" his father said.

"Isn't it what, Ernest?"

"Good to see our Michael."

"Of course it is." She blinked several times; her eyes were unfocused.

"Did you just get in?" Mike asked.

His father shook his head. "About an hour ago. We checked into that motel you told us about—the one across from the hospital. Seems like a nice place."

"I hear it's all right."

"Although it's not a Sleep Well." Mike's father's face broke into a teasing smile.

"No," Mike said, smiling faintly. "Say, why don't you have a seat? Dad, there's some chairs around. You could pull another one over."

"Who wants to sit?" his mother said. "We've been sitting all day, in the car."

"Oh . . . all right."

There were a few moments of silence. From other parts of the ward came the sounds of patients talking to one another; jokes, laughter. Mike glanced around. Leroy's new color television was on. The evening news. A group of patients stood around his bed watching it. Mike listened for a mention of Vietnam.

"How was the trip?" he asked. "When did you leave—this morning?"

His mother nodded. "Too long. And the roads are terrible. Those mountain roads this morning—why, they scared me out of my wits! Can't they put you in a hospital any closer?"

"No," Mike said, "there is none. I'm sorry about that. Why didn't you fly? There's an airport here. You could probably get a flight to Washington and then another one down here. Don't you think, Dad?"

Mike's mother shuddered. "Oh, God, no. You know I hate to fly. I'd rather drive."

"It wasn't that bad," his father said. "Once you get past Martinsville. A little long for one day, though."

"When do you have to go back—tomorrow? That's a lot of driving."

"I think we'll break it up going back. Come by here in the morning and get started around noon. Stop at a motel somewhere for the night, somewhere around—"

Mike's mother interrupted. "We brought some clothes for you, Michael, but we left them in the motel room. We'll bring them by tomorrow."

"Clothes?"

"A jacket and a pair of pants, plus some underwear. Oh, and a pair of shoes."

"Oh. . . . Thank you."

"You want to get up and around as soon as you can, you know. Try and get outside—get some fresh air."

"I can't. I'm restricted to this floor."

"Oh, God, they shouldn't do that to you. You don't look so bad. You haven't lost that much weight." Her voice sounded forced. "Let me see—"

"What—?"

She rushed to the head of the bed and thrust her face close to Mike's left ear. Out of the corner of his eye he could see her nose pointed at the side of his head, like the cone of an X-ray machine. Then she moved and studied his face from the front.

"Those aren't such bad scars," she said. He could smell her breath. "I wouldn't be worried if I were you. They'll fade away." She went back to the end of the bed and sat down on a chair.

"I'm not worried, Mother. Who said I was worried?" He smiled in what he imagined to be a benign, grateful way. "I'm just glad I'm alive."

"I'll bet you are," his father said. "That must be a terrible situation over there—just ter-rible." He moved his head from side to side in disapproval, his jowls shaking. He had put on weight, Mike noticed. Or had he? It was hard to remember; it seemed to Mike that he had been away for a long time. "Your mother and I watch the reports on TV every night," his father went on. He grimaced. "What I can't understand is how those Vietcongs can take those terrific shellackings and still go on. They lose thousands and thousands of men, week after week, according to the TV. It just doesn't seem reasonable to me." He stared down, frowning, as if blaming the enemy for their unreasonableness, then looked up at Mike and raised his eyebrows. "What do you think?"

Mike hesitated. "I—I don't know . . . I mean—I just hope it ends soon."

His mother said, "Are they going to operate again? You said on the telephone they might have to." She seemed not to have been listening at all.

"What?"

"Are they going to operate again? You said something about a metal plate."

"Oh." Mike smiled sheepishly. "No."

"No? But you said—"

"I know. That's what I thought. Someone in Da Nang told me that, I was sure, right after the operation. . . ." He thought back, trying to remember. "Anyway, the doctor here said no."

"Is he sure?"

"Of course he's sure."

"Then why did they tell you a thing like that?"

"I don't know." He smiled embarrassedly. "The doctor thinks I dreamed it." Suddenly he looked at his father. "Oh, by the way—did you ever get the message, the one from Da Nang?"

His father shook his head. "No, no message."

"No? That's strange." Mike tried to picture in his mind the USO woman in Da Nang. What was her name?

His mother said, "So that must mean they think you're all right."

"Huh?"

"If they don't have to operate again."

"Yes," Mike said. "Basically. I've got a few problems with my hearing and there's some nerve and muscle damage, but—"

"But your brain's all right? Isn't that what you told me the doctor said?"

"Yes, Mother, my brain's all right."

"Well, thank God for that. As long as your brain's all right."

Mike was silent. He glanced toward Leroy's bed. The crowd of patients was still there. Someone shouted at the television; someone else booed. The report about Vietnam must be on. Mike fidgeted.

"And you were right there in the middle of it, weren't you? Boy, that must have been something." Mike's father slowly shook his head. "Did you—*ah-hem*—adjust all right? To the situation, that is."

Mike hesitated, then said, "All right."

His father nodded. "That's a wonderful ability, to be able to adjust. In fact, it's a virtue, I would say. I've always tried to practice it myself, in all the situations we've found ourselves in." He glanced at Mike's mother, then looked back to Mike and spoke more softly. "Are you—*ah-hem*—going to have to go back? To Vietnam, I mean."

Mike smiled faintly. "No . . . I told you that, on the phone."

"I know you did. But are you sure?"

"Yes, I'm sure."

His father raised his eyebrows. "Who, uh, told you that?"

"The doctor."

"The doctor here?"

"Yes. Look, Dad, I don't have to go back, believe me. It's the policy: when you get wounded and sent back to the States, that's it, your tour is over, no matter how long you've been there."

"Well, that's a relief." Still he sounded tentative.

"Yes."

"And so—*ah-hem*—what's going to happen now? Will you—"

"Yes, Michael, how long do you have to stay in here, anyway?"

"I don't know, Mother. The doctor says he has no idea."

"Uh-oh, that's trouble."

"What?"

"Watch out for those doctors, Michael. They like to keep you in here forever."

"I don't think so, Mother."

"You don't know, Michael. You tell them you want to get out as soon as you can. The hospital's no place for you." She shuddered. "You're a healthy boy."

"I will, Mother, don't worry."

"You don't know, Michael. You start to get used to it—the routine. People become *addicted*. These doctors, they—"

"Mother, what are you talking about? Nobody wants me to stay here; they want me to *leave*. They need beds. They've got wounded coming in from Vietnam all the time." He thought of saying something more, than breathed deeply and forced himself to smile.

"That sounds reasonable, Nancy."

"Sure, it sounds reasonable, but I know what these doctors are like."

"Look, Mom, it was a doctor in Da Nang who saved my life. I wouldn't be here right now if it wasn't for him."

"That's a point, Nancy."

"Oh, all right, all right, all right—I won't say anything. I'm always wrong."

"It's okay, Mom, I didn't mean that. You can talk. . . . Actually, my doctor said I could probably go home soon. On hospital leave."

His father's face lifted. "Really?"

"Yes. Like, for a couple of weeks. When I get a little stronger."

"Wonderful! Hear that, Nancy?"

"Of course I hear, Ernest."

"That means you could be home around Christmas."

"That's right," Mike said. "But it isn't for sure."

His father beamed. "Wouldn't that be wonderful? We never imagined *that* was going to happen—not *this* Christmas." He turned. "Isn't that wonderful, Nancy? Our son home with us for Christmas?"

"Of course it's wonderful." She nodded matter-of-factly. "That's just what he needs—a little rest at home. Some good cooking. I'll bet the food in here is *ter*-rible. It always is, you know, in these hospitals—"

"It's not so bad—"

"Just wait, you'll get better in no time, once we get you home. You're not so bad."

"I know that, Mother." Mike looked away. He thought of having a cigarette.

"Well," his father said, his voice soft, "we're awfully proud of you, for what you did over there—"

"Thank you, Dad—"

"—for the way that you became a leader—"

"A *leader?* What do you mean?"

"What you wrote us. About being appointed a leader, in your group—"

"Oh, you mean a *fire-team* leader."

"Whatever it's called."

"That's no big deal."

"I'm sure it was."

"I'm telling you, Dad, it wasn't. The fire team is like the smallest unit there is. Four men. Sometimes three. Or two. Or whatever." He snorted slightly. "That's no big deal."

"Well, you might not think so—now. But your mother and I are very proud."

"Fine, thank you."

"And everybody else is, too. You have no idea how many people have been asking about you back in Kingston. They all think you've done an outstanding job." He shook his head with approval.

Mike breathed deeply. "Thank you. But I hope you haven't been telling them that I was a big leader over there."

"Just what you told us. . . . Oh, that reminds me." He held out the newspapers he was carrying. "We brought you some papers from Kingston, just as you asked us." He put them on the table next to Mike's bed. "And, uh, we sent a copy of this to you in Vietnam, but I don't think it would have gotten here yet—forwarded, I mean."

"What's that?"

From his inside jacket pocket Mike's father took out a piece of paper, which he unfolded, inspected, then handed to Mike. It was a photocopy of a newspaper article. "KINGSTON MARINE IN VIETNAM," the small headline read. There was a picture of Mike—his boot camp picture, with his hair cut short, a sullen expression. Mike read: "The son of Mr. and Mrs. Ernest Allison of 402 Meadowbrook Lane is currently serving a thirteen-month tour with the Marine Corps in South Vietnam. Michael Ernest

Allison, a 1965 graduate of Kingston East High School, where he played on the varsity football team . . ."

Mike looked up. "What's this? How did this get in?"

His father nodded solemnly toward the article. Mike read on: ". . . recently wrote in a letter to his parents, describing the situation: 'I am in combat—"in the field," as they say over here. It gets pretty scary sometimes, but don't worry, I am doing all right. It is a tough war but we are doing the best we can and I believe we are going to win. I have met several Vietnamese—I've even eaten meals at one of their homes—and I know how bad the Vietcong can treat them.' . . ."

Mike let the clipping drop to his lap. "What did you do?" His voice rose.

His father cleared his throat. "Why, I contacted the editor of the *Courier*—Carl Huddle—you've met him. He seemed very interested when I told him about your letter—"

"But I sent it to you—and Mom—not to him. It wasn't for the public—"

"I don't see what difference that makes."

"It makes a—"

"People want to read about Vietnam, Michael. All they get are these biased commentators on the TV networks who think they know so damn much. We've had dozens, literally dozens, of people come up to us and tell us how much they appreciated reading the article—haven't we, Nancy?"

"But—at least you could've asked me."

"I told you not to do it, Ernest."

Mike's father looked hurt. "I don't see what damage was done."

"I told you, Ernest."

Mike breathed deeply. "It's all right, it's all right. Forget it." He put the clipping on the table to his right. "It's done, anyway. Forget it."

"People want to hear from someone like you. We have an obligation—"

"It's all right, I said. Forget it—please." Mike looked down to the other end of the ward. The crowd around Leroy's bed had thinned; the news was over. Now Mike could see Leroy, his intestines lying on his stomach covered by a clear plastic bag, like a pile of shit.

Mike's father cleared his throat again. "I, uh, happened to stop by the Sleep Well motel the other day. . . ."

Mike let out a breath. "Oh?" he finally said.

"Everybody there wishes the best to you too."

"Thank you."

"They certainly think a lot of you there." Suddenly he smiled. "I always get a kick out of the way everybody there calls you Ernie. . . ." Mike said nothing. His father rubbed his chin. "Let's see, who else was there . . . ?"

Mike's mother said, "He looks tired, Ernest. Maybe we should go."

"No, no, that's all right," Mike said. "I'm all right." He smiled again, weakly, and looked from one to the other of his parents. "But tell me: how are you two doing?"

His father shrugged, raising his eyebrows in a self-deprecating expression, then turned to Mike's mother.

"Oh, my stomach's been off," she said, sitting up straight. "I can't eat a thing. But that's nothing new. Same old story. You don't want to hear about that."

"I'm sorry."

"And she won't go to a doctor. I've offered to send her to—"

"I've *seen* the doctor, Ernest—hundreds of them." Her tone was peevish. She turned to Mike. "They don't know what's wrong. All they want to do is operate—and I'm not going to let them!"

His father gave Mike a pained, aggrieved look, as if to ask, "What can you do?" Mike closed his eyes, then opened them.

"How about you, Dad? How are things at Barnett?"

His father frowned. "Not good."

"Oh?"

He shook his head vigorously; his jowls trembled. "There was a big strike last summer—I wrote you about it. Now Barnett is talking about closing the plant up."

"But . . . how can they? It's a new factory, practically."

His father set his face in a grimace. "They can do it."

"But . . ." Mike glanced from his father to his mother, then back again. "But what'll that mean for you, Dad?"

He spoke gravely. "We don't know yet."

There was a pause. "That's too bad," Mike said.

"It certainly is—it's a *shame*, if you ask me. After all that work we put in—and just when I feel I've finally got a team assembled that can deal with the situation. . . ." He shook his head; he had a pained expression. "I just can't understand how these so-called geniuses that are now running the show at Barnett can—"

"*Ernest!*" Mike's mother seemed to explode off her chair without actually leaving it. "For God's *sake!* Give your son a chance to talk, will you? He doesn't want to hear all that. Not now." Her voice was harsh and rasping; her eyes blinked rapidly.

"Mother, Mother, it's all right. Really—I don't mind."

"Well, *I* mind. I've had to listen to that stuff all day in the car. I'm *sick* of it—"

"Nancy, it's our future I'm talking about."

"Well, I know that, Ernest, but really—enough is enough. . . . Now go ahead, Michael, you talk. We came to listen to you. Go on, tell us about it." She drew herself up in her chair and lifted her head; her chin and nose were pointed at Mike.

"Tell you what?" Mike tried to keep his voice calm.

"Go on, tell us about it. Tell us what happened when you were wounded."

"But . . ."

"It'll be good for you. Go on."

He stared at her and then at his father. They were both staring back. Suddenly Mike remembered the lieutenant, looking down at his watch, telling Mike he had to move forward. But how could he? His face was covered with blood. No, that was only the dream. But what *had* happened? Was Longo all right?

"Go on," his mother said, "tell us."

Mike's heart beat fast. What did she want to know?

"I—"

A crash sounded at the foot of the bed.

"Ooooops—*damn* it!"

"*Ernest!*"

"What is it, Dad?"

"I dropped it."

Mike's father, reaching with his hand as if still trying to catch the brown paper bag that had just left it, stared down at his feet. Quickly Mike glanced around the room. Several patients were staring at them. A sweet, strong, familiar odor reached Mike's nose.

"What is it, Dad?"

He looked up, his eyes wide with innocence. "A bottle of sherry. I thought we might have a little drink together—ha-ha."

"That's *ter*-rible, Ernest—*ter*-rible! How could you *do* that?"

"It just slipped out." He looked down again. "That's a shame; it was good sherry, too. We had a glass in the motel before coming up."

"What are you going to do? *Phew*—it's beginning to stink!"

"Mother, take it easy, would you? It was an accident." Now some patients were laughing. Leroy stretched his neck trying to see.

"I know, Michael, but I told him not to bring it."

A ruddy-faced orderly, sniffing the air, came through the door.

"Hi, Carl," Mike said. "We, uh, had a little accident here."

The orderly examined the floor, then grinned at Mike's father. "I'll be right back," he said. "Don't worry about a thing."

Mike's father spoke to Carl's retreating figure: "Can I do something?"

"Don't worry, Dad, he'll take care of it."

A nurse walking by from the other end of the ward stopped by Mike's bed. "What's happened here?" she said. Her tone was smooth and calm.

"It's all right, Lieutenant Simpson," Mike said. "Carl's taking care of it. A little accident, that's all." She gave him a mildly puzzled look.

Carl came back with mop and pail. "No, no," Mike's father said, "let me. I'll do it." He tried to take hold of the mop.

Carl began to wipe. "Not to worry, sir. I'll have it up in a second." Mike could hear the crunching sound of broken glass. Lieutenant Simpson shrugged and continued on her way.

"See all the trouble you've caused, Ernest?"

He let out a breath. "Nancy, *please*, have a heart, would you? Do you have to keep jumping on me like that? You heard Michael: it was an accident. Be reasonable. You don't have to go into a rage."

"I am *not* in a rage—stop exaggerating!" Her voice rose piercingly. "You always do that. *You're* the one who dropped the bottle—"

"Mom, Dad . . ."

She got up from her chair. "I've got to go. Is there a bathroom here I can use, Michael?"

"Sure, Mom. Right out there to the right."

Carl pointed for her. "Just past the desk there, Mrs. Allison. On the right."

"Why, thank you," she said and turned and walked uncertainly away. Mike's father watched until she disappeared, then came to the head of Mike's bed and began to whisper.

"What? . . . Dad, that's my bad ear—I can't hear."

"Oh." He seemed surprised. He leaned across the bed and whispered more loudly. Mike could smell sherry on his breath.

". . . a terrific explosion in the motel room, just before we came up here . . . emotional outburst . . . just terrible! I didn't say a thing to set it off, either, not a thing—it just happened, out of the blue. . . ." His eyes opened wide as he whispered; he looked as if he were telling Mike something new, something of great interest to them both. Mike lay still, staring in front. Carl was bent over, picking up the last pieces by hand. ". . . and she just *refuses* to see a doctor. I've tried and tried, but she just won't go . . . It just isn't rational." He glanced quickly around, then straightened, clearing his throat.

"Thanks a lot, Carl," Mike said. "I appreciate that."

Carl grinned. "Forget it, jarhead. Why do you think they call us swabbies, anyway?" Mike smiled.

"Yes," his father said, clearing his throat again, "thank you very much, er, Carl. I'm awfully sorry about that."

"That's all right, Mr. Allison. It's happened to me too." He winked. "See you later, Mike," he said and picked up his mop and bucket and left.

"Nice fellow," Mike's father said. He glanced around the ward. "You must—I mean—are you—*ah-hem*—getting acquainted? With the other patients, I mean."

"Sure."

"That's nice. There must be some . . . interesting people here."

"Yes."

Mike's mother came back to the bed. "*Whew*," she said, "I can still smell it."

"Oh, please, Nancy, would you—"

"Mom, Dad," Mike interrupted, "I'm sorry, but I'm still pretty weak and I'm very tired. I think I'm going to fall asleep."

His mother's tone changed instantly: "Of course you are— that's only natural. Come on, Ernest, let the poor boy rest. Let's go and get some dinner—I'm *starving*." She smiled; it made her look much younger. She moved to the head of the bed and patted Mike's hair. "You get some rest," she said. Behind her, Mike's father gave an exaggerated wink.

"I will, Mom."

She bent and kissed his cheek. Suddenly Mike heard snatches of loud whispering: ". . . don't believe everything your father says—he exaggerates! . . . And never put anything in writing—I warned you! . . ." She straightened and went back to the foot of the bed.

"So long, big boy," Mike's father said, smiling. "See you to-morrow."

"So long."

They both smiled and waved as they walked out of the room.

Mike breathed deeply. His back was aching. He took his head in his hands and turned onto his side. He closed his eyes and in a few moments was asleep.

5

THE RIDE

Mike lay on the back seat of his parents' car, a blanket over him, afraid. What was to stop it? Another car suddenly smashing into theirs, for no reason, just a mistake. What was the power of a red light? He pictured himself lying on the pavement, mangled, dying; not even knowing the name of the person who had hit him.

"Ernest, watch out! That car is turning—what's the matter with you?"

"Nancy, please, would you stop hollering like that while I'm driving?"

"Well, I just wish you'd be a little more careful."

From where he lay Mike could see the side of his mother's face: her blinking eye and tensed, trembling mouth.

She jerked forward. "Watch out! Ernest, you almost *hit* him."

"Nancy, please! Have a heart, would you?"

"I'll have a heart, Ernest. Just pay a little more attention to your driving." She turned in her seat. "He got a ticket on the way back the last time, you know. For *speeding*."

"I know," Mike said. "You told me."

"He was way over the limit, too."

"Five miles an hour over—that was all he charged me with."

"You were going much faster than that and you know it, Ernest. You were *lucky*—that cop gave you a break!" She turned back to Mike. "They must have been talking for half an hour, the policeman and your father." She laughed. "I was beginning to feel sorry for him—you know how your father loves to talk!"

Mike smiled. His father leaned his head back. "He was a marine himself, by the way."

"Who?"

"The trooper. He told me—after I told him about your being in the hospital. He said he had been in Korea. . . . But he gave me the ticket anyway." He shook his head. "Now my damn insurance rates are bound to go up."

Mike pulled the blanket closer. He was cold. Why did he keep getting so afraid? Ever since they had left the hospital he had imagined gruesome accidents every time the car slowed down, stopped, speeded up. Was it still the shock of getting wounded? Or was it just that he was weak?

"Anyway," his father said, clearing his throat and leaning his head back again, "as I was saying before, it just doesn't seem reasonable to me, after all that work we put into making it a productive factory and giving all those people jobs, all of a sudden to give up on it, just like that. Does it seem reasonable to you?"

"No."

"And yet that's exactly what's happening. . . ."

They were on the open highway now—Mike could tell by the steady hum of the car—out of whatever town they had been passing through. He felt safer. Why should he feel safer, when the car was traveling at a greater speed? But their motion was regular, there were no stops and starts to excite his imagination. He felt lulled, too, by his father's talk.

"Does that make sense to you?"

"What?"

"I said, do you think that makes sense?"

"I . . . guess so."

"Are you sure you can hear all right? I won't talk if you don't want me to."

"No, no, that's all right. I can hear. Go on."

Death, Mike suddenly thought. That must be what was making him so afraid. That must be what happens when a person comes back from war: because in war death is always close, you get used to it; then when you get back you forget that the rules are different.

But had he ever really been that close to death? Mike thought back. He remembered how casually—even jokingly—death was referred to among his fellow marines. Deaths became reference points in everyday conversation—"the time that Hornet got zapped," "the time Zero got wasted," "the time the Streak bought the farm." Mike remembered his own close calls: the time Short-round got hit, when rounds kicked up a couple of feet away; the time he was "wounded" by the C-ration can, when the rounds were inches away; and his first real fire fight, when the Streak was killed—who knew how close the bullets had been then? *Ping, ping, ping.* Of course he had been afraid—but of something other than death, it had seemed: of the noise, the yelling; of the captain back in the Fort looking down through his binoculars. But of his own death? It hadn't really occurred to him. So why should he be afraid of dying now?

These were questions to write the Professor about, it occurred to Mike. With a pang he thought of the Professor's letter to him, resting in his inside sports jacket pocket. He needed to read it again—several times; there was much in it to think about; much about death.

"... Of course the damn union didn't help matters any by going on that strike last summer. That was a terrible thing to do. I told your mother at the time—didn't I, Nancy?—that this could be the end of Barnett in Kingston. ... The damn fools!"

Mike remembered the day the Professor had joined the platoon, fresh over from the States, wearing new, clean utilities, and jungle boots that still had all their polish. He had walked into the tent with Jeff and the other new marines, blinking behind his black-rimmed glasses—not military issue, but his own frames. He was a little shorter than Mike, thin; a strange build, Mike had thought. When he took off his helmet he revealed a short, boot camp haircut that looked out of place.

"Bill Pratt," he introduced himself as, shaking hands with Mike and Longo and Motor without any awkwardness. He seemed not at all disturbed by the scruffy, unkempt marines around him or their nicknames. Longo accepted his new fire-team member as he accepted everyone, with his good-natured, high-cheekboned smile—"Welcome to the Foreign Legion, man"—and began his questioning.

"Wow!" he exclaimed, after Pratt's first answers. "You went to college too? Where'd you go, man?" For the first time Pratt seemed embarrassed. His answer was barely audible. "*Yale?*" Longo shouted. "Man, we must have the best-educated fire team in the Marine Corps!" Excitement radiated from his face. "Hey, I've got it. We should enter that program on TV—what is it, that show with one college against another, you got to answer all the questions?"

" 'The College Bowl,' " Motor said. He sounded bored.

"Yeah, that's it, 'The College Bowl.' Think of it, man: we show up in flak jackets and helmets, M-16's. The other schools'll be so shook up they won't know what to say. We'd win easy. Yeah, why not? Let's do it."

"Why not?" Mike said, grinning, glancing at Pratt. "I'll go tell Captain Blood."

"Great. Do it, Crazy Mike. Have him cut us special orders."

"Wait—don't leave without me." It was Pogo. "I'll be on the team too."

Tracy said, "You're not going anywhere, Pogo. You never went to college."

"I did, too. The University of Nebraska. I went there lots of times. I knew this girl who was a student there and I used to visit her—"

"Shut up!"

Bill Pratt coughed into his fist. "Actually," he said, "I think it's a good idea, but I don't think the show is on the air anymore."

"Aw, shit." Longo seemed genuinely disappointed. "I bet we

could've won, too." Suddenly he smiled again. "So what'd you study, anyway, when you were at Yale?"

Pratt spoke in an unruffled, explanatory way. "I had intended to major in philosophy." *The Iceman*, Mike thought.

"Philosophy?" Longo was grinning again. "No shit. So you're gonna be a professor, huh? The Professor. Hey, that reminds me—we're the Ferocious Foursome again."

"No, Longo," Motor said. "The Fearsome Foursome."

Pogo said, "You're a professor? All right, I quit. Tracy, I ain't humpin' radio no more. I just got a deferment—I'm goin' back to school under the G.I. Bill. First thing I'm gonna do is burn my draft card."

"Shut up."

The Professor flashed a quick smile; he seemed not to think anything strange. Longo assigned him the Black Streak's old space in the tent, then he sat down and unpacked his seabag, arranging his possessions neatly. They included several paperback books, Mike noticed. Mike offered him a cigarette, but he said he didn't smoke.

On the Professor's first patrol they went down to Frontierland. The Professor, cover for Mike's point, moved quietly, which Mike appreciated, and he didn't get careless halfway through the patrol, the way Motor always did. He didn't sweat very much, either—nor did he head straight for the water bag when they got back to the Fort. They made no contact that time, but on their next patrol the Cisco Kid took a few shots at them. The Professor quickly whirled and returned fire with the rest of the marines.

Not even when the next swim call was announced did the Professor show any surprise. Without hesitating he joined it, and when the marines got to the beach he and Mike and Longo stripped down for the first shift in the water. The Professor was more solidly built than Mike had first thought, with a hairy, muscular chest. When Longo swam straight out the Professor went with him. "Longo, come back!" Captain Blood yelled, and Longo and the Professor swam back to where Mike was, where the three of them dog-paddled together. When Longo asked the Professor whether he had read *Catch-22*, he said yes.

Mike asked, "You play any sports at Yale?"

The Professor nodded. "Lacrosse."

"Lacrosse?" Longo grinned. "Man, you really were a preppy, weren't you?"

The Professor smiled quickly. "Yeah, I went to prep school, I admit it."

"Where?" Mike asked.

"Andover."

"Oh." Mike nodded. "That's a good one."

"Wow," Longo said, still grinning, "a real preppy. After all those fake ones I met at Monte Rio—I have to go to Vietnam to meet a real preppy."

In body surfing the Professor did it like Mike, with his head down and arms stuck forward, but after Longo explained "California-style" he tried it that way. Then they came back onshore, got dressed, and took their defensive positions while the other shift went in.

"Hey, Longo," Mike said, pointing at the swimmers, "get the cameras ready. It's the Invasion of the Naked Commandos. The VC are dug in all around us, ready to attack, but they're too embarrassed to look."

"Got it, Crazy Mike. The VC against the NC."

"Huh?"

"The Vietcong against the Naked Commandos—VC and NC."

"Oh—right." Mike glanced quickly at the Professor.

"They're going to have it out with leaflets instead of bullets," Longo went on. "The Hearts against the Minds."

"That's good!" Mike shook his head, smiling, trying to think. "Hey, how about this: meanwhile Rip van Winkle and Ma Barker are going to settle the whole thing with a body-surfing contest."

"Hey, Professor, come on, this is your big chance. You want to be in the movie or not?"

The Professor smiled cheerily. "Sure. What do I do?"

"What do you think? Fight!" Mike said. "There's a war going on. You're a professor—you're in charge of writing leaflets."

"But I'd much rather judge the body-surfing contest."

Motor, sitting a few feet away, said, "Uh-oh, another idiot. I'm getting too short for this shit, man."

Mike laughed. For the rest of the swim call he and Longo and the Professor made up imaginary scenes for the movie.

"... I think I wrote you about it at the time, didn't I?"

"Huh?"

"About the strike?"

"Oh ... yes."

"Do you remember what I said?"

"Well ... actually ... I'm not sure."

"Are you interested in hearing about it? If you're not, I won't go into it."

"No, no, I am. Go ahead."

"Well—ah-hem—first there was this meeting of the union ..."

The three of them used to talk a lot, Mike remembered—at chow, in the platoon tent, on swim calls, during breaks in their patrols, over bottles of Tiger beer at Rip van Winkle's. While the other marines discussed girl friends, cars, or boot camp days, Mike and Longo and the Professor would plan the movies they were going to make. They'd have arguments, too—"philosophical discussions," Longo called them—in which Longo, smiling, shaking his head, would marvel at the Professor's calm and detached way of speaking. The Professor, for his part, told Mike he thought Longo was "amazing—really amazing ... a *ballet dancer* before he was drafted—that's too much, it really is. He's really great."

It was in one of those "philosophical discussions" that the Professor talked about his reasons for quitting Yale and joining the Marine Corps. The platoon was set up on the beach during another two-day patrol. Longo and Mike and the Professor were eating chow in the evening while it was still a little light, making up movies with the cast of characters Longo had invented. Mike, under Longo's prodding, told the Professor his idea for doing a scene from *The Iliad*.

The conversation came around to beaches and vacations, and the Professor spoke of summers on Cape Cod, of how much he loved the ocean.

"Me, too," Mike said. "Ever been to Jones Beach? One of the best beaches in the world."

The Professor shook his head. "Actually," he said, "what I really love to do is sail. Someday—if I ever make it back—I want to take a year off and go sailing. Cross the Atlantic, maybe."

Suddenly Longo, with an incredulous smile, said, "How the hell did someone like you decide to come over here, anyway, Professor? What was it—some big existential decision or something?"

The Professor seemed embarrassed. "Actually, I guess it was, in a way."

"Shit, I figured," Longo said. "You intellectuals, man—always making these big theoretical decisions."

The Professor stirred his dinner over his homemade C-ration stove. It was ham and lima beans, Mike noticed, the one meal that everybody else hated. "What do you mean, Professor—an existential decision?" Mike asked.

"Well . . ." The Professor put down his can and rubbed his scalp, as though exercising his brain. "It's just that I came to the point where I felt I had to make a decision about the war, one way or another, and act on it. I mean, about myself and the war. What I should do."

"Man, that's easy," Longo said, holding up his hands. "Leave it alone."

The Professor flashed his quick smile. "No, I'm afraid I couldn't do that. It seemed to me that if you don't make a decision about something like that, then you're really not—well, *living*, if you know what I mean. What I mean is, you're not really taking charge of your life—"

Longo's voice rose: "You think you're taking charge over *here*?"

The Professor laughed. "No, what I mean is—by making the decision. Taking charge of that." He took a spoonful of his dinner. He ate all his C-ration meals the same way, slowly, with a distracted air, as though it didn't matter to him what he ate or whether he ate at all.

Mike said, "I can see that. But how come you made it?"

The Professor thought. "Well . . . it seemed to me that it came down to either going to Canada and becoming a draft dodger or going to Vietnam and fighting. I mean, it just didn't seem *fair* to me that I didn't *have* to make a decision, that I could just stay in school while other guys got drafted. I mean, what would I think about myself afterwards—after the war was over—if I had just kept avoiding it?"

"Man," Longo said, "at least you'd be alive. You sound like Crazy Mike."

"Really?" The Professor glanced at Mike.

"I don't know. . . . I mean—I just felt I had to do something."

"Exactly." The Professor took off his glasses and rubbed his eyes, then slowly and deliberately cleaned his glasses with C-ration toilet paper. Longo was right, Mike thought; he could picture the Professor in a classroom, leading a discussion. Next to him Longo was squirming where he sat. The thought occurred to Mike that the Professor and Longo were about as different as two people could be. "I mean," the Professor went on, "assuming that I get married and have children and everything someday"—he smiled again in an embarrassed way—"I don't want to face my kids and tell them that I avoided making a decision on the most important event of my generation by accepting student deferments."

Mike nodded. Longo said, "So what made you choose Nam?"

"Well . . ." The Professor folded his hands in front of him on his crossed legs and stared past Mike toward the ocean. "I guess it had to do with a lot of things. For one, I think there's a basic conservatism in my family that has—I admit it—conditioned me to some extent—if you know what I mean. I mean, I think that fighting communism might not be all that bad of an idea. If they're terrorists. Although I don't really believe in a big conspiracy or anything like that. And I do admit that Marxism has its attractions—as a philosophy, I mean. But what we're really dealing with is totalitarianism, anyway. . . . But it isn't just that—I mean, the politics of it. It had a lot more to do with something like the fact that I wanted to remain a part of my country—what the Greeks call *patria*—which doesn't necessarily have anything to do with government or politics or anything like that. I mean, if I went to Canada it might have meant that I'd never be able to come back again—legally. . . ." He looked from Longo to Mike. Suddenly he smiled. "And there *is* my parents' summer house on Cape Cod that I really like a lot and that I'll probably inherit part of someday."

"Yeah, fucking materialist," Longo said. "I knew it."

The Professor shrugged. "Sure. I suppose so. To some degree. But I like my family—basically—and I wouldn't want to be separated from them. Not for good."

"But that's the whole problem with this place—permanent separation. It happens all the time."

"Yes." The Professor smiled at Longo, then looked thoughtful. He spoke more slowly. "I guess that that had something to do with it too, actually—I mean, my decision. I guess that I thought—well, you know, war has always had an attraction. I mean, it seems to me that it is a situation where you can *learn* something—about yourself. You know, from being so close to danger and all that. Rather than sitting it out in Canada."

"Man, how can you learn anything when you're dead?"

Again the Professor smiled; he seemed to be enjoying Longo's frustration. "I know," he said. "That's a problem."

"A problem," Longo repeated, "what a way to put it!"

There was a pause. Then Mike said, "What about your parents?"

"My parents?" The Professor seemed annoyed. "What about them?"

"I mean, what did they think? About your decision?"

"Oh. Well. They tried to talk me out of it—my father, I

mean." He became thoughtful again. "I suppose it wasn't easy . . . inasmuch as his father had done the same thing—"

"He joined the Crotch too?"

The Professor nodded. "World War I. Fought in Belleau Wood. Anyway, I kind of suspect they were glad I didn't go to Canada." He turned away as though the discussion had ended.

"What does your father do, anyway?"

The Professor glanced at Mike. "He's a lawyer."

"Oh."

The three of them were silent. Mike lit a cigarette. He would have liked to have some bottles of Tiger beer for them to drink, to keep the conversation going.

Suddenly he said, "What about killing?"

"What?" The Professor laughed slightly, as if the question were absurd.

"No, I mean . . . I mean, I can see what you're saying, Professor, about being close to danger—death—and learning from it; like if you were just over here as a reporter or something like that—an observer. But we're not here just to be close to it. We're supposed to kill—"

"I know that—"

"No—what I mean is—what you said before, about having children: what if one of them asks about that? If you killed anyone. I mean, did you think about that when you made your decision?"

"Of course I did." The Professor sounded impatient. "Hey, I don't pretend to know all the answers—"

"No, no. I know. I was just wondering, that's all."

The Professor raised and lowered his eyebrows. "Well, it's just that . . . I guess I kind of figured that that's a part of war. It's like historical accident. I mean, it's just an accident that I'm the one who's over here at a certain time and place pulling the trigger. If it wasn't me, it'd be someone else."

"Unless everyone said no," Mike said. "I mean, made the other decision."

"Of course," the Professor said. "And that's the reasoning—I suppose—behind a lot of the people who do go to Canada. And I respect that. It's just that that's not the kind of thinking that *I* can act on."

"Man," Longo said, "you make it all sound so *reasonable*, like, so planned out; like everything's under control."

"Just the decision," the Professor said. "The initial decision."

Longo shook his head. "If I had been you . . ."

"But you were in the same position."

"Huh?"

"You didn't have to come over here."

"Man, I got *drafted!*"

"I know." The Professor's tone was matter-of-fact. "But you still didn't have to come here. You could have done a lot of other things—deserted, gone to Canada, Sweden, whatever. You didn't have to come here."

"Yeah, but . . ."

"And so in a way you made the same decision I did."

Longo picked up a handful of sand and let it sift through his fingers.

"That's right, Longo," Mike said.

Longo raised his shoulders. "But it wasn't *really* a decision. . . ."

Mike glanced at the Professor, who was cleaning up where he had eaten. He was always very careful about cleaning up, Mike had noticed, unlike most of the other marines in the platoon. Longo stretched. It was dark. The steady rhythm of the breaking waves seemed louder now.

"I don't know," Mike said, "maybe it wasn't really a decision after all. I mean, I can see it both ways." He waited, but neither Longo nor the Professor made any response.

Mike's heart was beating fast. What was happening? Why were they slowing down? He held his breath and listened. He heard other cars, the muted blowing of a horn. They were in a town. That was all. He kept listening. The car picked up speed. He let out his breath and relaxed.

"So would you agree with that or not?"

"What?"

"I said, wouldn't you agree?"

"Yes," Mike said, "definitely."

"I would too. Boy, I'll bet old Mr. Barnett is turning over in his grave. He was always very concerned about his workers, you know. . . ."

Death, Mike reminded himself, that was what he had been thinking about. Being close to death. Longo, it seemed to Mike, had had more experience with it than either he or the Professor—and not just because he had been in the war longer. Because of what he had been through before Vietnam. Mike remembered the time Longo had told about it. The three of them were talking about where they grew up; Mike told of how different Kingston, Virginia, was from New York and Long Island.

"Real redneck country," he said. "Lots of violence. People getting into some little argument and then blasting each other with shotguns. Goes on all the time."

"Sounds rather impetuous," the Professor said. "Why did you move?"

Mike shrugged. "My dad's company opened a factory down there."

Longo shook his head. "Man, that sounds like where I grew up. Violence. Lots of it. All the time."

"Really?" Mike said.

"Yeah . . . it got so bad, sometimes I thought I wasn't going to grow up—if you know what I mean."

"Really?" the Professor said, raising his eyebrows. "Pretty rough?"

"Yeah, it could be rough. I mean, I guess there were rougher places—like Watts, where they had those riots—but we weren't far away, man. I mean, Compton could be pretty rough too—parts of it."

"Oh, yeah?" The Professor seemed embarrassed by his own curiosity. "What was it like?"

"Oh, you know—gangs and rumbles and stuff like that. Just like on TV. Only worse."

"Really? You were in a gang?"

Longo shook his head. "My mother would've killed me, man. But I knew a lot of dudes who were. And sometimes there'd be these big fights—like, gang wars—and then they'd *make* you fight—on their side; beat you up if you didn't." He shook his head again. "Man, I remember this one time . . ." He looked from Mike to the Professor, then down, as if uncertain whether to go on. "A guy got killed—"

"Really?" Mike and the Professor said it together.

"Yeah." Longo kept looking down. "During a big fight. Beat to death with a pipe. Somebody stuffed his body in a garbage can in an alleyway and we all took off. Man, the cops came and everything. Took some dudes in for questioning. Nobody ever got caught, though." He glanced around.

"Wow," Mike said softly.

"Shit," Longo said, "there were some bad dudes where I grew up. Some of 'em are in prison now; some will be, once they get caught. Drugs, robbery, hijacking, murder—you name it. I'm lucky, man, I never got into any of that. . . . I mean, *really* into it." He let out a loud breath. "Two of my brothers, they weren't so lucky. One of them's a junkie; he's in bad shape. The other— we don't know where he is; haven't heard from him in years. Could be dead, for all we know." He stared in front of him. "You grow up like that and you really see a lot. I mean, like, in some ways it's good for you, I guess—if you don't get caught up in it. . . ." He shrugged. "I guess I was just lucky. My old lady kept me in line."

"But not your brothers?" Mike blurted out. "I mean, the two . . ." He could hear the Professor's disapproving sigh.

Longo shrugged again. "I don't know, man. I guess it just didn't work for them."

Mike nodded. "Well," the Professor said, "sounds a little different from growing up in Short Hills, New Jersey—or Garden City, Long Island, I'll bet."

"Yeah," Mike said. "Yeah."

* * *

". . . And they told me, when we moved to Kingston—Bill Singer, that is, who was president then—he made it very plain to me: Barnett was committed to Kingston. Committed. In fact when he asked me what I planned to do about living there, and I told him I thought I'd take an apartment, he said, no, no, go ahead, buy a house. And join the Rotary Club, and so forth—he was very explicit on that score—that he wanted me to become a part of the community. *Ah-hem*. And so I did. . . ."

And then there was the time they had finally got the Cisco Kid. Was that being close to death?

That was when activity around the Fort had begun to pick up, Mike remembered. Recently a patrol from second platoon had surprised a couple of VC planting a mine on a trail down in Hui Trong; they killed them both. And Blevins's fire team got another when they came across three VC leaving Ai Tu early one morning. The other two escaped, but Blevins, when he got back to the Fort, made a big deal out of the fact that it was he who had shot the one VC they did get. He lit up what he called a victory cigar.

But the Kid had been alone. It was on one of their regular patrols—just Mike's fire team plus a gun and Rain, the grenadier. They left the Fort at five in the morning and went down to Frontierland again, quickly passing through the vill. Mike looked for the girl with long black hair he had seen there the first time, but couldn't find her. Some time after noon they entered Ai Tu, on their way back. The day seemed to be even hotter than usual, although it was supposed to be nearing the end of the hot season now. Even the Professor was soaked with sweat. Mike had run out of water and now on the trail going through the middle of Ai Tu he looked around for a stone urn where he could fill his canteens. His back ached.

Suddenly there was a sound up ahead on the trail, then movement. Then—it seemed incredible to Mike—a figure with a rifle. He was waving! For a moment Mike thought it must be a marine from another patrol; there was a foul-up in scheduling. What else could it be? Or were the heat and his thirst producing a kind of mirage? Then there were shots.

They were close—from behind Mike—an M-16 on fully automatic. The figure up front wasn't there anymore. Mike moved behind a tree to the side of the trail and fired where the figure had been. The Professor, behind him, shouted, "He's down!" His voice was excited—more excited than Mike had ever heard it. Mike considered throwing a grenade.

There was silence. Mike glanced back. Everyone had taken cover. Longo got up and walked slowly forward. "You got him," someone said.

The body lay half on the trail and half off in a slight hollow. The chest was ripped open; red mixed with the black of his shirt. His shorts were black, too. His feet were bare and so was his head. Next to him lay an M-1 rifle.

"Hot damn, it's the Kid," Crane said. "The Cisco Kid. You got him, Longo. I'll be goddamned. You shot the Cisco Kid. Hot *damn!*"

There were more exclamations and more swearing and then the voices subsided as the patrol members stood and stared down at the body. Mike, looking with the others, breathed deeply.

"Damn, he's a young 'un, isn't he?" Brutus said.

"Yeah," Mike said, just to hear the sound of his voice. "Maybe it's not the Kid."

"Goddamn right, it's the Kid!" Crane sounded angry. "Don't you know an M-1 when you see it? That's the Kid."

Mike opened his mouth, then closed it. Crane was right, of course; it was just that it didn't seem like the Kid. Mike had always pictured him older, with a lined, leathery face, deeply tanned. But this—this body here—looked like a teenager's. His black hair was cut short and his skin was pale and smooth. He had muscular legs; he looked as if he would have been a good football player—a halfback.

"Look at them," Motor said, pointing. "Ho Chi Minh sandals, the real thing." Several marines nodded in agreement and now Mike saw the pair of rubber sandals lying a few feet away from the Kid's legs. Motor laughed joylessly. "Looks like he jumped right out of 'em."

"Yeah," Mike said again. He licked his lips, remembering his thirst. He started to say something, then stopped.

There was silence as the marines continued to stare. Mike glanced quickly at the Professor, who seemed deep in thought.

"Jesus, you were quick, Longo," Brutus said. "That's about the quickest I've ever seen. We ought to call you Wyatt Earp."

Mike smiled and glanced at Longo, but Longo made no response. He kept staring at the body.

"Quicker than me, that's for sure," the Professor said.

"Me, too," Mike said.

C.C. was swearing. "I just can't believe it," he said, "I just can't believe it!"

"What in hell you mumbling about?" Brutus said. "Spit it out."

"The one time I leave my camera behind Longo has to go and shoot the Cisco Kid. Man, I just can't believe it."

Mike stared again at the body. Why would anyone want a picture of it? The Kid's face looked hideous; his mouth was twisted with shock. Already flies began to buzz around his chest.

The Professor said, "Why do you think he jumped out like that, Longo?" His voice was calm, matter-of-fact. Longo, still staring down, shrugged and said nothing.

Crane spoke: "Hot damn!" He was excited. "I know why."

The others turned to him. "Why?" Mike asked.

"Because: the fucker wanted to get hit, that's why. Didn't you see him? He was waving!"

"Huh?" Brutus stared at Crane with an open mouth.

"That's right," Mike said, "I saw it too—I mean, I wasn't sure I was seeing right, but that's what it looked like. He was waving." Mike demonstrated how the Kid had appeared.

"Hell yes," Crane said, "he was asking for it. You remember Hornet, Longo, when he got zapped? The way he jumped right out, asking for it—it was the same thing. I'm not shitting you, man: after a while you start wanting it to happen. It's the same on their side—worse, probably. Hell, they don't get to go home after thirteen months. It's the war: too much war. Why the hell else would he jump out like that?"

There was another silence as the marines turned again toward the body with this new interpretation in mind. Mike, gazing along with the others, wondered what it was they were all looking for. For a moment he glanced up and saw the Professor staring at Longo.

"Cut his ear off," Motor said. Neither he nor anyone else moved. Then he said, "Anybody got an ace, at least?"

"Yeah," Brutus said, "I got one." He reached in a pocket and held it out. Nobody moved.

Suddenly Rain took it. Without a word he knelt down and put it in the Kid's mouth. "That's for Hornet," he said.

"And Streak," Mike said.

On his way back up Rain grabbed the rubber sandals. "You don't want them, do you, Longo?" Longo shook his head.

"Goddamn," C.C. said, "now that's a picture. Man, that's the picture of the year. Goddamn. I can't believe it—I just can't believe it!"

"Calm down, C.C.," Brutus said quietly.

The black ace of spades sticking out of the Kid's mouth looked like some kind of grotesque tongue. Now Mike realized why this was done: the card seemed to humiliate the dead body. Mike could almost feel the sharp edges of the card in his own mouth. Suddenly he shivered. It would make a good picture, he thought.

"Man," C.C. said, "you think if we hid the body, cover it up or something, it'd still be here tomorrow?"

"Come on, C.C.," Brutus said, "forget it. You fucked up, that's all."

"Why don't we take it back?" C.C. sounded serious. "Shit, yeah, Longo, ol' Captain Blood'll want to see it himself. Hell, the whole company will. Yeah, I'll carry him—by myself. All right, Longo?"

"Calm down, C.C.," Brutus said again.

"But I got to get this picture."

They began to step away from the body, as if sensing that the moment for taking a picture was gone.

"Okay, Motor," Longo said, "call it in; let's get going."

"Oh, boy," Motor said with what sounded like real enthusiasm, "they're gonna love this." He began to make his report.

Rain said, "Should we booby-trap him, Longo?"

Longo frowned and looked again at the body.

"We ought to, man," C.C. said. "Serves the fucking gooks right, one of them turns him over and eats a grenade for supper."

"How do you do it?" Mike asked.

"It's easy," Rain said. "We did it that time on Red River—remember, Longo? You—"

"Come on, Crazy Mike," Longo said, "let's go."

Back at the Fort there was a small crowd waiting at the opening in the barbed wire. Brutus handed the Kid's M-1 to Captain Blood and the captain held it aloft like a trophy. The marines cheered. That night at chow the story was told over and over of the way the Kid had suddenly jumped out, waving, and of Longo's amazing quickness. Crane asserted to whoever would listen his theory of why the Kid had jumped. He was drinking whiskey out of a pint bottle, Mike noticed. At the end of the meal Captain Blood told the marines that now they had to get Zorro. The marines cheered again.

"I think we should stop soon, Ernest."

"Certainly."

"I'm going to have to use the bathroom."

"Whenever you want."

"Oh, God, there hasn't been a place for *miles*. I *knew* we should have stopped at that last restaurant."

"We just passed a service station."

"That looked filthy. And don't go so *fast*, Ernest. No wonder we don't have a chance to stop."

"I'm only going the limit."

"You weren't before—I saw. You're going to get another ticket if you don't watch it."

Mike lay still, pondering a question, then made a decision. He sat up, rearranged the blanket over him and stared out the window.

She was right, he thought, there were no places to stop. They passed rolling farmland alternating with woods. The fields were brown and the trees bare. It was a bright day; it looked cold. Mike saw a tree line running between two fields and he imagined himself moving along it, stepping carefully, at the head of a patrol. What must it be like, he wondered, to fight a war in terrain like this, in this weather? Now they passed a thickly wooded gully and Mike saw troops sweeping through it on line. He smiled to himself. This must be another thing that comes from being in war—always interpreting terrain militarily, as if that were what the land is here for. Tree lines, hedgerows, ridges, hollows, rises, open spaces—none of these terms used to mean anything to Mike. Now he couldn't look at the land without imagining a patrol.

So many patrols! He thought back and one became another in his mind. He wondered whether he could remember every one. And yet right now there were more going on: people he knew were getting shot at, shooting back, killing, dying.

Suddenly he remembered a patrol: the time Longo had made his great leap. Why did he remember that one? Nothing much had happened. They had taken sniper fire from Hui Trong—it sounded like an AK-47; some replacement for the Kid, Crane said. And then the patrol—the whole squad, Tracy leading—spread out and went through the vill on line. Mike was ready, imagining at any moment the new sniper would jump out in front of him: this time Mike would be the quickest. There was a shout to his right—"Look out!" Mike turned and saw Longo in midair. Was he standing on something? It seemed as if he were suspended three feet off the ground. Then he landed and spun around, yelling at Mike and the Professor to freeze.

"There's something in that hedge," he shouted. They investigated and saw that it was a mortar round—a dud .81—rigged with trip wire. Tracy had them set a charge with TNT next to it.

"That was incredible, Longo," the Professor said as they waited for the TNT to explode. "The way you jumped—you seemed to be hanging in midair. How did you do that?" It sounded like a trick he wanted to learn.

Longo explained that he had seen the round at the last moment, even as he was stepping; his body just took over and leaped as high as it could. If he had stepped backward he might have lost balance and tripped it—because he was already stepping forward.

"Incredible," the Professor repeated. "That meant you didn't even have a good push-off for your jump."

Mike smiled. "We ought to call you Mao Tse-tung—the Great Leap Forward."

Longo didn't laugh. "Man," he said, "if I had tripped that wire it would've been all over—for all of us. That's pretty big stuff for a booby trap." He sounded shaken, unimpressed by his own feat.

"There's a gas station coming up," Mike said, "there, on the left." Immediately his father braked.

"Oh, good," his mother said. "I've got to go. Stop, Ernest."

"I am." The car slowed some more.

"I don't know, Ernest," she said, her face pointed forward. "It doesn't look like such a good place to me."

"Should I go on?"

"Oh, God, I'll bet there isn't another one for miles."

"I can always turn around and come back."

There was a pause. "No, no—that's all right—go on, stop, Ernest—*stop!* For God's sake, I have to go!"

He turned in and pulled the car up to a pump. The three of them got out. Mike walked with his mother to the side of the building, where she went into the women's room and he went into the men's.

Mike looked in the mirror. His face was pale except for his nose, red from the cold, and his scars, bright red; his hair stuck up. He looked like a scarecrow, he thought; a red-nosed scarecrow. Like Frankenstein. He patted down his hair.

Outside, he stood by the gas pump, smelling the fumes, shivering. How cold it felt! How different this was from the heat: it seemed to go right through him, right to his bones. How different this was from how he had imagined coming home would be.

The attendant, bent over the tank, nodded and Mike gave a slight nod back. He had a lean, pockmarked face, three-day beard, and slicked-down hair. For a moment Mike had the impression he was smiling.

The attendant replaced the hose on the pump, and Mike opened the door for his mother. His father took out his wallet.

"That'll be four dollars, even," the attendant said. Again he smiled at Mike.

Mike's father cleared his throat. "As I was saying before," he said, "my son here, Michael, just got back from Vietnam where he was with the Marines. We're taking him home from the hospital in Portsmouth—back to our home in Kingston." Quickly Mike turned toward the rear door and opened it.

"That *raht*?" the attendant said.

"That's correct."

The attendant made what sounded like a short laugh. "Guess they licked 'im," he said.

"What's that?"

"Sounds like they licked 'im good."

"Oh—ha-ha."

Mike stopped himself, turned, and glared at the attendant. Their eyes met, and now Mike saw it was a leering smile on his face. Suddenly he felt colder. He looked at his father getting into the car and then looked back, but the attendant had turned away. Mike got in too. As they pulled onto the highway Mike kept staring back.

"Whew! That place was *filthy!*"

"So was the men's room," Mike said.

"Next time let's stop a little sooner, Ernest. Be a little more considerate, would you? You always wait for the last second."

Mike's father nodded. "Did you hear that fellow's accent, Michael? He sounded just like the people in Kingston, didn't he?" Mike said nothing. His father leaned back. "I said he sounded just like the people in Kingston—his accent, I mean. Wouldn't you say?"

"I don't know."

"Kind of an odd fellow, wasn't he?" He sounded amused. "A character, I would say. . . . What was that he said?"

"I don't know."

His father cleared his throat and brought his head forward.

Mike stared out the window. They passed an old-looking trailer, its yard littered with junk. He thought about lying down again. But why should he lie down? Why had he lain down before? He was well enough to sit. He was well enough to walk around. He still had that pain in his head—although right now it wasn't so bad—but his neck was stronger. Not strong enough to fight someone, though.

Something seemed wrong. What was it? Mike glanced from his mother to his father. Both were quiet, facing forward. That was it: the quiet. It was too quiet. He thought of asking his mother to turn on the radio, but he knew she didn't like it—it gave her a headache, she always said. Besides, it was Sunday; the only thing on would be preaching or gospel music.

"So, uh, what do you think will happen, Dad?"

"What's that?" His father jerked his head back.

"I said, 'What do you think will happen?' "

"Oh . . . er . . . in what respect?"

"With Barnett."

"Oh, didn't I tell you? It looks as if they're going to open up a new plant in South Carolina. Orangeburg. There's no union down there, you know—but I hear it's full of coloreds—"

"No, I mean what's going to happen with you—and Barnett."

"Eh?" He moved his head to look in the rearview mirror. "What do you mean?"

"What's going to happen to you—if they close up the Kingston plant?"

"Oh . . ." His shoulders went up. "Well, early retirement has been mentioned. . . . Of course what happens to me isn't really the important thing—"

"What do you mean by early retirement?"

"I'd retire now, with a pension, instead of in four years."

"Oh."

"Well, you know, that's the trend these days. They don't have much use for you anymore if you're over sixty—or over fifty, for that matter. I was just reading an article in *Fortune* magazine . . ."

Mike gazed out the window. They passed a small, new-looking house with a wrecked car off to the side; strewn around the lawn were old tires, rusted farm tools, bottles. The next lawn had junk heaped all over its lawn too, including an old refrigerator lying on its side. On the door of the house hung a red-faced Santa Claus.

There was something wrong here too, something that was missing. Where were the people? That was it: didn't anyone live here? There—there had always been people; in the part Mike knew, anyway. Working in the paddies, going to and from villages, squatting outside their hooches, cooking, washing clothes, standing around talking, begging. There the houses had been close together. They had been neat, it now seemed to Mike— compared to these isolated farmhouses with their junk-filled lawns. And there had been color, too: all that greenness. So different from this cold, bleak, deserted countryside.

He thought of Crane. Was Crane back in the States yet? Did he miss Vietnam? Mike would bet that he did—in spite of how happy he had been to get out of the field. When was that? Mike tried to remember. Right after the new lieutenant arrived. No, that was wrong: Crane had never met the new lieutenant. He had left before; way before, in fact—a few weeks.

"*Whoopie!*" Crane had yelled when Jeff came into the tent and told him his orders had come through. "*Whoopie!*" He was going to Chu Lai—a desk job; leaving the next day. "*Whoopie!* No more patrols!" He swore cheerily then rummaged in his pack and pulled out a half-pint bottle. Jack Daniels, Mike saw. Crane sat down and opened it. The tent was nearly empty. Pogo was lying on his side, his knees nearly up to his chest, sleeping; Longo was writing a letter. Mike got up, moved over to Crane, and sat down next to him.

"Congratulations, man," Mike said. He held out a pack of cigarettes. "Smoke?"

"Yeah, sure, Crazy Mike, I'll take one of yours. I'm gonna cele-fucking-brate, as Short-round would say."

"I'm for that, man."

Crane lifted the bottle and took a long swallow. "*Aaaahhh . . .* God, that burns!"

Mike grinned. "I'll bet."

Crane licked the top of the bottle, then took a long drag on his cigarette.

"That's really great, man," Mike said. "I'm really happy for you."

Crane laughed loudly. "Damn right you are. You don't wish you were getting out too, do you?" He laughed again.

Mike shrugged. "Who wouldn't?"

"That's right, man—exactly right: who wouldn't? Who'd be crazy enough to want to stay here—right?" He drank.

"Right."

Crane said, "I'll bet I know what you want, Crazy Mike."

"Oh? What's that?"

Crane shouted in his ear, as if Mike were hard of hearing: "I'll bet you want a sip of Jack fucking Daniels!"

Mike smiled. "Who wouldn't?"

Crane held out the bottle. "Go ahead, Crazy Mike, have a drink on ol' Ichabod . . . Hot damn, I just can't believe it—I'm gettin' out—I'm gettin' *out!* Hot *damn.*"

Mike took the bottle and sniffed it. "Yeah, that smells like ol' Jack, all right." He put it to his lips and drank. "*Aaaahhh!*" He grinned at Longo, who shook his head. Mike took another quick sip. "Aaahhh! That's the kind of burning I like." He handed the bottle back. "Hey, Crane," he said, "remember that time I ate that hot pepper and almost burned my throat out?"

"Yeah, I remember. First day you were here—trying to get out of the field already!"

Mike smiled. He could feel his head becoming light already. "How about that time the Kid shot at us in Frontierland—when I cut myself on the C-rat can?"

Crane drank and handed the bottle to Mike again. "What about it?"

"Well, just that if I was trying to get out of it, I would've taken a Heart then, remember? How you wanted to give me one?" Mike drank. "Man, that's good. Where the hell'd you get that, anyway, Crane? Rip van Winkle don't sell that stuff, does he?"

Crane snorted. "I found it, man."

"Sure." Mike smiled knowingly. "Come on, where'd you get it?"

"I told you: I found it. Think I'd lie to you?" He took another swallow.

"All right, where'd you find it?"

"In a box of cookies."

"A box of cookies?" Mike held his smile.

"Yeah, no shit, a box of cookies. What're you, an M.P. or something?"

"Hell, no. I'd just like to know where I could get a box of cookies like that myself."

"You got to get it in the mail, that's where."

"Huh?"

"In the mail: you have your girl friend send it to you. Get it? You got a girl friend, don't you?"

Mike laughed. "Sure, lots of them. Good idea, man, good idea."

"No shit it's a good idea." Crane lifted the bottle in front of him. He shouted, "And here's to *you*, Captain fucking Blood, you can kiss my fucking ass!" He drank.

Mike laughed. "We're gonna miss you, Crane, we really are."

"Oh, yeah? What d'ya want me to do—stay in this fucking hole?"

"Hell, no; I was just—"

"Three more months," Crane said, "then I'm out—out of the whole fucking thing. Gonna go to New York and be a *civilian*." He drank again, then stared down in front of him.

Mike lit another cigarette. "What are you going to do, anyway, when you get out? You gonna go to medical school?"

Crane let out a loud laugh that soon turned into a cough. He drank more bourbon. "Shit, no," he said, "I ain't goin' to no medical school."

"Oh." Mike glanced at the bottle. There was about a third left. "Well," he said, "at least now you'll be getting as much of that as you want."

Crane gave him a sideways look. "Oh, yeah? What does that mean?"

"In Chu Lai—there's a club there, I bet. A PX, anyway."

Crane shook his head. "Uh-uh. Not in the rear, man. Once I get out of here I'm not touching the stuff. It's only the goddamn officers who need it in the rear. They hear a mouse fart and they're reaching for a bottle, shaking." Mike laughed. "You don't believe me?"

"Sure, I believe you."

Crane swore. "Uh-uh," he repeated, "I've seen what booze'll do to you—in my family. . . . Here's where you need it—shit! 'Corpsman! Corpsman!' And rounds flying all over"—suddenly he laughed—"oh, man . . ." He laughed again, then drank. "And does it get better? Does it get easier?" Mike waited for an answer, staring at Crane. "And you think I'm gonna go back and go to *medical* school?" He began coughing again, then forced liquor down his throat. "You don't think I've stuck my hands in enough people's guts? What the hell are *you* going to do—join some other war when you get through with this one?"

"No. I—"

"I'll tell you something: you're gonna wish you took that Heart—and two more like it. You think it's so fucking great over here—that it's all a big joke. But I'm telling you, it's real. Just wait till it starts getting to you. You'll do anything for a Heart."

He finished the bottle and got up. " 'Scuse me. I got to see a man about a bottle. Someone who owes me. Who owes me a lot." He left the tent.

Mike looked at Longo.

"Forget it, man," Longo said. "He gets that way sometimes."

"Really?" Mike moved over to him. "Shit. I thought maybe I said something wrong."

Pogo turned over where he was lying. "I don't see what's wrong with making it a joke," he said. "Better'n keeping it a war." His head, with his hair sticking out, looked as big as his body. "Well, so long, think I'll get back to this dream I was having." He closed his eyes and seemed to go right back to sleep.

Mike said, "Seriously, did I say something wrong?"

"Nah—forget it. Like he said, the war's got to him. I just stay out of his way when he's like that."

"I guess so."

Longo lowered his voice. "He wasn't kidding about doing anything for a Heart." He paused. "He almost shot himself once."

"Really?"

Longo nodded and glanced around the nearly empty tent, as though deciding whether to say more. "Brutus told me about it. It was right after that time we ran into all those mines on Red River—when all those guys lost arms and legs. Man, I would've hated to be a corpsman then. That goddamn colonel . . ."

Mike said, "You think that's why he's got this thing about officers—I mean, he's so angry at them all the time?"

Longo shrugged. "I don't know, man. Sometimes it's hard to say why, with a thing like that. It just happens. Because it happens—you know?"

Mike nodded. "But what did happen, anyway?"

Longo made a face. "We were going through this vill," he said, "and there were all these dead gooks lying around—"

"Really? VC?"

Longo shook his head. "Civilians. Farmers, man. Villagers . . ."

"Really? How come?"

Longo shrugged. "How come?" He smiled slightly. "No reason. They were in the wrong place. There had been maybe one or two VC in the vill, and so somebody from headquarters kept pouring in arty. Then we went in—our platoon—we were the first unit to enter. Man, there were dead gooks all over the place. They really got caught. Kids, babies, old people.... It was bad." He stared down. "And then this major from the S-3 tells us that we have to search for weapons. Anyone can be VC, he says. And so we had to go through all those bodies."

"No."

"Yeah. Man, 'search and destroy' is right. Only it was more like destroy and search." He paused. "Crane puked," he went on. "I don't blame him. I almost did too. And then right after that he tells Brutus that he's going to shoot himself. In the foot. He was all set to do it, too—there were snipers all around, he could've gotten away with it. But Brutus talked him out of it."

"Wow," Mike said.

Longo shook his head again; he had a trace of a smile. "The thing is," he said, "Crane really digs this place."

"What?"

"Yeah, he told me once. How he thinks it's so beautiful—you know, the countryside and people and all that. He really digs it. Wants to write about it someday, he told me. That's why he wants to go to New York—be a writer. And so it really tears him up, a lot of the stuff that goes on over here."

Mike thought. "I didn't know."

"He really needs to get out," Longo said. "I'm glad."

The next day a supply run came out by tank and amtrack carrying several replacement marines, including a new corpsman. He seemed opposite to Crane in almost every respect: short, a little pudgy, soft-spoken, smoking a pipe. Mike asked Longo what his name was going to be and Longo said it was obvious: the Doctor. Then, after shaking hands with most of the marines in the platoon, Crane climbed up on the amtrack and waved goodbye.

They passed a sign: STONEWALL JACKSON MEMORIAL HIGHWAY. Of course, Mike remembered, there *had* been a war here.

He gazed again at the passing tree lines and hedgerows, rises and hollows. Was there patrolling then too? But no mines or booby traps; and certainly no high-powered, automatic rifles that can tear a man's chest apart with a split second's burst. Still—all those big battles; Mike knew what a big battle was like. And with no helicopters. The wounded must have suffered—in this cold. Many must have died waiting for treatment.

They passed an old wooden farmhouse standing by itself near the top of a hill. And what was it like for the people, Mike wondered, when the Union Army came through? His high school history teacher in Kingston had emphasized that: the way the civilians in the South had suffered. Bad things had happened.

He remembered the time the PRU's had come out to the Fort.

"Holy shit, look at those guys!" Longo had exclaimed as the group of visitors climbed down off the tank and amtrack that had brought them out. "They look like a cross between Hell's Angels and hippies. How many are there? Quick—count. Twelve? Man, the original Dirty Dozen."

Several of the PRU's had hair coming down to their shoulders. There seemed to be no one uniform. Some had helmets, some floppy jungle hats, one a cowboy hat with a string tied under his chin; some wore camouflage striped utilities, some had regular ones. They carried an assortment of weapons: grease guns, submachine guns, carbines, rifles; several had machetes strapped to their sides. One of them shouted at the others and then went over to Captain Blood, accompanied by an American who had come out with them. Whatever the first one said seemed to have no effect on the rest, who continued to slouch around, lighting cigarettes, giving off surly looks to the staring marines.

"Man," Longo said, "they look like they'd as soon kill you as look at you."

C.C., snapping pictures, said, "Hey, who are these guys, anyway, Crazy Mike? What are PRU's? You're the big expert on the war."

Mike shrugged. "I don't know. Just what Jeff said—that they're supposed to be experts fighting Charlie."

"Man," C.C. said, "I wouldn't want those guys to come looking for me. How about the American, who do you figure he's with?"

"Marine, I guess," Mike said.

"He's CIA." It was Rain, standing behind them.

"Really?"

Rain nodded as he stared at the PRU's. "Provincial Reconnaissance Units," he said.

The Professor said, "That's right. PRU's. I thought that sounded familiar. I read something about them in *Time* or *Newsweek*." He studied them. "Yes, of course, they *would* look like that. Motley crew."

"What do you mean?" Mike asked.

"Oh, I don't know. Aren't they convicts or something? Rain probably knows more than I do."

"That's right," Rain said. "A lot of them get recruited out of prison to fight for the government. Some of them are murderers. They do, quote, special work—assassinations and stuff like that."

"*Assassinations?*" C.C. sounded outraged. "What do you mean, assassinations, Rain? There's a war going on—how can there be assassinations?"

Rain said, "Oh, like if there's a village chief who's really corrupt—too corrupt, even for this government—then they'll dress up like VC and go in and kill him."

"Really?" Mike said.

"Yeah," Rain said. "Some of them are Chinese."

"Really?" Mike turned to stare at them again.

"Man," Longo said, "these guys really *are* the French Foreign Legion."

Early the next morning Mike's platoon left the Fort and set up in an encircling position around Ai Tu. The PRU's, accompanied by two squads from the third platoon, went inside the village. Within an hour there were explosions and scattered firing. The word was spread: "They've got some!" Smoke arose—a hooch was on fire. The marines around Mike yelled in delight. Later there was more firing and more fires.

That evening in the Commissary Mike heard what had happened. The PRU's had singled out several villagers and taken them into a hooch for questioning. They told the PRU's the location of three VC hiding places—tunnels dug underneath hooches in the village. The PRU's and marines had gone there and dropped grenades down the holes, forcing the VC out. Six were killed and two captured, along with the villagers who had been questioned. Then the PRU's had set fire to the hooches where the tunnels had been found.

"A people of fire," Rain said. "That's what the Vietnamese call themselves. That's why they burn the hooches: they know what the villagers respect."

"That's what they should do to the whole country," Motor said.

"Damn," C.C. said, "I wish to hell I'da been there."

"Get some good pictures, right?" Mike said, smiling.

"Hell, no, man. I want to get some VC. That sounds like good huntin'—flushin' them out of their nest."

After chow Mike, Longo, and the Professor walked by the tent that had been set up for the PRU's. One of them was standing watch with a grease gun over the prisoners. The two VC were blindfolded, their hands tied behind their backs and their ankles tied together. Both looked young. The villagers squatted together on the other side of the tent. There were four of them.

"Look!" Mike said. "Look who it is." He and Longo and the Professor moved a couple of feet inside the tent and stared down. "It's Ma Barker."

She seemed oblivious to them. Her mouth was open and Mike could see blood. She was crying.

"Look at that," Longo said, pointing at the ground in front of her; there were three small yellow pebbles. "They knocked out her teeth. They must still be at her. I'll bet she didn't talk."

Mike looked from the teeth back to the woman, then up at the Professor. Suddenly both of them grinned.

"Shit," Longo said, turning away, "these guys are *mean*."

* * *

Although there was color here too, Mike had to admit: the red-dish dirt by the side of the road, the brownish orange of high-waving grass, black-barked trees with bright red berries. They passed a field where sunlight glinted off the stubs of cornstalks, like broken glass. Mike blinked.

That was when things had begun to happen at the Fort, he re-membered—after the PRU's had come out. Changes had oc-curred. For one thing, the company started losing more men to mines and booby traps. The second platoon, for some reason, was hardest hit. "Hard-luck Second," they were called. They must have lost a dozen marines within a couple of weeks. But Mike's platoon lost men too. Day-train stepped on a mine in Hui Trong that blew his foot away.

And then Mike came back from a patrol one evening and C.C. said, "Hey, Crazy Mike, you hear the news?"

"What's that?"

"We got a lieutenant."

"Really? Who is he? What's he like?"

"Nobody knows. He's in the CP getting the hearts-and-minds treatment from Captain Blood."

Suddenly the main topic of conversation became the new lieu-tenant. At chow that evening in the Commissary everybody seemed to have something to say about him, although no one had actually met him. "I heard he tried to get third platoon instead of us 'cause he heard we were a bunch of shitbirds. . . . Heard he told the captain he's gonna shape us up, starting with PT every morn-ing. . . . Heard he's gonna make everyone get haircuts once a week, just like boot camp. Even brought out a pair of clip-pers."

Blevins claimed that he knew where the new lieutenant had gone to college.

"Where?" Mike said.

"TCU," Blevins said. "Texas Christian. And he played on the football team and was president of his class."

"How the hell do you know that?" C.C. said.

" 'Cause. I heard it from cap'n's radioman, D.J. He was in there this afternoon when they were talking."

The next morning Jefferson came into the tent and said the new lieutenant wanted a platoon formation in five minutes.

"A platoon formation?" C.C. whined. "What the hell is that all about? I'm not going on no platoon formation. This ain't boot camp."

"Just shut up and get your ass ready," Brutus said. "There's nothing wrong with holding a formation: gives him a chance to see us and we'll get to see him. I like a man who isn't afraid to talk in front of a group."

The platoon fell out next to Jeff's tent—now Jeff's and the new lieutenant's tent—with much complaining and arguing. Some of the marines wore utilities, some were in shorts and T-shirts, some had no shirts at all. There were bare feet and boots, side by side.

"Goddamnit, C.C.," Jeff yelled in his high-pitched voice, "what do you think is, the *Army?* You know you can't stand in formation without your head covered. Get your ass moving— now, goddamnit! On the double! ... Rain—damn it!—go put your boots on." Mike watched as Rain hobbled back to the tent in the Kid's sandals. Jeff shouted at others to go back and put shirts and boots on; finally he called the platoon to attention, faced about as well as he could in the sand, and saluted the new lieutenant.

"Men," the lieutenant began, "I'd like to introduce myself." Immediately Mike felt his face get hot. The lieutenant spoke with a squeaky southern accent; he sounded as though his mouth were full of food. "My name is Lieutenant Farmer," he went on, "and I'd just like to say that I am looking forward to working with the first squad—I mean platoon." A wave of tittery laughter passed through the ranks.

"Quiet in the ranks!" Jeff hollered.

The lieutenant paused, then went on. "But the real reason for this formation is to hand out some promotions that have just come down from battalion headquarters. So when I call out your name please step forward."

Tracy was the first to go up—"Sergeant Johnson." Then Longo and Blevins, both promoted to corporal. After several marines from the second and third squads were called, the lieutenant read, "Lance Corporal Allison."

As though coming out of a daze, Mike quickly stepped out of the ranks, turned to his right, began to step and tripped in the sand, falling flat on his face. As he picked himself up he could hear C.C.'s shrill laughter.

"Goddamnit C.C.," Sergeant Jefferson yelled, "you're at *attention!*"

That afternoon the lieutenant began calling marines into his tent to speak with them individually. Mike, because his last name began with "A," was the first. Standing outside the lieutenant's tent, he spoke through the flap inside.

"Sir, Pfc.—I mean, Lance Corporal Allison reporting. To see the lieutenant, sir."

"Huh?"

Mike repeated it.

"Oh, come on in, Allison."

Mike took off his cover and entered.

"Nice to meet you, Allison," the lieutenant said, smiling, holding out his hand. He was Mike's height, a little stockier in build; about 190, Mike guessed. He shook the lieutenant's hand.

"Thank you, sir. Uh, nice to meet you."

They sat down on the lieutenant's cot. The lieutenant stared at Mike, still smiling. His eyes were pale blue; his skin very light and slightly freckled.

"I'm just trying to get acquainted," the lieutenant said. "Tell me, Allison, just how long have you been over here?"

"Four months, sir. Almost."

The lieutenant chuckled. "Well, I haven't even been with the platoon four days, so I guess I've got a ways to go." He glanced down. On his wrist was a large black skindiver's watch. "I'm sure you know better'n me how difficult it is fighting this war, what with all the mines and booby traps and such." *And such*, Mike thought—what was Longo going to call him? "Ah, let's see," the lieutenant went on, "you're in the second squad, Allison—right?"

"First squad, sir."

The lieutenant chuckled again. "I'll get it straight one of these days. Let's see . . . whose squad is that again?"

"Tracy's, sir."

The lieutenant frowned. "Tracy?"

"Oh—I mean, Corporal—I mean, Sergeant Johnson, sir."

The lieutenant nodded. "And how do you feel about Sergeant Johnson as your squad leader?"

"I think he's a good one, sir."

"Is that right? And who's your fire-team leader, Allison?"

"Longo, sir. Corporal Longo."

"Longo. Uh-huh." He stared at Mike. "You think he's a good fire-team leader?"

"Yes, sir. He's the best."

"Oh? And why do you say that?"

Mike hesitated. "Because . . . because he is, sir. Because he really knows things—like how to move—I mean, how to use terrain, things like that. When to call the guns up. He's really good. He's really quick, too. He made this one leap, it was incredible, nobody could believe it"—and he told Lieutenant Farmer about Longo's jump over the booby-trapped mortar round.

"Is that right?" The lieutenant's blue eyes looked dreamy. "And what is your job in Corporal Longo's fire team, Allison?"

"Point, sir."

"Oh?"

"Yes, sir. Although actually I'm about to be taken off it—becoming cover man again. The Professor's going to be the new point."

"The Professor?"

"I mean Pratt, sir. Pfc. Bill Pratt."

"Oh, I see. Well"—he smiled—"that sounds good for you."

"Yes, sir."

The lieutenant stared down at his hands. "I had a chance to look at your record book, Allison," he said, "and I noticed that you went to college for a while—a year, I believe. Is that right?"

"Yes, sir. A little over a year, actually."

"Is that right? And what made you quit, Allison?"

"I, uh, quit to join the Marine Corps, sir."

"Is that right? Was your father a marine?"

"Oh, no, sir." Mike smiled.

"I see. . . . Well, you must have felt pretty strong about it—joining the Marine Corps, I mean."

"Yes, sir, I guess I did. I mean, I did."

"What made you pick the Marine Corps, anyway?"

"Why? I guess—because they're the best, sir."

The lieutenant nodded and looked down at his hands again. They were large hands, covered with light-colored hairs on the back. "Yup," he said, "I guess I thought the same way as you, Allison. The best. That's what I wanted too." He looked up. "Take this platoon, for instance—would you say that right now it's one of the best—I mean, over here, fighting this war?"

"I, uh, don't really know, sir."

"Well, let me ask you this, then: do you think there's any room for improvement?"

"I, uh—yes, I'm sure there is, sir."

"And where do you think that improvement could be made?"

"Sir?"

"In what area?"

"I—I don't really know, sir. I mean, I guess just in fighting the war—getting more VC."

The lieutenant nodded as if in agreement. "Well, Allison, I'd like to work with this platoon and help it become one of the best there is in the whole Marine Corps." He raised his eyebrows. "Now how do you feel about that?"

"I think that's a good idea, sir."

"I'm glad you do, Allison. Now, I know that Sergeant Jefferson has been doing a fine job, filling in as platoon commander, and

I'm going to need all the help from him I can get, but there's going to be a few changes coming up and I expect everybody to cooperate. Is that clear?"

"Yes, sir."

"I'm glad you feel that way, Allison. You seem like a fine marine."

"Thank you, sir."

There was a pause. The lieutenant said, "Now, I'd like to ask you: do you have anything you want to talk about? Any problems?"

Mike stared off. *His back*, he thought: it felt as if it were going to kill him, sitting on the cot like that, half turned toward the lieutenant.

"No, sir."

"If you do, you can always come to me."

"Thank you, sir. . . . Uh, sir?"

"Yes?"

Mike hesitated, then blurted out, "I heard you were from Texas, sir. Is that right?"

Lieutenant Farmer smiled bashfully. "Why, yes, I am."

"Did you play football, sir—in college?"

"Why, yes, I did. Why do you ask, Allison?"

Mike felt his face redden. "Oh, I was just wondering, sir. I played some myself and I thought you looked like you did. End?"

"No, I was a guard."

"A guard? I mean, really? Sir? I wouldn't've thought that—I mean, guards are usually bigger. That must've been rough."

"Yeah, well, I guess I wished I was bigger sometimes." He chuckled. "What position did you play?"

"End, sir."

"That could get pretty rough, too."

"Yes, sir. . . . But not as rough as point."

The lieutenant glanced at his wristwatch. "Well, uh, thank you, Allison. That'll be all."

Mike got up, his face hot with embarrassment. "Thank you, sir." He began to leave, then stopped. "Uh, sir, I hope the lieutenant didn't mind me asking—about football, I mean. It's just that it's starting the season now and I've been reading about it in *Stars and Stripes*."

The lieutenant smiled. "No, it's all right, Allison."

When Mike walked into the platoon tent he was immediately met with questions: "What'd he ask you? . . . What took so long? . . . What's he like?"

Mike grinned. "He's all right. A little confused."

"Confused?" Rain said, squatting in his VC sandals in a corner of the tent. "Confused how?"

"Yeah, you know, like when I started talking about Tracy, the Professor, Captain Blood—he kind of wondered what was going on."

"Damn, you didn't," C.C. said, beaming at Mike. Mike grinned back. "Come on, what'd you talk about?"

"Oh . . . football."

"*Football?*"

"Yeah. He told me he played guard. Started telling me how rough it was. I told him point was rougher."

C.C. laughed. "Damn, I'll bet you did. You're crazy all right: Crazy Mike!"

Later, Mike asked Longo, "So what do you think, anyway? What's he going to be in the movie?"

Longo shook his head. "He's too dumb."

Mike laughed. "How about Dumbo? Or Goofy?"

Longo didn't smile. "Man, he doesn't need a name—he's got it already. Farmer."

"Yeah, but . . ." But Longo seemed uninterested.

". . . And of course the Japanese are in the act now too, which throws another monkey wrench into the picture. They come over here with their cameras, taking pictures of everything—and then go right back and copy everything they've seen. They're great copiers, you know, the Japanese. And then with their cheap labor—it's no wonder they can come out with a cheaper product, putting our people out of work. So what are you going to do?"

Mike hesitated. "I don't know."

"Exactly—and nobody else seems to either. . . ."

Mike turned and stared out the window. He noticed muted greens and yellows in overgrown fields, browns and rusty oranges in woods. Suddenly there was a field of dazzling, brilliant green, like an artificial football field on a color television set.

The changes the lieutenant had spoken of began to occur. The platoon's defensive positions on the Fort's perimeter had to be dug deeper and sandbagged thicker, which meant work parties for the marines who weren't out on patrol. The lieutenant checked the lines every night—sometimes two or three times the same night—and quizzed the men as to sectors of fire and principal directions of fire. There were rifle inspections after every patrol, and on patrol the marines had to carry extra ammunition and to bury their C-ration cans after they ate and to stay out for as long as the patrol was scheduled for. The lieutenant went on patrols himself—and night ambushes; he seemed to get even less sleep than the rest of the platoon.

Mike noticed changes in the marines' attitudes as well. Some of them resented the lieutenant—like Motor and C.C., who thought he was just trying to impress the captain. Stories were told about the lieutenant's mistakes and slips of tongue. But other marines, like Brutus and Blevins, defended him, saying that it took time to learn his job. Mike noticed that whenever the lieutenant was around a working party, the men would always work harder—no matter who they were. Once the lieutenant walked through the platoon tent unannounced; after that it was always kept neater.

Shortly after he arrived the lieutenant accompanied one of Mike's fire team's patrols to Frontierland. Just as they were beginning to pass through the village on the main trail, the lieutenant ordered Longo to stop and have his men search all the hooches.

"Aye, aye, sir," Longo said. "But sir, we've been down here before and never found anything. It's just a sleepy little village, that's all, sir."

"Is that right?" The lieutenant sounded dreamy. "Well, maybe it's changed some, then. Captain Matthews said there's been intelligence reports that there's a whole mess of VC sympathizers down here. So we'll just go ahead and do the search."

"Yes, sir," Longo said, turning away and muttering something about the lieutenant's intelligence.

Another time, on a patrol north of the Fort, the lieutenant somehow got turned around. He had his map and compass out and was studying both intently.

"But I know where we are, sir," Longo said. "We've got to cross that rice paddy and then go along that tree line."

"Uh-huh." Lieutenant Farmer's brow furrowed. "I'm sure you're right, Corporal Longo, but I just want to figure it out here for myself."

"Yes, sir, I understand, sir, but if you'd just look at the sun, you'd see." Longo shook his head as the lieutenant continued to study his map. "Man," he muttered, "why doesn't he just stay in his tent?" Mike quickly turned away, sure the lieutenant could hear.

". . . And all those people who are going to be out of work—what's going to happen to them?" There was bitterness in Mike's father's voice. "That's a terrible feeling, to lose your job like that, all of a sudden. That's what happened during the Depression, you know—only on a much larger scale, of course. It's just a terrible thing for a person's morale, sense of self-esteem. . . . In fact, some people never recover from it. . . ."

There was something else that happened then too, something important. Mike tried to remember. Tracy and his letter—that was it: when Tracy had to make his big decision.

"Goddamnit, I *told* him not to do it," Tracy said, sitting barechested in the platoon tent, glaring at the letter in his hands. "I *told* him! But he never *listens!*" The marines around him stopped what they were doing and stared. "Man," Tracy went on, making a fist, "if he was here right now I'd whip his ass. Goddamnit! That's what I ought to do—go up there and whip him good!" He threw the letter down.

For a few seconds no one spoke and then Blevins, puffing on half a cigar, said, "What is it?"

Tracy glared at him, shook his head. "Nothing—it's my business. . . . It's my goddamn brother. He just got over here. He wrote me."

"Really?" Blevins was wide-eyed. "He in the Crotch too?"

"No shit."

"Huh?"

"Nothing. Forget it." Tracy swore again.

There was another silence and then Longo said, "Where is he, man?"

Tracy let out a long loud breath. "Up north, by the Z. Ninth Marines."

Longo whistled. "Grunt?"

"What else? I am, aren't I?"

"Oh."

Tracy turned to face Longo. "I *told* him not to do it. All he had to do was tell his C.O. in the States that he's got a brother who's already in Nam. They wouldn't have sent him, that's the policy—no two brothers at the same time. But no, he wouldn't do it—afraid the war'd be over by the time I got back." He swore again and picked up the letter. "He's *always* been like that, ever since we were little. Always has to do what I do: ride my bike, wear my clothes, play the same position. . . . Once he took out my girl and then I did whip his ass. I can still do it, too—and he knows it."

A few marines laughed tentatively. "Goddamnit, it's not funny!" Tracy shot glares around the tent. There was silence. "Now I've got to decide what to do," he said.

Blevins, assuming a serious expression, said, "You mean you might get to go home?"

Tracy nodded but said nothing.

Motor said, "What's to decide, man? Go home. I would."

"Yeah," Longo said. "I mean, it's too bad about your brother being up by the Z and all that—but now you can get out. Just tell the captain. He'll radio the first sergeant and they'll cut your orders."

Tracy stared down in front of him. "I know," he said. "But my tour isn't up yet."

Motor snorted. "Who gives a shit?"

Tracy jerked his head up. "I do," he said. "I don't like to chicken out." Motor seemed about to say something more, then shrugged.

"How much time you got left, anyway?" Blevins asked.

"Four months. Tomorrow'll be just nine months in."

"Goddamn," Blevins drawled, staring at Tracy in amazement.

Tracy pushed his glasses up on his nose and turned again to Longo. "So what do you think, Ed?" he said. "You think it's turning chicken?"

Longo waved his arms. "Shit no, man. You've put in your time. What are you trying to prove, anyway? Get out. Hell, there's a reason for the policy. You know that."

"Yeah, I know." Tracy looked back to the letter. "But I don't like to quit—chicken out."

Pogo, lying between Tracy and Mike, turned over and said, "Then why don't you turkey out? Or something else—alligator out, or rhinoceros—?"

"*Goddamnit, Pogo, shut the fuck up!*" Tracy whirled toward him, putting up both fists. "I mean it. I'll beat the shit out of you!"

"Just trying to help," Pogo said and turned back. Mike had to cover his mouth to keep from laughing.

"Hey, it's not quitting, man," Longo said, in a soft, pleading way. "It's just following the policy."

"Yeah, but why didn't my brother follow it? I got here first."

"That's his problem. He went ahead and did it."

"Yeah, he did it all right, he always does it. . . . Goddamnit, you just can't tell him anything. He just goes ahead and does what he wants—and then *I* have to make the decision. Man, if he was here right now I'd whip his ass. He knows it, too." He sounded a little subdued. Then he looked down again. "Maybe I'll ask the lieutenant—see what he thinks, what I should do. Maybe he can help."

"Man, you don't need any help." Longo's voice rose. "Just go. Get out. You don't need to ask anybody."

Tracy shook his head. "I don't know," he said. "I don't like to chicken out."

In the Commissary that evening Mike asked the Professor, after most of the other marines had left, "So what do you think Tracy should do? I mean, what would you do if you were him?"

The Professor sat up straight. He answered quickly. "Well, I don't think it would affect me. I mean, if my brother were coming over."

"No? Why not?"

"Because. I would have made my decision to come over independent of his—or anyone else's. What he did would be his business. I would hope so, anyway."

"Man," Longo said, "you make it sound so cut and dry."

"But he's right, Longo," Mike said. "I mean, if you make up your mind to do something like that—like come over here—shouldn't you follow through with it?"

"Hey, look"—the Professor gave an uncomfortable smile—"I was just speaking for myself. I have no intention of telling Tracy—"

"No, no, I know," Mike said. "I was just curious—what you thought. I mean, it *is* a big decision, it seems to me."

"What are you talking about?" Longo's voice was excited. "What's so big about it?"

"It is," Mike said. "I mean, that's the way I feel."

"But the decision has been *made*—the brother made it for him—only one brother at a time. That's the policy."

"But it doesn't *have* to be," Mike said. "It's a policy, not a regulation. Two brothers *can* be over here at the same time—if they want to."

"Want to? What are you talking about, *want to?* Who the hell *wants* to be here?" Longo stared at Mike, then shook his head and looked down at his food.

"I was just thinking about it," Mike said. His voice felt cold to him. He turned to the Professor. "What about you, Professor? I mean, you've got a brother, don't you? What's he doing about the war?"

The Professor frowned. " 'Doing about it?' "

"Yeah, you know—like you, what you did. Decided to come over. He going to join the Crotch too?"

"No," the Professor said, "he can't."

"Can't? Why not?"

"He's too tall."

"What?"

The Professor nodded. "Six-seven."

"Wow . . . And he wants to, huh?"

The Professor shook his head. "Actually, he's pretty much against the war."

"Really?" Mike hesitated. The Professor bent to his eating, as if the conversation were over. "Does he go to Yale too?"

"No." The Professor smiled quickly. "He's the smart one in the family. He's at Harvard."

"Really? . . . Well, doesn't that bother you?"

"What? That he's at Harvard?"

"No—that he's against—"

"I know—just kidding." The Professor became serious. "No, why should it bother me? He has to make his own decisions. I respect that."

Longo and the Professor went on eating. Mike said, "Hey, did you write him about the movie? Tell him he can be in it too: the antiwar demonstrator." The Professor smiled slightly but said nothing.

The next morning Mike, on a work detail filling sandbags with the rest of the squad, watched as Tracy went over to the lieutenant's tent and called inside. Lieutenant Farmer came out and then the two of them talked. The lieutenant stood erect as he listened, his arms folded in front of him; Tracy, shorter than he by several inches, gestured with his hands and pushed his glasses up on his nose. He was wearing only shorts. His body was deeply tanned while the lieutenant's arms and face were red. When the lieutenant spoke he hardly moved his body. Tracy nodded, staring at the ground, then came back to the squad, looking not very happy.

"What'd he say?" Mike asked, putting down his entrenching tool.

"Oh, nothing."

"Nothing?"

The rest of the squad stopped work too and faced Tracy. They were all bare-chested and there was a strong smell of sweat in the air.

"He musta said something," Blevins said. He was panting, sweating more than most.

"He said I had to decide for myself," Tracy said. "He said nobody could make the decision for me."

"Jesus, no shit!" Longo sounded disgusted. "Big fucking help!"

"I know," Tracy said. "But he's right. It is a big decision. He said I'd have to live with it for the rest of my life."

"For Christ's sake!" Longo was lisping. "What does he know? He just got here. Oh, man . . ." Mike had never seen him so excited. "Don't you get it? They don't *want* you over here, that's why they got the rule. So if something happens, there won't be a big stink about it—you know, with parents and congressmen and all that."

"I know, Longo," Tracy said. His voice was firm. "But he's right. I've got to decide." He looked back toward the lieutenant's tent. "I could tell what he was thinking, though. He thinks it's chickening out."

"That's got nothing to do with it! The platoon's short, that's all he cares about."

Tracy turned back, frowning. "I'd like to beat his ass," he said.

And then he made his decision. It was right after their next patrol, their first platoon-sized one under Lieutenant Farmer. The first day out they lost a man to sniper fire—Bambi, from second squad; he had been a hurdler in high school somewhere in Ohio. KIA, right between the eyes. They set up on the beach again for the night, but this time the lieutenant sent out several ambushes as well as night listening posts, so there was no extra sleeping time. The next day they did an extensive search of the village where they had once found the VC leaflets addressed to black marines. In one hooch, hidden in a sort of homemade bomb shelter, they found a case of small bottles filled with liquids and powders. Doc, the new corpsman, said it looked like medicine, and Rain said it was VC, so the lieutenant decided to bring it back. Just as they were leaving the village a new marine from third squad triggered a booby trap—a hand grenade rigged waist-high on a tree—and had to be medevacked with wounds of the thigh and ass.

Finally, late in the afternoon, they reached Ai Tu. Mike was out of water; all he could think of was getting more. He had hoped that the lieutenant would let the platoon go straight back to the Fort—because it was late and everybody seemed tired, because they had searched Ai Tu so many times before—but he didn't. He ordered the marines to spread out on line and move slowly through the village, searching each hooch and checking everyone's I.D. "Man, that's like checking you guys for I.D.'s," Motor said. "I know all these fucking gooks."

Suddenly there was an explosion to Mike's right. A loud, powerful thud; a kind Mike had never heard before. A marine cried out. It sounded like Brutus.

"Corpsman!" It was C.C.'s voice. "Oh, God. Oh, God!"

Mike moved quickly toward the sounds. C.C. and Doc were bent over someone on a narrow trail in front of a hooch. Mike began to ask what had happened, but the corpsman moved and now Mike could see that it was Brutus. The end of one of his legs wasn't there. What Mike did see looked as if it were stuffed with something white and stringy mixed with something red, like spaghetti and sauce. He turned away.

Lieutenant Farmer brushed past Mike as he ran along the trail. "Keep it spread out!" he yelled. "Sergeant Johnson, get your men set up on the other side of that house!" He told his radioman to call in for a medevac.

The helicopter came in and took Brutus out. Then the platoon began to search again. As soon as the lieutenant was out of sight, C.C. went into the hooch near where the mine had been. Mike could hear him shouting and swearing, then the sound of slapping. A woman ran out, crying and holding her head. C.C. followed her.

"Fucking bastards!" His face was red and wet with tears.

There was smoke in the hooch. Fire appeared through the doorway. Mike turned and glanced at Rain, next to him. Rain was staring at the hooch without expression.

"It was an accident, Tracy," C.C. said. "I dropped a match by mistake."

Back at the Fort Mike stood by the wire with a full canteen, watching the last of the smoke come up from the vill. He drank and drank but still felt thirsty; his throat felt coated with dust. His whole body felt dirty, inside and out. He finished the canteen, then turned and went to clean his rifle.

The next day Tracy announced his decision. "That's it," he said, "I've made up my mind." Mike and the other marines in the tent stopped what they were doing and stared at him. "The hell with it," he said, "I'm going."

Immediately Longo spoke: "Way to go, man."

"I'm going to do it," Tracy said, as if Longo had argued with him, "I don't care what anybody thinks." He clenched his fists. "I'm going over and tell the lieutenant right now."

"Lieutenant's out on patrol," Blevins said.

"Then I'll tell him when he gets back, goddamnit. I don't care."

"Go tell the captain, man," Longo said.

"Uh-uh. I'll wait for the lieutenant. I don't care what anybody says. Even if they call me chicken. I'm going."

"Good for you."

That evening Longo pulled Mike aside by the water bag. He swore. "Tracy did it," he said, "what I was afraid of."

"What's that?"

"He told that"—Longo made a face—"he told the lieutenant to make me the squad leader."

"That's great, man. What's the matter?"

Longo grimaced. "I don't want to be squad leader."

"But . . . you'll be great. Christ, you don't want Blevins, do you? *Lightning?*" Mike laughed.

Longo shook his head. "But I don't want to."

"Ernest! Can't we have a little break now? I think we've had enough of Barnett for one day."

"But Michael said he wanted to hear about it—didn't you, Michael?"

"Now don't use your son, Ernest."

Mike's father raised his shoulders and slowly let them down.

Ahead, above the horizon, a vivid reddish yellow arose from a bank of gray. The gray was clouds, Mike realized, the first ones he had seen all day. They looked like a massive range of mountains in which a huge fire had broken out, or a battle.

"Look at that sunset, Michael! Isn't it just beautiful?" Her voice soared.

"Yes, Mother, it really is."

"Just *beautiful!* Makes me wish I were a painter—how I'd love to be able to paint something like that! Sunsets—I'd paint nothing but sunsets. . . . Remember the ones we saw in Florida?"

"Yes."

She sighed. "It's such a lovely time of day." Suddenly she turned. "What were the sunsets like in Vietnam? I'll bet they were beautiful too."

Mike hesitated. "I don't . . . I guess so."

"Oh—" She started to say more, then turned back to the front.

Mike stared out the side window at the pine forest they were passing. Darkness lurked among the trees. But how could that be—with so much light and color up ahead? But it was. It was as though darkness were a thing, not an absence: something that came up out of the ground when the sun got far enough away. How *had* the sunsets looked in Vietnam? Was that something Crane had noticed—was going to write about?

They had been quick—that was what Mike remembered.

Night came fast. He hadn't liked the night. It was cooler, yes, but in the dark he never felt as though he knew where he was going. Especially when he walked point—he hated that. At least, when he wasn't point, there was someone to follow—even on those moonless nights when the marines would be so close to one another there'd be constant bumping, like the first nights of training. But when there was no one in front it would feel as if each step were going over an edge. And who knew where Zorro was, waiting to attack?

Had they ever gotten anything on their ambushes? Mike thought back. Yes, definitely. Once an ambush from second platoon killed three VC right outside of Ai Tu. They really were VC, too: all had weapons. That was shortly after Mike had arrived at the Fort and he got the idea that ambushes like that happened all the time. There wasn't another successful one for weeks. Another time a fire team from first platoon brought back two prisoners. The marines had been moving into their ambush position near the shoreline when the point man exchanged fire with two VC about thirty meters away. The VC ran; the marines chased them. They found them in a hooch in a nearby vill, hiding under a bed. "Like hide-and-seek or something," one of the marines told Mike the next day. Mike saw the two VC, tied up and blindfolded, next to the captain's tent. They looked about twelve years old. Rain said they had just been drafted.

And then there was the time that Blevins's fire team was set up outside Ai Tu and saw someone coming out of a hooch. They opened fire, then went and looked. It was a woman, dead. But so what? There were plenty of women in the VC. But this one didn't have any weapons; and she was old. "Looked like a VC to me," Blevins said the next day, grinning.

But no, Mike had never gotten anything on any of his ambushes. Although that one time—who knew? Maybe he had. But what had *really* happened? It was the middle of the night. The ambush site was next to a cemetery; on one side was a small pagoda, half in ruins; on the other side, where Mike was set up, were fifty meters or so of open space and then a drop-off down to a stream. Lying on his stomach, Mike peered sleepily across the open space. There was half a moon and he could see a good way. Suddenly there was a figure in front of him. Mike's eyes opened wide; his body tightened. The figure was walking straight at him. Was it Zorro? Did he have a weapon? Confusion vanished as Mike gave in to his body: his finger squeezed the trigger, squeezed it again. For a moment the thought went through his mind that it might have been a woman.

"What is it, Crazy Mike?" Longo shouted from his position.

"I don't know. But I think I got him. Professor, did you see him?"

The Professor, lying a few feet to the side of Mike, said, "See who?"

Nobody else had seen him either. They waited while Longo, over the radio, requested illumination. The mortars dropped a flare over their position and the marines all looked. Nothing. But how could that be? Mike was sure he had seen someone. Although he did have to admit that he had been fighting off drowsiness for some time. It was just about at the end of their ambush so they got up and searched the area again before going back. Nothing. Maybe there was a tunnel, Mike suggested. "Yeah," Motor said, "and maybe it was a ghost coming back to his grave."

". . . And just wait till you see her, Michael. She's a real sweetheart. And she wants to meet you, too. I told her all about you."

"What? Who are you talking about?"

"You'll see."

Mike's mother turned around. "It's the desk clerk at the motel," she said, "in Martinsville." She winked at Mike. "Your father's developed a little crush on her—haven't you, Ernest?" She laughed. "Just don't talk to her too long, though. We want to eat as soon as we get there."

"Certainly."

"Your father," she went on, her smile fading, "he loves to talk."

Houses appeared more frequently now. The highway widened

and there were restaurants, motels, gas stations, supermarkets, automobile dealers, dry cleaners, a McDonald's. They were approaching Danville.

Mike's mother turned again. "Hungry yet?"

"I guess so . . . a little."

"Maybe we should stop here, Ernest. We're getting hungry. There's some good motels here."

"No, Nancy," Mike's father whined, "let's go on. It's just another half an hour."

"It's farther than that, Ernest"—her voice suddenly dropped—"and we're getting hungry."

"Look, there's the sign: 'Sleep Well at a Sleep Well, Martinsville, thirty-three miles.' See it, Michael? We'll be there in no time."

"Oh, all right, Ernest. You always get your way."

They drove into Danville, passing by factories, warehouses, run-down houses, tall smokestacks letting out thick gray smoke. It looked old, Mike thought, like a northern city. The sky, still a little light, seemed a pale, unnatural blue, like the sky at the end of a hazy summer day. Mike was glad they weren't stopping. He didn't like Danville. He had never been here before, but he had read about it: racial violence in the summer after his senior year. As Mike stared through his closed window at a group of young black men standing on the sidewalk, it seemed to him that the city was still dangerous. He realized he was afraid again.

They were back in the countryside now; it was just about dark. On the outside of houses, on trees on lawns, Christmas lights were being turned on. In front of one house was a Santa's sled. Through the windows of another he could see the black and white of a television screen. The evening news, Mike guessed: the reports from Vietnam.

It was after Lieutenant Farmer arrived, Mike remembered, that the activity at night began to increase. The lieutenant used to go out on ambushes himself—almost every night—leading them to new sites, some of them far from the Fort. A VC here, a VC there—soon it was no longer unusual for an ambush to report a success. Weapons were captured and documents taken from the bodies were sent on to higher headquarters. Documents, weapons, and medical supplies were also turning up in the searches of the villages that the daytime patrols were conducting. These searches used to be routine—go into a hooch, look around for a few seconds, and then leave; but now the marines were much more thorough when the lieutenant was on patrol, and even, after a few weeks, when he wasn't. One time in Ai Tu Rain found a submachine gun. It had been covered with black plastic wrapping and buried in the backyard of a hooch. "The ground looked kind of funny," Rain explained, "like it had been freshly dug up—and that's not where they'd be likely to put a mine." The lieutenant ordered the man and woman who lived in the house taken back to the Fort so they could be sent to battalion headquarters for questioning. Another time Mike himself made a find during a search of Hui Trong: a collection of empty C-ration cans, neatly stacked in what looked like a hidden compartment in a corner of an old villager's hooch. The old villager, speaking through Rain, claimed that he used the cans as dishes. But Rain said they were going to be used for making booby traps, so the lieutenant had the marines take the old villager back to the Fort too.

But none of the ambushes or patrols had yet to kill or capture the mysterious Zorro. He seemed to be stepping up his activity as well: wounding two from an ambush patrol in Frontierland, wounding three more outside of Ai Tu. And then came the night the second platoon's LP was attacked. It was while they were out on a two-day patrol, set up for the night on a hill eight kilometers northwest of the Fort. At about 0400 a three-man listening post, less than a hundred meters in front of the perimeter, came under attack. It lasted only a few seconds. A squad from the platoon went out and found all three KIA, their weapons and radio gone, their throats slashed. Mike had known one of the dead marines— Cochise, a black guy from New Jersey who used to talk about his wife a lot, who was half Indian. After that Mike began to hear stories about ambush patrols that weren't going to where they were supposed to, but rather were staying close to the Fort. Again there were rumors about a possible big VC attack coming soon against the Fort.

"Shit," Motor complained, "just when I'm getting short—watch, the bastards'll probably attack the night before I'm supposed to go home."

"It's because we're hurting them," Blevins said. "The last month we got more VC than we did the whole four months previous. Cap'n's pleased—I know, heard it from D.J. He thinks we're hurtin' 'em good."

"Really?" Mike said.

Blevins nodded. "Uh-huh. Cap'n just got word about some of those captured documents we been sending in. They say the VC's all upset because of all the kills we been gettin'. I know—D.J. told me."

Motor swore again. "Big deal. We zap one, they send in two more."

"Like Hydra's head," the Professor said, flashing his quick smile.

"Huh?"

"Oh, nothing."

"Oh, boy—finally! Martinsville."

"See, I told you." Mike's father leaned back. "It's been just thirty-five minutes—thirty-four, to be exact."

"Well, it's about time. I'm *starving!*"

Mike looked out the window. It was dark now, but the highway was bright with the lights of more restaurants, motels, service stations, passing cars. His father slowed for a traffic light. Death, Mike remembered, that was what he had been thinking about. How many had died here in Virginia? What would they have thought, he wondered, if they could see what this land had become? And the people who were here now, in their homes, eating dinner and watching television—did they ever think of the dead?

6

DINNER

Mike's father turned the car off the highway. "Look familiar, Michael?" he said. Mike glanced up at a large red-and-yellow neon sign: SLEEP WELL.

"Sure."

"Wait'll you meet the desk clerk," his father went on, "if it's the same one we had before. She's a real sweetheart." He parked the car in front.

"Now, Ernest," Mike's mother said, opening her door, "don't overdo it."

A short, thin, pimply-faced teenager in a wrinkled white cotton jacket opened the front door. "Evenin', sir; evenin', ma'am; evenin', sir," he said. He wore a red-and-yellow button on his jacket that read, SLEEP WELL AT A SLEEP WELL.

"Good evening," Mike's father said in a formal way. Mike nodded. He noticed finger smudges on both the inner and outer glass doors. Inside the lobby on the right was a glass-enclosed map of the United States showing the location of other Sleep Well motels; it too had finger smudges. Under it the brochure rack was half filled. A stand-up ashtray in the corner contained several butts.

"I'm going to the ladies' room, Ernest," Mike's mother said. "Check in fast so we can eat right away. I'll be right out."

"Certainly."

Behind the front desk a thin, blond-haired girl around Mike's age said, "Good evening. May I help you?" She wore the same button as the bellhop's. On the wall in back of her was a semicircle of bright red plastic poinsettias. SEASON'S GREETINGS was written in green underneath.

"Why, thank you." Mike's father spoke in a high-pitched, accented voice. He smiled. "Your name's Judy Beth, is that correct?"

"Yes, sir." She answered with a blank, wide-eyed expression.

Mike's father cleared his throat. "My name is Allison. My wife and I stayed here a couple of times before. We were here just recently. Do you remember?"

"Sir? What night was that?"

"Let's see . . ." He turned to Mike. "It wasn't last night. . . ." Mike looked away. "We were in Portsmouth last night—at the hospital." He turned back to the desk clerk. "It was the night before, I believe."

"Oh, yes, I remember. You were on your way to Portsmouth. Would you like a room for tonight?"

Mike's father cleared his throat again, cocked his head to the side, and half turned toward Mike. "This is our son, Michael. We just picked him up at the hospital."

"Hello," Mike said.

Judy Beth turned to him. "Hello, nice to meet you."

"I think I told you the other night, Judy Beth, Michael here just got back from Vietnam. He was wounded over there. He's with the marines."

"Yes, sir," Judy Beth said, "I remember now, you telling me about that." She turned to Mike. "You must be awful glad to be back." Mike nodded. He was standing very straight.

"He's going to spend Christmas with us," his father said. "We live in Kingston, you know."

"Yes, sir. I remember you telling me."

"We all feel very, very grateful."

"Yes, sir, I imagine you do."

"Considering the . . . circumstances."

"Yes, sir. I don't understand it a whole lot—I mean, what's going on over there—but I just think it must be terrible." She looked at Mike. "I'm real glad you're back, and I sure hope you're going to be all right."

Mike nodded again. "Thank you," he said. He realized he had a miserable look on his face. He tried to smile. "Thank you very much."

Judy Beth turned back. "Would you be needing a room for tonight, sir?"

"Oh . . . yes." Mike's father turned to Mike. "What do you think, Michael—two rooms, or—"

"Yes, two rooms, Dad."

He smiled at Judy Beth, clearing his throat. "If you have them. . . . Mrs. Allison is with us too."

"Yes, sir, we've got them. Would that be adjoining rooms?"

"Oh, I don't know. . . . What do you think, Michael?" He smiled again at Judy Beth. "Michael's the expert in the family when it comes to—"

"Adjoining will be fine," Mike said. "Can we register now?"

"Yes, sir." *Don't call me sir*, Mike wanted to say.

Just then his mother came up to the desk.

"All set with the rooms? Come on, let's go and eat. I'm starving!"

Mike's father inclined his head. "Nancy, you remember Judy Beth here, don't you? Judy Beth, this is—"

"Yes, yes, I remember. . . . How do you do, Judy Beth, nice to see you again. . . . What's the matter, haven't you registered yet?" She turned from Mike's father to Mike, glaring.

"Right now, Mom, we're doing it right now."

"I warned you," she said, "it'll take him all night."

"We're doing it—"

"All right, you do it. I'm going in and getting a table." She marched into the restaurant.

Mike's father peered at the registration form through the bottom of his glasses. "I think I told you, Judy Beth," he said, "that Michael here used to work in a Sleep Well too—in Kingston."

"Is that right?" She gazed blankly at Mike.

"How many summers did you work there, Michael? Was it three or four?"

"Three."

"And it was quite an experience, wasn't it?"

"Yes. Excuse me, Dad, but I've got to go to the men's room. I'll see you in the restaurant. . . . Nice to meet you, Judy Beth."

"Nice meeting you, sir."

They sat at one of the center tables of the long, narrow dining room. There were no other customers.

"Didn't I tell you, Michael? Isn't she a sweetheart?"

"Sure."

"I just can't get over it—how pleasant the people are down here. I mean, in this general area, Kingston included."

"Well, I don't think she was so wonderful," Mike's mother said. "Pretty plain, if you ask me. Michael can do a lot better than that—can't you, Michael?" She gave him a wink.

"I wasn't speaking about her looks in particular; I was referring more to her disposition. Although, I have to say—"

"Oh, I guess I was mistaken. . . . Well, come on, let's order. I'm starving! You know how these southerners are—slow as molasses!" She laughed and opened her menu.

"I'd be willing to bet we get served very fast," Mike's father said. "You know why I say that, don't you, Michael?"

"Yes, Dad."

"You do? Why?"

"Because we're the only ones here."

"Precisely." He laughed silently.

"What are you going to have, Michael? A nice steak?"

Mike opened his menu. "I don't know, Mother."

"Go ahead, get a steak—we can afford it." Her voice dropped. "I think you'd better. 'The only ones here' is right—that's a sure sign of a lousy restaurant. At least you can't go too far wrong with a steak."

"I wouldn't say that, Nancy. I had a fine dinner here the last time. What was it I had? Chicken—?"

"Oh, boy, don't go by your father, Michael. You know him, he just likes to *eat*, period!"

Mike studied the menu. There were southern fried chicken, roast chicken, ham steak with pineapple, pork chops with apple sauce, fried Gulf shrimp, sirloin steak (New York cut), and chopped steak. With salad and potato.

A waitress came up. "Evenin'," she said. She was a black-haired, middle-aged woman, thin and short, wearing a black satiny dress with white trim, the same kind of dress the waitresses from the Kingston Sleep Well wore.

"Good evening." Mike's father spoke in a formal manner.

"What would you like?" The waitress held a pencil to her pad.

"Oh, let's see . . ." He opened his menu. "What do you suggest?"

"Go ahead, Michael. You order first."

Mike looked up. "I guess I'll have the steak, the sirloin. Rare." He chose his salad dressing and potato and then said, "Do you serve beer?"

"Yes, sir. Pabst, Budweiser, Schlitz."

"I'll have a Pabst."

"One Pabst."

His mother ordered a chopped steak, medium rare, and then his father asked, "What can I have, Nancy?" He turned to the waitress and smiled. "I have to check with the boss first."

"Oh, Ernest, you can have anything you want."

"Anything? How about the fried shrimp?"

"You know what you're not supposed to eat."

He smiled again at the waitress. "See what I mean?"

"Oh, come on, Ernie, let's get going. Order the chicken."

"Fried chicken?"

"No—roast!"

"Ha-ha-ha." He handed the waitress his menu. "You heard the

boss." She wrote on her pad and then he said, "Er, excuse me, but what is your name?"

"What?"

"I said, what is your name?"

She collected the other menus, then stepped back. "Well, my name is Barbara, but everybody calls me Cricket."

"Cricket? That's an interesting name." He cleared his throat. "Well, Cricket, is it possible to order a glass of sherry?"

"No, sir. Only beer."

"Just like Kingston," he said to no one in particular. He turned back to Cricket. "That's where we live—Kingston, Virginia. Do you know where that is?"

"Yes, sir. 'Bout a hundred eighty miles over yonder." She nodded to the west.

Mike's father laughed amusedly. "That's exactly right, Cricket. We're driving there tomorrow. Are you—*ah-hem*—from around here?"

"Yes, sir. Martinsville. Born and raised."

"Oh, come on, Ernest. Let her do her work."

"Well, since you don't have any sherry, Cricket, then I'll have a beer too."

"Yes, sir. What kind?"

"*Ouch!* . . . I think I just got kicked—ha-ha. . . . Oh, it doesn't matter. Whatever Michael, our son here, is having."

"Pabst."

"That would be fine."

"Two Pabst." Cricket turned and went back to the kitchen.

"Ernest! You know you're not supposed to have any beer."

"Nancy"—his voice was a gentle whine—"this is a special occasion. We've got our son back with us."

"I know that, Ernest, but you're still not supposed to have any." She said to Mike, "He's impossible: he always has to do what you do."

An elderly couple, both wearing black, entered the restaurant and sat down at a table near the cash register. Mike's father leaned toward Mike and spoke in a conspiratorial way: "Say, I didn't know you were old enough to order beer in a restaurant."

"I'm not," Mike said.

His father smiled. "I guess she thought you were, though."

"I guess so."

"Well, if you're old enough to go over there and fight, I should think you could at least order a beer. *Ah-hem.*"

Cricket came back to the table with their beers.

"Why thank you."

Mike's father leaned toward Mike again. "I wonder why they call her Cricket. Sort of looks like one, doesn't she?" He chuckled. "Seems a bit of a character, I'd say; a little on the sour side. . . ." He straightened and poured beer into his glass. "Well, here's to our son's return," he said, raising his glass, "his—*ah-hem*—home-coming."

Mike raised his too and they drank.

Mike's mother laid down her fork. "Michael," she said, "your father and I have been talking."

"Oh?"

"Yes."

"About what?"

"Well, we've been thinking about moving."

"Really?" She nodded. "Where?"

"To Florida."

"Really? Great."

"With all this happening at Barnett—and the way it looks now that your father's going to get early retirement . . ."

Mike turned. "What do you think, Dad? Do you want to go down?"

His father assumed a pained expression. "I don't see why not. There doesn't seem to be anything for me to do in Kingston. Barnett certainly has no further use for me."

"Wouldn't that be nice?" Mike's mother beamed at Mike. "If we could get some nice little place down there, somewhere not too far from the ocean?"

"Sure. If that's what you want."

"I think it is, Michael. We're getting to be that age, you know. We're not getting any younger, that's for sure. Your father needs a rest." Mike nodded. She continued, "You know, Michael, I've read that Florida has some very good colleges. Maybe you'd like to go to school down there when you get out."

"Maybe."

"You get the G.I. Bill, don't you?" his father asked.

"Sure," Mike said, "everyone does."

"That's a terrific deal—for going back to school, that is."

"But I'm not sure what I'm going to do when I get out. I haven't decided yet."

"I don't blame you," his mother said. "Get a job for a while. There's nothing like work: work is the best thing for anybody."

"Personally," his father said, clearing his throat, "I think education is very important. And it's getting more and more so every day. It used to be that a high school diploma was all you needed; then it was a college degree. Now it seems as though everybody is getting into some kind of graduate program. You just can't get enough education—especially if you're going into business—"

"Maybe he wants to work for a while, Ernest. Let him make his own decision. . . . I think there's lots of jobs in Florida, Michael; it's really growing down there. Remember all those motels we saw? I'll bet you could get a job at a motel down there easy."

"I'm sure he could," Mike's father said, "after all his experience at the Sleep Well." He smiled.

Mike took a deep breath, staring down at his plate. Almost half of his steak was left. He looked up. "I may want to do some traveling," he said.

"Traveling?" His father looked puzzled.

"Yeah. Traveling."

"Traveling where, Michael?"

He turned to his mother. "Oh, I don't know—I've got some places. . . . Look, I told you, they don't know if I'll get a medical discharge or not. I may be in the service another two years."

His father said, "I can't see why they'd want to keep you in—if you don't have to go back to Vietnam. You—*ah-hem*—said you didn't have to go back. Isn't that right?"

"Yes. That's right."

"Well, thank God for that," his mother said. "What's the matter—steak too tough?"

Mike sighed. "No, it's fine, Mother. I'm just not that hungry."

"You've got to eat, you know—if you want to get better."

Mike said nothing. He hesitated, then reached in his jacket pocket and took out a pack of cigarettes. He opened it, took one out, and lit it. "By the way," he said, "when I, uh, get home, I'd like to make some phone calls, if it's all right with you. I mean, long distance phone calls. But I'll pay for them."

"No problem," his father said, wiping his lips with his napkin. "You don't have to pay us anything."

"That's all right—I want to. Some of them might be pretty expensive."

"Who are you going to call, Michael?"

Mike glanced up. "Oh, some people. . . . A family out in California, for one. Compton, California. That's one of the places I might want to go to. . . . It's near L.A."

"L.A.?" His father smiled. "That's what they say in San Francisco. But they get offended if you say that in Los Angeles. At least they did when I was out there—but that was over twenty-five years ago. Barnett had their sales convention out there and—"

"Who are you going to call in California, Michael?"

Mike stared at his mother. "A family—of a friend of mine. I mean, he was a friend. A buddy." He shifted his look to his father, then down to the table. "My squad leader. Actually, at first he was my fire-team leader, then he became my squad leader. He's the one who made me fire-team leader. He was my best friend over there." Mike pushed his plate farther away. "He got killed," he said, watching his hand holding the cigarette, "at the end—when I got wounded." His voice sounded far away to him. "Anyway, I want to call his mother—his parents—and talk to them. That's all. I think I should."

There was a pause. His father said, "Certainly. Go right ahead. Make any calls you want."

"Thanks." Mike took a deep drag and blew it out.

"What, er, was your friend's name?"

"Longo."

"Longo? Italian, huh? We used to have a Longo in the plant on Long Island. He was from New Jersey, originally. I think you met him once. He—"

"No," Mike said, "he wasn't Italian."

"Oh? What was he then?"

"He was black."

His father's brow furrowed. "Hmmm, that's strange. Sounds like a typical Italian name to me."

Mike took another drag. "Yeah, well, he was part Italian—I mean, his father was—is. Half, I think."

"A mulatto, then."

"I don't know, what you call it."

"Then he must have been fairly light-skinned."

"Yeah." Mike crushed out his cigarette. Suddenly he looked up. "He was in the theater, Mom—I mean, before he got drafted. In college—he quit college too—he was an actor, a dancer . . . a real talented guy."

She blinked. "Is that right?"

"Yeah . . ." Mike looked down again. "Anyway, there's some other calls I have to make—people who got killed, families. . . . One guy from Florida—Fort Lauderdale. He was black too." He snorted. For a moment he smiled. "Anyway, I just feel that I have to, that's all."

"Certainly." His father cleared his throat. He spoke softly. "You must have met quite a variety of people while you were in Vietnam." Mike nodded. "And this friend of yours—what was his name?"

"Longo."

"No, I mean his first name."

"Oh . . . Ed."

"He, er, was quite a person, you say?"

"Yes." Mike's voice was like a whisper.

"You said he was your leader?"

"Squad leader, yes."

"So he must have had some leadership abilities."

"He could have led the whole platoon—or even the company."

"Is that so. . . . He must have been quite a person." Mike stared in front of him, unmoving. His father slowly turned his head from side to side. "That must have been quite an experience," he said. "Certainly one that I've never been through." He looked at Mike and raised his eyebrows, as if to ask a question. Mike hesitated, then reached in his pocket and pulled out another cigarette.

Cricket came to the table. Mike's father said, "Don't you—*ah-hem*—want a doggy bag for that steak, Michael?"

"I don't care."

Cricket said, "You want me to wrap it up?"

"Oh, Ernest, haven't you had enough?"

"I meant for Michael."

"We've got plenty of food at home."

"But he might get hungry tonight." He smiled at Cricket in an amused way. "He's a growing boy, you know."

"You want it wrapped?"

"Michael?"

"I don't care," Mike said. "Sure, go ahead."

"But don't you try to eat any of it, Ernest. You've had enough tonight."

"Certainly not." He smiled at Mike.

Cricket said, "You folks want any dessert?"

"What do you—?"

"No." Mike's mother's voice was harsh. "No dessert."

Mike's father laughed. "I think that will be all for now, Cricket. Thank you very much. It's been a pleasure. *Ah-hem*. We'll take our check whenever you're ready."

"Yes, sir." Cricket took a step back from the table and put her hands at her sides as if standing at attention. "Excuse me," she said, more to the table as a whole than to any one person, "but didn't y'all say y'all was planning to drive Kingston way tomorrow?"

Mike's father smiled in a gently amused way. "That's *raht*, Cricket."

"Well, then maybe y'all'd be interested in knowin' what we jes' heard on the radio in the kitchen. I would, if'n I was you." She paused. "Says it's supposed to rain tonight and then turn to freezin' some time in the mornin', then either freezin' rain or snow the rest of the day. A real bad storm, supposed to be." She paused again. "These roads 'tween here and Kingston can be raht dangerous when they git wet. There's this one turn called Lover's Leap where there's accidents regular. Just last week a semi jack-knifed and went off the road, killed the driver and some other folks." Mike's mother gasped. "Jes' thought I'd let y'all know. I'll have yer check in a second." She stepped forward, took up plates and went back to the kitchen.

"Oh, no—that's *terrible!* What are we going to *do*, Ernest?"

He raised his eyebrows. "It shouldn't be too bad, Nancy. We've been over those roads several times now—once when it was raining—and I don't think—"

"But if it's *ice*? Oh, God. I know those roads. She's right: they're *terrible*. I don't know, Ernest, maybe we should stay another night."

He grimaced. "I really should get back for that meeting tomorrow, if at all possible. If they close the roads, that's one thing, but as long as they stay open, then I'm sure it'll be all right. We'll take it easy."

"Oh, God, you'd better."

Cricket came back with a hunk of aluminum foil and the check. Mike got up. "I'm going to the lobby, " he said, "to buy a newspaper. I'll see you out there. Thank you for the dinner."

His father nodded graciously. Suddenly his mother got up too. "Wait. I'll come with you, Michael. . . . We'll meet you by the room, Ernest." The two of them left.

* * *

Outside, by the back parking lot, Mike stood with his mother, waiting.

"Oh, God," she said, shivering, "what are we going to do? Those roads are terrible!"

"Mother, it'll be all right."

"How can it be all right, Michael? You don't know what it's like. Those roads are bad enough when it's *dry*—all those curves! Why, it makes me dizzy just to look out the window!" She shivered again. "These mountains—I *hate* them. . . . I think we should wait another day."

"No," Mike said. His voice felt cold to him. "We should go tomorrow."

"I don't think so, Michael, not the way your father is driving—"

"Oh, he'll be all right, Mother."

"Are you kidding?" Her voice pierced him like a weapon. "You don't know, Michael: you haven't been watching—you're back there lying down. When he got that ticket, he had no *idea* how fast he was going. Why, he had me scared half to death! And it wasn't the first time, either. I know: I've been watching him. His driving is really getting worse. I'm frightened, Michael. I really am."

Mike pulled his jacket close around him and turned away. Next to where he was standing was a neat row of small spruces hung with white Christmas lights. Behind them the ground rose sharply; taller, unplanned pine trees grew on the slope, looming over him. Were they really going to leave tomorrow? He kept picturing their car swerving down a steep mountain road, out of control.

"It's because he's thinking about that damn company all the time," his mother went on, "that's what it is. You don't know what I've been through, these past few months—ever since that damn strike." She turned toward him. "I know he wants to talk about it, Michael, but it's not *right*: he's *obsessed* by it. And that's not good for him, either—especially while he's driving. He doesn't pay attention. I get so afraid he's going to have an accident, I can't relax at all. . . . So please, Michael, don't ask him any questions about business tomorrow, all right? Wait at least until we get home. Then you can ask all you want. All right?"

"Okay, okay," Mike said. "I won't. Don't worry."

He looked up. The sky was blank. He breathed deeply, smelling the pine and spruce; he thought he could smell the coming rain, too. He remembered boot camp: getting up at five in the morning and standing in formation in the freezing darkness waiting for chow. He remembered winter evenings when he was a boy—how much he had hated the cold and dark! He shivered. Was he really going to become a hunter?

"You know, Michael, I don't want to alarm you, but I'm really worried about your father. He isn't well."

"Oh?"

"We went to the doctor last week and his blood pressure is way up. The doctor told me if he doesn't watch it he's going to have a heart attack. Now, I know I sound terrible sometimes—and I'm sorry, I really am—but I've got to take care of him. You know how he is: he's like a little boy; he just wants to eat and drink everything he sees. So please, Michael, while we're home, do me a favor, would you? Don't encourage him. He's going to want to do everything you do—especially now during the holiday season—but he just can't. All right?"

"All right, Mom."

"And another thing, Michael. I just want to tell you: I'm sure you needed to smoke over there, with all that pressure—but try not to smoke *too* much, would you? It's not good for you—especially right before you go to sleep. Besides, your father doesn't like it; you know that."

"Yes, Mother."

"Now I'm not trying to tell you what to do, Michael—just a little friendly advice."

"Thank you."

"Remember: you're back now."

Mike let out a deep breath. "I know that, Mother."

"Life goes on, you know. You've got to try and forget—"

"I'm not going to forget!" His voice rose; his body stiffened.

"Oh, I know, I know. I didn't mean that. I'm sorry. . . . I just meant that you've got to keep living, that's all, you can't be tied to the past. I'm sorry about your friend, Michael, believe me. But for God's sake, let the dead alone—"

"I—"

"Oh, here he comes! Finally. I'm *freezing!*" She laughed with relief. "I'll bet I know what *he* was doing: having a little chat with his *girl* friend. Your father! He just loves to talk."

PART
THREE

7

THE BATTLE

Mike sat in the chair by the table next to his bed, facing the television. It was a color television. He wondered whether the Sleep Well in Kingston had replaced their black-and-white sets with color ones too. They would be heavier to carry when they needed repair; more tempting to steal. He took a pack of matches from the ashtray on the table next to him and lit a cigarette. The matchbook was just like the ones in Kingston, as was the ashtray itself, both with the Sleep Well emblem. He looked around the room. The rust-colored bedspread and yellow draperies were the same too, as was the black vinyl chair he was sitting on. On the wall over the bed was a painting, a ship at sea. His eyes came back to the television.

Should he put it on? This was a treat, wasn't it—his own color television? In the hospital there was an old black-and-white one in the lounge that seemed to be broken half the time. Leroy, though, down the ward from Mike, had his own color set; a good one, too—Japanese. Mike liked to watch the evening news by Leroy's, always with other patients crowded around, interrupting the war reports with comments, boos, cheers.

From the table next to him he picked up the newspaper and

found the television listings. "The Karen Eliot Comedy Hour" would soon be on, from nine to ten, and then a documentary about the Marine Corps in World War II. Mike snorted. He hoped he'd be asleep by then. On other channels were situation comedies and a special on whales. He put the listings aside.

He inhaled deeply. His mother was right, he thought, he was smoking too much. He could feel it in his lungs. It was why he wasn't sleepy yet, he suspected: the tobacco made his heart beat faster. In Vietnam he had smoked two to three packs a day; now he was smoking almost as much.

A loud rumble came out of the wall; Mike jumped in his chair. What was it? The heater. Why so loud? The heaters in the Sleep Well in Kingston didn't make that much noise. How was he going to get to sleep with that thing going on all night? He put out his cigarette and lit another. He figured he would feel exhausted soon, all of a sudden, in spite of his smoking—and if he didn't, he could take sleeping pills. In the hospital he took two every night. He liked that: not having to worry about falling asleep, not having to still his mind when he lay down, knowing that something would do it for him. It was like not having to worry about the future. Wasn't that what being in war was like? With so much death around, so much pressure, who could worry about the future? Who could think about giving up smoking?

He had aspirin, too, in case the ache in his head got worse. It was aching now, but only a little. At first in the hospital Mike had asked for something stronger than aspirin, but his doctor had said it wasn't allowed—not for a head wound. Leroy was on something stronger. Sometimes in the night he'd cry out in pain, and then the night nurse would come by and Leroy would beg for more drugs. He wasn't the only one: others would cry out too; sometimes there'd be a scream from a nightmare. The first night Mike had heard the cries his heart had begun to pound. Someone was dying, he was sure. After a few nights he'd hear them and go right back to sleep. In the morning the patients would joke about needing a fix.

Mike peered inside his cigarette pack. There were plenty left.

And if there weren't, he could always go down to the lobby and get more. In the hospital he didn't even have to leave his floor; there was a machine in the hall outside his ward. The showers were just outside the ward too—hot showers, anytime Mike wanted. His sheets were changed twice a week; the room temperature was always just right. The chow wasn't that bad—not after Vietnam—and there was a hamburger place on the first floor if he wanted to pay for it himself. Plus there was the enlisted men's club for beer.

Maybe he should have a beer now, Mike suddenly thought; maybe that would make him sleepy. Another Pabst. Why not? Just get up and go downstairs, buy one from Cricket to take back to his room. It was allowed, people used to do it all the time at the Sleep Well in Kingston. He might wake up his mother, though; she was a light sleeper. But so what? He could do anything he wanted.

If he went down for a beer then he could talk to the desk clerk again. What was her name? Actually, Mike thought, she wasn't so bad-looking; just dumb. She reminded him of someone he used to go out with in high school. Judy Beth, that was it. *It must be so terrible over there.* What had she meant by that?

He picked up the newspaper again. It was from Roanoke, a Sunday paper in several sections. The front-page headline told of a local judge arrested for fraud; below that was a story about an Army unit that had been ambushed in the Central Highlands. It was the same story that had been in the Norfolk paper that morning, but Mike read it again. The company had lost ten men killed and thirty-nine wounded; in their counterattack they killed ninety-two of the enemy. It read like an almost routine event, but in Mike's mind the account came alive with the sounds of explosions and screaming, the confusion of scrambling desperately for cover, firing at unseen targets, the sight of gushing blood.

On the next page he found another headline: DEATH TOLL MOUNTS IN VC MASSACRE .... OVER 200 TRIBESPEOPLE KILLED. Mike read this story again too.

He went on to other sections. VIETNAMESE MOTHERS FIGHT

VC TERROR ... BOSTON COEDS PETITION AGAINST WAR ...
POLITICAL LEADER SLAIN NEAR SAIGON ... VIETNAM VET
GOES BERSERK, SHOOTS THREE. A letter to the editor called on
antiwar students to stop protesting and to fight for freedom in
South Vietnam instead.

Mike put the paper back on the table. From his inside jacket
pocket he pulled out two envelopes. One was very thick and had
smudges all over it; on the upper left hand corner was written,
"Lcpl. W. Pratt, APO 96318, San Francisco, CALIF." Mike
stared at it, weighing it in his hand, inhaling and exhaling smoke.
Then he put it aside.

From the other, smaller, envelope he extracted two pieces of
notepaper held together by a paper clip. On the first one he read:

Dear Mom and Dad,
As you have probably learned by now, I have been wounded.
Please do not be alarmed. I was hit by rifle fire in the side of my
face and neck, but I am doing all right. Tomorrow I will be flown
to the Philippines and soon I hope to be home and seeing both of
you. Don't worry.

Love,
Michael

The second one read:

Dear Mr. and Mrs. Allison:
I've written this letter just as your son wanted me to. It is an
honor to be able to help someone who has done so much for us
all. I feel very proud.

Lucy Chandler, USO

Mike studied the handwriting. It was up and down, a little plump,
easy to read. "Michael," on the first note, lay scrawled across the
bottom of the page like a child's writing—or a madman's. Finally
he put them back in their envelope, then on the table next to him.

He looked at his watch. "The Karen Eliot Comedy Hour" was
just beginning. They'd be watching it in the hospital, Mike knew,

crowded around Leroy's bed, laughing and hissing when Karen Eliot made jokes about the president, cheering and booing when she referred to the war. He got up and turned on the set. After a minute the picture appeared. Karen Eliot was on stage, wearing a glittery, full-length, blue-black dress, laughing. Mike listened to her monologue. Then a commercial came on and he turned the volume all the way down and went into the bathroom.

He looked in the mirror. Was his mother right—were his scars fading? He touched them with his fingers. Had the desk clerk seen them? He picked up one of the glasses on the sink and took it out of its white Sleep Well wrapper. The glass wasn't glass at all; it was plastic. He snorted. Color television and plastic glasses. He filled it with water, took a sip, then went back to his seat.

Quickly Mike got up. On the screen a man dressed in camouflaged utilities was waving a miniature American flag while carrying what looked like an M-16. Mike turned on the volume. The man in utilities shrugged; the laughter died away. The next skit came on, an old man with white whiskers chasing a young woman in yellow shorts. Mike turned the volume back down.

In his seat again he lit another cigarette. His gaze settled on the telephone. Maybe he should call down for a beer. *Hey, Judy Beth, this is Crazy Mike up in 235. Come on up.* Was that what his father had in mind? Just like on R&R. Mike's face became hot. Why should he feel embarrassed? He did what everyone else did—just about: stayed in a big hotel and got himself a whore. But why had he picked Taipei? For no good reason. Because Rain had told him what a great time he always had in Taipei. Rain loved Chinese women; they might not be the most beautiful, he said, but they're the best at pleasing a man. Mike told him about the whore he had had in Okinawa, on the way over—the first time he had slept with a woman. She was good, he said.

What was the one's name in Taipei? Chi Lin, that was it. Even while he was in bed with her, he'd forget it—and then rack his mind trying to remember. Not that she was bad; it was just that she wasn't sexy. With her cheerful smile and short, plain hair, she looked more like someone's sister than a prostitute. If only he had

had Lou's girl—Lou, his buddy from boot camp whom he had run into in the hotel lobby; with her low-cut black dress and long, straight, shiny black hair, she had turned Mike on. But instead there was Chi Lin's incessant questioning: "What's'a matter? What's'a matter? No like Chi Lin? What Chi Lin do wrong?" Later, talking to Lou, Mike found out why she had behaved that way, why all the prostitutes were so afraid: because if their customers complained to the manager he would beat them, and if he kept getting complaints they'd get fired. They all had big families to support, Lou said.

Mike's last morning he had spent talking with Lou in the hotel bar, drinking one bloody mary after another. It was dark in the bar and cold from air conditioning; Mike kept forgetting what time of day it was, how much longer before his flight left. He and Lou talked about their boot camp days, what had happened to their buddies since then. Lou told Mike that Smitty was dead.

"What?"

"Yeah," Lou said, "didn't you know? Got zapped first week over. Stepped on a mine and blew himself away."

"No," Mike said, "I didn't know."

Lou asked Mike what it was like where he was. Lou was stationed in Da Nang, working in an office at division headquarters. As Mike spoke of the constant patrolling, booby traps, mines, fire fights, walking point, Lou shook his head and bought them more drinks.

"Man," he said, "I wish I was in the field—no shit, even with all that stuff you're talking about. I hate it where I am."

"Wish I had clean sheets and three hots a day," Mike said.

"Yeah, but there's a lot of shit going on."

"What do you mean?"

"Bad: drugs and racial shit and stuff like that. I really get scared sometimes, I really do." Lou went on to tell of fights between black marines and white NCO's—"lifers"—of knifings and sometimes even shootings. Of marines dealing hard drugs and getting arrested. "Man, I keep my nose clean. I've heard stories about the brig you wouldn't believe. That is one place I do not want to end up. A white guy like me gets sent there and he's had it." Mike frowned. He told Lou there were no drugs where he was. "How about the racial stuff?" Lou asked. Mike shook his head. "It's bad where I am," Lou said. "Anytime I see splibs together I get the hell away."

Lou was becoming drunk, Mike could tell. His eyes were red and watery, his speech slurred. Mike was surprised at how much he himself could drink. He counted the bloody mary's he had had and realized he had never drunk so much alcohol in his life as he had in the last few days. He wanted to have more. It seemed as though as long as he kept on drinking and talking he wouldn't have to go back; time would stop. He kept glancing around the bar for Lou's hooker.

On the flight back Mike became very thirsty. He slept and when he woke he was covered with sweat. He smelled—different from the way he did in the field—and when he got off the airplane he felt uneasy, as if Da Nang had changed. He realized it had: it was cloudy. It was the end of the hot season, still very hot and even more humid.

Inside the terminal Mike bought a can of soda at the canteen. Next to him a South Vietnamese soldier was trying to buy sandwiches. The enlisted man behind the counter told him he couldn't. "No Vietnamese money," he said. "Only American." The Vietnamese soldier kept talking back in his own language.

Suddenly Mike spoke: "I'll pay for the sandwiches." He gave the cashier the money.

The Vietnamese smiled at Mike, patted his arm, then motioned for Mike to follow him across the room to another Vietnamese, this one with the markings of an officer. The two of them spoke together, and when they finished, the officer addressed Mike.

"Thank you very much."

"Oh, you're welcome, uh, sir. Do you . . . speak English?"

The officer nodded, smiling. "Yes. I went to Georgetown University. My name is Major Nguyen. I am pleased to meet you."

They shook hands. "Pleased to meet you, uh, sir."

The major asked Mike where he was stationed. When Mike told him, the major frowned. "I think that that is not a nice place for Americans," he said. "There are many, many revolutionaries from that area where you are."

Mike stood up straighter. "It's getting better," he said.

Major Nguyen peered at him. "I think it must be very hard for you," he said. "Our country is very different than yours. You must feel very bad, so far from your home. Is this true? Do you?"

"I . . ." Mike assumed a serious expression. "I mean—it's something we have to do." He wanted badly to drink his soda but felt he should wait. He had never spoken with a major before.

"Yes," the major said, nodding, "I think you have to—now. Do you know what I mean?"

"I'm—not sure."

The major's dark eyes opened wide again. "Before," he said, "when it was only the Vietcong we had to fight—then we were able to do it ourselves. But now . . ." He shook his head. "Now that the Americans are here, it is the North Vietnamese we have to fight—and they are too much for us. They have good leaders in the North. I know, I come from there. Ho Chi Minh, he is up here"—the major raised his right palm to the level of his eyes—"but here, in the South, our leaders are only here"—he held his other palm by his waist. "The North have the Russians and the Chinese. And so we have the United States. Do you understand?"

"I—"

"What happens to our country is no longer up to us. It is hard, I think, for you to see that—you are so rich and so powerful—you can do anything you want. But now you must fight for us. You have to. Do you understand?"

"I . . . think so," Mike said.

Suddenly the major smiled. "But please, may I have your address? You have been very nice. I would like to write you."

"Really?"

"Yes. Perhaps you can visit someday. Do you like to hunt?"

"I . . . I mean—I'd like to."

"When there was peace we used to hunt many times in the mountains. Very good."

Mike sat down on one of the wooden benches and wrote his address on a piece of the Major's notepaper.

He spent the night in the same transit housing shack where he had slept his first night in Vietnam. It was full, as it had been then, of marines fresh over from the States, along with those returning from the hospital and from R&R. Mike slept poorly, and the next morning, with the day again cloudy and hot and sticky, he felt as if he hadn't rested at all. Around him in the shack the new marines talked of how much they wished they were somewhere else. He went out on the road and hitched a ride on a truck.

When he got to battalion headquarters Mike jumped off the truck and started for the company office, a plywood shack among rows and rows of same-looking buildings. Off to his left came the loud report of artillery. Mike remembered how he had jumped the first time he had been here—unable to distinguish between incoming and outgoing. He felt as if he were coming home—as if he had been away for a month. He couldn't get rid of a feeling that something important had happened. Had the VC finally launched their big attack against the Fort?

Inside the company office Mike saw Lieutenant Farmer talking to the first sergeant.

"Lieutenant!" Mike blurted out. "What are you doing here?" The first sergeant glared at Mike. The lieutenant turned around. His boots were scruffy; the gold bar on his cover was so tarnished it was hardly visible; his face and arms were somewhere between red and brown. "I mean, uh, hello, how are you, sir? I was just, uh, wondering, what the lieutenant was doing back here—why you're not at the Fort?"

Lieutenant Farmer smiled. "Oh, hi there, uh . . . Allison—isn't it?"

"Yes, sir. Lance Corporal Allison. Just reporting back from R and R, sir."

"Oh, so you don't know that we've moved?"

"Moved? No, sir. Moved to where, sir?"

"Right here, for now."

Mike was conscious of the first sergeant's continuing glare. "But—where are we going? Sir?"

The lieutenant inspected his big black skindiver's wristwatch. "That's what I hope to find out, shortly. I've got a meeting with the captain in five minutes. If there's any word, I'll pass it on down. Don't worry." He talked in a folksy way.

"Yes, sir." Mike asked him where he should go now and the lieutenant gave him directions. He left the office and walked toward another cluster of plywood shacks. Suddenly he saw Ski passing an empty C-ration can like a football to another marine. Mike began to run.

"Hey, it's Crazy Mike!"

"Ski! Where's the platoon?"

"In there, Crazy Mike." He pointed to one of the shacks.

Mike went inside. On either side was a row of cots on which marines were sitting and lying around, playing cards, reading, sleeping; scattered on the floor were weapons, clothing, candles, gear, empty soda cans. In one corner Rain was squatting in his VC sandals, studying his phrase book. Blevins, shirtless, half a cigar in his mouth, looked up at Mike and smiled. There were several marines Mike didn't know. At the far end of the shack, sitting cross-legged on the floor, his hair freshly cut, was Longo, reading a letter.

"Hey—Longo."

He looked up. "How's it going, man?"

From the cot next to Longo a marine sat up. He had a thick black mustache. "Hey, Crazy fucking Mike!" He spoke in a raspy voice.

For a second Mike hesitated, then said, "Short-round!" They shook hands. Short-round was even shorter than Mike had remembered. "What're you doing here?"

Short-round scowled. "What the fuck you think—I'm here on a fucking USO tour?"

Mike smiled. "You mean you're back with the platoon? How's your leg?" Short-round shrugged. "Great," Mike said. "Good to have you back."

Short-round emitted a disgusted snort. "That's close." He swore again. "Two months I got left, and they send my ass back to the field. That's the fucking Crotch for you. What a suck-ass outfit! Man, the Air Force knows how to live. Cam Ranh was like being back in the States—hot chow, clean sheets, round-eyes— you don't even know you're in a fucking war. It's like a country club down there: swimming pools, beaches—and you don't have to set up no fucking machine guns when you go for a swim, either. This place sucks."

Voices answered him from different parts of the shack: "So go join the Air Force, Short-round. . . . What do you mean, there's a lot of bennies up here—look at all the farms for sale, cheap. . . . Why don't you go tell the colonel you don't like it—he'll let you go. . . . Go eat shit!"

"Anyway," Short-round said, looking down and then back again at Mike, "I hear you're the team leader now."

"Yeah," Mike said. He glanced at Longo. "I was, anyway."

"It's okay with me," Short-round said. "I don't want to do no leading. I just want to get the fuck out of here. I caught another bust, anyway, down at Cam Ranh. Back to pfc."

"Oh? What for?"

Short-round shrugged. "Who the fuck knows? Disrespect or something—some candy-ass Air Force sergeant . . ."

Someone shouted, "Thought you liked the Air Force, Short-round!"

He sat down, and Mike took off his flak jacket and helmet. "So what's going on, anyway?" Mike asked Longo, who was reading again. "I just saw the lieutenant. He said something about leaving the Fort."

Longo spoke without looking up. "Word came down three days ago; we packed up everything and yesterday we pulled out. Now we're here, waiting. That's all I know. Don't worry about your gear; I took care of it."

"Thanks—"

"You got to watch your gear real close back here, Crazy Mike." Mike turned. It was Blevins.

"Oh?"

Blevins nodded. "There's all kinds of stealin' going on. They come in first night we was back and went through this place good—while we was out standin' lines. Money, cigarettes, poncho liners—all gone. They took a box of my cigars. Plus they took C.C.'s camera."

"No!" Mike glanced around the shack. "Where is C.C., anyway?"

"Probably out lookin' for his camera," Blevins said. "He's madder'n a hornet, I'm not kiddin'. He said he'd kill the guy who stole it."

"Wow." Mike frowned. "Who's doing the stealing?"

From his cot Short-round laughed huskily. "That sounds like Crazy Mike—'Who's doing the stealing?'—like someone's going to say, 'Oh, I am.' "

"No, I just meant . . . We never had any stealing at the Fort— what's going on?"

"It's the new guys," Blevins said, "that's what I figure."

"I didn't steal nothing." It was one of the marines Mike didn't know. He was sitting on the cot next to Blevins, cleaning his black-rimmed eyeglasses. He was very plump.

"No, it's the guys back here, I bet," Short-round said, "the ones stationed in headquarters—'in the rear with the gear.' All these guys can think about is how much stuff they're going to take home with them. That's what it was like down in Cam Ranh: everybody stocking up at the PX all the time. Those guys don't have to fight."

Mike shook his head. He sat down on the cot by Longo and lit a cigarette. His back ached a little; he wondered whether he still smelled.

When he saw that the other marines had gone back to what they were doing, he said, "Hey, Longo, what's going on? I mean, why'd we leave the Fort?"

Longo looked up. "*Why?* You think there's any *whys* in this war, man?"

"No—I mean—"

"Only thing I know is we're supposed to wait. Scuttlebut has it we're going up north—the whole battalion. Army's taking over down here."

"Really? The Army?" Longo said nothing. "But—what about the Fort?"

"What about it?"

"The Army going to take it over?"

"Fort's done closed up, man. It *isn't*: no more. We folded it up; it doesn't exist."

"What do you mean? I mean . . . nobody's going to replace us there?"

"Uh-uh."

"But . . ." Mike hesitated. He glanced quickly around the shack. What was wrong with Longo? "But what about those vills . . . what about Binh Le?"

Rain, from his squatting position, said, "You ever see a friendly vill after Charlie's been through with it? Won't be a hooch left standing, not a one."

Mike breathed out loudly. "Jesus . . . Who made the decision?" Longo let out a short, dry laugh. "How about Captain Blood— what does he say?"

"He don't say nothing, man: he's gone."

"Gone?" Mike caught his breath. "What do you mean?"

Longo looked up. "Oh, yeah, you weren't here. He got orders for a desk job at regiment. Out of the field; two days ago."

"How come?"

"*How come?* I don't know, man—that's another *why.* 'Cause officers don't have to spend as much time in the field, that's how come. They're more delicate than we are, or something. I don't know."

Mike hesitated. "Who's the new captain?"

"Name's Francis."

"What's he like?"

"Seems okay. Lettin' us grow mustaches, anyway. But he's big on haircuts."

Mike glanced around the shack again. He had the uneasy feeling that everyone was watching him. He lowered his voice. "What did Captain Blood say—when you closed the Fort?"

"What could he say? It wasn't his doing. He was glad to get out of the field. Who isn't?"

"Jesus," Mike said, "after all that work—"

Longo laughed again. "What work, man?"

"You know—in the vills."

"So we ran a few patrols. What did you think—we were going to stay there forever?"

"No. . . . It's just that—we were really getting to know the place."

"So you ate a few meals with some old gook. . . ." Longo looked down at his letter.

Mike frowned. "Where's the Professor?"

"Got dysentery. He's in Da Nang, NSA."

"Bad?"

"Not bad enough. He'll be back."

Mike nodded. Blevins was watching him, he could tell. Suddenly he said, "Pogo—where's Pogo?"

The talk near him quieted. Short-round sat up again. He gave a quick, almost imperceptible shake of his head.

Longo looked up. "You didn't hear?"

"No. What happened?"

"Zapped: the last patrol we ran at the Fort."

"No. . . . Really? . . . How—where?"

Longo turned to the side. Rain said, "Frontierland—just outside it."

Blevins said, "Man, you shoulda seen what we did to that vill down there—you'd be proud, Crazy Mike. About burnt the whole place down."

"Really?"

"Ai Tu, too," Blevins said. "Charlie can have that place. There ain't much left."

Mike put out his cigarette and lit another. He spoke softly to Longo. "That's too bad, about Pogo. I mean, it really is. Did he, uh, I mean—did it happen right away?"

"Yeah," Longo said, "right away. . . . So how was your R and R, anyway?"

"Okay."

Short-round said, "You eat pretty well?"

"Yeah. Had a little Chinese food; mostly steak."

Short-round laughed. "That's Crazy fucking Mike for you—talking about food on his R and R!" Mike hesitated, then laughed too.

Someone said, "Hey, Crazy Mike, is it true what they say about slant-eyes? That their cunts are slanted too?" It was the same marine who had spoken before, the one sitting next to Blevins.

Mike looked at him a second. "Find out for yourself," he said, then lay down on a cot and tried to sleep.

A brand-new station wagon rode through a suburban neighborhood on what looked like a bright autumn day; an announcer told how roomy it was. *If only they had stayed at the Fort*, Mike thought. Then none of the rest would have happened. Who had made that decision, anyway? How could they just give it up like that? The marines *had* been making progress—Binh Le *had* become a friendly village. It took time, that was all.

If they had stayed at the Fort then Mike would never have gotten drunk that night and done what he did. That was right, he told himself: that argument with Longo never would have happened. But he wasn't afraid to remember it—what did it matter, really? A stupid argument, that was all. People have arguments—they have fights; brothers fight all the time. And Longo was like a brother, wasn't he? Actually, Mike could hardly remember what had happened.

It was the—what?—third day Mike had spent at battalion headquarters. Third or fourth, anyway. Mike and the rest of the platoon had been staying busy, getting resupplied, cleaning their rifles and gear for the lieutenant's constant inspections, getting haircuts. They were eating three hot meals a day and sleeping on cots at night—when they didn't have to stand perimeter duty. Every day it seemed as if there was a new rumor as to where they were going: afloat as the next Special Landing Team, up to Con Thien, out to Okinawa until the battalion got up to full strength, on a big operation in the same area Red River had been. Mike had a new member of his fire team, Wiggins, the young-looking, over-weight marine with black hair and black-rimmed glasses who had spoken to Mike his first day back. Right away he told Mike he had a bad knee and shouldn't be in the field.

That evening, just before chow, Rain and C.C. came rushing into the shack.

"We scored, man, we scored," C.C. said, grinning. They began pulling bottles of Tiger beer out of their flak jackets and utility trousers. The bottles kept coming out, like a magician's trick.

"All *right!*" Mike shouted. He tried to give C.C. money for some of the beer, but C.C. wouldn't take it.

"I'm not spending any where I'm going," he said. Rain refused it too.

"Man, you should have seen him," C.C. said, pointing to Rain, "with his VC sandals on, squatting with this gook dude, making a big deal. Looked like they were a couple of Charlies plotting some big ambush or something." He laughed.

The last bottle C.C. pulled out was different from the others. It was a clear bottle with brown liquid in it and a screw-off cap. "Man," he said, studying it, "this looks like the same stuff my daddy used to get from his favorite bootlegger down in Missis-sippi." He screwed off the cap and sniffed. "Oh, God, I didn't think they could make it any worse'n what he drank. This stuff is nine parts used diesel oil and one part water buffalo piss." The marines laughed. C.C. sniffed again. "Make that used water buf-falo piss. No wonder that gook threw it in for free."

"Let me smell," Mike said.

"Watch out, man," Longo said, "that stuff'll kill you."

Blevins laughed. "If anyone drinks it, it'll be Crazy Mike."

Mike took a sniff and made a face. C.C. laughed. Suddenly Mike put the bottle to his lips and drank.

"Told you," Blevins said.

"Oh, God, you're right, C.C.," Mike said, "it's the worst I've ever tasted. And I've had some bad stuff, too."

C.C. put the beer in the middle of the floor for whoever wanted it. Mike opened a bottle and took a long swallow, trying to put out the burning in his throat. Other marines cursed the taste of the beer, but Mike said it was good.

Away from the others, Rain pulled something out of his side trouser pocket to show to Mike. In his palm were three or four dirty-looking cigarettes.

"What's that?"

"What do you think?" Rain said. "A little puff-puff." Mike gave him a puzzled look. "Grass, man. Mary Jane."

"Really?" Before Mike could say anything more Rain put the cigarettes back in his pocket.

Mike drank more beer and then he and the others went to chow.

There was some kind of stew that night. It tasted like C-ration stew, but Mike ate a lot of it. He wondered whether he was putting on weight—after his R&R and now with no patrolling and all the food they were getting. Plus the beer. Wiggins, sitting across from him, stuffed stew and bread into his mouth. With his small pointed nose and pudgy cheeks he looked like a pig.

Short-round told about the latest rumor he had heard, that the battalion was going on a big operation in the A Shau valley.

"Where the hell's that?" Ski asked.

"You better start finding out, man," Short-round said. "It's Number Ten Land. You know that bullshit they tell you in boot camp about how you will fear no evil in the valley of death because you are the meanest motherfucker in the valley? Well, the A Shau valley makes the valley of death look like Disneyland—I mean, the *real* Disneyland. Like, you go up there and you don't come back."

Wiggins gulped. "Uh-oh," he said, "I think I just got dysentery." Everybody laughed.

C.C. said, "Hey, Crazy Mike, you hear about Crane?"

Mike stopped eating. "No. What happened?"

C.C. laughed. "It's all right, man, nothing like that. We heard it from some guy in third platoon who was down in Chu Lai. It seems ol' Crane got so drunked up one night he walked into the officers' mess and tried to piss all over everybody—right in the middle of chow!"

"No! Really?"

"The truth, man. They were going to throw his ass in the brig—"

"The brig?" Mike swore. "He didn't go to the brig, did he? I heard that's a bad scene."

Short-round said, "No, we heard he got off 'cause he's been to the field and is up for a Bronze. They busted him a grade, that's all."

"But that really took balls, didn't it?" C.C. said.

"Ol' Crane has some balls, all right," Mike said. "I think I'll drink a couple to ol' Crane tonight."

"How about Tracy?" Blevins said. "You hear what happened to him?"

"No, what happened?"

"Jeff got a letter a few days ago. About the first day he's home he runs into a demonstration; some guy waves a VC flag in his face, so Tracy punches the guy out, right in the nose. Breaks his fucking hand. Wants to know if he gets a Heart for it." Mike laughed. "But the thing is," Blevins went on, "what got him so worked up"—he glanced around the table—"wasn't so much the flag, it was that the guy waving it looked just like Pogo. . . . That's what he wrote, anyway. . . . Of course he didn't know."

Mike assumed a serious expression. "Pogo was all right," he said. He smiled. "Hey, what was Pogo's real name, anyway?"

"Oh, God, what a name! Whipple?"

"Roger Whipple," Ski said. "Can you believe it?"

Mike shook his head slowly. "He was all right."

"Hey, speaking of names," Ski said, "you hear what happened with Short-round? First day we were here, he's walking by a mortar pit and C.C. yells out, 'Hey, Short-round!' Man, you shoulda seen those mortarmen scatter. Funny as hell!"

There was a pause, then C.C., frowning, said, "Now I'm not the violent sort, but I believe I'd do worse than that to the first person who tries to wave a Vietcong flag in my face. I mean, I don't care if it's a girl, I'll punch her goddamn teeth in. I will. I hear there's a lot of girls doing that now, too. College girls. Freaks."

"No, you're not violent, C.C.," Short-round said. "That's close. How about that time you took on a whole company of M.P.'s in Okinawa?"

"Oh, hell, that was different. I was provoked. That's what I mean: I don't ever get violent unless I'm provoked." The marines at the table laughed.

After another pause, Mike said, "Hey, C.C., you hear anything about Brutus? How's he doing?"

C.C. turned toward Mike, then looked down. "Yeah, I got a letter. . . . Says he's gonna go out for the wheelchair Olympics. . . . No, not really; he was kidding, I think. I mean, he says he's gonna be able to walk—maybe; artificial leg."

Mike waited a moment, then said, "How about Motor? You get to see him, Short-round, before he rotated?"

Short-round snorted. "Yeah, I saw him—right before he left. That bastard. Starts rubbing it in, how I've still got two months to go and he's going home. Pissed me off. I told him I hope his plane crashes." He laughed hoarsely.

After chow they all went back to the shack and drank more beer. There were more stories about the Fort: Ai Tu and Binh Le, Zorro and the Cisco Kid, Pogo, the time the Black Streak got killed. Mike told about the time he got drunk in Binh Le with Rip van Winkle and had to go on a two-day patrol the next day, how hung over he was. "Fuck it!" he shouted. "Ain't got no patrols

tomorrow. Ain't no more Fort. Gimme some of that buffalo piss!"
He grabbed the bottle of whiskey from under C.C.'s cot and held
it in the air. "To Crane!" he said, and drank.

"Jesus, 'Crazy Mike' is right," Wiggins said. "I'd never drink
that stuff."

Mike pointed at Wiggins, wiping his lips. "The hell you
won't," he said. "Wait'll you been here a while: you got no idea
what you'll do. You'll see." Wiggins gave him a disgusted look.
"You'll see."

Mike turned away and grabbed C.C. by the shoulder. "Hey,
C.C., let's have a drink." C.C. shook himself loose. "Come on,"
Mike said, and put the bottle up to C.C.'s lips.

C.C. pushed it away. "Uh-uh," he said, "I'm not drinking that
stuff."

"Come on—"

"No!"

Suddenly Mike raised the bottle and took another swig. He
grinned. "Hey, C.C., you get a picture of Rain and that gook
squatting together, down by the wire? . . . What's the matter,
C.C.—can't find your camera?" C.C. turned away.

Mike pulled out his cigarettes, dropped them, picked them up
and lit one. He glanced around the shack. Where was Longo? He
wasn't here; Rain wasn't either. Where were they? Why hadn't
they asked Mike to go with them? Mike took another bottle of
beer from the center of the floor; there weren't many left.

The events of the night began to become confused in Mike's
mind. There was a big argument among the marines in the shack
about the war and how the Marine Corps should fight it. Like the
South Koreans, someone said: wipe out all the villages friendly to
the VC. No, said another, stay out of the villages, just go after the
big units—invade North Vietnam. Forget about this place, someone else said, everyone go home. Mike tried to tell about his talk
with Major Nguyen; he held his hands the way the major had to
show the difference in leaders; the United States had committed
itself, Mike said, it had to stay. He realized no one was listening.

Where was Longo? At one point he noticed there were only a couple of inches left in the whiskey bottle.

He went over to C.C. and put his arm around his shoulders.

"Hey, C.C., you're all right. . . . I was just kidding, before—I mean, about your camera—"

"Forget it—"

"No, man, I've got to tell you—I understand—I mean, about the whole thing . . . what it means. . . ." Mike wiped his mouth. It was hard to get his words to come out right. "I mean, that whole thing—I understand it. . . ." What was his point? The more he talked, the thicker his tongue became. "I mean, about taking pictures . . . being in a war . . . the mind like a camera . . . no emotions . . ." Finally he stopped. C.C. was staring at him. His face looked different: it had angles and lines that had not been there before; his eyes were sunken. Now there were two faces, four eyes. Mike tried to focus. Why was he looking at Mike that way? Had Mike said something terrible? Did C.C. want to fight?

Longo would understand, Mike suddenly thought, what he was trying to say. He looked around, squinting. There was no more beer. He ran out of the shack.

He decided to go down by the garbage dump, where Rain and C.C. had gone before. Maybe that was where Rain and Longo were now. There were always villagers hanging around down there; Mike could buy some beer, anyway. He wanted to squat and talk with a villager, the way Rain had done. If Rain and Longo were there then they could all go to a villager's house and eat and drink with him—and smoke marijuana. Mike was ready to. Why hadn't he told Rain before?

It was a bright night. The moon and stars were out. Was it a good night for the VC to attack? Rain would know—Rain knew everything. Suddenly Mike remembered he hadn't cleaned his rifle.

He was down by the garbage dump. No one was here—no villagers, no Longo, no Rain. Where had everyone gone? It smelled. A voice said, "Who's that?" Mike jumped. It was a marine on guard duty. Of course: no one was allowed down here at night. "Eat shit!" Mike yelled and ran back the way he had come, giggling.

Where did he go then? He wasn't sure. He kept walking—walking and walking, looking for Longo.

Someone stopped him.

"Where are you going, marine?"

It must be an officer, Mike thought. "Back to my platoon, sir," he said.

"Oh? . . . Tell me something."

"Yes, sir?"

"Have you seen the elephant?"

"What?"

"The elephant—have you seen it?"

"What? Sir?"

"Have you been to town and seen the elephant?"

"I . . ."

Suddenly the officer giggled, then walked away.

He must be drunk, Mike thought. He remembered what Crane had said about officers in the rear getting drunk all the time. But didn't the French Foreign Legion used to get drunk too? He thought of the whiskey that was still in the shack and decided to go back.

But which way was back? Where was he? He stopped and tried to think. Suddenly he saw two marines coming out of a shack. Was it his? He went to look. The marines were black. They disappeared around a corner. No, it wasn't his shack—but what were those marines doing, sneaking around like that? Thieves. Mike thought of what Lou had said and kept glancing around as he walked.

Mike realized he was lost. Lost? What did that mean? How could he be lost if he was still inside the wire? Why couldn't he find his shack? They all looked the same: row after row of darkened plywood buildings. Perhaps he had found it, had been passing by it time after time without knowing. It occurred to Mike that maybe he'd better pick one out and look into it. But then he might be taken for a thief: marines might jump him. He walked faster, turned another corner. He was the only one out, everyone else was where he should be. What if the VC attacked? He had no weapon; he was separated from his unit. All the officers were drunk; the enlisted men were thieves. How could marines steal from one another? Didn't they know what they were here for? He began to run, then fell. He picked himself up and fell again.

At one point he seemed to come to, standing in front of a shack. Somehow he knew it was his. He went inside and saw a faint light at the far end. Three marines were sitting on the floor around a candle; one of them was Longo.

He looked up. The light from the candle cast shadows above his cheekbones, hiding his eyes. "Hey, it's Crazy Mike," he said. He sounded drunk. "Join us, man. I was just telling these guys about the movie. . . . Crazy Mike is in the movie too—aren't you, Crazy Mike? . . . He doesn't give a shit; he knows it's not real. . . . Come on, man, have a seat." Now Mike saw that Wiggins was one of the other marines; the third was a new one too, whom Mike didn't know. He went to his cot and sat down.

"I can't."

"Why not?"

"Got to clean my rifle."

"Come on, man." Longo was smiling. "Have a seat."

Mike shook his head. "Got to clean my rifle." He pulled his M-16 out from under his cot.

"What for?"

"Because . . . got to."

"What are you talking about?"

"Because . . . maybe there's an attack tonight. VC."

Longo laughed. "You're talking crazy, man. Come on down here."

"Don't laugh! I'm not crazy. I'm here to fight."

Longo turned back to the others. "Crazy Mike is a little crazy sometimes, but he knows it's all a movie—don't you, Crazy Mike? He knows you can't take it serious."

"I'm serious. You get me? I'm serious. Don't tell me what to be."

"Hey, what's wrong? What's with you, anyway?"

"Just shut up."

"What is it, man?"

"I'm serious, that's all. I'm serious."

"Hey, man, I *know* you." Longo's voice was pleading. "You're beautiful: you're a beautiful person—"

"Shut *up!*"

"Come on, man . . ." Longo reached with his hand. "Come on and join us." He touched Mike's leg.

Mike jumped off his cot. "Just shut up!" He shoved Longo back. "Leave me *alone!*" He glared down at Longo, his fists clenched.

Longo, half lying on the ground and half sitting up, a puzzled half smile on his high-cheeked face, didn't move. He said, "Take it easy, man."

Suddenly Mike opened his fists and turned around. He sat down on his cot, picked up his rifle again, and started to take it apart. His mind went blank. How could this be? How many times before had he done it? He put down the rifle and stretched out on the cot.

Mike closed his eyes and clenched his right fist. He brought it up to his mouth and rubbed his lips against the hair on the back of his hand. He groaned. *I was drunk,* he told himself. *That was all. I had too much to drink. It was that gook whiskey.* And Longo had been drunk too—or something, from the marijuana. The way he had just lain there on the ground, looking up—that wasn't natural. Why didn't he do anything?

And the next day? Mike groaned again. He didn't want to remember. He had been hung over, that was all: that was why he hadn't done anything. That goddamn Blevins.

Mike had awakened with the worst headache he had ever had in his life. His head felt as if it had been split open. He reached up and felt it to make sure it wasn't. Then he went outside and vomited. Still he felt sick.

Then it came to him: Longo, the night before. Immediately he thought: who had heard? What did they think of him? He tried to remember: everyone had been asleep; nobody had heard. Except for Wiggins and the other new one. And they didn't count. He didn't like Wiggins anyway. Why did he have to get Wiggins?

He went back inside the shack. A few marines were cleaning their gear, but there was no Longo. He must be at chow already, Mike thought. He walked quickly to the mess tent, trying not to vomit, and got in line. When he swallowed, the taste in his mouth made the nausea worse. He glanced around him, at the rows of plywood shacks where he had wandered the night before. Now the whole area was filled with noise and activity: trucks and jeeps moving about, the blasts of artillery and mortars going out, marines walking with purpose to and fro. Near him in the chow line Mike could hear marines talking excitedly about where the battalion might be going. What did it matter where they went? What did any of this matter? It seemed incredible to Mike that he was a part of it. All he wanted to do was get away: go somewhere else, someplace where nobody knew him—where nobody knew each other; where people didn't ask questions.

There was a voice behind him: "Hey, Crazy Mike." He spun around, then immediately felt dizzy. "How're you feeling, man?" It was C.C., smiling. Snatches of their talk the night before came rushing into Mike's mind. His face became hot.

"All right."

"All right, bullshit!" C.C. laughed. "Ain't nobody drinks like that and is all right the next day. God, you look terrible. You puke?"

"Yeah." Mike tried to smile.

"Damn, you were drunk," C.C. said. "I ain't seen anyone that drunk since before my old man left home. You remember that stuff you were telling me?"

Finally Mike managed a smile. "Yeah, sure," he said. "Sorry about that. I mean, I didn't know what I was saying."

"Don't be sorry, man. Hell, I kept trying to tell you: it was only a camera, I just get pissed off when somebody steals anything from me; I hate it. But there was no way I could tell you anything last night. You were really going on." He kept smiling and staring. "Damn, you were drunk."

Mike nodded. "I know." Why did C.C. keep staring at him? Mike tried to hold C.C.'s eyes. Suddenly he remembered the way C.C. had looked the night before; he turned away.

"You seen Longo yet?"

"No. Why?"

"Just wondering. I saw him talking to the lieutenant before. Maybe there's some word out, where we're going."

"Maybe. I'll let you know if I hear anything."

"Thanks, Crazy Mike." C.C. smiled again. It was a different smile, it seemed to Mike, from his usual admiring look. "Damn, you were drunk." Finally he moved away.

After what seemed like hours Mike got his B-ration scrambled eggs and coffee. He walked around the mess tent with his tray, looking for an empty seat. Then he saw Longo, getting up to leave.

"Hey," Mike said. "Longo."

Longo turned. There was half a smile on his face. His eyes were bloodshot. "Hey, man, how're you doing?"

"Not so good," Mike said. "I already puked once. I feel pretty sick."

"Yeah, that stuff'll do it to you. Bad stuff."

"Yeah, I guess so. I guess I should have listened to you." Mike licked his lips; they were very dry. "Kind of having a hard time remembering what happened. I mean . . ."

"It's okay, man, forget it." The half smile seemed frozen on Longo's face. "It was bad stuff, that's all." He moved his shoulders slightly up and down.

A wave of nausea swept over Mike. He rubbed his forehead. "Yeah, well . . ."

"Eat your chow, man—get something in your stomach. It's okay, really."

Mike clenched his jaw muscles. "Yeah, I guess I'd better. . . . I'll see you later. What's going on today, anyway? Any word on where we're going? I heard you were talking to the lieutenant."

Longo shook his head. "Nothing, man."

After breakfast Mike cleaned his rifle. He still had a headache and felt nauseated but not as bad as before. He was very thirsty; he kept refilling his canteens from the water bag by the platoon shack. In the afternoon Lieutenant Farmer held a rifle inspection. Wiggins's rifle wasn't as clean as it should have been, Mike knew, but it passed, and Mike said nothing about it.

Then, in the evening, as Mike again filled his canteens from the water bag, he heard someone behind him say his name. He turned and saw Blevins, a three-inch cigar stub sticking out of his mouth, smiling.

"Hi, Blevins," Mike said.

Blevins, chewing on his cigar, said, "I heard 'bout what you did to Longo last night." His eyes were fixed on Mike. He had just got a haircut, but his usual blond cowlick still stuck up at the back of his head.

"Oh?"

Blevins nodded, taking the cigar out of his mouth. "Reckon it's 'bout time someone did it," he said. Mike said nothing. Blevins kept smiling, his eyes crinkling at the corners. "Some of us in the platoon's been wonderin' 'bout you—the way you and him's been carryin' on." Mike frowned. "It's good to see him put in his place, if you know what I mean." He pulled on his cigar. Suddenly the thought occurred to Mike that Blevins would look and sound this way thirty years from now; that he had grown all he was going to grow. "Reckon one of us ought to be squad leader," he said. "Least we got a white man runnin' the platoon now." He nodded at Mike again, knowingly, then turned and walked away. Mike stared after him, at the blond cowlick bobbing up and down on the back of his head.

Mike snorted through his nose, clenching his fists. *That god-damned redneck: I should have shoved his fucking cigar down his throat.* Why hadn't he? Why hadn't he even *said* something? Because he was too slow—again. Even more so because of his hangover; no reflexes at all. But if Mike ever saw him again . . . He picked up his pack of cigarettes, pulled out the last one, and lit it.

But who were the "others" Blevins had mentioned? That night at chow Mike kept darting looks at the marines around him. Was it C.C.? Ski? Wiggins was no longer playing up to Mike, he noticed. Did Wiggins think there was something wrong with him? Mike make a point of sitting next to Longo.

The next day the Professor came back. He had lost weight; his face was pale and his cheeks sunken. He looked as if he had just come out of a month in the library. When he heard the news about the Fort closing up and Captain Blood being gone, his only reaction was a shrug. When he heard about Pogo he was silent. At a fire-team meeting Mike introduced the Professor to Short-round and Wiggins. "So you're the fucking Yalie philosopher," Short-round said. The Professor gave him his quick smile, as though not at all bothered by Short-round's abrasiveness. Wiggins seemed to idolize the Professor, asking him question after question about Yale.

At noon Mike and the Professor and Longo stood in the chow line, together again for the first time.

"How was your R and R?" the Professor asked.

"All right."

"What's Taipei like?" Mike shrugged. "Any good buildings?"

Mike said he hadn't seen much of the city. "But I ate pretty well."

The Professor spoke about his own plans for R&R—"If I last that long," he added with a quick smile. His family had friends in Tokyo whom he was going to visit. "But I really want to go to Kyoto," he said. "I hear there's some great temples there. Plus get a look at the countryside; it's supposed to be really beautiful. If you guys ever get another R and R, I could probably arrange it so you could stay with these people too."

Mike mumbled a thank you. Longo said, "Man, if I ever get another R and R, I know where I'm going."

"Where's that?" the Professor asked.

"Same place I went the first time. Hawaii. That's the place for me."

"Good body surfing, right?" Mike said.

Longo shook his head. "Man, Hawaii's got everything. Volcanoes, beaches, jungle, fields, mountains—you name it; all in this one tiny place. . . . Man, I took this one trip to Maui, way out in the boondocks, and it was like paradise, I'm not kidding. The people are so friendly—like, to anyone who comes by, automatically. They don't even think about locking their doors—it's like they've never even heard about crime." He smiled wistfully. "I mean, I know there's problems in the cities—like, with crime and prejudice and all that—but I never saw it. I met some really beautiful people there, really beautiful. I've *got* to go back." Mike turned toward the front of the line, watching Longo at the side of his vision. Longo was staring off, a trace of a smile on his face. He went on: "Man, if I ever get out of this madness and learn how to fly, that's what I'm going to do—that's my dream. Get a job with United Air Lines—"

"What?" For a moment Mike laughed.

Longo looked at him. "Yeah, United does all the flying between the States and Hawaii." He turned away. "Have a pad somewhere on Maui and spend half my time there and half in the sky. Make enough bread to send some home to my mom. . . ."

"That's great," the Professor said. He talked of his own dream—to sail across the Atlantic someday. He loved sailing, he said: the feel of the wind and spray on his face, the smell of saltwater, the sense of freedom—"Probably something like what you feel when you're in a plane." Then he said, "How about you, Crazy Mike? What's your dream?"

"Me?" Mike smiled self-consciously. He thought of his plans to stay till the war was over, to live and work with the Vietnamese. Should he tell them of his talk with Major Nguyen? He shrugged. "I don't know."

That night Sergeant Jefferson rushed into the shack. "Saddle up! We're going—now! Move it!"

The marines jumped off their cots, laced their boots, and grabbed their gear. There were swearing and yelling and shouting back: "Where the hell we going? . . . What the hell's it all about, Jeff?"

"Squad leaders up! Meeting with the lieutenant—ASAP!"

Longo and the other two squad leaders left the tent with Jefferson while the rest of the marines continued to get ready.

In a few minutes the squad leaders came back and called meetings of their own. Longo said, "Recon patrol's in trouble—on some hill about twenty clicks west of here. Our platoon's been picked to go in and bail them out. Choppers're going to take us in."

"Choppers?" Mike said. Longo nodded.

"How many gooks are there?" It was Blevins.

"They don't know—anywhere from a company to a battalion." Longo paused; nobody said anything. "Nothing's for sure yet; we just gotta be ready. If we go—it might be any minute. It'll be a hot LZ, that's for sure."

The hubbub inside the shack resumed. Mike felt grateful for it; it was like a cover for what he was feeling. *Choppers*, he kept thinking, *coming down to a hot LZ*. . . . What was wrong with him? He had been shot at before. But it wasn't just being shot at: it was going in a helicopter, and at night. Just the thought of it made him feel sick. For a second he thought of Crane and how Crane almost shot himself. He lit a cigarette and tried to concentrate on the talk around him. No, of course he wasn't going to shoot himself. Wiggins was scared too, Mike could tell. His face was white; his eyes darted around uncontrollably. He looked like a pig.

A half hour went by. Jefferson came back into the shack.

"As you were! Standby over."

"What happened?" voices shouted back.

"They got lifted out—that's all I know. Hit the sack."

Half the marines seemed to be swearing and half smiling. Mike slapped Wiggins on the back. "Too bad," he said.

"Shit," Wiggins said, "I didn't want to go on no chopper."

"Yeah, well, you go on what they tell you to go on," Mike said, feeling a sudden surge of anger. Then he unlaced his boots and put his rifle away.

The next day word finally came down that they were leaving: the entire battalion was going north to join an operation that had already begun. That afternoon the marines in Mike's platoon watched as helicopters filled the sky.

"Jesus, it looks like locusts," C.C. said, as the choppers hovered and then landed on a flat, open area next to the battalion perimeter. Out of them jumped the first Army troops from the unit that was to replace the marines.

"Look at C.C. drool," Ski said, laughing. "He wants to do some *hunting!*"

Short-round swore. "All those choppers for one company? What have they got—one for each man?"

The marines kept staring. Rain said, "One of the Vietnamese words for helicopter is *dragonfly-machine*. Now I see why."

That evening the soldiers came to the marines' chow line wearing camouflage-striped utilities and silver-colored helmet liners. "*Woof, woof!*" the marines shouted. "*Doggie, doggie!*"

"Jesus!"—Short-round was disgusted—"that's just like stupid fucking jarheads for you: in the middle of a war they try to pick a fight with their own allies."

The next morning Mike's battalion began its move, getting on trucks and driving to Da Nang. At the airfield they waited and waited in the hot sun, bunched together in the backs of the trucks. They had on full packs with shelter halves and Mike's back began to ache. He wanted to take off his pack and sit down, but there was room to do neither. Wiggins kept asking whether he could get something to eat at the canteen; Mike said no.

"Why not?" Wiggins asked. "It's right over there—I'll be right back. Even if we start loading I'll make it back."

"No."

Short-round seemed jumpy. He swore. "If we don't move out soon, I'm going there myself," he said, "and I might not come back."

"Good," Wiggins said, "I'll go with you."

Mike laughed as if Short-round had been joking. He found himself wishing he were just a point man again—why did he ever agree to be fire-team leader? Meanwhile the Professor took a paperback book out of his helmet and read.

Finally they loaded up on C-130 cargo planes. They waited again, then they flew and landed at Dong Ha. It was cool and overcast when they got off the airplanes. Mike stood on the runway and stared around him. It was a huge base; it sprawled for miles. Everything seemed dirty: the trucks lined up at the edge of the runway, the marines in the ground crew with their brown-colored flak jackets, the slummy-looking buildings in the distance. It reminded him of New York City.

"Where are we going?" Wiggins asked. "When're we gonna chow?" He was afraid, Mike could tell. But of what? They had been told Dong Ha often received incoming, but nobody in the ground crew seemed worried about it. He told Wiggins to shut up. Mike's back began to ache again; all he wanted to do was take off his pack.

They spent the night in plywood shacks like the ones down south, only dirtier. When Mike woke the next morning he didn't know where he was. There was a commotion outside and everybody rushed to the doors to look. A few curls of smoke rose in the distance; somebody said that the base had just been mortared. It seemed very far away to Mike. A few marines laughed.

Right after chow that morning Longo came back from a meeting with the lieutenant and gave the squad the word: their company and one other were going out to help a battalion from the Ninth Marines that was on a hill fifteen miles west, surrounded by NVA.

"How're we going?" Mike asked.

"Trucks," Longo said. "The hill's right off Highway Nine. When we get there further orders will be issued. Any more questions?"

"How many gooks are supposed to be out there?" Blevins was staring hard at Longo.

"Might be a regiment."

Blevins didn't move. Short-round swore.

"How about our packs?" Mike asked. "Do we leave them here or bring them?"

"Bring 'em," Longo said. "After we link up with the battalion that's surrounded, we stay with it for the rest of the operation. Who knows how long that's gonna be."

"What's the name of it?" Ski asked.

"Boone," Longo said. "Operation Boone."

They got on the trucks and headed west. It was cool; the sky was a dirty gray. It felt like a chilly autumn morning, Mike thought, like the day of a football game. Lieutenant Farmer was in Mike's truck, constantly checking his wristwatch. He passed the word to be on the lookout for possible ambushes.

The countryside changed from flat and sandy to large round hills, dark green, thick with vegetation. Was this where Major Nguyen used to hunt? It occurred to Mike that he'd much rather be here when there was no war. Then he would go hunting too. He'd be good at hunting: he liked to do things by himself. He didn't want to tell people what to do; he didn't want anyone telling him what to do. He didn't want to be here at all: he didn't like this part of the country. What did he know about fighting a war up here? He was used to the heat, to passing through villages on small patrols, searching hooches and checking I.D.'s. Here there were no vills. What if they got ambushed? They wouldn't stand a chance.

Mike glanced at Longo, trying to catch his eye; but Longo was gazing out to the side, frowning. He looked cold. Mike turned to the Professor; their eyes met. Mike tried to smile; they both looked away. His back began to ache again. If only he didn't have this pack—then he'd feel all right. He heard firing in the distance.

The trucks speeded up, then slowed. The marines became quiet. Wiggins swore. "Why the hell did they pick us for this, anyway?" he said. "We're not ready."

Lieutenant Farmer smiled thinly. "Well," he said, "I guess

that's what the Marine Corps is all about." Mike couldn't tell whether he was afraid or not.

Someone pointed up ahead. "There it is!" Mike could see a hill, standing by itself. Firing was coming from it. In front of it was what appeared to be the remains of a village, with hooches smoldering. Under the gray sky it looked like a painting: static, distant, something only to look at. Mike wished he could remain static himself.

Then the marines were jumping off the truck. Mike did too. Lieutenant Farmer shouted, "Keep it spread out! Squad leaders up!" Mud from the road splattered up to Mike's face. He yelled at his fire team to spread out. There was an explosion nearby. Mike hit the ground.

Now he was running, clumsily, his pack bouncing, following Longo along the side of the road and then along a path. Again there was an explosion and the ground seemed to shake. The firing was near, Mike could tell: AK-47's and M-16's. But where was the enemy? They must be dug in. There was a din of firing now. Mike's ears hurt.

"Get down!" Longo shouted. "Fire!" But it seemed as if everybody was already down. Mike settled in the slightly muddy dirt and fired himself. What was he firing at? A tree line to the front. To his left he saw Short-round and the Professor jump into a crater. There was another crater just beside it. Wiggins jumped into it; Mike did too. He heard rounds going by above his head.

Then there was whistling, and then explosions: mortars were coming in. "Corpsman! Corpsman! . . . I'm hit, I'm hit! . . . I'm dying!" Who was that? Was it one person or more? Mike couldn't tell. He didn't want to move. He felt Wiggins's body next to his: heavy, inert. "Goddamnit, Wiggins, fire!" Mike shouted, and raised up for a second and fired himself. But where was the enemy? Somewhere, Mike knew: they had to be responsible for this snapping above his head. He heard more screaming. Suddenly he thought how strange it was that only a few feet away where the trucks had been it was perfectly safe. Why didn't he just go back? Who would know? Go back and shoot himself. But no, he couldn't do that—he couldn't think of it. What if he shit in his pants? No, he wouldn't do that either. He fired again. "Fire, Wiggins!"

Mike's magazine was empty; he needed a new one. Good—something different to do. But could he do it? His fingers were fumbling; he knew it was taking too long: like a dream, where he couldn't do anything right. . . . Finally he got the magazine in. He stuck his head up for a second and fired again—at a tree line a hundred meters in front of him; he tried to keep his rounds low, imagining that there was someone over there like him, sticking his head up every few seconds. He thought: they should have this happen to them too. He shouted at Wiggins: "*Keep firing! Keep firing!*" His voice was like a club, pounding Wiggins on the head.

Someone shouted behind him: "*Move it! Move it!*" He recognized the high-pitched voice: Jeff's. But Mike didn't move. Jeff couldn't mean him—how could he move? It was all he could do to keep firing—and keep Wiggins firing too. His pack felt like a hundred pounds on his back. If only he didn't have it!

Suddenly there was someone else next to him in the crater. Longo. Where had he come from? Another of Longo's tricks.

"How you doing?" Longo's face was very close to Mike's. His eyelashes were quite long, Mike noticed, and curled. His wide nose was shiny; below it were the beginnings of a soft black mustache.

"All right," Mike said. "What the fuck's happening?" His voice sounded rough to him; it felt good. He thought about having a cigarette.

Longo turned and looked out above the top of the crater, then brought his head back down. "It's bad, man—we walked into it. Everybody's pinned down. They got a machine gun set up in that tree line and they're trying to come around in back of us. Using the mortars to split us up. It looks like we've got to move up. Shit."

Mike nodded knowledgeably, but he thought: how did Longo know all that? Longo continued, shouting in Mike's ear, "Take your team up to that hooch"—he pointed—"use grenades to go in—but I think it's empty. Watch your ammo!" His lisp was pronounced, Mike noticed. Then Longo was gone.

Mike turned on his side toward the crater next to him. Were Short-round and the Professor still there? He shouted, "Short-round! Professor! We're moving up—to the hooch!"

"I can't," Wiggins said, as though Mike had spoken to him. "I can't, I can't! . . . My knee!" He was crying, Mike could see. Had he shit in his pants? Mike quickly looked but saw no stain.

"Bullshit! You're *going!*"

"No—"

"You're *going! Goddamnit!*" Mike's voice boomed. "We're going up there—together—*you hear me?*" He grabbed Wiggins's flak jacket and pulled, but his hands lost their grip. He grabbed again, tighter, hurting his fingers. "Come on, *goddamnit!*" He shouted again toward Short-round and the Professor: "*Cover us!*" He listened for their firing and then, not sure whether he heard it or not, he pulled. This time Wiggins moved.

They ran, then flopped down behind a small mound next to the hooch. "Keep firing!" Mike shouted to Wiggins. "It's all right, just keep firing! It's all right—there's no one in the hooch!" But how did he know? He didn't. He wanted it so. He looked behind. He saw the top of a helmet in Short-round's crater.

"Come on!" Mike shouted, "*move up!*" Suddenly he heard whistling and put his head down in the dirt. He tasted the dirt. He tried to press his body closer. He had a thought: *I like the taste of dirt.*

Behind him and to the right there was a string of explosions. Then Short-round and the Professor were next to him.

"Why don't we go in the hooch?" It was the Professor. His face was red; his glasses were cock-eyed. But he sounded calm.

"All right," Mike said, "all right, let's go in the hooch." He turned to Wiggins; Wiggins had taken off his pack. Mike was about to shout at him to put it back on when he thought, *I'll take mine off too.* He did.

They went in, took positions, then began to fire through openings—a door, a window. In the corner Mike noticed a shrine like the one in Rip van Winkle's house. Suddenly there was an explosion above them.

"Fucking *rocket!*" Short-round yelled; he sounded hysterical. But Mike almost laughed. Bits of something came raining down on them and now Mike wished he had on his pack.

"That's good, Wiggins," he said, "that's the way: keep firing."

Then Longo and Blevins and the rest of the squad were in the hooch too. It filled with the sounds of swearing: "Goddamn bastards! . . . Motherfuckers! . . . Fucking gooks!" Ski's was one of the voices; so was C.C.'s. Suddenly someone yelled, "There's too many fucking *people* in here!" Mike smiled. He felt glad for the crowd, for the bodies close to him; it was like being in the ocean, bobbing in the waves. He wanted them all to stay here.

"Keep firing, Wiggins!" Mike yelled and stuck his own rifle out the window. "Motherfuckers! You bastards!" How good it felt to scream! To hate! "Come on, Wiggins, shout! Let 'em hear you!" Mike turned to his right and watched C.C.: he was like a madman, screaming one second, then flopping his machine gun on the ground where the door used to be and firing. Next to him was Blevins; he looked toward Mike and their eyes met. "Kill 'em!" Mike yelled, and Blevins swore out too; both of them went back to firing.

Suddenly Rain was on Mike's left, firing out the same window as Mike and Wiggins. Every few seconds he'd stick out his grenade launcher—*phonk! phonk!* He worked quietly, smoothly, like a machine. Mike realized it was the first time he had ever seen Rain in action like this. He was good, Mike thought; he was good. Mike began screaming less and firing more, like Rain.

Now Longo was next to him, crouched down, the radio up to his ear. He was shouting, "But I *can't*—that's where the machine gun is!" Mike had never heard him lisp so bad; he felt embarrassed for him.

Mike could hear the voice come back through the handset: "*One Alpha Actual, start moving your squad toward the tree line. Now. You've got to reach Three Bravo. They're cut off. Do you read me? You've got one minute to start moving out. Over.*" It was Lieutenant Farmer—his unhurried, dull, plodding voice. Mike had a picture in his mind of the lieutenant looking down at his watch.

Longo sputtered, "But—we can't, it's—"

Lieutenant Farmer's voice interrupted: "*Start moving, One Alpha—one fire team at a time. Out.*"

Another blast above. "*Rocket!*" Mike curled up, putting his arms around himself. Should he go back and get his pack?

"Oh, shit!" Longo said, "Oh, *shit!*" For a moment Mike thought he was crying. Then Longo said, "Blevins—you and your men—let's go!"

"Huh?" Blevins gave a wide-eyed look.

"Rain, too." Longo seemed to be speaking to nobody. "C.C. stays here. Cover."

Mike began to speak. "Ed," he said, "wait!"

Longo turned to him. "What?" His face seemed twisted, ugly with pain. Mike had to force himself to look at him.

Mike opened his mouth. "I . . ."

"You cover and then follow us," Longo said. He shook his head, grimacing. He swore. "I can't . . . Shouldn't have . . . So stupid!" Suddenly he glanced back. "Why? . . ." Then he was gone.

Mike shouted and he and his fire team and C.C. fired together through the door and windows of the hooch; the sound of their firing was like a roar, reverberating in what was left of the inside. It seemed to comfort Mike, blotting out his thoughts. He wanted it to go on—on and on, never stopping.

Suddenly Short-round yelled, "They're hit! They're hit!" He sounded hysterical. "They're out there—in the open! Oh, fuck!"

"Where?" Mike tried to sound calm. He popped his head up for a second but could see no one—just the bare, crater-marked earth; beyond that a blur of trees. He put his head back down and a burst of rounds went over him. "Where? Are you sure?"

C.C. jumped back. Where was he going? Was he running away? Then Mike saw him on the ground, blood gushing from his arm and shoulder.

"Corpsman!" Mike screamed. "*Corpsman!*" Short-round let out a string of obscenities, as though C.C. had got hit on purpose. He jumped away from C.C.'s machine gun, as if it were a snake.

Wiggins was sobbing. "Please, God, I don't want to die, I don't want to die! Oh, please, God, please . . ."

"Shut *up!*" Mike grabbed Wiggins and shook him as hard as he could. "Shut the fuck up!" With a great effort he threw Wiggins to the ground.

The Professor, kneeling over C.C., was bandaging his arm. *Oh, God*, Mike thought. *Oh, God. What am I going to do?*

"Longo!" he yelled through the front of the hooch. "*Longo!*" There was a burst of machine-gun fire and Mike put his head down.

What should he do? He stuck his rifle out and fired. If only he could just stay here and do that! He drew his rifle back and listened to Wiggins cry.

"Goddamn it, Wiggins, *fire!* You bastard!" Then Mike said, without having thought it, "We're going out there, Wiggins, we're going out there! Bill, help Short-round cover for us! One of you work the gun. We're going out there! Come on, Wiggins!"

"No—no—no!"

Mike raised his head, clenching his fists. What could he have done? Would he have gone out there?

But he was going to—yes, he was going to! Wasn't he? When he stood up, dragging Wiggins with him, the ends of his fingers digging into Wiggins's flak jacket, full of pain.

"Cover us, goddamnit!" The Professor, now with C.C.'s machine gun, said something Mike couldn't hear. He shot looks around the hooch, tried again to see outside. Then he crouched, one arm on his rifle, the other on Wiggins, and prepared to leap.

Two things happened at once: he spun around, and he felt a tremendous ache in his jaw, an ache that could never become undone, it seemed to him. He had more thoughts: so this was what it was like to get hit. Was he going to die? Now he was lying on the ground next to C.C. He could taste blood—blood and dirt, mixed together. Was it his blood or C.C.'s? He didn't care; just to taste something. He felt the Professor wrap a bandage around his head.

Did he stay conscious? He couldn't tell. He thought he heard Blevins's voice: "Longo's still out there!" Then what was Blevins doing in here? The hooch seemed to be crowded again. With all the strength he had left, Mike strained to listen. Then there was the sound of explosions nearby. "Mortars!" someone yelled. "Incoming!" Mike became afraid. The thought occurred to him that he didn't want to die.

He was being carried, roughly. *They're going to drop me*, he thought. *Why should they help me?* If only he could make it to where the trucks had left them off: that peaceful area. That was where he wanted to go. *Maybe that's why they're helping me: because they want to go there too.*

And then what? He was in a truck, then a helicopter; then he was in a hospital. The lieutenant was there. He was telling Mike he had to go back to the fighting. Mike knew he had to: he could hear Longo's screaming—"I'm dying! I'm dying! Help! Help!" When he woke he heard mortars hitting outside. Or were they artillery? Then he'd fall asleep again and have the same dream.

On the television a woman was opening a refrigerator packed with food. Mike picked up the cigarette wrapper from the table next to him, felt inside with his little finger, then crumpled it and threw it across the room. He picked up the ashtray and pulled out a butt that had an inch of tobacco left and put it between his lips. He struck a match and drew it close to him, watching his fingers tremble. The flame seared his eyes and he squeezed them shut.

Suddenly he got up, went into the bathroom, and stared in the mirror. Was this his face? It looked like a madman's: his mouth hanging open, his hair sticking up, his eyes with a wild, glazed look.

What are you back for? Why were you chosen?

He sucked more smoke from the butt, then turned on the tap water and held it under, listening to it hiss.

He walked back to his chair and sat down. From the table next to him he picked up the thick and dirt-stained envelope, took out the folded-up sheaf of papers inside, and began to read.

8

THE LETTER

Dear Mike,

Sorry it has taken me so long to answer your letter, but we have been on the move quite a bit, plus with the monsoon in full swing now—it rains all the time (it seems)—letter writing becomes rather difficult (and anything else, for that matter). In any case, this is not an easy letter to write. Forgive me if I make it short—but I'd better get it on to you, as we're about to move out again.

Longo died. Right away, in the first part of the battle that first day on Boone, when he was trying to move up from that hooch we were all crowded into. As far as I know his death was instantaneous—machine gun got him in the chest and stomach; I think a round went through his heart. (I saw him; there was no pain on his face.) A little after you were taken away our artillery finally zeroed in on that machine gun position so we were able to move up okay and drag Longo back.

Then things got bad again. Mortars came in on us and there was a hell of a lot of attempted maneuvering going on but actually very little movement. One of the rounds landed just about on top of Wiggins—he didn't have a chance; his body was almost in pieces. (Nobody saw him get it—it was during a sustained mortar barrage and we were all under cover at the time; the wonder was that he wasn't too. I'm afraid the inescapable conclusion is that he got up in the middle of the barrage—for whatever reason. I'm sorry.) Anyway, it went on like that for the rest of the day—mortars and arty back and forth, a few meters here gained on the ground, lost over there; more machine-gun positions to knock out. The next day too: up at five, fighting by six; break for the night around eight or so. Ski got wounded pretty bad in the leg—we heard he might lose it (C.C. might lose his arm, too); Lieutenant Farmer got hit in the hand and forearm but refused medevac and stayed with us. In all, the platoon lost four KIA—Cullinan and Healer from third squad, in addition to Longo and Wiggins—and twelve wounded. (For a while we were down to fifteen men in the whole platoon; Blevins was acting squad leader after Longo got hit.) The third day, the same—with a little hand-to-hand thrown in. Finally, that afternoon (I think) the weather lifted just enough to allow some close-air support to come in. That seemed to make a difference—that plus a couple of companies from a battalion of Ninth Marines that suddenly showed up out of nowhere (to the rescue at the end of the movie?)—or else the NVA simply got tired of it all and decided to pull one of their disappearing acts, taking off into nowhere (how do they do that, anyway?—take little pills? immerse themselves in disappearing ink? or maybe they're not real: material for the avant garde). Anyway, the *Stars and Stripes* (always traditionalist—no experimental innovations, thank you) had it as this big frontal assault at the end with John Wayne, etc. leading the way, knocking out hundreds of slimy gooks with one hand and singing the Marine Corps Hymn with the other. Ho hum; it was nothing. I think the body count was close to a hundred, which got regiment all excited. And that was about it.

LATER. Sorry my account was so brief. I almost mailed it the way it was, but then decided I owe you a little more. (Not that you owe *me* anything, by the way—I didn't really do anything at all—put a bandage around your head, called for help; so please forget it. Was really glad to hear you made it, by the way; Blevins was sure you hadn't.) So it will be even more delayed—I hope you'll forgive me—although I don't really have a hell of a lot to add to what I've already written. I'm afraid I don't have it in me to go over the details of those three days; besides, I'm sure you can imagine what it was like: fighting, fighting, and more fighting; passing beyond exhaustion and then beyond that. It just kept going on and on and then it was over.

As to your other questions. To be truthful, they did not make a whole lot of sense to me. Actually, I found your whole letter a bit confusing. Disturbing, actually. It was like a dream —parts of it, anyway—so dark, ominous (ever see any movies by Ingmar Bergman, Swedish director?): I became afraid for you—and still do, when I reread it, trying to understand what you are getting at, what actually happened. That NVA in the hospital with you in Da Nang—the one who was trying to commit suicide—did you ever find out what happened to him?

Sorry—got to go again. Truck escort duty: serving as "security escorts" for truck convoys on Route 9—i.e., giving the NVA even more of a chance to ambush us. One gets the unmistakable feeling that it's only a matter of time. Talk about being expendable!

LATER. No ambush but we did take some sniper fire coming back in. The new machine gunner, Palmer, was hit in the leg—a nasty, very bloody thigh wound that Doc did a great job patching up. You never met Palmer. I did—barely. Nice guy; from Seattle (although he and Rain didn't know each other; didn't really like each other, as far as I could tell). Now we get to see what the next machine-gunner will be like. It goes on.

Sorry if I sound a bit jaded, but that's exactly how I feel right now. Worse, actually. It is pouring like hell outside and I am crouched under a leaking shelter–half tent, slowly getting soaked to my bones. We're still up north—looks like we're going to stay up here; now doing security duty at a big artillery installation called the Rockpile; which means either serving as sitting ducks on the lines or going out on patrol and becoming sitting ducks out there. ("Ducks" is right—in this weather!) I feel less as though we're fighting in a war than we're caught in one.

Anyway, back to your letter. (This isn't going to be easy.) Are you trying to say that the lieutenant had something to do with Longo's death—that his "stupidity" in sending Longo forward when he did is to blame? (You are so cryptic in parts!) All I can say is: no, I do not agree. The lieutenant was passing down an order—just as we all do, even us lowly fire-team leaders. (I got your old position, by the way; never felt invested with such hollow authority in my life! "Pass the word down"—a tape recorder could do it! There are three of us now: me, Short-round, and a new man, Reynolds. I am still point—Reynolds is just too new, and Short-round is a wreck. Really bad. So it is really a two-man fire team.) Certainly the decision to send Longo forward at that time may very well have been "stupid"—but so what? What were we doing there, anyway—on Operation Boone? After the NVA withdrew and we were able to reach the hill it was pretty obvious that it wasn't really necessary for us to be there in the first place—the battalion on the hill had been holding out all right. But if the idea is to fight the enemy wherever he is, then I can see why we were there (not that I go along with that idea). I'm sure a lot of "stupid decisions" are made all the time over here, but I suppose that's true of all wars. (And all human activity?—"dominated by decisions made in the teeth of reason," as one of my teachers said.) So I'm not sure what you mean by "finding out what really happened and doing something about it."

And what's this about Blevins? No, I do not see him as some sinister force in the platoon (neither he nor anyone else, by the way, left Longo out there to die; Longo died instantly, and nobody knew he was hit till they came back to the hooch we were in)—nor am I at all surprised that he once made a racist remark. Blevins is a juvenile, essentially (although I must admit he did rather well as acting squad leader during the battle; he seems to respond favorably to the lieutenant)—given that and where he is from, I rather think it would be surprising if he didn't make a racist remark once in a while. (Blevins, by the way, is rotating tomorrow. Happy as hell—got cigars from God knows where and has been handing them out. I told him where you are and he says he's going to try to look you up. Hope I didn't do wrong. Everyone says hello; everyone who's left, that is. Most of them were surprised you're still alive.)

LATER. As I said before, Short-round is pretty bad. He's got about three weeks to go and I don't know whether he's going to make it. Just now he failed to clean his rifle for inspection. Just kept repeating over and over that it didn't matter, he isn't going to use it anyway, he's not going to fight anymore. I tried to tell him that *I* know that—it's all right—just go and clean your goddamn rifle. Finally he did. The lieutenant seems to be handling it pretty well—seems to sense that Short-round is beyond any kind of browbeating, flag waving, appeals to conscience, etc. He's really had it. Remember how he sounded when he came back from the hospital—that brash complaining all the time, like some comedian with the same routine? He still complains but it isn't funny anymore; there's no life in his voice. He went to Doc after Boone and told him that he'd better find something wrong with him, it was either that or the brig, because there's no way he can fight anymore. Now whenever firing breaks out he just flops down on the ground and covers his head with his hands, like a little kid afraid of the dark.

Rain, by the way, is still with us too—although he is also due to rotate soon—another couple of weeks. I asked him the other day what he was going to do now; he said he didn't know; he had just been turned down for another extension of his tour over here. He has to leave. What a mind-boggling notion! He is upset because he has to go—while a few feet away sits Short-round, so desperate to get out it seems he might die of the wait. Rain is really a strange case, I have discovered.

LATER. It finally happened: we got ambushed. Not as bad as I had expected—only a little ambush, not the all-out annihilation we've all been anticipating like the one that wiped out an entire company from the Ninth Marines a few weeks back (how reassuring it is when stories like that filter down to us!). No, this was probably just a platoon or so of NVA. We—our platoon—were serving as truck convoy escorts again, when there was the usual crackle, the same old sinking feeling inside, then the rush of adrenaline as responses took over: we returned fire (an incredible amount), the truck drivers floored it (those trucks *can* go fast), and away we sped with only a casualty or two. Superman (remember him?— from third squad: first name's Kent) got a bit stunned when a round grazed his helmet (no medevac), but my new man, Reynolds, was hit rather soundly in the shoulder. He's gone.

I almost mailed this letter (for about the third time), but first I read yours again, and then decided to write some more. I think I've answered all your questions (and so I'm not sure why I'm still writing), but there's something about your letter that really gets to me, I must admit: it really *does* have a nightmarish quality to it; yet when I stop to think about it I realize you're probably in all kinds of comfort—clean sheets, hot chow, etc. etc.—the kind of comfort I don't even dream of anymore. In other words, the nightmare is over *here*. And yet when I read *my* letter (which I did, right after yours), everything seems so normal and sane. I tell myself that maybe I should try and make things sound more terrible. (There—a little mud on the page—get the idea?)

Not that I begrudge you your comforts, by the way—you earned them, certainly; nor do I envy you for what you've been through—are still going through, I'm sure. Please write back and let me know what the doctor says. Are they going to operate again or not? That part was a little confusing. I must say, the idea of someone cutting into my head and putting in a metal plate makes me cringe.

LATER. We just got some replacements for the platoon—eight, I think, in all. I've got another new one: North. Looks quite young—or have I gotten that old? (Saw myself in Doc's shaving mirror the other day: a couple of gray hairs.) From California. Seems very gung-ho. Small: "Mighty Mouse," I want to call him. (But it seems we've given up assigning nicknames.)

Anyway, I've got one more thing to say and then I'm going to mail this. Here goes. (I might as well jump right in; I think that's the only way I'll ever get it out.) It happened the third day of the battle, sometime in the afternoon, I think. (The usual designations of time somehow lost their meaning during those three days—time was divided into fighting and not fighting, that was about it.) We had been stuck in a ravine, raked by machine-gun fire and with mortar rounds crashing down all around us. It was pretty bad: in fact it seemed to me that we were just waiting to get hit—all of us; too exhausted to do anything else; as though it didn't matter anymore what happened to us; just to have it over with. I really think I was beyond caring—or almost, anyway.

And then, suddenly, everything changed. It was one of those things that cannot be explained afterward—even to oneself: why didn't it happen a minute earlier, or a minute—or an hour—later—or not at all? Why *that* particular moment? It seemed no different from any other. I don't know; I had just about lost hope; yet at the same time some part of me seemed to sense that it was all going to be over soon. Someone—the lieutenant?—yelled out, "Let's go!" (as he had yelled before, but to no effect)—and then—for no reason—we did. Just when it seemed the most hopeless for doing so: we all got up and charged forward, firing as we ran. We flopped down, fired, then charged again. Miraculously, not one of us got hit.

Rain and I were together. He had no more rounds for his grenade launcher and Short-round and I really had no more fire team; so he kind of attached himself to me—although I never gave him an order or anything like that: he always seemed to know what to do better than I. He was really good—just kept going on and on, oblivious to any sense of his own self being in danger. When he ran out of rounds for his grenade launcher he'd pick up a rifle (from one of our casualties) and fight with it.

The next time we flopped down (Rain first—I was following *him* now) we found ourselves in a fighting hole already occupied by two others. My first thought—since we were on the flank—was that we had gone a little too far over and had stumbled into one of second platoon's positions. Although I knew that they couldn't possibly have moved up this far already—they had just made it up to *our* lines, before we had set out on our mad charge. And then I had another thought: that whatever platoon they might be from, wasn't it peculiar that they should both be Chinese Americans (or some other kind of Orientals)—two of them together in the same fighting hole, like brothers? (Needless to say, my mind at that point was not functioning very sharply—at some things; yet so many thoughts in such a short time!)

And then I realized who they were. Right there, right in front of me, a matter of *inches*, not even feet or meters: the famous unseen enemy, NVA. No longer phantoms, no figures of the imagination, but real live human beings (what you must have thought when you saw that suicidal NVA in the hospital). Young ones, too: I think that was the first thing I noticed (after all the other wild guesses). Maybe sixteen or seventeen; and scared (you know how good you get at sensing *that* over here). And the other thing that I realized (somehow, not by any rational thought process) was that they represented no danger to us. None at all: I just knew it. They both had weapons—AK-47's—but these were lying on the ground next to them; and the NVA themselves were in a kind of half-lying, half-sitting position, staring at us as though they had been waiting for us all along. I was so astounded I didn't know what to do.

But Rain did. He pointed his rifle at the first one—the one on the left, he looked a little older—and fired, and then he turned to the second one and shot him too. I said—after hesitating, I don't know how long, a few seconds, I guess—"Why?" And then I checked myself. I'm not sure why. I think—well, maybe I was afraid that Rain was going to turn his rifle on me too. (I must admit I've never felt very trusting of Rain.) I guess that went through my mind. But I did repeat it: "Why?" That was all I could say. He shrugged. "Not worth anything as prisoners," he said, and then actually fingered the collar of one of them (we were now lying beside them, hugging the dirt ourselves, bullets flying over our heads), and said, "privates." I barely glanced at what he was fingering—a sign of rank, I suppose. I don't know what I thought—all kinds of things were going through my mind (or maybe nothing was). I was thinking of my *safety*, for one thing—how far into the NVA's lines had we gone? Were there others nearby? Where was the rest of the platoon? Why had he shot them? Maybe it was a good thing: now we don't have prisoners to worry about, now we can just do what we have to do. It *simplified* things, I remember at one point thinking (and I was *so* tired). And besides, after all: they *were* the enemy: maybe they were the same ones who had killed Longo. I tried to feel anger toward them. I tried to feel that Rain had acted out of anger—that he had a right to do what he did, after all he had been through.

The battle went on. The others caught up to us; we advanced some more; the NVA held. But our movement seemed to provide a spur to the rest of the company and the other companies: everyone was moving up now—more than we had the whole previous day. We were able to reorganize a bit, take care of wounded— even ate some. I had a cigarette—with Rain; as though there were now some bond between us. It was the first cigarette I'd had in I don't know how long (I'm not a smoker). We talked in grunts and monosyllables about how we felt (right out of a war movie); but the strange thing was—even stranger than that—was that I found myself unable to look at him. I mean, I *looked* at him, but I couldn't hold it—not for more than a couple of seconds. I kept wondering whether I was afraid of him.

LATER. Still haven't mailed this. I suspect I know why. I just received a letter from my brother—who is always writing me—in which he again begged me to tell him what is going on over here (he always does: he is really fascinated by the war—used to read about it much more than I did). Again I wrote back without giving him what he wants—all the gory details.

Yet when I write to you I am able to say what I want. It's because you've been here, of course—and everything is just so different over here: war is such a completely different world from the one we've been brought up in. I think I realized something like this after the battle, when we had to search through all the NVA bodies for weapons. It was really an incredible scene: all these bodies lying around, some of them really stinking (I was on the verge of throwing up several times); and there we were, picking through them like vultures; then afterward sitting down right next to them, chowing down (a chopper had just brought out cases of C rations): eating, sleeping, shitting, pissing—going on with our lives as if everything were normal. How can someone who hasn't been here (or in some war) understand that?

LATER. Mortared last night. I remember how afraid I used to be of getting mortared when we first moved up here: how quickly one adapts! Now it is almost routine. Well, not quite. I mean, the initial fear soon passes—when you realize you're still alive (and then you can always swear at the enemy for disturbing your sleep and show how hardened you've become). But that cry of *Corpsman!*—that, I think, I'll never get used to. And then all those cries from men in pain, from men dying. Last night there were three: all from third squad (all fairly new ones, too; one of them had been here only a week; he was KIA). The other two were pretty bad. Doc was upset, I could tell.

LATER. Caught a cold on our last patrol—a miserable, drenching affair in which we lost a man from third platoon to a sniper, KIA. Can you believe it? A *cold* in Vietnam? I find myself wanting to go to the Yale Infirmary and get put in bed for a few days. (It really is cold over here, by the way. I don't know what the actual temperature is, but sometimes it feels like it's freezing. This morning I could see my breath. Which is all very disconcerting.)

Perhaps it is this sense of disorientation that has led me to my latest discovery. I have been thinking a lot about what I wrote—that the reason this letter is getting so long is that I can communicate with you in a way that I can't with others (like my brother). And then I realized: but I could mail this to you at any time and simply write another. No, there is something else. I remember when I first began this letter, how strange I felt breaking the news about Longo: almost as though it were *I* who was killing him—by telling you about it. Because until you find out from me, Longo will still be alive for you.

LATER. Cold is worse. Others are coming down with it too. (I sneakingly suspect a connection between all this cigarette smoking I've been doing and my cold; I can feel that my resistance is lower.) Short-round is begging me to give it to him—he stands out in the rain and purposely lets himself get soaked, trying to get pneumonia. I remember once at Yale one of my classmates did the same thing to get out of an exam. Then it was funny; now it is pathetic. Every time I hear a shot (like last night when someone on the lines opened fire on some supposed movement—how easy it is to imagine movement over here!), I immediately think of Short-round, wondering whether he has finally decided to shoot himself through the foot or hand. (Two more weeks for him to go, by the way.)

Sorry, got to go: rifle inspection.

LATER. But what if it *weren't* two more weeks? What if Short-round had to stay here indefinitely—until the war is over? What if we all had to? I think you once suggested that. (Or were you only trying to provoke me into an argument? I really had a hard time, sometimes, figuring out when you were serious. Just like my brother.)

I keep thinking of something else you once said: the time you compared us to the Greeks in *The Iliad*, camped out on the shores of Ilion, eating lamb and drinking wine. (You kept surprising me like that: sometimes you seemed to be cultivating a wild-man, redneck image, other times trying to show off how many books you had read.) Actually, I don't think we're like the Greeks at all—and not just because we have no lamb or wine. I mean, can you imagine them fighting the Trojan War with a thirteen-month rotation policy? (Who would get to share in the spoils at the end?) And would the Greeks have let their commander-in-chief—L. B. Agamemnon Johnson—stay back in Attica the whole time? Sometimes I think the arguments one hears over here about how to fight the war really do make sense: invade North Vietnam or get the hell out, drop a few nukes here and there; burn all VC villages to the ground. I mean—can you imagine the Greeks having a weapon that would destroy Troy but not using it?

I always thought their motivation for fighting their war was pretty flimsy—some Trojan pretty boy stole one of their wives—who cares? But now I wonder. I mean, what are we trying to do over here? Spend thirteen months encamped on the metaphoric shores of this tiny country (so much less powerful than we are), foraying out once in a while to do battle against an enemy we have no grudge against, trying to win—what? Booty? Spoils? Women? No: the *hearts and minds* of these *other* people—the ones caught in between—whom we never really have any contact with anyway. Even down by the Fort—how much contact with the people did we really have? (Those ridiculous I.D. checks all the time—I think that if I were Vietnamese, I'd get pretty angry after a while, showing the same damn card over and over, having these big strangers come into my home whenever they felt like it.) And then at the end of thirteen months, whether we have accomplished anything or not—killed any enemy, taken any cities, won any "h&m's"—we go home (if we are still alive; sooner, if not). And then what? Forget about it and resume our normal lives?

But my real question is (and I'm not sure what the hell started me on this—but it looks like I get an almost full night's sleep tonight—drew last watch—and I've got another inch or so of this candle left; so I think I'll write a little more before I sack; North, my new bunkie, is a very sound sleeper): what if it should turn out to be ten years that *we* have to stay over here—that *I* have to—as it was for the Greeks? Could I do it? Would I have chosen to come over here in the first place, if that had been a possibility— even a remote one? I can't imagine it—not like this, anyway: living in tiny tents (when we are lucky), eating bad food out of little cans, alternating between mud and heat—not to speak of mines, mortar attacks, ambushes. Ten years? *Then* I think I would need the lamb and wine, the prospect of rape and spoils. Why did they do it, anyway? It was their destiny, of course. And yet—at the same time—wasn't it also their choice?

I mean, perhaps it would be better if we had come here because someone's wife had run away, or because we wanted (subconsciously) to give in to the bestial side of our nature: at least then we'd be fighting to the fullest extent of our powers—rape, pillage, burn. (And then, maybe, wars wouldn't be fought anymore— doesn't someone say that in *War and Peace?* Prince Andrei, I think. Fight it like the South Koreans, he says—the hell with making distinctions between military and civilians: kill everyone, take no prisoners; and then war would be so terrible that no one would ever resort to it.)

LATER. And I thought I was going to get so much sleep last night! When I finished writing I lay down to my eagerly anticipated six full hours (!!!), but it seemed that the sleep goddess wasn't favoring me. I was exhausted—I'm exhausted all the time, that's nothing new—but my mind kept thinking of the Greeks on the beach, Longo was filming it; Tolstoi was there too, playing Zeus. My brother kept arguing with me: he wanted to play Hector, I was Achilles. Did I ever sleep? I don't know; if I did, my dreams were about the same thing.

Anyway, I've got a few minutes now before we go on patrol, and maybe I can wind this letter up, if I can get down something that occurred to me last night as I was trying to sleep. It is this: at least the Greeks had a role for *destruction* (as flimsily motivated as they seemed to be—and as flimsily motivated as the *gods* seemed to be, too: wasn't it Discord who started the whole thing, for no good reason?—but then, I suppose, the Greeks were making a point about *discord*).

What made me think of this was something that happened in

the battle, on Operation Boone. It was on the third day (sounds rather biblical, doesn't it?), when the skies finally lifted a bit and the jets were able to come in for some close-air support. We had about had it by then—I don't know how much longer we could have gone on fighting; I had never felt so exhausted in all my life. But there they were, swooping out of the skies, these screeching godlike machines with their awesome loads of destruction (including napalm). What a sight it was! The mushroom clouds, the billowy flames—what special effects! And the noise—no comparison between that and what we had thought was loud: this, surely, was sight and sound of other dimensions. As I was watching it I realized that this, then, is what war is *really* about. After all we had been through—all the grinding, numbing, unhumanly exhausting business of battle, all the individual effort: here were the gods come out of the skies to show us lowly mortals what every war must come down to: power. Power and destruction: the power of destruction, the power to kill. This is all we are here for; nothing more.

Did I say "watched"? I make it sound as if I were sitting back in an easy chair. No, I didn't merely watch; I was not sitting back. I cheered. Yes—with all the others around me: suddenly all exhaustion gone, raising our fists and cheering wildly, screaming at the top of our lungs, we cheered the way a child might cheer at his first fireworks exhibition—no, more strongly than that, much more strongly: we cheered with passion, the kind of passion a child never knows. (When I look back on it now I think I must have been mad: Edmund O'Brien at the end of 1984, cheering for Big Brother.)

That is why I can't write to my brother of what goes on over here—of what goes on *inside*. The morality, values, etc., that we are brought up with have nothing to do with what goes on in a war. Except, perhaps, for the *unofficial* morality: e.g., John Wayne war movies. But, unfortunately, they have nothing to do with war either—really; which is why Longo's idea was so good: we *do* understand war movies—everyone does—much better than we understand war itself.

LATER. Just got a big resupply—rain suits for everyone! They are not bad—light, can be rolled up and put in one's trouser pocket.

Both jackets and pants. We can wear them on patrol—they don't seem to cut down on one's mobility at all. Good old U.S. technology and industry at it again. (Our *deus ex machina?*)

Big rumor that we are going to Khe Sanh. Rain called it the "new Con Thien"—only even more remote, surrounded by even more NVA, taking even more incoming. North says he hopes that we do go—he wants some "action"; he's tired of this "small stuff"—wants to be in a "really big battle." I can sense his envy whenever we talk about Boone. (What would he have thought about our patrols down at the Fort! I find it hard to believe myself that we used to go out with so few men: up here a platoon is a small patrol. I once told North about our "swim calls," but he seemed unimpressed: "I didn't come over here to do no hanging out on the beach." Nor does he think much of my books— "What're you lugging those around for?") I'm sure he will do well—he has so far—but for some reason I find his talk unnerving. I must confess I do not want to go to Khe Sanh; perhaps I'm just getting tired of all the mud and rain and never seeing the sun; this perpetual cold I seem to have. ("And you *asked* for this?" Doc always says.)

LATER. Short-round's had it. Last night. Ambush. Bad. We went out in the afternoon—the whole company; after an eventless patrol set up for the night on a couple of adjoining hills. A listening post from third platoon got hit almost as soon as it left the perimeter to move into position. Of the four men in the LP, two were killed (instantly); the other two wounded bad. One of the ones who was killed had just joined the company—literally; two days ago. His first patrol. Short-round couldn't take it; started screaming. Now I know what the words mean: stark-raving mad. I think it is the worst thing I have seen in my life. How can I say that? Can it be worse than death? I have seen dead bodies, have smelled them rotting; I have seen legs and arms lying next to men still living; I have seen their faces (and turned mine away). Yet never have I felt the way I did when Short-round began screaming, his arms and legs flailing uncontrollably. At least those other things—they were all human: but Short-round was a thing possessed. It took five of us to hold him down (and you know how small Short-round is) while Doc gave him some kind of injection.

I hope I shall never have to see it again. (North was one of us who held him down. He reacted as if it were hand-to-hand combat: with a sudden fierceness and tremendous energy that almost matched Short-round's. He will be good in battle, I am sure. Afterward he said nothing.)

LATER. The battalion chaplain was just here—held a memorial service for all those who died on Boone—and since. How strange it was to listen to him, to his talk of sacrifice, honor, peace, and freedom. He read a quote from the Bible, that one about "greater love hath no man" than he who lays down his life for his friends. I couldn't help thinking of Longo, of what he would have thought of his "sacrifice": how acutely aware Longo always was of his own loss of freedom (how he cherished what little he had—the freedom to imagine!). I found myself resenting the chaplain's explaining—in his way, using his words—the death of this person whom he had never met, who meant—means—so much to me. I found myself wondering how his counterpart from *The Iliad* would have explained it—that Ares got angry because Longo didn't take the war seriously enough? Or because Longo didn't cast him in the movie?

And what of the NVA—do they have memorial services too? That time just after the battle when we were wandering among their bodies, searching for weapons—something happened then I haven't told you about. Or rather, something didn't happen. I wasn't really looking for weapons; I was trying to find those two that Rain had killed. I don't know why. Just to get another look at them, perhaps—maybe one was still alive. No, I knew they were dead (I had seen them die, not three feet away). I think I wanted to find out something about them—anything—I.D. cards, pictures, letters from home, diaries. Something to tell me who they were, some clue to their existence.

But I couldn't find them. All the bodies looked the same. After a while I stopped trying. After a while I realized it didn't matter. What did it matter about any of them—*who* they were, whether they had families, or didn't, whether they chose to come here or not? What difference? They were all dead, that was all that mattered. Suddenly I thought: what difference was there between them and me? Do I exist any more than they do? The war exists:

we don't. No wonder Short-round is so afraid: not of dying, but of dying over here. Because over here, death has no meaning. I remember how I used to think that war is the ultimate reality—that in war one could really learn something—about life, about oneself. Now it seems more like the ultimate unreality. (How does that speech of yours from *Macbeth* go? "A tale told by an idiot, full of sound and fury, signifying nothing"—yes, but over here it is not life but *death* that fits that quote.)

LATER. This evening a few of us who were with the company down south (there are only a few now) began talking about the "good old days"—the Fort, Captain Blood, Zorro and the Cisco Kid, Ma Barker and Rip van Winkle, Fantasyland and Frontierland, etc. (Did "the Fort" really exist? I sometimes wonder. It's really weird—sometimes when I think back to those days, I have this vivid picture in my mind of Longo on the beach, megaphone in hand, directing this huge epic movie.) Someone put in a few words about "ol' Crazy Mike" and how you used to "recite Shakespeare in the middle of a fire fight." (Actually, I always thought you were a bit of a ham—no offense—although wasn't it Longo who was always prodding you into it? As I remember he seemed to get a special satisfaction out of that *Macbeth* quote.)

Eventually—ultimately?—the talk came around to Longo, and it turned into a kind of unofficial "service for the dead" for him, with those of us who knew him telling our favorite Longo stories. (I still can't get over the way he jumped over that rigged mortar round that time—he seemed to be stepping in midair!) Then somebody—Doc, I think—said, "What do you think Longo is up to now?" Making a movie—what else?—someone else said, and then it really *was* like the old days, as we tried to figure out what the movie would be like. Maybe he's got together with Cecil B. De Mille—can you see it, the two of them up there, working on some big epic? Then someone else remembered that Walt Disney is dead now too—can you see that?—Longo and Disney together? What role do you think he'll have God play, anyway?

LATER. Rain just left. I don't know why, but I was sorry to see him go. Another link with the Fort gone, perhaps. I talked to him just before he got on the truck; asked what he was going to do now.

He was definitely getting out of the Crotch, he said—talked as if it would never be the same without him. (I'm still not sure why they won't let him stay in—something about wanting him to train people in the States rather than letting him fight anymore over here. But he's just the kind of person we need to fight this war!) Then gave some dark hints about what he might do, delivered in his usual laconic, enigmatic way: join some mercenaries he's heard of based in Thailand, fighting in Laos and Cambodia; or go to Biafra (like someone he knows) and fight there; or "something else." What? As I was listening to him I thought about the PRU's that once came out to the Fort; and it occurred to me that perhaps the South Vietnamese government has the right idea: wars *should* be fought by convicts—murderers, people with no allegiance except to violence. (Remember the way Rain looked at them when they first came out?—he seemed to sense that he was one of them.) What are we "normal" people doing over here? What is Short-round going to do when he gets back?

We shook hands before he left. I said nothing about the two NVA. I had the feeling that in a few minutes he would forget I ever existed.

LATER. It is late at night and I am writing by candlelight. North asleep. I feel I don't care whether the NVA see my light or not—it is more important to write. (Or do I really want to get hit?—just a little wound, in the shoulder, perhaps—the left shoulder, so I can keep on writing. No, I don't really want that—although I did have a mild case of diarrhea this morning, and it occurred to me that perhaps it is a recurrence of that dysentery I had just before we left the Fort—the doctor had told me that might happen. "It occurred to me"?—more like I am hoping like hell it is. No—that's not true, either. The thought went through my mind, that's all.)

Word came down today that we are going to Khe Sanh after all—leaving tomorrow. It seems there is something big brewing up there. (I'm not supposed to be telling you this, by the way: that was part of the word we got—we're not supposed to tell anyone in our letters. Can you believe it? Whoever passed that one down really does think he's in a war movie—one of those World War II ones where some English-speaking Germans infiltrate the post office. Incredible.)

I do not want to go. All right, I admit it: I'm scared. Why should I be scared? Whatever happens at Khe Sanh can be no worse than what I've been through already. (Strange how at moments like this I find myself actually *missing* what I've been through: not necessarily the battle itself, but that feeling of fearlessness that comes as one passes through stage after stage of exhaustion. There just isn't any room or energy for fear. As though we become machines—firing our rifles, reloading, dashing ahead a few meters, getting down, throwing a grenade—a matter of conditioning. Now I know how all those huge battles of past wars could have been fought: we fight as long as we are properly oiled and fueled. Or die.)

I keep thinking of that suicidal NVA next to you in the hospital in Da Nang. Why was he trying to kill himself? Was it simply his conditioning at work—or was it that the war meant so much to him? Now when I think about my reasons for coming over it seems that they are just that—reasons, words, excuses. What if my grandfather had never been to war—would I still have come over? Where is the necessity for my being here?

Perhaps I never should have written this letter. I think I should say no more.

Best,
Bill

9

SERVICE FOR
THE DEAD

The screen was black and white. Crewcut young men in T-shirts and utility trousers waved from the deck of a ship; behind them was the sea. It was World War II, Mike realized—the documentary. They were marines. He folded the Professor's letter, put it back in its envelope and placed it on the table next to him. He turned again to the television.

There was a closeup of two marines with their arms around each other's shoulders, laughing; one of them had a mustache. There was a marine who was reading a letter, puffing on a cigarette. The camera cut to another, a grim set to his thin face, tattoos on both arms; he seemed ready to fight. Two others, realizing the camera was on them, began to clown, pulling their hats down over their faces and sticking out their ears and tongues. The camera switched again, to a marine who frowned and moved away. He was afraid, Mike knew. Another one, all by himself, stared blankly out to sea. A gust of wind stirred a short lock of his hair; he turned and gave the camera a puzzled look, as if not sure why it was there, or why he was. He looked young, Mike thought—they all did, much younger than they used to look. Suddenly he got up, went to the television and put the sound on, then returned to his seat.

The narrator was reciting a list of the marines' names. It was Cliff Morgan, the movie star. He had once fought with the Marine Corps himself, Mike knew. He had a deep, gruff voice that he usually used in gangster or police roles, but now he spoke in a subdued, flat tone.

"What kind of men were these marines?" he asked. "They were simple, ordinary men, most of them. Men from places like Brownswood, Texas, and Glen Ridge, New Jersey; Flat River, Missouri, and Columbus, Montana; Pittsburgh, Chicago, and Detroit. Some of them had fought before, at Tarawa and Guadalcanal, Saipan and Peleliu; some of them were barely out of boot camp, still only boys. Tomorrow morning they will begin the battle for a little piece of land called Iwo Jima, and none of them will ever be boys again. In the next thirty days, almost six thousand of them will die."

On the screen the battle began, but Mike could no longer see it, could only hear Cliff Morgan's voice as he described what went on. Mike's lower lip was trembling and his eyes were filled with tears.

"The assault at Iwo Jima is what the United States Marine Corps is all about," Cliff Morgan said, "young men advancing into the very face of death, thousands of miles from their homes, fighting on in spite of their leaders and buddies falling dead and wounded all around them, fighting on in spite of exhaustion, beyond exhaustion, fighting on. Fighting until they could fight no longer and then fighting some more."

Mike sobbed. His chest heaved and tears streamed down his cheeks. The sobbing was accompanied by a whiny sound high up in his throat. It grew louder. Why was he crying? He had seen films like this before—ever since he was little. Why was he crying for them?

A commercial came on. A chorus of show girls danced and high-kicked around a new color television set. Mike stared at the screen, breathing heavily. What had happened? Was he all right?

It was the faces: seeing those faces and hearing their names, knowing that some of them would die. But of course they had to: it was history. Hadn't he known when he used to watch these films that some of them would have to die, that this is what war means—is all it means, for those who have to fight it?

He thought of getting up and turning off the television. But would it happen again?

The commercial ended and the documentary resumed. The marines were on the island now. There was footage of explosions, men running, firing, throwing flames, killing Japanese. There were more explosions, weapons smoking, bodies floating in water. The landing beaches were strewn with marines, dead and dying. Still the battle raged on.

"What kind of men were these marines?" Cliff Morgan asked again, his voice still without emphasis. "They were men willing to leave family and friends and go halfway round the world, to fight an enemy that had proclaimed war until death. They were simple, ordinary men who somehow became extraordinary in battle, not only in killing but also in saving, in risking their lives time after time so their buddies might live. They were men who, for a few brief moments, became the very best at what they were doing, who afterward would never be the same again."

"No, no!" Mike shook his head, sobbing. "I'll go—I will, I will!" The sound of his own voice surprised him. For a moment he thought of his parents in the next room. "I don't care!"—he nearly shouted it—"I want to go back! . . . Please—let me go—let me do it again!" He put his head down in his hands and let himself cry.

In a while he looked up at the screen again, at the marines fighting and dying. Were there children who were watching now too, he wondered, wanting to go to war themselves someday, to become someone else?

Through his sobs he spoke again. "I'm sorry," he said, "I'm sorry, I'm sorry . . . I'm so sorry."

WORLD WAR II
Edwin P. Hoyt

"MANAGEMENT
MUST MANAGE!"*

MANAGING   69986-9/$4.50US/$5.95Can
Harold Geneen with Alvin Moscow

"Sensible advice from the legendary practitioner of superior management, ITT Chairman of the Board Emeritus, Harold Geneen."°   —*Publishers Weekly*

THEORY Z   How American Business Can Meet the Japanese Challenge
William G. Ouchi   59451-X/$4.50US/$5.95Can

"Powerful answers for American firms struggling with high employee turnover, low morale, and falling productivity."   —*Dallas Times Herald*

HYPERGROWTH   The Rise and Fall of Osborne Computer Corporation
        69960-5/$5.95US/$7.75Can
Adam Osborne and John Dvorak

The personal account of the Silicon Valley megabuck bust that stunned the business world.

An Avon Trade Paperback

FROM PERSONAL JOURNALS TO BLACKLY HUMOROUS ACCOUNTS

VIETNAM

DISPATCHES, Michael Herr

01976-0/$3.95 US/$5.50 Can

"I believe it may be the best personal journal about war, any war, that any writer has ever accomplished."
—Robert Stone, *Chicago Tribune*

A WORLD OF HURT, Bo Hathaway

69567-7/$3.50 US/$4.50 Can

"War through the eyes of two young soldiers...a painful experience, and an ultimately exhilarating one."
—*Philadelphia Inquirer*

NO BUGLES, NO DRUMS, Charles Durden

69260-0/$3.50 US/$4.50 Can

"The funniest, ghastliest military scenes put to paper since Joseph Heller wrote *Catch-22*"
—*Newsweek*

AMERICAN BOYS, Steven Phillip Smith

67934-5/$3.95 US/$5.75 Can

"The best novel I've come across on the war in Vietnam"
—Norman Mailer

COOKS AND BAKERS, Robert A. Anderson

79590-6/$2.95

"A tough-minded unblinking report from hell"
—*Penthouse*